AVENGING FURY

AVENGING

FURY

John Farris

A Tom Doherty Associates Book
New York

AVENGING FURY

Copyright © 2008 by Penny Dreadful Ltd.

A Forge Book
Published by Tom Doherty Associates, LLC
175 Fifth Avenue
New York, NY 10010

www.tor-forge.com

Forge® is a registered trademark of Tom Doherty Associates, LLC.

Library of Congress Cataloging-in-Publication Data

Farris, John.
    Avenging fury / John Farris.—1st hardcover ed.
        p.   cm.
    "A Tom Doherty Associates Book."
    ISBN-13: 978-0-312-87732-3
    ISBN-10: 0-312-87732-3
    1. Psychics—Fiction.   2. Time travel—Fiction.   3. Las Vegas (Nev.)—Fiction.
I. Title.
    PS3556.A777A95   2008
    813'.54—dc22
                                                        2008005131

First Edition: May 2008

Printed in the United States of America

0 9 8 7 6 5 4 3 2 1

AUTHOR'S NOTES

On page 51, The Actor is quoting John Keats.

Part of Flicka's lament on page 171 is adapted from remarks attributed to the songbird Mariah Carey.

The next-to-the-last line on page 175 is courtesy of Willie Nelson (who ad-libbed it in the movie *Electric Horseman*).

Because this is, after all, a novel, I've made a few changes in the landscape of Las Vegas. The megaresort Bahìa I've placed where the MGM Grand usually is. "Concordia Hospital" doesn't exist. Neither do Virgie Lovechild's digs. I've poked fun at a few actual entertainers and Vegas icons, who are probably used to it. Others named in the book are merely figments. Show business "celebrities" come in two distinct categories: the synthetic and ephemeral, who are easily mocked. And the true originals, who can never be replaced. Like Willie.

The description of a time machine as "a great cellophane butterfly" is taken from Ray Bradbury's fine story the "F. Scott/Tolstoy/Ahab Accumulator"; additional embellishments are mine.

The lyrics for "Jesus Hot-Wired My Heart," the chain gang's lament on the Dumas line, and "Rat Alley Moan" are by the author, a long-neglected songwriter.

Finally: there are three or four fragments of W. Shakespeare within Delilah's many discourses; everything else she has to say is my invention.

ONE

> . . . BUILT IN TH' ECLIPSE,
> AND RIGGED WITH CURSES DARK . . .
>
> —JOHN MILTON, *LYCIDAS*

(The crazed, the futile, the damned. Hardbodies of both sexes. The cheesy egos. Those who lack pity, tolerance, or shame. Castouts and castaways. The carelessly spawned and heartless young. Those with visions to pursue or sell. Those who maim their spirits skipping out on life. The self-indulgently cruel. Those who know the lingo but lack the moves. Those with perpetual night in their eyes. Those who just want the money. Caged birds with no voices. Amateurs at everything. Las Vegas can wake up the harlot in a spinster church organist. It isn't sensible to set foot in a place that's out to rob you, but there it is, that irresistible siren song of commerce and show business. Twenty-four hours a day, every minute of it game time for the true predators.

Where there are predators, there also are skilled hunters, a very few to be sure. But always the best at what they do.)

... The strong winds that afflicted the Las Vegas area and caused some temporary power outages had abated and the clouds were breaking up as the cold front passed through, affording glimpses of a waning moon above the summit of Spring Mountain.

The hunter wouldn't be needing the moon tonight. At four thousand feet Tom Sherard had settled into his hide overlooking the Lincoln Grayle Theatre, approximately one-quarter mile away at two o'clock and seven hundred feet below his rocky perch. He sat cross-legged in spite of the painful stress on his bad knee, the stock of the .476 Holland & Holland rifle against his shoulder as he calibrated the scope.

Southeast lay a golden field of shimmering lights sown like the wages of sin across the high-desert floor. A toy version of King Arthur's castle and a Sphinx-guarded pyramid at one end of the Vegas strip; a red ribbon of roller coaster around the tip of the Stratosphere Tower at the other end.

Below Sherard, the terrace of the theatre looked like the flight deck of an aircraft carrier, with huge concrete planters for trees and three fountains, not operating at this hour. The superstructure of the theatre, five stories of beehive glass cut like a diamond into thousands of facets, filled the front of a cavern that had been blasted out of the mountain to accommodate the theatre and kitchens where assembly-line meals were prepared for sixteen hundred guests on show nights.

The hunter couldn't see past the facade from where he was, but he knew from the Magician's Web site what the semicircular lobby inside looked like: gold-veined travertine floors and eight chandeliers resembling stalactite sculptures in an ice cave, each weighing a quarter of a ton.

A pair of night watchmen in a golf cart were moving slowly around the terrace. He sighted in on one of them, crosshairs just below a jowly neckline, feeling now the familiar slow-boiling anticipation of a blood stalk at the root of his throat, in the pulses of his temples.

The watchmen concluded their circuit of the terrace. A door opened in a wall bearing a fifty-foot-high mosaic of Lincoln Grayle. The golf cart disappeared into the lower depths of the theatre complex.

Sherard moved the stock of the custom-made rifle from the padded shoulder of his hunting jacket. He closed his eyes, clearing his mind of the shot he was going to make, and waited.

Eden Waring ran through the levels of the darkened theatre and crossed the lobby, emerging into the brilliance of ten-k floodlights aimed at the theatre's facade. The temperature behind the cold front had dropped to the midthirties at this elevation. She was still perspiring from the heat of the menagerie tunnel and began to shudder as she turned and backed away from the entrance doors, circling a fountain, keeping it between her and the were-beast she was certain would be coming after her.

As she moved she had a look around the empty terraces, glanced at the stars appearing now in the sky. One hand against her breasts, cupped over the talisman that His Holiness had provided for her. She was bleakly aware that whatever papal blessings accompanied it would be of only limited value. Bertie Nkambe had believed in her own talisman—and look what it had gotten her. None of her powers had been adequate to anticipate and deflect an assassin's bullets.

Now that she was out in the open, fear evaporated from Eden's skin. Bertie lay gravely wounded in Concordia Hospital, but Eden felt satisfaction in remembering what the Magician's face had looked like after she'd smashed most of it to a pulp. The sharp neck of the wine bottle was still in her left hand. Probably futile as a weapon, given the power coming her way, the retaliation she had provoked.

She let go of the ugly little talisman and wiped the hollows of her eyes. The drops of Grayle's blood and her perspiration that she flung from her fingertips appeared to hover in the floodlit night a few feet from her, taking on some of the fire that seemed also to grow within the crystal chandeliers visible inside the theatre. Light of her Light; a subconscious recognition, a gift of apprehension as, there on the terrace (where it seemed to Eden she had been waiting until half past Eternity instead of less than a minute), something was happening.

The most wonderful *something* she had known in her life. Nothing compared with the sight of an ordinary golf cart coasting out of a doorway in a wall near the left foot of another huge version of Lincoln Grayle, this one composed of many thousands of black and white tiles. You couldn't look anywhere in or outside his theatre without encountering the likeness Eden had done a brutal job of deconstructing only minutes ago.

Eden wasn't thinking about that right now. She could only smile incredulously at the sight of Bertie Nkambe behind the wheel of the cart as it crossed the terrace on a diagonal, coming straight for her. Bertie looking in the pink instead of unconscious beneath a ventilator mask in the hospital Eden had left a little less than three hours ago. Bertie, giving her a familiar blithe wave along with a big white dimpled smile.

Incredible to see her, but wonderful: of course she knew about Bertie's considerable healing powers. . . . Eden could not control her tears.

"Bertie!"

"Hi."

"But you—"

"C'mon, we'll take a ride. Tell you about it."

"No! Bertie—Grayle—he—we've got to—"

"Hey, nothing to worry about! I saw him. He's down and out. You clocked him good."

"Saw—?"

Bertie braked the golf cart a few feet from Eden and beckoned, still smiling, a hand jauntily on one hip. Didn't appear that a single hair on her head had been disturbed by the Magician's hired assassin. To Eden's weary eyes Bertie looked as if she'd spent hours getting made up for a cover shoot.

"Time for us to skedaddle outta here, Eden. Saddle up and let's ride, partner."

Still Eden hung back, light-headed from confusion, the conflict of her senses.

"Bertie, where's T-Tom?"

"Tom?" Her smile changed, just a little, as if she'd heard something obscene.

"Didn't he come with you? He's—" Eden took a couple of steps toward the golf cart, shielding her eyes from the hot glare of a nearby floodlight. She failed to notice the crimson drops of moisture she'd discarded into the air rearranging to spell out a warning:

BEWARE

"—Supposed to be here," Eden concluded weakly. "I left him a note?"

Bertie's good humor vanished. Her back hunched like that of a sullen cat. She looked around the terrace swiftly, then in a moment of apprehension raised her eyes to the cliffs flanking and rising above the Lincoln Grayle Theatre to the darkness of the sky.

Bertie's sharp eyes seemed to elongate as she took in the silent seated form of Tom Sherard, a distant wink of light off the lens of his rifle scope. Her recognition of danger was swift but not as swift as the bullet Tom sent her way. The .476 slug took out two ribs and splashed most of one lung, knocking her flat and hard beside the golf cart.

A human being and most animals would have died instantly from hydrostatic shock. But this Bertie wasn't human, only a cunning copy. A copy struggling to assume yet another form on the deck as the big bellowing echo from the Holland & Holland reached Eden's ears. Sure as hell wasn't Bertie getting up quickly on all fours, claws grating stone, blood billows issuing like condensed red breath from its mouth and coal-black nostrils.

Eden recoiled from the scorch of a hot floodlight. The were-beast making a howling effort to achieve its full shape from the abandoned from of Bertie Nkambe—the Magician's last great illusion—wasn't having an easy time coordinating the shift. Mindful of the sharpshooter on high, it turned and loped awkwardly toward the safety of the theatre. Still incomplete and lopsided from the drag of a Bertie-leg, knee to foot, that remained unassimilated, a sight that wrenched Eden's violently beating heart.

Then Tom fired again, hitting and disabling a shoulder of the beast.

The were-beast plunged through a glass door and skidded ten feet on slick travertine, then collapsed out of rifle range in a spill of coughed blood.

There was another message in the air for Eden made of her sweat and tears, a message from the center of her being:

DESTROY

Eden looked up to where she thought Tom must be, but she couldn't locate him. She walked deliberately across the terrace as the were-beast crawled along the floor inside the theatre, howling miserably. It left a blood swath beneath great blazing chandeliers that were as white as ice sculpture.

(Ice, glass—what did it matter? What mattered was to focus properly, channel the Dark Energy that Eden felt as a hot-wire tingle across her scalp, causing the hair on her head to stand and strain at the roots.)

A smoke-tinged rosette opened in one of the facets on the hivelike facade. And she hadn't even been trying, just gave it the merest glance, the cosmic heat converging from both eyes as another blister formed on her lower lip.

The talisman smoked between her breasts. Her nipples were electric. Eden was on fire, but it was a fire she could bend outward and direct according to her will—it meant her no harm. She looked up again, past a few clouds to a starfield across the heavens. Those stars assumed, from a cataclysm of seething light and energy, a familiar form: her own. Recognition gave her cheer and a confidence that was beyond godlike.

(Better not to leave any part of it standing. Not a single magical door or tunnel through with the Magician might make his escape.)

Eden stood ten feet from the facade of the Lincoln Grayle Theatre, perhaps twice that distance from where the deformed Magician was making an effort to put his final act together—

—And dropped a quarter ton of melting chandelier on top of him.

The feline shape was indistinct within the crude drop of molten glass. Only the grotesque hyena head and strong shoulders of the tiger were still visible. Its screams were difficult to bear. Eden added another slow-moving mass of molten glass to what was already on the floor, continuing to pile it on until all the chandeliers were melted and down. They composed an ingot like a softly pulsating, liquid star eight feet deep on the travertine floor.

The glass would, perhaps, take a week to cool and harden completely.

Eden backed away from the theatre until she came to the outer edge of the terrace. Her celestial simulacrum lay cozily on the brow of the mountain, immensely radiant. Stars in her eyes, stars in her hair. All of them spinning in concert with her earthly mind waves. She looked down and saw that she had risen a couple of feet above the terrace floor. She felt a curious lack of childlike wonder. Still she enjoyed her casual buoyancy, a bodiless sort of freedom, along with the light show playing in her brain as she initiated the meltdown of the theatre's facade, more slumping tons of sizzle glass.

But the added weight was too much for the terrace supports and the whole thing collapsed suddenly. Eden thoughtfully watched it go, great smoking globs of glass and slabs of concrete tumbling down the mountain, setting trees aflame, filling a third of the parking lot and blocking the four-lane parkway, the only road from the valley floor to the theatre.

The floodlights were out. The Magician's show had gone permanently dark.

Beginning to feel depleted, Eden let herself drift a few hundred feet through the dark rising cloud of smoke and dust until there was solid ground beneath her feet again.

In his hide from where he had shot the were-beast, Tom Sherard packed up his rifle and scope. Then he took out his cell phone and dialed a number in Rome, a number so private that fewer than ten people in the world had it.

He left a message for Pope John XXIV. Then he went down the mountain in search of Eden, still feeling dazzled and shaken by what he had seen, the chaos her passions and wild talent had wrought.

OCTOBER 27 · 1:09 A.M.

Bronc Skarbeck's cell phone, which played the first eight bars of "The Stars and Stripes Forever," woke him up in the bedroom he shared with his teenage mistress. Bronc, in spite of the injuries that had been done to him at the abrupt conclusion of his military career, remained intensely loyal to his country, but not to the fools, connivers, and outright traitors (in his estimation) who were currently in charge.

"General, it's Perk. Sorry about the lateness of the hour, but there's been—we don't know everything yet, but it looks serious."

Perk, for Elizabeth Ann Perkins, was Lincoln Grayle's executive assistant. Too smart and efficient to bother him with anything short of devastating news, probably involving the Magician. Grayle had been in town for a few days, so it wasn't a plane wreck.

"Out with it, Perk."

"They're calling it a landslide. Took out the facade of the theatre and all of the terrace. The slide is blocking the Grayle Parkway and covering two of the parking lots."

"When did it happen?"

"A little after midnight, according to the sheriff's office. A helicopter's up there now, assessing the damage."

"Casualties?"

"We don't know yet; reports are still sketchy."

Skarbeck knuckled the crown of his head. Nearly flat front to back, crisp military haircut, dyed pimento red in defiance of his years.

"Why call me? Where's Linc?"

"That's just it, General. I don't know. He might still have been at the theatre when it happened. But he hasn't answered his cell phone. Now that I think about it—" A tremor in her voice, then she resumed, low and fretful, "Oh, I *hope* he wasn't just driving away when it all came down."

Skarbeck flinched slightly. "Take it easy, Perk. Did you try Linc at home?"

"Yes, sir. They haven't seen him since late yesterday afternoon."

"When did you see him last?"

Beside Skarbeck on the round bed, the size of a circus trampoline, Harlee Nations stirred in pearl-gray sheets, rolled over on her stomach, and smiled with her eyes closed, her youthful, creamy face enlivened by the romance of a dream.

Skarbeck, pleasantly distracted, passed a hand over the firm contours of her truly wondrous ass. Her skin tone like balm to his calloused hand. The phosphor of his commando's chronometer shed green light on his inamorata like the aura of a séance. Harlee read rock music and hairstyle magazines exclusively although she had graduated high school, valedictorian of her class, at fourteen. She liked to drive very fast in her candy-apple red Viper V-10 and was taking lessons on handling the new Ducati bike he'd given her. For exercise she was serious about fencing, belonged to a local club, and practiced three times a week. She smoked a little dope with Skarbeck when the mood was right, and her pet name for him was Wonder-cock.

Give Harlee a couple of years—he knew this from experience with others her age—and she would become a major-league ball buster. While he grew older, once again burning himself at the stake of his obsession.

"Perk, you there?"

"Oh—yes, sir. I was thinking. There was a three-hour dress rehearsal for Linc's new show; that was over about eleven o'clock. So he was in his suite when the girl showed up."

"Girl?"

"She told me that she had an engagement with Linc, which I thought was pure horse puckey. I mean I've heard that one before. But—"

"Describe her."

"Well—midtwenties, if that. Attractive, but no raving beauty. Strawberry blond, deep tan. Her left eye turned in a little, but that didn't detract from—"

Skarbeck felt a sudden chill.

"So who was she, Perk?"

"Wouldn't give her name. But Linc knew her. From the way she talked, the message she wanted me to give to Linc, there obviously was a relationship. She was nervous, but very determined to see him."

"What was it she wanted you to tell him?"

"She said, quote, 'I want Linc to know that what began at Shung-waya must be finished tonight.'"

"Shung—? What or where is that?"

"I don't know, sounds African, doesn't it? And he just came back from Africa not too long ago, so I thought, hmm. You know. Anyway, I repeated what she wanted me to say to Linc, and tired as he must've been, he sounded really pleased. Wanted me to bring her right on back to his suite. And that was the last time I saw him. It must have been about a quarter past eleven. Most of the cast and crew were already out of there, and I left a few minutes later."

"So chances are Linc could still be there, spent the night with his visitor. Okay, but we don't know if the theatre was damaged inside by whatever caused the rock fall." Skarbeck paused. "The road's blocked, you said, but there are a couple of other ways out, aren't there?"

"Yes. Two tunnels through the mountain. That's how the night crew made it out, or so I was told. Most of them are in the parking lot now, waiting to be helicoptered down the mountain."

Skarbeck, not exactly fearing the worst, still felt a stirring of tentacles in the lightless deeps of his paranoia. What if Grayle had been buried under tons of rubble in his sports car? The General had cast his lot with Grayle after an unfortunate alliance with the Multiphasic Operations and Research Group, known as MORG. But without the Magician's power and money his ambitions would be little more than rubble too. And he was sixty-five years old. The hand that was straying over Harlee's lovely body trembled, and this slight seismic disturbance was enough to make her flinch and sigh through parted lips. But she didn't wake up. He envied her blissful sleep. He had a prostate the size of a baked potato and could count on being up three times a night to piss, depending on how much he'd had to drink before bed.

He suspected cancer but by God there wasn't going to be any cutting. No resultant impotence and adult didies for Bronc Skarbeck. If it was there like a bad seed in the prostatic tissue but failed to metastasize, then he might squeeze out another eight or ten years. Statistics favored a final round of longevity. Time enough for his comeback, a takeover of the government that had, as he devoutly believed, betrayed him and snatched his honor away. His first attempt had been aborted by the girl with the wayward eye described by Perk. But at the time he hadn't had the Magician as chief plotter and cohort.

"Perk, I think all we can do for now is just hang and wait for Linc to contact one of us. Meantime you should get in touch with the insurers. I'll want an estimate of damages soon as the sun comes up in the morning."

"All right."

"Rocks are always falling off mountains. That's what Lloyd's is for. And listen: don't worry. Could be that Linc decided to wring some suspense out of this unfortunate occurrence. Crank up the old publicity mill. His kind of brainstorm, wouldn't you say? 'Lincoln Grayle's Real-Life Miracle Escape from Death.'"

Elizabeth Ann Perkins laughed uncertainly.

"Sure. He might think of something like that. Disappear for a few days, scare the hell out of all of us. All for the good of the show."

"With his TV special coming up during November sweeps. Spectacular timing. Ratings could be through the roof this time."

"Yes, that would be— General Skarbeck, I have another call! Then

I'd better be going over to Grayle's Mountain, see for myself how bad things are."

"Good. You do that. Stay in touch."

Skarbeck folded his cell phone and continued to sit on the low bed, scratching his still manly, convex chest through a blizzard of graying pelt. He was thinking of something Lincoln Grayle had said to him a couple of evenings ago while they were assessing Plan A on a terrace of the Magician's house in the deep blue and orange of high-desert sunset out there on Charleston Mountain.

We are plotting tonight what will become the myths of tomorrow.

Spoken with that prankish grin of his that on occasion could produce goose bumps on the forearms of a battle-tested hard-ass old Marine commandant.

Skarbeck drew the back of his hand across his nose and smelled blood.

It was leaking from one nostril. He had decided that the nosebleeds were a result of ingesting the testosterone booster known commercially as Uptight, which was an imperative for keeping his dick at DEFCON ONE during the delights of the bedchamber Harlee provoked in her soft, insinuating fashion and with her splendid nakedness. Uptight was a potent vascular dilator hacked off shaggy stumps in a Japanese rain forest. Emperors and warlords for millennia had been fortifying themselves with it. But just a smidge too much of the powdered lichen could raise his systolic pressure to three-alarm status while charcoaling the dyed roots of his hair.

Skarbeck padded into the master bathroom, a palace within a palace, marbled and skylighted for drinking in the stars while soaking or steaming. He stuffed a ball of cotton up his nose. The dribble of blood had him wishing for the physical immortality that only Lincoln Grayle possessed (Skarbeck never thought of him as *Deus Inversus,* in order to keep a firm focus on the reality of the here and now that he inhabited).

Or was Grayle the only immortal in his large coterie?

Skarbeck had never pried, but he did have an occasional tremor of suspicion about the luscious girl in his bed. A time or two during the weeks since she had moved in, Skarbeck had seen something pierce her facade of pubescent artlessness—calculation in sage-green eyes that suggested she was not exactly what he had assumed her to be. Not a fragile reed inside a great body, clueless about the big bad world, but imperial in manner and heritage, timelessly wise. That made him wonder if she had another master to whom she was devoted. After all, the Magician had introduced Harlee to him. A gift of the Magician. The analog of which was the Trickster. Possibly she was a part of the intrigue surrounding Grayle at many levels of his purpose; a spy, in fact.

Skarbeck was no dummy, in spite of being willing prey to his libidinous weakness. The Magician knew his history: Skarbeck's obsessive need for young, unplundered (except by Skarbeck) pussy. That weakness, along with an untimely binge after he was passed over for Chairman of the Joint Chiefs a little more than a decade ago, had resulted in the kind of salted-wounds humiliation only the media can provide.

He was dead certain that he'd been set up by his enemies at the Pentagon and on the Hill. After rehab he was no longer a drinking man, the only positive outcome of his ordeal, but his thirst for revenge remained far stronger than a repressed appetite for Tennessee sipping whiskey.

So immortality was beyond his grasp. But vitamins, herbal tonics recommended by his associate Dr. Marcus Woolwine, and spec-trochrome therapy, or SCT, prescribed by Lincoln Grayle, tilted the odds (should the self-diagnosis of cancer be wrong) in favor of his reaching an eighth decade still reasonably hale, faculties intact. His face and body viewable from all angles in mirrors mirrors mirrors enhanced confidence and morale. The vaunt of an eagle, the gang-sterish hauteur that lifetime military hardcases often possess, and well-hooded scheming blue eyes.

At the moment, however, his eyes revealed a certain uneasiness.

He knew the identity of the girl Perk had mentioned, the one pay-ing a late call on the Magician. Whom Grayle might have been enter-taining still before the cliff face fell. She was Eden Waring—the Avatar, by virtue of her psychic prowess. And recently she had become the obsession of Lincoln Grayle, the human aspect of Mordaunt, *Deus*

Inversus. Who believed that he could control the Waring girl's powers. For what purpose? Grayle hadn't been forthcoming; need-to-know basis, whatever. Skarbeck was cautious about trying to fathom the dark side of his employer.

But he knew more about Eden Waring: paranormal, dangerous, godlike. Not inhuman, however, and assuredly not immortal.

Then there was the matter of Eden's doppelganger, whom Skarbeck had heard about but not seen. Eden's mirror image, from a parallel universe (according to Lincoln Grayle, but he'd said it with that teasing smile of his, so who knew), a recent arrival in Las Vegas, where the weird and otherworldly seemed to be commonplace, at least around showtime. The dpg apparently was another project of Dr. Marcus Woolwine—psychiatrist, mesmerist, and bioengineer—who had dealt with her once before and not to his advantage. Grayle had hinted to the General that doppelgangers could travel through time. Skarbeck had reserved comment (no business of his, actually) except for a nod to indicate he was open to possibilities while privately thinking that physical near-immortality was one thing (he had read enough of the ancient histories, half a million years' worth of the continuum of life on earth, to acknowledge that it was a near-truth). But flitting around centuries past and future, cutting across parallel universes? *Bullshit.*

Not that he really cared. He was committed only to what Lincoln Grayle wanted from him, and covetous of the astounding resources the Magician could bring to Skarbeck's objectives: literally the wealth of an entire planet.

"Is it your nose again?" Harlee said.

She was leaning against a marble pillar in the wide entranceway to the bath and spa, partly and beguilingly obscured by a pedestaled urn of red roses. Dreams were dissolving in her eyes. There was about her an air of arrested motion, like someone who has missed a cue to begin her life.

"Not serious," Skarbeck assured her. "What woke you up, babykins?"

Harlee shrugged. "You weren't there."

She straightened and came toward him, treading lightly and with a diffident hunching of her shoulders as if, until he beckoned, she was unsure of her welcome.

"And you missed me."

"Yesss." Rising on tiptoe to give him a kiss. Those exquisite painted toenails. She had a breathy little voice that reminded him of Marilyn Monroe. But when they had watched *Some Like It Hot* and Skarbeck had pointed out to her the vocal similarity, Harlee had wrinkled her nose and said with great though unwitting comic timing, "But she was a blonde."

Now Harlee said, with an urging lift of her chin, "Are you coming back to bed, Daddy?"

"Soon as I pump ship," he promised.

"I'll hold it for you," the sloe-eyed girl said. "You like for me to hold it while you're whizzing, don't you?"

So that's how it went, with Harlee cuddling behind him, arms around his waist, fingers delicately agrip, his heart glowing, their love a thing of many mirrors. Nudity, he thought, while waiting patiently to pee, was charming in children, innocently erotic in the pubescent young, grotesque in bodybuilders and those high-fashion models who skip too many meals. There was pathos in the nudity of the very old. As for the in-between years, bodies were what you made of them. Skarbeck still took pride in how he looked, and his reflections of self-approval added kick to Harlee's intimate fondling.

And so to bed for a half hour of gentle romping, sensual kinsmen of the night. Afterward, Harlee asleep again in his arms. His heartbeat was troublesome, a long while coming off its high; but a lovely wind swept his senses, cooling embers of rut.

He stayed awake for some time, alert to a brooding intuition that the rock fall on Grayle's Mountain might have more ominous implications than he'd originally thought. Probably it would be a good idea to drive out at first light, have a look-see.

1:55 A.M.

. . . Tom Sherard drove the back roads of the valley and desert until at last he saw her, a lone slow-moving figure at the side of a long straight road to nowhere.

He slowed the rented SUV to a crawl and kept pace with her and she never looked his way. She walked with her head up, eyes fixed on the dim mountainous distance.

He pulled ahead of her, turned the SUV in her direction, all lights blazing. She must have been nearly blinded, but she kept walking until he got out and stepped into her path. Then she just stood there, swaying a little, looking intently at his face. Her own face was grimy, her clothing filled with dust. Breakouts on her lower lip from hives. She began to tremble, as if she were just feeling the cold.

"Where are we, Tom?"

"I don't know."

"Then let's stay lost. For a little while longer. Can't we, Tom?"

She fell forward then, eyes closing, as if she were falling out of the sky.

6:58 A.M.

. . . The ringing of Sherard's cell phone shocked Eden from her doze.

She left his side, where she had been warm and content, crept out from beneath the thin blankets on the bed they shared in a nondescript motel, the first they had come to, in a desert town that might have been in California, or Utah. The room had a single inadequate radiant heater and the floor felt like an ice rink to her bare feet. Eden rummaged in the pockets of his hunting jacket and came up with the phone. Answered.

She listened for twenty seconds, let out a soft cry as she sank down trembling on the side of the creaky bed, turned her face to Tom.

He raised his head, blinking to get the sleep out of his eyes, and stared at Eden.

"Is it about Bertie?" he asked.

"She's awake and alert. Still on the ventilator but doing, they s-said, miraculously well."

His face relaxed into an expression of gratitude and then irony at the echo of the word *miraculous* somewhere in his mind.

"All right, then. That's my girl. She's begun to heal herself."

"C-can she do that?" Eden blubbered.

"In many instances. Will you please get under the covers? You're shaking to pieces."

She had never felt more naked than in this decrepit room, four stained walls, a loose window that let in a whistling wind, a bed, the man she had made love to in the shower, soapy and voracious, then again minutes later in the bed. He was now looking at her with unexpected composure when she'd dreaded that he would push her away from him like a cheap pickup he already was tired of, regretted. She was embarrassed by her body and bones, the sores on her lower lip, the still-unbanked fire in loins and breast. Not because he'd done badly by her but because each orgasm she'd experienced had seemed only a promise of greater bliss to come.

"It's all right, Eden," he said, sympathetic to the rage of emotions in her face.

"Oh, no, how can it be all right?! I went haywire; betrayed Bertie, my *God,* insulted us both, not to mention the memory of my—"

He reached up impatiently with both hands and pulled her down hard on top of him, Eden gasping in surprise. The rough stuff a new slant on the man and the situation. But his hands relaxed immediately while still keeping her close.

"We were both haywire, as you put it, for a time, and with damn good reason. I didn't know if you were alive or dead. Drove aimlessly, one road after another. How did you manage to get so far so quickly? No, it doesn't matter. The look on your dirty face when I found you. I had to make love to you as quickly as I could, and nothing short of a bullet in my own heart could have stopped me. Quite the typical aftermath of a successful hunt. That's one aspect of it. But we made love to bring ourselves back to life. Now we will deal with it. Nothing has happened for us to be ashamed of, or grieve over, or waste time in recriminations."

"How can I d-deal with being in love with you?"

"But you're not, Eden."

He held her face against his chest while she shuddered in protest. Then, to her chagrin and sudden panic, he began to laugh.

"Nothing's funny! And how do you know what I—"

"Affection, gratitude, youthful desire is what you feel. Everything that we hope may define and enrich our long-term friendship."

"We haven't had the chance to—"

"I have no misgivings about making love to you, Eden. We've behaved humanly, not badly. But—"

Eden thought she saw herself, vaguely, a diminished spirit in the high gloss of the pupils of his eyes. She was very still against his body, afraid of what he must say next. Obeying the wants of the flesh had broken something that might not be repairable—a valuable charm that had bound the three of them in a magical circle.

"—But I would feel badly should I use this night as an excuse for an affair that would be good for neither of us. Tonight may have been fated; now we must try to get on with what is most important in our lives. Think about what lies ahead of you, Eden. And for Bertie and myself. You've grown in your powers, awesomely so, but only half of Mordaunt and what he represents lies buried behind us. You are still missing someone of vital importance to your evolution as the Avatar. Cry now if you must; but let that be an end to it."

After half a minute the motionless Eden said, "I won't cry."

"Not yet. But you will."

"I think I have to . . . go away for a while. By myself."

"Of course."

"I don't know what I'm going to say to Bertie."

"Shouldn't that be up to me?"

"Damn, damn, *damn*."

"But she will get over it."

"So sure of yourself, aren't you?"

"Not in these matters."

"Will I have to hate you before I get over you?"

Unhappiness in his eyes. "I said I was out of my depth here."

She dug her fingers into his shoulders until he winced, Eden a creature of unrest, kneading away her growing frenzy and her own sense of loss. She tossed her hair out of her eyes. Hollywoodish.

"Screw her; leave her."

"You haven't been listening worth a damn."

"Then say what I want to hear!"

"I've told you the truth. Now take your well-earned holiday and think it over, Eden."

"I can bring this room, shit, this crummy goddamn motel down around our heads. I can destroy both of us here!"

"You can do disastrous things. I bear witness. Go ahead, throw all of your toys out the window and break your crayons. It won't change the picture of yourself in your coloring book."

Eden slumped against him with a low and mournful sound.

"All right, little beauty. All right, now."

He stroked her rigid shoulders and the cold nape of her neck.

"Just hold me a little while longer, Tom." Her body quaked but her voice had lost its spiteful grit.

"For as long as you like."

"And tell me that you're hurting. Even though it's not much of a hurt."

"If I confess to that, you'll know rather too much, won't you? Could present an obstacle in the relationship we must work very hard to maintain."

"Oh boy, all the answers. The voice of pure reason. Tom Terrific, truth-bringer."

"Speaking of hurts, actually it's your bony knee digging into my bad one, and that does hurt plenty. I may whimper."

Eden shifted her weight, briefly thinking about giving him a hard nudge in the groin with her knee. Those little sulfurous bubbles of spite still showing up in the bloodstream. But she was deadly tired and, after strenuous sex, parts of her body felt like leftovers from *The Rape of the Sabine Women.* Presumably he was already sore enough.

She kissed him, sensing no reluctance on his part, relaxed and let her mouth linger beside his, lips moving speechlessly. Then she rolled away and raised herself on one elbow, looked at him. Eyes drowsy, refocusing slowly.

"I do love you. Someday you'll know how much. Our relationship will just have to live with that. Now let's get out of this dump. The wind coming in around that window is beginning to depress me. Whether or not Bertie can heal *her* wounds, how easy can that be, and meanwhile she'll need us."

7:06 A.M.

Bronc Skarbeck left the walled compound of his house overlooking Lake Las Vegas and picked up 515 north in Henderson, endured heavy traffic until he switched to Charleston Boulevard. He drove his Aston Martin west past golf courses and a desertful of closely packed housing developments that, even in the best light the new day offered, looked to Skarbeck like instant slums.

Half a dozen miles from Grayle's Mountain he tensed up, seeing clearly the immense damage that had been done to the theatre. The avalanche pile also was visible, a miniature mountain with a thin horizontal streak of smoke and dust still hovering over it.

He'd left Harlee slumbering. Didn't know how long he would be gone, but she was good at amusing herself: hair, nails, exercise classes. And she was computer literate, probably since kindergarten, a devotee in fact. The furious, fantastic, arcane games that made life itself, what used to be real life, seem drained of ardor and promise to an entire generation. Once he had asked her (addressing the back of her head) why she spent so much time on the Internet, and Harlee had answered with religious intensity, "Because it's there." The Web. The Net. What meaning did that word have for them? Security. Dive right in. For Harlee there was almost nothing as satisfying as a good chat room on the Net. A cozy cybersite with a dozen good friends using aliases. When she was unplugged for any length of time she became listless, vaguely apprehensive. Hard drives had become the culture's frontal lobes.

Two Metro police cars were parked at an angle and nose-to-nose across the entrance to the four-lane Lincoln Grayle Parkway, a wide avenue through more desert, with date palms on either side and tall Italian cypress trees planted along the median. Bronc showed his driver's license and his business card identifying him as former Marine Corps Commandant D. W. (for Dwight Willis) Skarbeck, U.S. Marine Corps (ret.), now Chairman of the Board of Lincoln Grayle Enterprises. He drove on. Sprinklers were active amid the cypresses. A few hundred yards in toward the mountain he came to the gated entrance to the theatre itself, three stories high with waterfalls in a desert garden on either side of the gates. Beyond them was the rubble perimeter of the ugly landslide.

More cars there. The pileup, covering at least twenty acres, included blobs of smoking glass, uprooted desert trees, great blocks of concrete with inch-thick lengths of twisted rebar embedded, some boulders the size of ready-mix trucks, and, undoubtedly, a large quantity of mangled rattlesnake colonies.

Stupendous. Already he was thinking, *It had to be an explosion of some kind.* The melted glass.

Skarbeck got out of his tiger cat of a car. It was a chilly morning. He wore his black leather bomber jacket over a mock wool turtleneck, and he hadn't forgotten his hiking boots. Elizabeth Ann Perkins was similarly outfitted. Her cropped, bleached hair looked crisp as honeycomb.

"Jeez, can you imagine?" Perk said, wide-eyed.

A helicopter from a local TV station flew low over their heads. A yellow Clark County fire truck was leaving; no blazes in the nearby sagebrush to put out.

Bo Wilfers, who was Vice President of Operations for the Grayle Theatre, was walking toward them down the middle of a dry

streambed. He'd apparently been reconnoitering. Bo had the wad-
dling midsection, the sluggish big-boned grace of an ace athlete
turned boozer.

"How're you, General?"

"Bo. Anyone able to get up there yet?"

"Couple of engineers. Cort McAllister from the night crew."
There was a crackle of talk on Bo's walkie. He answered, then listened, reported the news to Bronc: "Structurally the theatre's looking
fine. It's just the terrace and most of the facade that's gone. The funic-
ular to the terrace was taken out, but a freight elevator on the north
side of the carpark is untouched. We'll be able to get the menagerie
out and relocated to Snow Lake Ranch soon as the curators show up."

"What about Grayle?"

"No sign of him," Bo said with a frown, looking over the landslide
behind him. Twenty feet high in places. All of them thinking the
same thing, but no one wanted to put the ultimate curse on the situation. Elizabeth Ann had her fingers crossed behind her back. Seeing
that gave Bronc a prickly neckline, hint of yet another disaster to cut
the ground from beneath his own feet. He ran his tongue over his
teeth, tasting a residue of Harlee, her piquant flavor. A black bird
soared smoothly down on a current of air from the heights of the
mountain range and took up a vigil on a branch of an arrow-shaped
conifer stuck at a sharp angle in the morass.

Bo's walkie crackled again. "Yeah, on my way," he said to someone inside the theatre.

The freight elevator was large enough to lift a ten-ton truck two
hundred feet to a warehouse cut into solid rock. Above this storage
area were kitchens where meals for sixteen hundred guests were prepared on show nights. From there they walked through a wide passageway to the lobby.

Emergency power was on. But the lobby, with a weak inflow of
light from the rising sun, was a hive of long shadows and shattered
decor. Bronc upped the illumination with a million-candlepower
floodlight. He sniffed deeply; he had a good nose for the residue of
explosives. Because what he saw on the 150-foot curve of travertine
floor amazed and perplexed him. Heaps and globs of melted glass

below the skeletal bronze remains of eight large chandeliers. But there was no indication that there had been a fire hot enough to do such damage. Not a trace of smoke. Nor for that matter did he detect the fumes of dynamite or Semtex.

Bo cautioned, "Glass is still hot, so be careful where you walk."

"Bo, just what the hell happened here?"

Bo could only shake his head. Perk said in a voice filled with awe, "Never in my born days."

Bronc walked around a coalescing whalelike pile of glass, avoiding little semihardened rivulets extending several feet from the mass. His powerful light revealed something kerneled inside: a dark, vague form. His heart jumped.

"Oh, my Lord," Perk said softly. "What *is* that?"

"Animal, I'd say."

"But could it be—"

"Human? Don't think so. Wrong body shape, and the size of the head—"

The brilliant reflection from the glass hurt Skarbeck's eyes. He aimed his light away from the curious cryptlike blister on the marble floor.

"Bo, can you find out if any of the big cats Linc uses in his act are missing from the menagerie?"

"Check on that right away."

"Perk, I don't remember how to find my way back to Linc's dressing suite."

"I'll take you. But we already know he's not—"

"I want to look around anyway." He glanced up, wondering why, if there'd been enough heat generated in the lobby to melt glass, the sprinkler system hadn't functioned. "And, Perk. Get me all the tapes from every security camera, inside the theatre and out."

"The insurance investigators will be asking—"

"Uh-uh. I want to see them first."

Tom Sherard and Eden Waring had breakfast at a Denny's in North Las Vegas. Eden forced herself to eat a bite, then two bites of omelet, then turned ravenous while looking over the morning papers.

Alberta ("Bertie") Nkambe, twenty-year-old superstar model and celebrity *vivant* from Kenya, had made the front pages of the *Las Vegas Sun, USA Today,* and the West Coast edition of the *New York Times.* The stories were all slanted the way Tom had predicted they would be. Bertie had been lunching with a friend after a fashion show at the Bahìa megaresort on the Strip and, struck by stray bullets, was the innocent victim of a love-triangle shooting. The designated victim and her companion at lunch, Charmaine Goferne of Atlanta, Georgia, and the lovelorn assassin, one Cornell Crigler of Las Vegas and an employee of Nevada Gambling Control, were dead. Cornell from a self-inflicted wound moments after the fatal shooting. As was Charmaine's boyfriend, a detective sergeant with Atlanta PD named Lewis Gruvver. He had been shot once in the temple earlier in the day in his and Charmaine's bungalow at Bahìa. Same gun. Mr. Crigler had left a wife and several kids. Messy, but with that familiar inevitability that made the case a quick wrap-up for the local cops.

And all of it was complete fiction, Eden knew; Bertie had been the real target. Mordaunt may have thought he could handle Eden, but not Eden and Bertie together. Another miscalculation. Charmaine was another poor soul captured by the gravity of the irresistible Trickster and put to his purposes. She hoped Crigler and Charmaine, released from thrall, would have a nice extraterrestrial rest somewhere else. While Mordaunt the shape-shifting Trickster remained earthbound, immortal and thus sentient but helpless inside his glass display case until the last tick of Eternity.

My pleasure, the Avatar thought, with malice that was followed by a dreary shudder.

Eden ate the last portion of her omelet. A double scotch would've tasted wonderful with those somewhat bland eggs. Tasted wonderful anytime. The breakouts on her lower lip hurt. Hives. One minor consequence of all the Dark Energy she had channeled; probably she was lucky that her back teeth hadn't melted along with those chandeliers. She was using hand sanitizer on the blotches but it would be a couple of days before they dried up and meantime she felt and probably looked like a wreck. Stress was responsible for the early onset of her period. Too bad there were no taut, terrific, maintenance-free superbodies to go with superminds, Eden thought, with a savage cynicism that surprised and then depressed her.

Sherard was checking e-mails on his computer. He looked up at her.

"*Habari gani?*" Eden asked.

"Joseph is on his way from Nairobi." Joseph was Bertie's father. "And her brother is coming from Paris."

"Family. They'll be a great help to her." Eden smiled weakly at Tom and looked away. Blue morning distance. Sere mountains. And then—ta-da!—there was Las Vegas. You could dress up the landscape with comedy architecture but still it all resembled distressed property in hell. It was Lincoln Grayle's town, and she wondered how many of the Trickster's minions were still orbiting his defunct nucleus. She hated the place. Her heart was breaking here.

Another naked, lingering look at her lover-by-chance, while his attention was elsewhere. Tom Sherard, idealistic to a fault, although his own heart in their hour of intimacy had revealed its flaw, that buried vein of fool's gold.

"Let's go see Bertie," Eden said. "She's wondered where we are."

"How do you know that?"

"How do I know anything?" Eden said with a shrug.

His Holiness Pope John XXIV has his evening meal served to him on a tray in his papal apartment study, having canceled a formal dinner with visiting prelates from several Eastern European countries. He pled indisposition due to a stubborn ear infection, but his real purpose is to confer with the shade of a young Arab prince who had been a rare and promising moderate with growing diplomatic influence in the venal, superheated atmosphere of Persian Gulf politics. His older brother, jealous of his popularity, had had Rahim assassinated six days ago.

The Holy Father's day job, according to a principal tenet of the Catholic religion, is God on earth. He was born Sebastiano Leoncaro in the Italian Piedmont, one of his numerous human personae throughout millennia. As the senior member of a council of twelve Old Souls, he is the supreme voice of the Caretakers, responsible for matters of policy, assignments, and the inevitable fitness reports: none of the ancients, including Leoncaro himself, has achieved the state of cosmic perfection represented by a star in the firmament. They all have struggled, earthbound, for hundreds of thousands of years to give guidance to the human race, that hodgepodge of fledgling souls incarnating every day to begin the arduous task of defining themselves. A long learning process even for those who have achieved a satisfactory degree of advancement in less-demanding cosmic outposts. Earth has its beauty spots but it also has Malterrans, who are here to harass and hone the human psyches of the Little Souls to a fine edge of homicidal fury.

Leoncaro, the Light on earth, has an opposite number: Mordaunt, *Deus Inversus,* darkness that only supernal light may penetrate. The Caretakers, able to influence but not interfere directly in the actions of men, however stupid and harmful to their progress, have had some interesting times with Mordaunt, who can interfere as much as he pleases while treating the human personae of the Caretakers to horrors and bloodbaths.

Twelve Caretakers have never been enough, particularly with the population of the medium-size and overburdened planet soaring to six billion. But twelve is a sacred number in celestial dynamics. Not to be trifled with. Because of attrition from overwork (even the hardiest of ancients eventually fray and lose their pep in service to the Little Souls), there always is a need for replacement council members. Leoncaro has trained his share. Zachary, an Echelon 3 in the hierarchy of prospective Caretakers, is one of them.

While he eats his broccoli and pasta and sips white tea for his digestion, Leoncaro says to Zach, who is seated on a small sofa in the study, "I'm reluctant to put you in the field again so soon. You've made your contribution as Rahim, and earned a holiday."

"I should have seen it coming. Abdallah has the brains of a cabbage. I always thought it would be Fouad."

"We move on," Leoncaro says. "To Las Vegas."

"From one desert paradise to another," Zachary says. "From the Empty Quarter to empty pockets."

"Good to know that being blown sky-high in the royal yacht didn't vaporize your sense of humor."

"What's going on in Glitter Gulch?"

"By way of explanation," Leoncaro says, passing a linen napkin edged in gold thread over his lips, "perhaps I should introduce you to someone."

He holds the napkin away from himself and gives it a significant shake. From the loose cloth tumble spheres of sapphire and ruby light that, whirling giddily, arrange themselves into the fair figure of a young woman, the flame ruby of her hair slowly paling to strawberry blond. She turns when fully formed, smiles gracefully at her mentor, then turns again and, still smiling, acknowledges the shade of the late desert prince with a courteous nod. She remains facing him with an easeful radiance, steadfast as the evening star, hands folded at her waist.

"This is Eden Waring," Leoncaro says. "The Avatar."

"Beautiful," Zachary, appropriately mesmerized, says to his boss. "But she is not one of us?"

"No. Eden is, however, a prodigy and a blessing, a soul enlightened through many incarnations; perhaps this will be her last stay on earth. We would like for it to be a long and useful stay."

"What powers does she possess as the Avatar?"

"Eden is a prophetic dreamer. She has psychotronic capability and access to great stores of cosmic energy, employable through a little talisman that I provided her, accompanied by a portion of humbug and balderdash. But talismans require a story if they're to be effective."

"Oh, sure."

The talisman that Leoncaro speaks of, a small twist of an unidentifiable metal that the vision of Eden wears mounted on a gold chain around her neck, exhibits pinpoints of twinkling light.

"Also Eden possesses the left-handed art: she can produce her doppelganger almost at will."

"Two of them?" Zachary says with a perplexed smile. "An embarrassment of riches?"

"Hardly," Leoncaro says, suddenly grim. "But we'll come to that. You should understand that although Eden is well centered, mature and resourceful for her years and a born leader—she was captain of her basketball teams in high school and college—the suddenness with which the mantle of Avatar was thrust on her left Eden in a low state of emotional turmoil verging on morbidity. Adding to her problems was Mordaunt—in the persona of Lincoln Grayle at his most seductive."

"An illusionist, isn't he? I saw him one time on telly."

"*Was* an illusionist." Leoncaro permits himself a few moments of satisfaction at the thought. "Having seen Eden in action, I chose to put her at great risk once more, along with another gifted young psychic, Alberta Nkambe. I sent them after Mordaunt."

The holographic Eden looks around at him. Leoncaro nods and she seats herself on a corner of his desk, gazing serenely at painted cherubs on the study's ceiling.

"It didn't go all that smoothly," Leoncaro continues. "Miss Nkambe is recovering from gunshot wounds in a Las Vegas hospital, another of the Trickster's machinations. But because he coveted Eden—or the monster offspring he was confident she would bear him—Mordaunt apparently was a little careless. And Eden buried him. Rather, she buried a teratogenec nightmare, the shape Mordaunt had assumed in order to be able to mate with her, under half a ton of melted glass in the lobby of the Lincoln Grayle Theatre."

"Nice going," Zachary says with an admiring whistle. "She can deliver the goods. So Mordaunt is—"

"Entombed. But still immortal."

"Then you would like me to—"

"No, no. I've already arranged for the necessary disposal through the good offices of the *Crucis Aurea*. Wouldn't do for the beast's remains to end up in a desert landfill with coffee grounds and unpaid bills, a Dumpster shrine for the Wicked of his Lasting Dark who flocked around Mordaunt in his prime."

There is an interval during which the Holy Father sucks at a bit of broccoli stuck between two gold-crowned teeth. Finally he reaches in with a thumbnail to dislodge it.

"That would seem to be that," Zachary says, certain that there must be a great deal more on Leoncaro's mind.

"Following the Holocaust we succeeded in disciplining Mordaunt, reducing his power by half, by isolating the masculine and feminine halves of his black soul. That formidable effort cost us three Caretakers, and I've suffered for years with headaches like rock crushers."

Zachary nods in respect for what had been a fabulous feat of will. First the council's outrage; then the power of many suns, the purest light in the universe, had been channeled through a psychic prism of all the Caretakers to split the soul of the dark god Mordaunt in a supernova instant. Like taking a bright razor to a fat plum, by way of a mundane analogy. The masculine aspect of the Trickster's would continue to be, as always, bad news for humankind, but the feminine soul had been consigned to a chain gang in rural Georgia in the 1920s, installed in a physical body whose punishing workday was destined to repeat metronomically, in that dusty little corner of a parallel universe, until the stars went blind. Or had something gone awry with the Caretakers' scheme?

"I'm afraid so," Leoncaro says, anticipating what the late Rahim's question will be. "As I told you, one of Eden Waring's talents is her ability to produce the doppelganger. A reverse-image replica in flesh, blood, and all-too-human longings. Subject to certain laws of physics. The dpg was nonetheless under full control of her homebody."

"But all doppelgangers are devious in their desire to acquire identities of their own."

"Only Eden, in the ancient tradition of the Eponym—the Namegiver—may grant her dpg independent life. Which, although she was inexperienced in occult matters, Eden knew instinctively not to do."

"In spite of the wiles of her lookalike?"

"Because Eden was uncooperative, the doppelganger named herself—which doesn't count, of course, except for vanity's sake. She chose Guinevere—'Gwen' for short. The heart of the matter is, through no fault of Eden's, Gwen has gone missing."

"How can that be?" Zachary says, quietly amazed.

"While masquerading as Eden, Gwen attracted notice from Lincoln Grayle. He must have observed almost immediately that she was only a doppelganger. But he had a use for one of the dpg's special talents, which is the ability to travel through time."

"Oh-oh."

"Yes."

"But if *Gwen* is under Eden's control—"

Leoncaro gestures with the hand that bears the papal ring that millions of the laity yearn to kiss while down on one knee in a holy place.

"She isn't. Eden was here, in my study, four days ago. She told me that she had lost contact with her dpg."

"How? That would violate physical law, not occult tradition."

"Merely conjecture; but Mordaunt may have invented a means to disturb the electromagnetic synchronicity of homebody and dpg. If she were temporarily not subject to Eden's volition, Gwen may have been persuaded to . . . do the Trickster a little favor." Leoncaro makes a wry face. "Whether Eden can regain control of her doppelganger before serious mischief occurs is a problem Eden has lacked the time to devote herself to."

Zachary studies the representation of Eden Waring, ever smiling, that waits attendance near him, trying to envision—through her astute good-natured eyes, the untiring but polite gaze now fixed on him—the rough were-beast she put paid to, damned to a stretch of time it could be hoped would equal that of a prehistoric insect drowsing in a hardened ooze of amber.

Mordaunt.

Or, more accurately, the masculine aspect of the entity. Cruelty suppressed, rage inhibited, his gross and evil powers reduced by the Avatar to the mildness of a baby's fart.

"So it must be the other half of Mordaunt's soul we need to be concerned about now," Zachary says.

"It would be negligent and reckless of us to assume any less." Leoncaro is grim in his concern.

"And you want me to help Eden Waring?"

"With Bertie Nkambe laid up for now, and Tom Sherard attending to a vital matter I am about to propose to him, she will be needing someone else she can count on."

"I have your authority to do a Takeover?"

"Certainly. Time is of the essence. Because of her treatment of the so-called Great One, Las Vegas has become a dangerous place for Eden."

"I haven't had much experience with Takeovers," Zachary muses. "I'll be responsible for two human entities, not one."

Leoncaro's mouth turns down at the corners. "Do we need to have this conversation?"

"No, Holiness. But . . . I may have to shadow Eden for a while until I come across someone suitable for a Takeover."

"'These troublesome disguises which we wear,'" Leoncaro says, quoting from *Paradise Lost.* "Remember that you're dealing with an Avatar. If Eden senses that she's haunted, it will not be beneficial to her morale."

Tom Sherard and Eden Waring were permitted ten minutes with Bertie Nkambe in the critical-care unit of the hospital.

Bertie's hair had been shaved from one side of her scalp and she had drains in her head. The swollen face would have been unrecognizable on any of the magazine covers where Bertie had been appearing since she was sixteen. Her brain was still edematous but the damage to her right temple, done by a bullet that had already passed through Charmaine Goferne's body, had been repaired during five hours of surgery. Bertie was on a ventilator because a second bullet had collapsed a lung. The third shot had shattered her right wrist as she tumbled out of her chair to the floor of the terrace café at Bahìa, where she'd been lunching with Charmaine, a sad tense lunch for Bertie as she peeped the other girl's mind and discovered that very little of humane intent or social consequence remained there, thanks to Mordaunt.

Bertie was conscious but, intubated, she couldn't talk. Even subvocal conversation with Eden, a skill they had been practicing during the months Eden had spent at Shungwaya, came hard for Bertie.

—Lincoln Grayle? *Mordaunt?*

—Done for. It's finished.

—How?

—Relax, I'll show you.

Eden held Bertie's left hand in her own hand, careful not to disturb the drip line inserted into the large vein below her middle finger. She gently massaged with a thumb the underside of Bertie's wrist, exciting a current that rose as waves of imagery to Bertie's brain and caused her own body to tremble.

—*Awesome.*

—Why, thanks.

—You okay?

Eden looked around the circular critical-care unit, which was crowded with flattened folk behind gauzy partitions, some as bad off as Bertie, others possibly worse: major coronaries, accident victims hung slackly in glistening graceful drip lines, cheating death to the *whuff* of ventilators and the ping of exotic medical monitors, lines of vital signs like unfolding waves across the screens. The nurses all had the serious faces of high calling.

—Guess so.

—No. You're not. You're running on empty. It's like you're thin skin and bone and I can see the light passing through you.

—Come to think of it, I probably could use a nap.

—Don't go yet.

Bertie's eyelids flickered. She looked at Tom, waiting at the foot of the bed, rangy and high shouldered, intently studying her, a little knob of muscle in one cheek the only indication of unhappiness.

—Tell Tom . . . I love him.

—I will. But he knows, Bertie.

—You've got the shakes.

—More like heebie-jeebies. I'll be all right. Tom wants to be with you now, Bertie, and they didn't give us much time to be in here.

The respirator chuffed and sighed.

—Wait . . . Eden. What about Gwen?

—Oh, don't know. I have to find her. She'll keep, wherever she is. Bertie, the whole world's been calling. I'll get back to some of your people for you, let them know how you're doing—and Joseph, hey, didn't I tell you? Joseph and Kieti are on the way to Las Vegas!

—Wonderful. Tell them . . . not to worry. But this is going to take a little time. I have a lot of work to do inside my brain. It's like . . . an earthquake knocked everything off the shelves.

Eden gave up her seat beside the bed to Tom, smiled at Bertie, a smile that went flat against her teeth in an involuntary grimace. She kissed her fingertips and brushed them across Bertie's humid brow, then fled the room.

In the bathroom down the hall Eden dropped clumsily to her knees and with a dismal quaking gave up her breakfast. Then she sat back nerveless and cold against a tiled wall, too worn out and sick with guilt to want to show her face to anyone ever again. Because she had seen in Bertie's almond eyes recognition of what Eden had hoped to withhold—in spite of the fact that Tom was still all over her skin, a flushed erotic malady, and there was that chiming in her heart whenever she glanced his way. Even in the mummylike limbo provided by painkillers and massive hits of antibiotics and antiinflammatory drugs Bertie couldn't have missed it.

To make the hell that she wanted, childishly, to writhe in more of a torment, Eden understood that the contempt and anger she wished Bertie to feel would never be forthcoming—the animus that only a spitting catfight, a howling siege of recriminations, might subdue. No, in her inevitable hurt Bertie would find the largeness of soul to forgive Eden. There was a simple truth here: Tom was Bertie's one true love, always would be. Every truth enrages someone. It was Eden's rage that had her in hell, not the presumption of guilt. She bumped the back of her head against the wall. Again and again, figuring this out.

Someone else wanted to use the bathroom. Eden was feeling pulses again from the head-banging exercise. A warm-up flow of blood. Her hands had almost stopped tingling. She felt cranky and slightly ridiculous sitting there, out of excuses. She wanted a drink of water.

It was Tom Sherard waiting outside. He smelled the lingering airs of her purging with a twitch of his mouth she couldn't interpret either as sympathy or disgust. Well, all right then.

He left the door ajar, took Eden gently by one arm and led her away.

"Hold up your head, now." She lifted her head with a tense smile. "And for all our sakes, Eden, stop beating yourself up."

"I've stopped."

9:38 A.M.

In his Moorish-style house of cool arcades and spacious windows framing blue water or desert hues of sage green and dusty rose, Bronc Skarbeck sat in his leather-paneled study running surveillance tapes from the Lincoln Grayle Theatre complex. Twenty-three different cameras that had recorded comings and goings during a two-hour period from ten p.m. to shortly after midnight of the present day.

Some of the cameras were stationary, others panned 180 degrees.

Fast-forward and it was like watching an old-time silent movie comedy, the jump and scurry of forms, disjointed zipalong action, except there was no culmination, no merry slapstick finale to be savored.

Skarbeck was familiar with most of the area the cameras covered. Four different angles on the scimitar curve of the marbled lobby. Five angles inside the dinner theatre and on the stage, a multilevel marvel of technology and engineering by the whiz-kid illusion-design team of an imaginative showman. The old flea-flicker smoke-and-mirrors magic game elevated exponentially, combining circus with the pyrotechnics of a space-shuttle liftoff. Two hundred twenty-five dollars a ticket, no seniors' discount or group rates, which price included a palatable three-course dinner with a choice of red or white wine before the show. They were serving mostly Aussie imports now; California vintages had become too pricey. The all-new Lincoln Grayle show, now indefinitely postponed, had sold out four months in advance.

Skarbeck flinched at the thought of refunding approximately thirty-two million dollars. Or, worse, permanently shutting down due to the loss of the star attraction.

While he sped through the tapes he was averaging a phone call every three minutes. What to do about this, say about that? The news trickling in ranged from hopeful to near calamitous, depending on whom he was talking to. Lincoln Grayle's Shelby GTO had turned up in the garage of the only mechanic Grayle allowed to touch it, out by Nellis Air Force Base. So that somewhat lessened the chance that Grayle had perished in the gigantic rock slide. On the other hand, he could have called for a limo. It likely would take about three weeks to blast, bulldoze, and truck away all the debris from the base of the mountain to find out what or who might have been, lucklessly, beneath the roar and smash.

Skarbeck preferred to believe that the Magician had been resting up in his dressing room when the avalanche occurred. But nothing on the tapes he'd viewed so far supported this hope. Needless to say, Linc didn't have surveillance cameras in the dressing suite.

But if he were still alive, why the hell couldn't he at least let Skarbeck know?

The dress rehearsal for the new show had ended around eight o'clock. By ten thirty the theatre and support complex were nearly deserted. Late deliveries for the kitchen stores and wine cellar had ended. Meetings of zookeepers, the show's cast and backstage crew, the tech people, the kitchen and wait staffs, were over. Four security guards, a couple of engineers, and the menagerie's vets were still around: one of Lincoln Grayle's snow leopards was about to deliver cubs. Elizabeth Ann Perkins also had lingered, should Grayle need her for something.

And a little before ten p.m. Eden Waring had arrived.

Business or pleasure?

The tapes he was watching didn't have her walking into the theatre, standing there in that big lobby a little uncertainly, maybe, then being noticed by one of the security techies in the bunkered room with all the TV screens, who alerted Patrol or maybe Perk herself to find out what Eden wanted. Skarbeck didn't see any of that and wasn't particularly interested. What he wanted was to see her leaving, with or without the Magician. Or had Eden left at all before the big slide, the unexplained melting of eight huge chandeliers? Bronc Skarbeck had a mystery to solve. But he was objective, pragmatic. A man to keep his head even with the world out of warp. Eden Waring didn't scare him. She only made him think about things he didn't want to think about.

Harlee Nations came into Bronc's study while he was on another phone call. Harlee wasn't wearing the usual teenager grunge. She dressed up to be casual. Three thousand dollars' worth of Hermès stuff; and she was barefoot. Touching. She'd had her morning swim in the lap pool, done another mile on the treadmill in the poolside gym. Unusual for a sixteen-year-old with a heaven-sent body to pay so much attention to physical conditioning. Also she watched what she ate. No fast food for Harlee and she never touched "sweetsies," her name for candy or desserts.

She stood a few feet behind his high-backed leather swivel chair, visible to him on the blank face of one of the monitors. There were three on his boomerang-shaped desk. The two other monitors were running tapes simultaneously.

Skarbeck terminated his call and swiveled around to face her with his terse, slightly canted smile of admiration. He put the tapes on pause.

Harlee kissed the top of his head where his scalp showed in a small brown oval.

"What's going on, Daddy?" she said in her wisp of a voice, green-gage eyes catching sunlight from prisms of leaded glass in the windows.

"There was a rock slide at the theatre last night."

"Ohh. Was anyone hurt?"

"We don't think so. I'm looking at tapes for around midnight to see—uh, if it might have been a minor earthquake. I could go for a fresh cup of coffee."

"Sure. Then if it's okay I'm going to meet a couple of friends at the Grand Canal Shops. We'll probably do lunch too."

"Need some money?"

"Oh, I guess three hundred. I won't splurge, Daddy."

Bronc took out his bankroll and slipped some fifties from his money clip.

"Have a good time," he said indulgently.

"Thanks. I'll be right back with your coffee."

Skarbeck took off the tapes he'd been looking at and considered those that remained in the big carton on one end of his desk. He selected one marked MENAGERIE TUNNEL/2300 HOURS, and another that afforded a 180-degree continuous pan of the lobby, 2400–0200 hours. He ran the tunnel tape first, and saw nothing of interest until shortly before midnight.

At eleven fifty-six, according to the counter in the lower left of the frame, two figures appeared. Bronc slowed the tape to normal speed. The camera angle and the low after-hours lighting in the tunnel prevented him from seeing all but the basic structure of their faces. Nonetheless, from the shape of the man, the way he walked, or prowled, that wily grace, he had to be Lincoln Grayle. The young woman keeping him company had a bottle in one hand. Too big for Pepsi. It had the canister shape of a wine bottle.

She stopped, swaying tipsily, and swigged. Grayle paused too, leaned against a tunnel wall. There was some dialogue between them. The young woman overgesturing in an impassioned but well-soused manner. Grayle patient, watchful, perhaps, with folded arms.

Then she lurched toward the Magician, bottle in the left hand and behind her hip. For a moment her face turned toward the camera, flaring into a clarity of features as if flashgunned. Skarbeck hit Pause. He studied her. Yes. He was looking at Eden Waring.

Eden put her right hand on Grayle's opposite shoulder. Then around to the back of his neck. She tried to snuggle against him. Still talking. He appeared not to like having her on top of him but made no attempt to push her away. She put her head down against his chest and dropped her hand to his crotch, began to grope him.

Skarbeck wished he knew what was being said at that moment, but probably even a lip-reader wouldn't have been of much help to him. Lincoln Grayle with his shoulders against the wall and the Waring girl trying to get into his pants.

Then Eden appeared to collapse. The Magician's hands were at his sides, obviously he hadn't struck her. She was all of a sudden dead-slack against his body, like a fainting spell, and knock-kneed.

When he tried to lift her up and move her away from him, Eden recovered. Skarbeck saw, in her left hand, the wine bottle that for a time had been out of sight. She rammed the bottle butt-first into Lincoln Grayle's face and there was a dark spume of blood as his head snapped back.

She hit him again, backhanded with the bottle, which broke jaggedly in two against a cheekbone or the top of his skull. Her quickness and the savagery of the attack amazed Skarbeck. He had to see it again. Then once more. Then the tape ran on and Grayle sprawled on the tunnel floor, hands raised weakly to protect himself, but obviously he was all but unconscious.

For a few moments Eden Waring stood over him in a lethal sort of crouch, the sawtoothed part of the wine bottle poised near his bludgeoned face. Grayle gestured weakly, unable to defend himself.

Jesus.

But she didn't do it. Eden apparently said something final to him— as if anything remained to be said—with an angry jerk of her head. Then she backed away, turned, and walked quickly out of range of the surveillance camera, not drunk at all in Skarbeck's estimation.

Precision and brutality. Eden Waring had set Grayle up, probably having known what she was going to do even before she arrived at the theatre. Skarbeck could admire that sort of purpose and the nerve necessary to pull it off.

He watched Lincoln Grayle, barely moving, casualty of an intimate war Bronc had been unaware of, lying on the floor of the menagerie tunnel until the tape ran out.

There was no follow-up tape of the tunnel that might have told Skarbeck how long the Magician had lain there bleeding. The security bunker wasn't manned after eleven p.m. If one of the veterinary crew still in the menagerie had heard Grayle call for help during the few minutes from midnight to the moment the towering glass facade of the theatre had slumped down like fiery lava from the mountain, piling up on the terrace and ultimately causing its collapse, Skarbeck would have been alerted right away and Grayle would be in a hospital now with plastic surgeons considering how to rebuild that famous face, resurrect its nuances of dark romance and canny mystery.

So Linc had managed to leave the tunnel without anyone to help him and go—where?

Skarbeck started the lobby tape.

Each tier of the eight identical chandeliers, powered down to a dappled glow after-hours, had the tightly joined facets of a dowager's diamond bracelet. They reflected light from the terrace floods through the glass of the lobby doors. Part of the terrace was visible as the camera panned. He noticed movement out there. Skarbeck paused the tape and tried to make out what was happening through the floodlight glare on the lobby doors. He recognized a security patrol cart, stationary, but because of the camera angle he would've needed computerized enhancement to identify who was standing beside the cart.

Even without enhancement, the figure was unmistakably female. Miss Waring again?

He fast-forwarded until the camera had returned to that area of the terrace about which he was most curious. Pause.

The same figure, and now, at the outer edge of the camera's eye, a hint of someone else.

Exasperated by his limited apprehension, Skarbeck let the tape move on. When it panned back to that glimpse of terrace that was beginning to obsess him, he paused again.

The figure that had been standing by the golf cart wasn't there. Something else was, much larger than a human being. Dark and cat-like, thrashing on the terrace floor as Skarbeck rolled the tape forward and back, again and again.

On the next pass by the camera the beast had definition and was closer to the theatre, on the move and dragging something that looked like—

Looked like, almighty Jesus, a human leg.

Skarbeck blinked and fidgeted while the camera panned away. When it returned almost dead-center on the lobby doors he saw that the thick sandwich glass had been broken out of its chrome steel frame, and the animal, bigger than any panther Bronc had seen—no, the color was throwing him off, that jet inkiness, this cat had the heavyweight body of a tiger. With a large, ugly, doglike head. Night-marish, even without the fifth appendage, a lissome length of woman's leg hanging from the beast's shaggy underbelly. Worse, leaving a swath of blood or excrement across the travertine floor while, in the floodlit exterior, Eden Waring followed with the measured steps and clasped hands of a processionist.

Another astonishment: a thin radiance, a lance of light, beamed out from somewhere near her breastbone, and her eyes were vividly aglow in an otherwise shadowy, somber face. The upward-slanting beam of light she seemed to project connected with a chandelier above the crawling, obviously wounded beast. The chandelier erupted like a phosphorous torch, whiting out the tape until the panning camera moved on.

Another twenty seconds before the camera returned to that exact angle, where it captured an elongated, molten glop of what had been crystal chandelier engulfing the silently screaming creature on the lobby floor.

What wonders were these?

Skarbeck heard a shriek behind him. He jumped as if a knife had been thrust between his shoulder blades.

He looked around to see his delicious teen companion, Harlee Nations, lose her grip on the mug of black coffee she had brought him. Her head fell back and she crumpled bonelessly in a dead faint on the Spanish tiles of his study.

5:22 A.M.

In the ninth hour of the high-stakes Texas hold 'em game that had begun the night before in one of the plush card rooms of Bahìa, Cody Olds was reasonably sure he knew who the big winner was going to be, with $180,000 in a pot that was still building.

Four of the six players who had begun the game had quit the table: the cross-dressing heart surgeon from Dallas; the German arms dealer who looked like Beethoven; the hip-hop record producer, a sharp dresser who had a silly street name and carried a covey of adoring chocolate chippies around with him; and a sixtyish comedienne and longtime Vegas favorite who had a butch haircut, a twinkle, and a salty leer. Along with The Actor, she had kept the verbal action lively ("I named my last dog Oedipus Rex; he had a lot of mother issues"). When she left the game with a grand sigh after mucking a pretty good hand, The Actor had looked up at her with exaggerated pity and said, "Glut thy sorrow on a morning's rose, Nadine."

Then, as he pondered the cards on the flop, he'd said, "Nadine and I have always been on the verge of getting it on, you know. But somehow it never happened. One of those great unconsummated romances, like Hemingway and Garbo."

"Marlene Dietrich," Cody had murmured. "Wasn't it?"

"You were never going to get within sniffing distance of *my* organ grinder 'long as I was buying the drinks," Nadine had retorted as she was leaving the card room. She had handed out C-notes to the casino employees who had kept the game running smoothly with new decks when requested and providing liquid refreshment, a buffet, lots of bowls of ice, and hot moist towels for the players.

The Actor had kept their little break going by taking a sip of the apple juice he drank exclusively while playing poker. He had been nominated four times for Academy Awards and had won twice. He read good books and collected Impressionist paintings.

"Only those with some experience in living know how to age well," he had said to the hip-hop *artiste*, who was in his young thirties, played poker recklessly and without flair, and had no idea of what The Actor was talking about.

The Actor played now with a leisure that somewhat masked his ferocious desire to destroy everyone else in the game. He was probably the best bluffer Cody had ever met. Cody was no slouch at the gull either. He had inherited a sparse and stoic expression that went back a ways on the family tree—his father's side—to one of the original mountain men of the early 1880s. The eyes like chips of obsidian. The rest of him—his build, bold chin and cheekbones, hair as black as an Indian pony's mane—was pure Navajo.

Two sevens and the jack of diamonds had been dealt on the flop. The Actor, who was sitting across the table from Cody, now might be holding quads: two sevens down, two on the flop. But at least trips, Cody thought.

With two jacks in the hole, Cody was already secure with a full house.

The Actor went all in: another eighty thousand. So this was going to be the ball cruncher of the all-night game. The Actor had to be smelling a possible full house in Cody's cards. Either he had the nuts and Cody could save himself an expensive call, or The Actor was running a bluff with only three sevens. And why not? He played aggressively and bluffed with panache; he'd taken two big pots already against weaker players when they had better cards. Most actors who were any good at poker were lamentably short of easy tells, and adept at spotting phonies. Part of their professional training, Cody assumed.

Cody thought he had spotted something, though, during previous sessions when The Actor was in town. He tended to be more talkative when he was running a bluff. And it was his nature to relish gutting an excellent player holding a hand that should have won the pot. Persuading Cody to fold a full house would juice him for a week. In spite of long hours at the table with only a couple of breaks, The Actor's eyes behind lightly tinted glasses were otherworldly bright, like the mystical jewel in a toad's forehead. Yeah, he was up to stealing another pot, Cody thought, a little dry in the mouth but otherwise nerveless. Not the impression he conveyed, however, worrying a stack of chips with his left hand. Letting the suspense build.

They looked at each other, minds locked in contemplation of their strengths and rivalry.

"You don't talk much about yourself, Cody. I've noticed that."

"Not all that much to talk about." He had a low-pitched, square-shooter's voice, pure western Americana as to accent, the sort of voice ad agencies employed to sell rugged pickup trucks on TV or persuade people to eat more beef.

"Not married, I presume."

Cody considered an answer.

"The only woman I ever wanted to marry is married to my best friend."

"Oh. That is a dilemma."

"No, I wouldn't say so. I just go on lovin' them both and it's good enough for me."

"Men less wise than yourself would consider it a tragedy." The Actor had another nip of apple juice, not taking his eyes from Cody's face as he enjoyed Cody's other, presumed dilemma: to call or not to call. "You know, it's a toss-up whether more tragedies are born of vanity, or of love." He paused and let a smile uncurl. "Or is love just another form of vanity?"

"Beats the hell out of me," Cody said, wondering what movie that was from.

"Well, it's been enjoyable, Cody. Most enjoyable. But now I believe the moment of truth is at hand." The Actor's smile became a little cozier as he watched Cody with crafty passionate eyes.

Cody abruptly called, then flipped over his cards.

For a moment The Actor had an expression of airy surprise, like a man taking a misstep off a blue-sky girder. He looked for salvation on Fourth and Fifth Streets, the skid row of back-broke poker players. The dealer laid down a six of spades and a king.

"Nice doin' business with you," Cody said.

The Actor drew a long theatrical breath. "I may be screwed, but tell me I don't deserve it."

"You don't," Cody said, casting an eye on the card-room major-domo, who came over to box up his chips. Two hundred forty thousand for a night's recreation. He'd won bigger, and he'd lost his share. "Trips usually get the job done."

"I don't suppose I can interest you in one more turn of the cards for, say, fifty thousand?" The Actor wheedled. "Just to give me a little taste of satisfaction after such a disappointing night?"

"Nope," Cody said. And, unexpectedly, he winked. "I'm afraid of you gamblers." It was the pure-luck factor involved in high-card that made him leery. For thrills he rode roller coasters.

"I do have an early call, so I should be on my way to the set. But tell me: how did you learn to size up people so well?"

"People are easy," Cody said. "Horses, they're hard."

Tom Sherard was waiting at the north end of the Lincoln Grayle Theatre's parking lot in the light of three emergency flares, antacid-pink semaphores to the sky above, when the helicopter arrived, huge and thundering. Sherard flew helicopters himself and as this one was landing he identified it as one of Sikorsky's S-80 superlift models. Three General Electric engines. Its hover shook him and sucked the air out of his chest. Super Stallion. They had been built for the U.S. Navy and Marine Corps, but Sherard observed as the helicopter settled down a hundred feet from him that it had no military markings. The Stallion could carry a couple of pilots, a crew chief, and fifty-five troops, or a max payload close to seventy thousand pounds.

With his head down he walked through a squall of dust and fumes toward the helicopter. Ten men—he assumed they were all men—disembarked. They were anonymous, all about the same size in dark gray paramilitary or SWAT gear, but Sherard didn't see any automatic weapons. Sidearms only, probably Tasers.

The team leader of the *Crucis Aurea* Flex Force met him halfway.

An old, old religious cult with a benevolent name, with rituals, meaning, purposes unknown to Sherard. He shivered in his sheepskin-lined leather jacket.

"Tom Sherard?" He had an accent. Italian, Tom thought. The team leader glanced at the distinctive, hardy-looking blackthorn cane, as aggressive in appearance as a cudgel, that Tom was leaning on. It was his ID. He had left his other cane, of mopane wood with the gold head of a lion, in Eden Waring's care, and for her protection while he would be away.

"Yes."

"A skiing accident?"

"No, I was shot." More ID. The leader nodded. Sherard motioned behind him. "There's a freight elevator to a lower theatre level two hundred yards west of here. It's locked down for the night. Code card. Only the security patrol can operate it. But there's an outside emergency staircase next to the elevator shaft. That gate is locked also, although it shouldn't be a problem to you."

"How many security, please?"

"Unknown." Sherard gave him a handheld computer. A big fork-lift was being driven off the helicopter. Followed by a flatbed truck. The nine other paramilitary types hopped aboard the truck, which was driven straight at Sherard and the team leader. He got into the front seat next to the driver and gave directions with one hand. Tom was helped aboard the flatbed by two team members. Nobody spoke. As they headed for the base of the mountain in a jostling rumble in the waning minutes of desert night, a cold night still, the forklift trailed the truck. The team leader studied the floor plans of the theatre and support complex.

Twenty seconds after they reached the outside concrete elevator shaft and accompanying emergency stairs, they had blown the hinges off the steel gate at the foot of the stairs and were storming up to a warehouse beneath the kitchen level.

Tom had problems with steps because of the knee that his wife's assassin had nearly blown away on a New York street. By the time he made it to the warehouse, two security guards were down and were being cut loose from Taser wires and the intruders had a code card for the freight elevator. Two team members were using paintball guns to blot out the eyes of the security cameras.

The elevator went down to where the forklift was waiting at the edge of the parking lot. The *Crucis Aurea* team went upstairs to the kitchens, then down a wide tunnel to the lobby. More cameras got the blackout treatment.

Sherard saw it for the first time in the concentrated glare of several flashlights.

Eden Waring's work: a blister of smoky-veined glass more than four feet high, containing the remains of the were-beast Tom had shot twice from his mountain hide above the now-missing terrace of the theatre.

The team leader made the sign of the cross in the air above the crystal tomb, saying something in Latin, throwing *Mordaunt* in twice. Sherard wondered if he might be a priest. He was the only one of them who had ventured close to the encapsulated entity.

The forklift arrived. Maneuvered into position, it raised the heavy glob of glass off the travertine floor and they all got out of there.

Elapsed time since the Super Stallion had landed was just under six minutes.

Now they were bearing the were-beast away, to the grave that had been chosen for Grayle/Mordaunt. *Deus Inversus.* The cloven hoof. Old Slick himself. So many names through millennia that applied to a singular evil.

As they lifted off in the helicopter Tom Sherard kept his eyes on the now-shrouded blister lashed to pad eyes on the floor. It gave off heat in the confines of the Stallion's belly. It had a brimstone odor. Men with their helmets and face shields removed stared, some in stupefaction tinged with horror. Small crosses clenched in their fists. Others refused to look at the accursed thing.

The core of the blister in which the beast lay had not solidified, according to the thermal imager that monitored what was going on beneath the metallic silvery shroud. On the TI screen, deep heat shimmered spectrally around the blunt, obscene head.

They flew southwest across the bare bones and dry sockets of Mojave, moonlit sand basins and soda flats, toward the port of Long Beach, California.

Tom thinking, *If only it stays this easy the rest of the way.*

But what did Eden's power, combined with the Dark Energy of the universe, mean to a relentless and immortal soul?

6:55 A.M.

From the lounge of the spa where he'd had his daily therapeutic massage, Cody Olds looked down on a floodlit half of an outdoor basketball court. A slender girl, five-nine or -ten, wearing blue spandex and a Lakers jersey that hung past her hips was moving side to side on the court, dribbling, bursts of toned speed and quickness, sure-handed with the ball, putting on a show, although she couldn't have known anyone was watching her.

Left hand, right hand, behind the back, then the crossover dribble and eyeblink-quick she was up, draining left-handed jumpers from fifteen feet or better, waving bye-bye to the basket, hand at a forty-five-degree angle to her outstretched arm like she'd been taught to do at a good basketball camp when she was a kid. *Swish-swish.* Then varying her routine by not shooting off the dribble, passing instead against a slant-webbed backstop behind the goal with a small square-target painted on it, no-look passes, plenty of zip on the ball. College girl, he guessed, wondering where she played or if she still did.

Cody had played basketball himself, in high school, then two years at Northern Arizona University in Flagstaff before a fall down a mountain that killed his horse and left him with a fused backbone and plenty of morning pain. He couldn't sit a horse for longer than twenty minutes nowadays, and long contemplative trail rides into high country had been one of his abiding pleasures.

No, the girl didn't play anymore. But still loved the game and was thinking about the Lakers–Spurs exhibition tonight at Thomas and Mack.

Cody wondered where that insight had come from. He even looked around; it was as clear in his mind as if someone had spoken to him. But he was alone in the lounge. Nevertheless, his lightly oiled skin prickled, as if something were slithering up the back of his neck.

He didn't know the girl. He was sure of that. She wasn't someone to drift out of a man's mind once he laid eyes on her.

He continued to watch the workout she was putting herself through. Face agleam with sweat in the floods. Never changing expression.

A show of thoroughbred grace in animals and women just naturally refreshed Cody's day, brightened his outlook in a way that even a big winning hand at poker didn't seem to do anymore.

She was a redhead, more of a strawberry roan shade, and wore her hair scrunchied back and off her neck while she worked on her game. *Swish.* Those long tanned supple legs had a lot of jump in them even though she wore a knee brace. Right knee. Big-time college ball was harder on the ligaments of a woman's knees than the knees of a male athlete.

Didn't know who she was, but he felt a powerful urge to become acquainted; that tingle across his shoulders wasn't just because of his recent massage. He *had* to get to know her. Intuition again?

But he was standing there in a spa bathrobe behind floor-to-ceiling windows that didn't open, and she—something about how hard she was working, the grit effort she put into every move, with an undertone of, to give it a name, driving anger, suggested that she wanted to be left alone.

Man trouble? At her age, what else?

She only thinks she wants to be alone.

And where did he get that idea? Cody clenched his shoulder muscles as if warding off a persistent psychic prodding. Maybe his long night of high-stakes poker had overtaxed his brain and nervous system.

Five minutes to shower and towel off, throw on a change of clothes, get himself out there.

Before this filly decided she'd had enough and walked away, becoming unfindable, leaving him with a nagging sense of loss for many a day.

Life seldom announced its critical turning points. Afterward you always knew. But by then all you might have to show for your knowledge were regrets.

Cody was not one to sit in a melancholy mood waiting for a spark to appear in yesterday's ashes. And he didn't have anything going right now. Which, for a single guy in Vegas, was almost unheard of.

Eden still couldn't believe he had left in the middle of the night without waking her. Surreptitious moves were not Tom Sherard's style. He'd left very little in the way of explanation—only that His Holiness had personally asked him to do this thing, oversee the disposition of Mordaunt's earthly remains. A note from Sherard on her computer was the first thing Eden had seen when she woke up at five o'clock after a night's sleep that had been more stressful than soothing, like an entrance exam to hell.

Well *shit*. And she had made love to this man not twenty-four hours ago, holding back nothing of herself—one way of putting it; she felt like a jilted heroine in a Victorian romance. Aside from her very personal feelings okay, what sort of team play *was* this?

Because Tom had been the one to insist, until Alberta Nkambe's prognosis turned favorable and they could take her back to Shungwaya for recuperation, that they not split up. Las Vegas was still a dangerous place for them, particularly the helpless Bertie. And there was Eden's task, which she had yet to begin, of retrieving her wayward doppelganger.

He had left Eden with Simba, the gold lion's-head walking stick. As if Tom thought that the cane would be of more use to her while he was traveling an unknown distance with an entity she had subdued but still feared. Dreaming through a wretched night of its watchful dormancy in that thick coating of glass, shaped in dreamtime like a flawed eye with a sunken squamous pupil. The damned thing almost never left her thoughts! Tired as she was after a long workout, bent over on the rubberized outdoor basketball court with heaving breasts and tugging with both hands at the hem of her purple jersey, those hot spots of melting chandeliers still swayed in the front of her mind.

Ten thousand years from now none of this is going to matter.

Which was what Eden usually reminded herself when she was at the limits of frustration or deeply funked.

Yes, but. Having become acquainted with *Deus Inversus,* she couldn't be so sure of that anymore. Which left her sure of nothing at all.

Her legs, unused to the practice grind, were hurting. *So shoot some free throws as part of the cooling-out routine, then walk back to the bungalow.* Sauna, shower, the sun would be well up by then. Breakfast on the terrace, a protein shake if she couldn't get anything else down. Then an hour of computer chat with her mother, Betts, and Eden's best chum, Megan Pardo in San Fran, and it would be time to visit Bertie. Afterward take Bertie's father, Joseph, and her brother Kieti to lunch at Bellagio. A big pair of shades, ponytail, and baseball cap; the idea of walking around town didn't worry her too much, although Tom had said—

"I have two tickets to the game tonight. Courtside."

Eden flubbed a free throw. *Now what? Or who?*

The ball bounced back to her from the backstop. She leaned left to snatch it up, finding comfort in the spread of her fingers on the thick black welts of the women's NBA pro model, holding it chest-high as if it afforded protection from whatever stranger she was about to have a look at. Deep breath, just a casual glance. His voice hadn't startled her. It had a comfy gruffness. Fatherly sound. *Time to quit now, Eden, come in for supper.*

Yes, sir. Soon as I hit ten in a row.

He wasn't the old bird-dog, quail-hunting type she'd expected to see. Youthful lines, someone who kept himself up. Gleaming raven hair brushed straight back from a spacious forehead and curling up toward his ears at the collar line. A Mount Rushmore sort of face, only bronze with flared cheekbones, his skin unlined except for little folds at the corners of a wide amiable mouth. Well trimmed but full mustache, no vanity piercings. A couple of rings on his long fingers looked like tribal jewelry: silver, topaz, turquoise. Six-three, she guessed. An easy, idle, cowboy kind of stance; and yes, that *was* a somewhat kicked-around old John B. Stetson in his hands.

"You'd be a Laker fan, I'm guessin'."

Eden didn't acknowledge his question or his existence until she'd drained the next free throw.

"I'm for whatever team Steve Nash is playing for," she said, waiting for the ball to carom back to her, not looking around again.

"Kobe's got that toe problem," the cowboy said, to keep the conversation going. "Looks like he's on the DL once the season starts."

Eden nodded slightly, still not turning around. Eyes narrowing in concentration, she hit her next four. He didn't say anything else but she knew he hadn't budged, was still watching, and Eden was thinking that she liked the set of his mouth. She hadn't had a good look at his eyes. Maybe wasn't all that interested.

The cowboy said, "I'd never quit until I made my ten. Miss one in a game, twenty in a row at practice."

Eden nailed her fifth and sixth free throws, took two deep breaths. "What if you missed two in a game?"

"Didn't often happen. Well, I stayed in the gym all night if I needed to. Until they threw me out."

"I was like that," Eden said. *Seven, eight.* "Sometimes I hid in the locker room, then I'd shoot with the lights out if there was moon enough that night."

"Where did you play college?"

"Cal State Shasta." *Nine.*

"Division One?" He was impressed. "I was at Northern Arizona. Got hurt the spring of my sophomore year. Broke my back."

Ten.

Eden didn't want to shoot anymore, but she felt momentarily at peace. With the basketball under one arm she walked to the bench where she had left her towel and sweats. Glancing at the westerner. Not giving him much to read in her glance. The sky had brightened, there were pink bands of cloud overhead. He had dark eyes, angular beneath a slight jut of brow. She made a guess at his age: midthirties.

"How did you break your back?"

"Horse shied on a high trail I ought to have had the sense to avoid. Loose shale, and there was some ice left from winter. Do you ride?"

"No," Eden said. She pulled on sweatpants and dried her face.

"I'm Cody Olds," the cowboy said.

Or maybe he was only part cowboy: he wore a good-looking tweed jacket and a cashmere turtleneck with his Wranglers and polished boots. Coca-Cola cowboy, Eden thought, dimly recalling a song from a Clint Eastwood movie.

"Hi." She hesitated. Then gave him the name on her Kenyan passport, the name she was registered under at Bahia. "Eve Bell."

He smiled. "On for the game tonight, Eve?"

Eden smiled back. And shook her head, a minimum of rejection.

"No."

He didn't look put out or flustered. She hadn't knocked the wind out of his sails.

"Then let me make you a gift of my seats. In case there's a special fella you'd rather be there with."

Eden tilted her head as if there were some density to this proposition, and blew him off again. But mildly.

"Can't accept. That is way too generous of you. Cody."

Saying his name indicated that, marginally, he was still in play, and she waited with a tone of interest to see what this Cody Olds would come up with.

He nodded. Looked thoughtful. "Then why don't we make the tickets the stakes in a friendly wager."

Eden began dribbling her basketball, figure eights around and between her spread legs, alternating hands, never looking at the ball. Looking at him.

"For instance?"

"It's been, I'd say, half a dozen years since I picked up a basketball. So allow me two practice shots, third one will be the money ball."

"From where?"

"Half court."

Eden laughed. "You're hustling me."

"Ma'am, on my word of honor."

She liked the way he said things. *Word of honor.* And he had that depth in his voice so that he didn't sound incredibly bogus.

"You'll have me feeling like a thief and a skunk, Cody."

He rubbed one side of his chin, scraping a little stubble that wasn't unbecoming. "Suppose you gave me an edge; you know, house vig."

House vig. So he was your basic degenerate gambler, Eden decided. Bet on anything and everything. What the hell, so far he was doing okay.

"Name it."

"I swish the ball, you buy us dinner before the game. If I catch iron but no bucket, game only; and I promise I will have you back on your doorstep by ten thirty."

"Oh, now I'm buying dinner." But she had begun to respond to that old game-day competitive sparkle. She made it appear as if she were having a tough time deciding. Then went full power with her smile. "Let's see what you've got, Cody."

Cody Olds took off his tweed jacket and folded it carefully over the back of the bench. Then he removed his boots and boot socks. Did a stretching routine, upper back and shoulders, some deep knee bends. Eden tossed him the ball. Smaller size, ounces lighter than his hands remembered. He bounced it a few times, getting back the feel, then walked to center court, all business now that the wager was set.

It hurt him to jump, she could tell that. The bad back. She was moderately sympathetic. Playing with pain. He couldn't be that hard up for a date. Wanted to win, prove something to her.

Cody put too much on the ball his first try and he was off form, a little awkward. His shot was high and to the left and just did connect with the backboard. He put his head down and bounced the ball a few more times, looked up, looked around at Eden.

"Okay if I move?" he said.

Eden made a magnanimous "whatever" gesture with both hands.

"I'm better when I move," he said, sounding like Robert Redford as the Sundance Kid. Then, quicker than Eden had imagined he could be, he dribbled to his left, squared up to the basket, and launched his jumper. Great form. He'd been a player, all right. She sensed as soon as the ball left his hands that it was good.

Swish.

Some people were just born to win.

Cody walked back to her, limping a little to belie the easy confidence that was native to him: he'd stubbed a couple of toes on his left foot. Eden was nearly expressionless, hands on her waist. Trying not to laugh at either of them.

"You cheated a couple of steps," she pointed out. "That wasn't in the vig."

"You'd break my heart for a couple of steps?" He exaggerated the limp and, feigning helplessness, dropped to his knees in front of her.

"I break hearts on Thursdays and Saturdays," Eden said dispassionately. "I guess you're safe. What time's the game tonight?"

"Seven thirty," he said, getting back on his feet and trying not to wince.

"Why don't we eat afterwards, then? I like junk at a game—you know, nachos, popcorn. Couple of beers."

"Where will I meet you, Eve?"

"I'm on bungalow row. The big one with the rain forest in the orangerie. There'll be some guys parked out front in a van, but they won't bother you if you wear that Gabby Hayes hat and talk cowpoke."

Cody Olds gave her a look. Some guys parked out front in a van? He knew that Bahìa's so-called bungalows were reserved for glam politicos, celebrity bling, kingly charlatans of commerce with their thirty-thousand-square-foot homes, art collections, transatlantic yachts, a stain of plague in their greed.

Eden politely ignored his speculation and said, "How about seven o'clock, Cody?"

7:10 A.M.

General Bronc Skarbeck looked around the lobby of the Lincoln Grayle Theatre and said, "Jesus Diddly Christ! You're telling me some guys in SWAT gear came in here with an industrial forklift the size of a John Deere Harvester, lifted that hunk of glass off the floor, and carted it out to a, what? *What* kind of helicopter?"

"I don't know for certain," said one of the security guards. "Never got a real good look. But it was at least the size of one of the Chinooks the Hundred and First used for deployments behind the Iraqi lines during the Gulf War."

Another guard said, "No, I think it was a Seahorse or whatever they call those boogers the Navy uses for minesweeping. Anyway, after they loaded up what they come for, big as she was that helo took on off out of here like a turpentined cat."

"What direction?"

"South, southwest maybe."

"And what were you doing while they were making their getaway?" Skarbeck asked.

"After you collect ten amps' worth of voltage, General, you don't feel like doing much of anything for a while. Gar-on-tee."

Bronc shook his head, although not in disappointment. A well-planned and executed entry had taken place, and they'd known just what they were after. No deadly force had been required or, judging from their lack of armament, contemplated. He couldn't make the least sense of it. They hadn't taken, as far as he knew at this time, anything of real monetary value. He repressed a superstitious shudder, thinking of what lay in the heart of that big glass blister. Skarbeck, after a restless night of disturbing dreams, was half convinced that, in his fixation on Eden Waring, the mortal Magician had made himself a victim of an illusion even he couldn't control.

Elizabeth Ann Perkins came over to Skarbeck with a cell phone, saying, "I've got Dr. Woolwine for you."

"Thanks." Before taking the call he sensed an absence and looked around again, scowling. Said to Perk, "Where's Harlee?" She had insisted on coming with him in spite of the fright she'd received yesterday while looking at one of the surveillance tapes. Now she had wandered off. Perk didn't know to where. Bathroom? "Find her," Skarbeck said.

Harlee Nations had taken advantage of her first opportunity to slip away from the others in the theatre lobby. She went immediately to Lincoln Grayle's dressing suite, where, to her quick appraising eye, everything seemed in perfect order. She was very much at home there. No sex with Grayle, ever, but that was okay. It allowed for adulation in its purest form.

Some of the Magician's collection of antique posters and props of other master illusionists was nearly three hundred years old. In the vicinity of Harlee's true age.

Harlee was something of an illusionist herself.

Upstairs, in the spectrochrome chamber of the duplex suite, she stripped to the skin and lay on the massage table, which was equipped with a keypad she could employ with the fingers of her right hand while flat on her back. Choosing from an array of colored lights projected through ordinary glass filters on an overhead grid, aligning them in combinations the length of her fine naiad's body, unblemished as polished ivory. The movement and duration of each precise beam, some as narrow as piano wire, were controlled by a computer program designed for her physical needs, the contours of her body alone.

Ten to twelve minutes of colored-light therapy, two times a week. Along with a few good pharmacologically engineered naps to speed her through the duller decades, condensing years into dreamlike moments, Harlee had stayed vital and refreshed in the blood throughout her long history.

At the end of World War II Harlee had regressed to and remained in the physical state of a sixteen-year-old, finding it to be a useful age for her line of work, which was the subjugation, manipulation, and—at Mordaunt's pleasure—total destruction of innocent or unwary souls coasting through life like so many mallards on a placid pond. She had a fully finished adult brain and was sexually mature, with the agility, stamina, and wiles of youth. Retaining everything she had learned during her extended stay but with enough mental capacity that she wasn't in danger of memory suffocation.

Colored lights, principally indigo and hues of purple, applied to the hindbrain and several glands and other organs were all she required to maintain her dewy, delectable self. But which light, and how long it needed to be focused on the pineal gland, or the thalamus, or the soles of the feet—that was the biogenetic art of it. You had to be in the know.

Harlee's deep knowledge, courtesy of the Great One—as his acolytes referred to Mordaunt—went back a few thousand years. Most of the ancient texts that contained techniques for achieving extraordinary life spans no longer existed. They had been burned or hammered to bits, condemned as sorcery in great libraries like those of Sumer, the Egyptian mystery schools, Pergamus, Carthage; and mighty Alexandria—seven hundred thousand scrolls up in flames thanks to Mordaunt, who had always felt that unenlightened souls should remain so as long as possible. The burning of the Library of Alexandria had represented the greatest loss of human wisdom and esoteric knowledge ever concentrated in one place.

By contrast, what the present generation knew—in spite of telescopes in space, supercomputers, models of DNA codes—about mankind's origins, history, and potential would fit into a rural book-mobile. It was an age of enormous hubris and abysmal spiritual ignorance; of moral dilemma and blood hatreds and epic human conflicts. Pretty much business as usual, as it had been for millennia. Mordaunt liked things that way, and he was the consummate Arranger.

But his human persona the thaumaturgist was missing, trapped in an alternate, aberrant shape, and although she could feel the vibrational imprint of where Grayle had lain only thirty-six hours before, she took no reassurance from it. Harlee felt bereft, directionless, and a little scared.

How could she help him? What would he now expect of her, as leader of her own lay circle of Malterran souls? Another time, Mordaunt could have survived anything that the Avatar bitch so wrongly named "Eden" dished up to him, but with half of his unconquerable soul temporarily unavailable, he had been all too susceptible, anticipating the pleasure of fathering a hybrid entity of such evil and catastrophic power that the world would tremble at its birth.

Harlee weathered a spate of jealousy. She couldn't bear children and she had no extrahuman powers; all that she'd ever had to offer Mordaunt was her devotion. And her skills as an assassin.

Get on with it, then? Harlee mused, as she concluded her spectrochrome session and began to dress. When Mordaunt returned (she didn't think *if*; there was no way to conceptualize such a dire thought) he surely would understand that, despite his fixation on the Avatar (*really*, she thought, reverting momentarily to her teen persona, it was like some pimply boy with a crush on a *cheer*leader), Eden Waring's continued presence on earth only added insult to the injury she had done him.

But to act without the express consent of the Great One, Harlee knew, could be a grave miscalculation on her part. You didn't fall out of favor with him and expect leniency. What you got was an exercise in bitter remorse, bodiless in darkness absolute and everlasting.

Harlee didn't like the idea of being without a lovely body to pamper, clothe, flaunt on a dance floor. A shape to drive men half out of their gourds. And fucking was the greatest.

Mordaunt had left the building, but there might be a way of communicating with him.

Harlee slipped into her sandals, locked up the spectrochrome chamber, and went to the Magician's walk-in wardrobe, two floors packed with costumes from past editions of his spectacular shows. Most of the stuff was behind glass on mannequins that mimicked the Magician's form. Scarves, capes, superhero masks, Elvis-style jumpsuits. The mannequins had ovoid heads but no faces.

Harlee glanced around but kept her nostalgia in check. After all, wasn't it just a little creepy?

There was a small elevator concealed in a back wall of the wardrobe. It operated by handprint only. She was identified and permitted to board. The elevator was large enough for two, or maybe a closely packed ménage à trois. The machinery hummed and Harlee slowly descended into a grotto beneath the dressing suite that was known only to a few trusted associates of the Magician.

Mineshaft rock walls. A constant temperature of fifty-seven degrees. She stepped out of the elevator and saw herself in the mirror-like surface of a steel vault door. It took up half of one rough wall of the grotto. On the two other occasions she'd been down there Harlee had wondered how they had managed to get something so massive into such a small area. Lowered it, perhaps, through a deep shaft in the mountain that afterward had been filled in with concrete, a continuous day-and-night pour like they built Hoover Dam that time.

There in the steel vault, both a retinal and full-body scan were required, followed by a voiceprint ID as a triple security backup.

Harlee spoke her name, which unlocked a magnetic-stripe reader. Harlee swiped the key card that she carried in her wallet. After that, a turn of the wheel on the door—slender Harlee needed to put her shoulders into it, straining—and she was ready to enter a vault more fabulous than King Solomon's mines.

The chrome walls inside had a golden sheen from two thousand years of legendary, looted treasures: Greek, Etruscan, Incan. Gold from the repository of the Knights Templar, once located at the end of a deep passage beneath the medieval castle of Gisors in France. Gold stolen from numerous Vicars of Rome who were as venal and acquisitive as Mordaunt himself. The long-missing trove of the Confederate States of America. The contents of the Lost Dutchman mine. And so on. Most of the gold, about nine and a half billion dollars' worth at yesterday's spot price, had been turned into uniform one-kilo bars that were neatly stacked as high as Harlee's head on five-foot-square pallets.

She liked gold jewelry, but the metal in brick form didn't seem very useful or whet her appetite. It was only another way of keeping score in that boring masculine game of world dominance.

Nevertheless, the Magician, showing off his hoard, had been almost childishly gleeful.

"Power corrupts," he'd reminded Harlee. "But it's gold that has always owned the wills of ambitious men. You're looking at the reason human souls were created to be slaves to *my* will."

There were other vaults around Vegas town, including a small one at the General's house, and they also were filled with gold bars, kilo-size down to ten-ounce wafers. Mordaunt had accumulated bulk silver and platinum as well, filling many cavernous rooms of a salt mine he owned in Kansas. He possessed as much of the yellow metal as any two of the world's central banks. When the complex deal that Bronc Skarbeck was in charge of rigging (it had something to do with fraudulent short positions on commodity exchanges and financial instruments called "derivatives") brought about the collapse of the world's currencies (only two of which were even partially backed by gold) and then an economic smash-up of unparalleled severity, Mordaunt would be in a position to name his price for whatever was worth salvaging.

But he was missing. And so was the red crystal skull usually kept in this vault.

The skull was Harlee's reason for being there. She needed the resonance and magnetic induction of that occult instrument to help her clearly define her purpose in this crisis. If there was a way that Mordaunt could still communicate with Harlee, then it would be through the astral properties of the crystal skull.

The crisis had deepened. Harlee was distressed enough to let out a long wail of frustration.

ABOARD THE *STELLA SALAMIS* · SAN PEDRO BAY, CALIFORNIA · 1415 HOURS ZULU

Tom Sherard watched from one of the bridge wings of the 480-foot container ship of Cypriot registry as the Long Beach Harbor pilot was dropped a half mile outside the breakwater and the ship's captain ordered full ahead, course heading ninety degrees.

Below him on the long foredeck of the *Stella Salamis,* sixty-two sealed steel containers were closely lashed together, one container height from the deck of the freighter, with open space where the one and two hatches were located. Among a miscellany of goods bound for three Central and South American ports, the "said to contains" on cargo manifests were several tons of hair dryers, laptop computers, halogen light bulbs, two thousand cartons of breakfast cereal, six thousand pounds of John Grisham novels translated into Esperanto, and pharmaceuticals for sluggish bowels.

There was a 1,250-pound item unlisted on any manifest: a giant glass bead containing were-beast remains and bound for the deepest hole in the eastern Pacific Ocean, just off the continental shelf and almost due east of the Bay of Fonseca.

Only a mile out and Sherard was feeling queasy already in weak sunlight on a moderate sea. He had been given Transderm-V patches by the ship's cook and medic while he was getting settled into a snug cabin off the boat deck, but the medic had cautioned that the patches, while calming his stomach, might cause hallucinations. Tom had decided it would be worthwhile trying to get his sea legs before resorting to the antinausea medication.

The wind was in his face at twelve to fifteen knots, and there were offshore clouds with tremors of lightning. Other freighter and Navy traffic was strung out in the road, north- and southbound. At full ahead the ship was rolling slightly.

The *Stella Salamis* had a polyglot but apparently sharp crew of eleven. Most of them understood or spoke enough English to get by: it was their universal shipboard language. The captain's name was Riklis, nationality unknown to Sherard. He was a small trim man with alert black eyes, a half-inch-thick wedge of black eyebrows, and a squared-off beard with a comber of white in it. He spoke the best English. Tom, officially known as the Person in Addition to Crew, was the thirteenth man aboard. If that made anyone uneasy, he wasn't aware.

Captain Riklis turned the ship over to the helmsman and came outside to keep Sherard company.

"You are not a sailor."

"First ocean trip."

"Ah. Well, we expect a routine voyage. The Pacific hurricane season is nearly over. There is a small disturbance out there"—he nodded to starboard—"two hundred miles, but no threat to us. The bad ones, you know, begin in the Gulf of Tehuantepec, and travel north with great speed along the coast. Treacherous. But this is a good ship. Would you like coffee?"

"Not right now. Thank you, Captain."

"The good ship *Salamis*. Do you know about Salamis?"

"Greeks against the Persians, wasn't it? About 500 BC."

"Ah. That one. An epic sea battle. But this ship is named for the old city and port on Cyprus. Where the apostle Paul began his missionary work."

"Is that where the *Crucis Aurea* was founded?"

The captain looked away from Sherard.

"Sorry. I do not know that name."

10:04 A.M.

Bronc Skarbeck left a quarter of a million dollars' worth of Aston Martin on the wide cobbled parking apron of Lincoln Grayle's digs halfway up a steep slope of Charleston Mountain, an architectural grand slam of a house with a pagan-palace feel to it—all those terraces and cantilevered decks, in form like an inverted pyramid securely anchored in bedrock. The thrust levels afforded vistas of mountains crackling with fall color, already snow-dusted across the highest peaks, and of bleached-bone desert way out there on the California side. There was a bite to the intoxicatingly pure air at this altitude. Hawks and kites were on high soar in the nearby blue, resembling totems of some hallucinatory, rain-dance religion.

Over speakers both inside and outside the house Skarbeck heard the Christmas music, much of it inane ("Rockin' Around the Christmas Tree") that Lincoln Grayle enjoyed listening to year round.

He took the elevator in the garage to an aerie deck to confer with Dr. Marcus Woolwine, a many-faceted genius with no taint of scruple in his makeup. Skarbeck had encountered Woolwine at times when their otherwise dissimilar careers converged during covert operations, most recently at the ill-fated Plenty Coups facility that the Multiphasic Operations and Research Group (MORG) had built a few years earlier, digging into tribal grasslands of the Crow nation in southern Montana like a huge open-pit mine. MORG was now defunct, but Skarbeck—blessed, for once, with an accurate sense of the inevitable—and Dr. Woolwine had skipped out of a deteriorating situation before the hue and cry, hearings on Capitol Hill, and subsequent criminal charges.

An accupuncturist was working on Dr. Woolwine in the bracing outdoors beneath two heat lamps.

At eighty-plus years the biogeneticist (among his several areas of legitimate as well as peripheral, witch-doctor-style expertise) was in crackerjack condition. Strict diet, Eastern physical disciplines, periodic injections composed of living animal and human embryos. Mysterious transfusions were rumored. Hyperbaric chambers. All that—and for all Skarbeck knew, the ritual sacrifice of young virgins both male and female—kept Woolwine at the top of his game.

One of his specialties had been to take natural-born killers and improve their lethality. Through electrical and pharmaceutical interventions he teased, twisted, rearranged brain dendrites or entire masses of lobe. He could hypnotize a timber rattlesnake and wear it around his neck like a lei to pool parties.

And, most useful to Mordaunt, he had devised an effective means of separating Eden Waring from her doppelganger.

"Almost finished here?" Skarbeck said to the relaxed Woolwine as a needle thinner than a human hair was withdrawn from below an armpit. "We need to talk." He was still uneasy, with a prickling premonition of a disaster in motion.

When they were alone and Woolwine was sitting up on the massage table, having pulled on a loose-fitting buttonless peasant shirt with a rough weave, he shook his head and said, "I have no idea of what happened to the Great One. Although I don't think we ought to presume that he is, ah, deceased. 'Death' as we know and experience it is not a reality that applies to our, ah, employer."

"Oh, no?" Skarbeck said dourly. He described what he had seen on the surveillance tapes, and told Woolwine about the predawn heist of the were-beast's remains, which were slowly hardening in their glass teardrop.

"Was it him, do you think?" he asked Woolwine.

"Quite possibly," Woolwine replied, frowning.

"So he's dead, all right."

"Of that, as I said, we can't be certain."

"Then we had damn well better get him back. *It* back. Whatever."

"Where were the, ah, remains, taken?"

"I'm working on that. Nothing so far. But the girl probably knows."

"Eden Waring, obviously, is to be approached with the utmost caution."

"That's where you come in, Dr. Woolwine. Although you didn't handle her so well the last time, up there in Plenty Coups."

Skarbeck saw an expression of dismay in Woolwine's eyes as he slipped on his mirror-finish, titanium-rimmed space cadet sunglasses.

"I would not care to be in a position of trying to control the power of the Avatar. Her dpg, that's another matter."

"The replica who calls herself Gwen?"

Woolwine lifted his face toward the clouds. Skarbeck saw, like a circling eyespot, a hawk reflected on one metallic lens of the wraparound sunglasses.

"She may prove to be more valuable to us than Eden Waring herself." Woolwine nodded approval of this observation, then paused to pour himself a healthy cocktail the color of pond scum from a thermos. Skarbeck refused an offer to sample the drink with a curt shake of his head. Woolwine sipped, made a savoring sound with his lips and tongue, and got down from the massage table. "But right now I have only the vaguest idea of Gwen's whereabouts. Come with me, General Skarbeck. There is something you should see."

Skarbeck accompanied the resident genius to the next level of Lincoln Grayle's house, Chuck Berry's rollicking "Run Rudolph Run" surrounding them on hidden speakers.

"Where are we going?"

"There is a slight chance Gwen may have returned by now."

"Returned from where?"

"Jubilation County, Georgia. If indeed she did manage to get there yesterday."

"It's only about a four-hour flight from Atlanta."

Woolwine chuckled.

"I'm speaking of Jubilation County as it was on a particular day in the summer of 1926."

Woolwine paused before a locked door at one end of a wide hall, beyond which was another terrace and a pale vista of mountains that appeared as remote as a moonscape.

"Oh, for Christ's sake," Skarbeck said. *"Time travel?"*

"Well, yes. Doppelgangers are adept at it. But to make matters just a *little* more difficult for our resourceful Gwen, the Jubilation County she was seeking lies in a parallel universe, one in which a single day is repeating endlessly. A universe, you might say, that developed a bad case of the hiccups."

In response to Skarbeck's stony expression Woolwine placed a finger to his lips and with a card key unlocked the door to Gwen's suite.

"Actually the difficulty factor in finding that particular 'Jubilation County' was, as you can imagine, increased exponentially." Woolwine lowered his voice to a near whisper before stepping inside, motioning for the General to follow. "Also, the act of inserting herself into a microregion of such a complex nature, potentially disrupting the symmetry of repetitive time, might create incalculable havoc. The mathematics of complexity theory are, I admit, beyond my ken."

To Skarbeck the multilaureled geneticist and accomplished mind-bender might as well have been babbling in tongues. When he followed Woolwine into the spacious Japanese-style suite, his displeasure was transmuted to amazement: Gwen the dpg was seated at a small writing table with folded hands, head tilted forward in contemplation of a red crystal skull. He blinked, then realized that he was seeing only a holographic likeness.

"What the hell—"

Woolwine blocked his further progress with a cautioning hand.

"No, no, don't disturb it."

"*It?*"

"Or the zero-point energy field around Gwen's image, which is her point of reference once she is ready to return to this little corner of the continuum. Provided she is not enmeshed in a sticky paradox. And her return involves, perhaps, the additional burden of a hitchhiker."

"What are you talking about? Who or what was she after in Jubilation County?"

"The feminine half of the soul of Mordaunt."

Skarbeck felt a disturbing tingle at the back of his neck. He rubbed slowly, unable to look away from the intimidating red skull with its flashy grin.

"What *is* that boogeyboo?"

"A source of polarized occult power that is, not to quibble, stupendous. Without the crystal skull I doubt Gwen could have made it out of this homely harmonic, let alone to another, plasma-shielded cell of our universe. Assuming she is there now, once again in the flesh, and not somewhere irretrievable in space/time, ricocheting at the Planck energy level as if she were in a cosmic pinball machine." He shrugged. "A brave girl. But so many ifs." Woolwine looked unwell. He licked his lips and took deep breaths. "And now you know as much as I," he said to Skarbeck. "I really must quit the room. I have a pacemaker, and the vortex spiral in here is redlining me."

"The *feminine* half of his soul? What sort of psychobabble bull-shit are you—"

"We had best hope that it's all true, inasmuch as we may never set eyes on him, I mean the masculine aspect of Mordaunt, again."

"I'm working on it. Too soon to make that judgment."

"Nevertheless—" Woolwine, gasping a little, made for the door. Skarbeck followed, closing the door behind him. In the hall, Yuletide sentiments that no one had had the nerve to deprogram caught up with them: Bob Seger and the Silver Bullet Band rocking out with "Sock It To Me Santa." Woolwine gave his lungs a lift and smiled thinly. "Nevertheless, Gwen may prove to be our only hope of, ah, continuing employment, with access to Mordaunt's cornucopia. I admit I have rather enjoyed the rarefied heights of the stinking rich."

Skarbeck included himself with a nod.

"But I'm thinking we don't need either of them. Not as long as we still have Eden Waring."

"The Avatar. Yes. Marvelous powers. Unfortunately, there is no darkness in her."

Skarbeck studied cameos of his own face, reflected in metallic lenses below Woolwine's sweaty brow; there was a vertical groove deep in Skarbeck's forehead like a fault line over the epicenter of his disaffection. "There's darkness in us all, Dr. Woolwine. What the hell, you're a Freudian—"

"No, no, I'm not a Follower. I invented my own discipline: psychoneuroendocrinology."

"That so? Anyway, it's the self-destructive urge, the gambler's secret desire to lose, the 'bad twin' syndrome—well, she's already got one of those. You know what I'm talking about. Don't tell me Eden Waring is any different from the rest of us. Being the Avatar doesn't automatically promote her to fucking sainthood. If the worst has happened to our good friend and patron Lincoln Grayle, then it will be up to you to dig into Eden's psyche and wake up whatever hound of hell is lurking there. On *our* leash, of course. Whatever you call yourself, you've got the know-how."

Woolwine said with a nervous wince, "But I'm not so sure that I—"

"Don't kid me. I'm a big fan of your work. And I'll remind you that I have plans of my own, no matter what condition Mordaunt might be in right now. I have no intention of abandoning them because of a little setback. Who knows how much help the Waring girl could be to us."

"I only meant to say that attempting to manipulate Eden Waring could result in a phase transition of our own cosmic cell—in other words, a severe case of the hiccups."

Skarbeck showed him a flash of an edged smile.

"But you'll do it anyway, won't you? Not just for the money. When it comes to crunch time for hotshots like you and me, it's all about the size of our balls."

ABOARD THE *STELLA SALAMIS* · 29° 48' N 117° 13' W · 1340 HOURS ZULU

The rolling seas of Baja California had been a little too rough to make sleep easy or profitable. After three hours or so Tom Sherard gave up the effort and left the small passenger cabin he occupied to prowl the ship with bleary eyes and a brooding mind, winding up on the bridge with the salt wind in his stiffened face. Starkly tired but uninvigorated by the elements. Wondering hopelessly how it could have gone any differently with Eden and himself, always returning to the same conclusion.

He had taken Eden because she wanted to be taken, and because his emotions were overcharged; every moment with her after he'd found her footloose on a desert road had had a hallucinatory vagueness about it. Her mother's lovely eyes and her mother's strange magic invested in the quaking, exhausted girl. Control of himself had always been an absolute in Sherard's life, a personal bulwark that had stood no chance against the force of his blood at their first intimate touching. Interesting, he thought, how much of what one assumed was inviolable in one's nature or character could be demolished by a fleeting look in a young woman's eyes.

A look he was sure would be there again, the next time he saw her.

He was willing to be hard on himself now, after some rather fatuous remarks to Eden that hadn't served either of them too well. But what was the point of going down that twisted road; it was done. Sex with Eden, physically so satisfying, had left him tremulous inside, a kind of moral palsy to give it a name.

The breadth of the sea, with the Baja peninsula a tan scrawl far to port beneath lowering, green-black clouds, was intimidating to Sherard. He felt a pinch of dread at each impact of tons of water breaking over the bow of the ship, which now seemed insubstantial in such risky seas. Spindrift glazed topside surfaces and tasted bitter on his lips.

Out of his element here.

So he'd betrayed himself, not to mention Bertie, but still he wanted Eden. Her scent and bodily warmth, his own sensual greed, was too much with him.

The slow uplift and plunge of the freighter, bow pointing down toward unimaginable deeps.

Sherard kept his footing, but there was nausea high in his throat. He wanted, wanted Eden—adrift without her, as lonely as he'd ever felt in his life. The full and only truth. Own up to it and get on. For now his hastily arranged voyage served two purposes. They soon would be well rid of a monster. Meanwhile, in relative solitude, he would have a few days to pull together his scattered resources.

Regain his own trust.

But there was the guilt, always the burrowing-in guilt, at not fulfilling his self-appointed role as guardian to two beloved young women. Leoncaro's express desire had been for Sherard to see a terrifying job through to the end. All right, then: the Magician had left the building—rather, his theatrical haunt—clinging to the side of a mountain. Leaving behind those who had served him. God only knew how many of those there were, what horror they represented.

Eden was nearly alone back there in Las Vegas. She and Bertie had the Blackwelder people watching over them, to be sure, and Sherard thought that Eden would spend most of her time at hospital. He had left Eden strict instructions—too strict, it seemed to him now, curt perhaps. And it might have been a mistake not to awaken her when he was leaving.

If he knew Eden—sometimes he thought he did—she just might be resenting that. In light of their new, obsessively smoldering, contentious relationship.

The horizon looked darker to Sherard. The weather seemed to be worsening as the *Stella Salamis* steamed south toward the Middle America Trench.

Bloody hell.

LAS VEGAS · 5:15 P.M.

With the General fully occupied and planning to be out of the house for the evening, Harlee had invited her crew over for a swim, some goofing, a gabfest, and catered barbecue.

Five girls. They stretched and preened and tanned and did their nails. All of them had the patter and midteen exuberance of Harlee herself, and all were wrenchingly gorgeous in their next-to-nothing thongs as they lounged around the blue Chiclet of a swimming pool. On his way out Skarbeck paused to look them over from an upstairs arcade. *My house is your house, sweet darlings.*

He was able to put a couple of names with the correct faces and bodies. Devon was the tall one with copper tresses spilling over freckled shoulders like ribbon waterfalls. Her wide-set gray eyes were as cool, as mystical, as Irish fog. Bare-breasted, she was doing Qigong exercises. What an eyeful. Then there was Honeydew, with that shockwave of blond hair, three shades of blond. As fresh, nervy, and playful as a baby tiger. Except for graceful Devon, they were noisy but not unmannered, punctuating fragments of cross-talk with little shrieks of glee or a disparaging groan. Speckling the scene with argot. Ginky. Flam. Sloth. Cryp. Random. Supa-dupa.

Harlee had deflected most of Skarbeck's questions about her crew: where they all came from, etc. Just as she politely but firmly deflected questions about herself. For all he knew she might have walked, fully formed, out of the hard glitter of desert sunrise one morning not long ago. Ignorance of her origins made his possession of Harlee feel less secure, but it was an unspoken part of her bargain with him, so he let it go.

He assumed that most if not all of Harlee's crew were attached to men like himself, the real pros of the high castles, the fantastical facades of Vegas that lined the Strip, otherwise known as death row for the self-indulgent. Their expensive casual clothes, running heavily to hip-hop, cholo, or tough chic—bandanas, leathers, swagger chains, gaucho pants, designer denim—their jewelry, and the cars they drove said that money was no concern of theirs. All they needed to do was ask for it.

When Skarbeck lingered a little too long, unabashedly voyeuristic, the sybarites noticed and acknowledged him—all save oblivious Devon in her free-flowing meditative state—Harlee having the last hand wave and greeting, passing on an airborne kiss, subtle dismissal in the gesture.

As soon as the General had left the premises and Devon concluded her Qigong patterns, frivolous talk ended and Harlee's crew gathered around her.

All expressions serious, solemn. No tears, but Flicka, a Finn-Indonesian mix of wonderful genes, was biting her full underlip, which resembled a piece of exotic, peeled fruit. Harlee remained on her feet, moving among her huddled crew like a lioness with cubs to feed.

Reese was the first to speak, and finished speaking with an apprehensive shudder.

"Is it, like, for real? What we saw? He's dead?"

Nic looked up from a golden nail on the toe she was fondling and said curtly, "Reese, chill. Honey, the Great One can't die." She recrossed beanpole legs styled for jaunting. Her dark eyes were rudely painted; in her casual carnality she was as scary as a young tarantula.

"Can't D-I-E," Devon repeated in a near whisper from the stillness of her lotus position.

"That's right," Harlee affirmed. "But no shit, he's in a tough spot."

"Do you think he's hurt?" Honeydew asked anxiously.

"What do *you* think?" Nic said. Her eyes had a splendid radiance in the light off the surface of the pool. "The bitch Avatar dropped half a ton of molten glass all over him."

Reese shuddered again and hugged herself. Her eyes were the size of moonflowers in a petite face. She was still beaded from a dip; her dark wet hair curled down her back like swimming snakes. "But w-what will they do with him now?"

Harlee said, "Some storm troopers moved in early this morning, scooped up the glass mound he's buried in, and made off with it. Bronc is trying to find out who they were and where they took the Great One."

"'Storm troopers' be kinda out-of-date," Nic reminded her.

"Paramilitaries, whatever. Big woo."

"*Crucis Aurea,*" Devon said wisely, her eyes focused on a patch of sky overlaid with the celestial gold of Renaissance art.

"We won't bother with them," Harlee advised her crew. "They're too hard to find anyway. But I think you all know who we're going after."

"The Avatar?" Flicka ventured, and hunched her shoulders warily.

"Not gettin' soft, are you?" Nic said. Very PMS today, for which the others usually forgave her.

"Oh, fuck you, Nic. It's just that she's, you know, volatile."

"But human," Harlee reminded them.

"Girl, you don't tell me to fuck myself," Nic said to Flicka.

Flicka's cheeks reddened. "You are so not the Terminator you think you are."

"Ah-*nohd,*" a couple of the girls chorused.

Harlee soothed Nic, who needed a lot of handling, by stroking the back of her head and long-stemmed neck. "Love your new crop, Nicole. Who did it, Sergio at Caesars?"

"Supa-dupa," Reese said, another peace offering.

Nic smiled snarky at Flicka, who accepted it with a slight glower.

Devon unlimbered and put her chin on the laced fingers of her hands. So to business.

"Do you think the Avatar is still in Vegas?" she said to Harlee. Harlee nodded. "Darn tootin'."

"Isn't that kind of a forties expression, Harlee?"

"I don't know. But I like it. *Loved* the forties. 'What's knittin', kitten? Let's cut a rug.' Bobby sox. Hubba-hubba."

"No, that's Barney Rubble," Honeydew corrected.

"*The Flintstones!*" Reese said.

"You're thinking 'Yabba Dabba Do!'" Flicka corrected Honeydew's correction. "And it's Fred, not Barney."

Devon looked serenely from one face to another, loving them all. Gentle Devon always used a thin-bladed knife for her stealthy assassinations, because there was little external blood and almost never a distressing outcry. Nic, on the other hand, excelled at Ninja hand strikes or with the occasional blunt instrument. Flicka was a poisoner. Discreet. Untraceable stuff. And Harlee—

"No more dork-outs," Harlee said. "Yes, I'm sure Eden Waring is still around town. Because we know the supermodel won't be leaving the hospital anytime soon, if ever."

"She's at Concordia?" Honeydew asked.

"Uh-huh. Whizzed by there this morning," Nicole said. "They got strict traffic control on the grounds; everybody gets stopped and questioned. And there must have been six of those, you know, satellite-uplink trucks sittin' around. Security inside, forget it."

"Are you still with that pimped-out low-ridah hardtail?" Honeydew said with an indulgent smile. "Really ought to give it up, Nic, before your spine gets so bad you can't wear stilettos."

"Pimped-out? Girl, you don't know biker edge when you see it. And it sure beat all hell out of drivin' a cage, even if it is a sixty-five 'Vette."

Reese said, "I heard that Virgie Lovechild can't get a camera on the floor where the Supa's probably veging with the other postop brain farts. And how much d'you suppose it's worth to Virgie, a shot of the Supa comatose in CCU? Fifty dimes from one of the tabs?"

"'Next on *Entertainment Tonight*,'" Honeydew drawled, doing her knockoff of a showroom-spiffy talking head. "'Teen Supermodel's Brave Fight for Life.'"

"I think she's older," Reese said. "Like, she's been doing *Vogue* covers practically forever."

"Speaking of security, the Avatar probably has plenty of her own," Flicka said.

"She's awesome at taking care of herself," Reese observed with a grimace, hugging her knees as she looked up at Harlee. "Those surveillance tapes, what a come that was. Like, *omigod.*"

"Scared?" Nic said, with a mean torque to her shapely lips.

"Chill," Harlee reminded her again, looking at Reese, then answering the question in the girl's eyes. "So one thing we know, the Avatar for sure will be spending a lot of time with her best bud." Harlee had another thought. "She might be staying there too, like in a VIP suite, with the Supa. Critical care, that just means somebody's watching the patient all the time, what else can they do for her? She'll make it or she won't."

Other heads nodded. Flicka made slow circles in the pool with her hand. There was a good smell of ribs cooking on an adjoining patio, visible through an archway in an adobe wall. Mellow western sunlight tinted all of their faces and flawless figures.

"Okay," Harlee said after a silent minute. "We know Virgie is the best at scoping out celebs. Half of the hotel employees on the Strip bird-dog for Virgie Lovechild and her pack-a-razzies." She pronounced it "rotsies," for "paparazzi." "Virgie may already have a glimmer where the Av is hanging. Devon and I have been, like, cultivating Virgie. She'll play ball."

Harlee paused, and smiled.

"As for security at the hospital—all of you guys will look just darling in paisley. Questions?" Another pause. "Fine. Let's chow down."

Even when he played poker all night, which wasn't that often—a couple of times a week if he was in Vegas for an extended stay on business—Cody Olds was still young enough to snap back fully refreshed and in physical trim after a three-hour nap in the cool darkness of his modest condo in a high-rise building a few blocks east of the Strip.

But on this late afternoon, with a date for a basketball game in less than an hour, Cody felt as if he had a weird kind of nonalcoholic hangover.

He was almost a nondrinker; wine or brandy sometimes, a glass of celebratory champagne on three yearly occasions: his mother's birthday, his own birthday, and the anniversary of the wedding of his two dearest friends.

He'd been awake for about five minutes and in the bathroom, naked and brushing his teeth, still with a dream in his mind sticky as cobwebs and, unlike most dreams hazily recalled upon waking, vivid in detail, imagined with an artist's eye. This dream had been about the attractive, athletic girl on the basketball court outside Bahía's spa. But they weren't playing ball. And the name she'd slyly given to him was not her true name.

So there he was with her on a windy mountain beneath lightning that laced a rolling dark sky in far northern New Mexico: the mountain called Dzilth-Na-Dith-Hle ("Dee-zee" in modern vernacular), a place profoundly sacred to the Navajo nation—Cody's mother's people—known to themselves as Diné. And in his dreams "Eve Bell" was really Changing Woman, soon to give birth to twin warrior sons, who, according to this crucial Navajo legend, were to rule the destiny not only of the historic tribal land of the Four Corners but of the universe itself.

Face-to-face with Estsan Natlehi—Changing Woman—Cody saw only the parlous lightning in her eyes. He was trembling in his dream, chastened by her stern beauty, terrified of her lodestar power. But it was the unique masculine power in him that Changing Woman had sought and needed: without Cody Olds, only half Navajo, the mythic twins couldn't be born.

Not a part of the legend as he remembered hearing it.

But he wasn't about to challenge the will of Changing Woman. The fate of the Wolf Spider clan, all of the Diné, the entire human race, depended on him.

Cody stopped brushing and rinsed. Stepped away from the basin. Five minutes after abandoning bed and dreamtime he had retained a straight-up erection, rigid as a railroad spike. He entered the thirty-six-nozzle Swiss shower, like a roomier version of the Iron Maiden. Turned it up full blast. No use. Changing Woman—or was it "Eve Bell"?—had him by the heart, and he couldn't refuse the lightning that needed discharging within his own hard grip.

So down the drain washed the human race. Cody couldn't laugh. He felt a little depressed about masturbating. And apprehensive about something he couldn't name.

Legends? Perhaps.

Or the truth implicit within the germinal legends.

He was dressed to go out when his cell phone rang.

Cody didn't have much use for cell phones and he loathed e-mail. But his legal-eagle mother and his brother Ben were gadabouts in their various quests, and there was no better way to keep in touch with them.

"Did you have the damned thing turned off last night?" his mother demanded.

"I played poker until five this morning."

"How much did that cost you?"

"I won, Ma."

"I know of a good legal offense fund that could use a whacking big donation."

"Wrote the check already. And one to Diné Citizens against Ruining Our Environment."

"That's my boy."

"Where are you, Albuquerq?"

"Benjamin and I are both mired in the depths of that open sewer that flows into the once-majestic and pristine Potomac River."

"Oh, Washington. Class-action again?"

"Betcha bottom dollar, Cody."

"I thought you said suing any branch of the United States government was an exercise in monomania, like tryin' to stack BBs on a greased plate."

"Before I join our ancestors, Cody, I plan to see to it there's not a strip of hide left on any ass that has the bad judgment to still be hanging around the Bureau of Indian Affairs." A late bloomer in career matters, Marie Olds had finished at the New Mexico School of Law when she was forty-six. She had since made up for lost time through sheer velocity.

"Ben there? Let me talk to him."

"No, he's out wolfin'. You would not believe how many single women there are in this burg. Some of them not half bad. And how their eyes do light up when they get a load of my Benny. They positively drool. It's almost disgusting."

"Ben knows how to handle the D.C. scene. Did you get the leasing and drilling stopped up around Nageezi?"

"We did. Indefinitely. The gas companies are in an uproar. Well, Jesus, how my heart bleeds. The greedy bastards. Eighteen thousand wells already in the San Juan Basin. But the Diné are supposed to give up sacred lands because BLM studies say that's where the biggest deposits are. So much for cultural sensitivity. They're already blaming us for the next energy crisis, which as we know are self-fulfilling prophecies."

"Are you takin' your beta-blocker, Ma?"

"So we're supposed to forgo our heritage to keep the rest of the country warm and cozy? While the Diné get gypped in pipeline and royalty deals and most still heat their own homes with firewood? What little they can afford. On what I hope is a more positive note, what are you up to in Vegas?"

"We're opening a show of Carrie Ballantyne's work at the gallery. You know Carrie. Ma, gotta run. Date tonight."

"Cody? Listen to your mother for once. Those showgirls either have a couple of kids tucked away in a double-wide, or else they're riddled to the gizzards with STDs that don't even have names yet."

"She's not a showgirl. College graduate. Played basketball."

"What does she do now? Deal blackjack?"

"No. I think she's private stock, old family money, probably a few of 'em way up there on the *Forbes* big-rich list."

Cody had no idea from where that assessment had come. But he had been around his share of scions. Some good and thoughtful kids indifferent to privilege. And a good many snotcases, wastrels, or stone losers. "Eve Bell" had, if not inherited money, an aura of special breeding.

"Really? Well, you might talk to her about the plight of—"

"No, I won't. Love you, Ma."

7:12 P.M.

When night began to fall on the high desert and the El Dorado of glitz took on added brilliance against an indigo sky, activity quickened in the tarnished old Airstream caravan wedged into the walled backyard of Virgie Lovechild's digs, off Koval and behind the parking garages of several mammoth Strip hotels.

Hers was the only remaining private residence in a four-block area of apartment complexes with optimistic names like Paradise Valley and Blue Heaven Gardens: for the most part they were cheaply constructed two-story oblong buildings like those that overshadowed Virgie's half acre for most of the day. All of the area was destined to be gobbled up by the oncoming sprawl of ever-more gigantic megaresorts like Wynn's and the Venetian, but thus far she had resisted all offers for her property. Virgie liked it there for, among other reasons, the fact that she was within walkie-talkie range of the major Midway attractions.

Virgie spent ten hours a day, seven days a week, minimum, in her cluttered office, usually a sweatbox in spite of two air-conditioning units taking up most of the available window space. She employed two assistants during busy nighttime hours. They worked the phones and computers, keeping tabs on nearly every social, political, and entertainment personality who set foot in town, plus a horde of the once fashionable, the newly notorious, the glamorously criminal, and the genuinely odd ducks who slipped into the population for a few hours or days to work their purposes. Virgie had both a phenomenal memory of and voracious appetite for faces—thousands of them. Recent plastic surgeries never deceived her. She was on good terms with the Las Vegas Metro police, who sometimes requested her services to deliver an elusive thief or homicide suspect. She traded tips with casino security honchos who kept track of the movements of known cardsharps and wired-up chiselers.

To maintain the pace Virgie also employed, nearly around the clock, highly mobile photographers with whom she was in constant touch. She made their livings and hers off what her Pack of Rotsies (as Harlee Nations had dubbed them) digitally forwarded to her: candid celeb shots that were then peddled by her syndicates to the worldwide gossip press. She filled special requests, but Virgie, in spite of being tempted at times by the prospect of large fees, was loath to shovel dirt, even if the purpose was to bury someone hugely deserving, like a particularly venal politician or scumbag wife-abuser. Virgie cherished her near anonymity and stayed out of the social whirl. Nobody in her adopted hometown knew much about her, including her cop friends. She left her digs only on rare occasions, for a dental appointment or to have her hair done before her bowling night. There was a NO SHIT/BAD DOG sign on the partly open gate in front of Virgie's midfifties stucco bungalow with its dilapidated palm trees and an old Chevy with a flaking vinyl top and hardening of the rubber hoses in the carport. But Virgie's only dog was a nonthreatening pedigreed bichon frise named Snowjob. Virgie herself was just an old dame of uncertain origins, like a good many other loners who had migrated to the high desert during the last couple of decades of hectic expansion. If pressed by one of the regulars during her bowling night at a hundred-lane complex out on the Boulder Highway, Virgie would say—cribbing from the immortal Gypsy Rose Lee—that she was descended from a long line her mother had listened to.

Virgie had a cigarette cough like a goose's honk, smart neon-blue eyes, and bright yellow hair; on sagging freckled skin her collection of aging tattoos looked like epidermal roadkill.

Truth to tell, Virgie was as socially undesirable as her manner was coarse. She had never met a Hollywood legend or *wunderkind* song-bird or other postulants of fame afire in the lamps of their celebrity, in all her years of pursuing them from her cramped Airstream redoubt. But, seeing familiar faces even in her sleep, intimate as she had become with their luminous lives (the godlike auras Virgie her-self helped to maintain), she considered them all family.

Virgie had made it through sixty-odd years without a husband, therefore no chick and no child. No ties existed or were possible with those few blood relatives still living in Blackpool.

No, the closest thing to children of her own were the somewhat bland but stylish and very lovely up-to-the-moment teenage girls who had started coming around a few weeks ago and by now had more or less adopted Virgie—for Christ's sweet sake—as if she were some sort of school project. But, no, that wasn't being fair. Virgie was the one who had been unable to resist striking up a conversation with Irish-tongued Devon at the hairdresser's. They were just a couple of innocents in a place where innocence was tops on the menu for the two-legged carnivores who abounded in Dazzle City. They were awed by her deep wellspring knowledge of **celebrities,** starstruck and idolatrous like so many girls their age. Wanting to be in the know, Virgie had accepted, now welcomed them. They were on her mind a fair amount of time lately. When they didn't show up outside the Airstream, timidly tapping, for several days, bringing little treats for her and Snowjob—fresh baked fudge, gourmet dog cookies—Virgie became concerned. All those carnivores on the prowl. She had no idea where her girls lived or went to school, who their parents or guardians might be. Seemed much too young to be emancipated juveniles. But on that score Devon and her best friend, Harlee, were supermum, as reticent as Virgie herself.

Fair enough. One thing she was sure of, inasmuch as she was a shrewd judge of character: the girls who had captured her fancy (Virgie having come to that tempered age where beauty in the female pleasantly diverted her heart without risk of a romantic seizure) were not high-priced specialty hookers, wearing little-girl frocks, large hair ribbons, and Snow White–style buckle shoes to assignations. Virgie shuddered at the thought of rich, fatty, cologne-stinking carnivores fingering, *oh God,* those delectable bosoms and bottoms.

Virgie was on one of her six phonecams when the girls appeared around seven fifteen, Devon carrying a beautifully wrapped box of the white chocolate, cherry-stuffed fudge that Virgie adored, in spite of how bad the sweetsies were for her precious remaining teeth. She already had more gold crowns than all the royal heads of Europe.

"No, Satch," Virgie said, blowing a two-foot stream of cigarette smoke from her nostrils, "p'raps she—or more likely it's a drag queen—*looks* like Divinity." Satch, a new hire, was on the other end of the connection and had just sent a candid for Virgie to vet. "*Walks* like Divinity. Even smells like her, God forbid. But she/he is pure wannabe; Divinity herself is front and center at Beyoncé's show right now with her ex—no, the middle one, the Brazilian jujitsu champion—and with Enchante, her side dish of the moment, steppin' out tonight with Slyrap Sho'Doggie. Do trust me on this, ducks, I always know whereof I speak."

Virgie swiveled around and said to one of her assistants, a black kid with a dagger goatee and a head that looked like a burnt cornfield, "Bluesie, where's my ID on George's new squeeze? I'm guessing she's one of the Italian imports he enjoys with his Verdicchio di Villa Bucci."

Bluesie danced fingers over his computer keyboard, eyes a few inches from the flat-screen monitor. "Not in our files."

"'Not in our files' is never a satisfactory answer, Bluesie. Now, *dig.*"

Deborah, a Goth girl with fat ankles and a habitually pursed little mouth who hated the sight of Harlee and Devon, clicked off on another cell and said, "Sean and Justin and three unidentified flying bimbos just got off the Warner jet at McCarran."

"Is Sydney still roving the airport?"

"Yeah."

"Get her. This could be juicy. Have Brinkman back Syd up at the hotel, stake out the sneak route on the subbasement level at Mandalay Bay. He knows the drill." Virgie swiveled back to her visitors, deposited a crummy half inch of cigarette remains in a smokeless ashtray, and accepted the gift of homemade fudge with her jutting gold-lined grin.

"Sean and Justin?" Devon said, wide-eyed. "Really? Where might they be staying?"

"The Four Seasons. Under their usual aliases. Sorry to disappoint, but I mayn't give those out. My sources are unimpeachable, but it's very hard to gain a competitive edge in this town."

Harlee, who had clapped a hand over her mouth, released it and sighed ecstatically. "I am hot to death for both of them!"

Virgie said, lighting up a fresh gasper, "But when last you came wasn't it Josh you were hot for?"

"No, Josh is *so* last month. Jason's my real pash, if I had to choose. But didn't I read in *Teen People* that Jason is going to marry what's-her-name? On the Disney Channel? With the flam dimples?"

Virgie enjoyed a clearing-out cough before taking her first drag on her Virginia Slim. "Talking about Pyxis O'Rourke? Don't bet on wedding bells: Pyx is acey-deuce but he wears the Victoria Secrets in all of his relationships. It's strictly PR, luv."

"Omi*god*! Jason? Those beautiful abs? Just can't believe it!"

"Oh, yes. Jase has been beaten bloody behind more than one leather bar in Twinkie Town. I do have a great set of pix, but I won't sell them until someone else outs the lad. I seldom wear a scruple on my sleeve, but he *is* a dear. We may only hope the unthinkable doesn't happen, and they fail to dump him in time outside Cedars emergency department when next he has the urge to be savaged by gangbangers."

"I'm nauseous," Harlee said, swallowing hard as if it were true. Using that breathy Monroe voice she knew full well made Virgie desperate to cuddle her. "Oh, well. *Suum cuique.*"

Devon gave her a look with a slightly raised eyebrow. Nobody said that anymore.

"'To each his own,'" Deborah translated. "*You've* studied Latin."

"Once upon a time."

"Where do you go to school, Bishop Gorman?"

By way of a further reply Harlee provided Deborah with a flat LD/YD stare (Lie Down/You're Dead) that returned Deb to her multiple phones in short order. Chicken-hearted in spite of her piercings and Goth facade.

Virgie was on another call and didn't pick up on the swift change in Harlee's demeanor.

"Okay . . . okay. But caution is our watchword. He's mobbed up and the entire state is posted off-limits to him. You know they will smash more than your camera at *Figaro*. But, I agree, it's much too juicy to pass up. How many times has she been nominated? And five kids back home in Connecticut, including that cunning young dwarf she adopted whilst she was filming in Thailand last year? Let me think. At auction, conservatively, should you catch them locking lips, thirty dimes. But you are not worth ten cents to me in a body cast, so do take care."

"It is ever so amazing to me," Devon said when Virgie returned her attention to them, "how you know just *everything* about anyone who is someone in Las Vegas."

"Make that the whole wide world," Virgie amended. "At a certain status level, of course. Sooner or later they all come trooping through our pleasure palaces. And none of them would feel at home— neglected, actually—if flashcubes were not constantly going off in their pampered faces." Virgie broke open the gift box, made appropriate sounds of delight, then offered fudge to the girls, who quailed at the thought of patches and declined the treat. Virgie made no offer to Bluesie or Deborah, who cast a petulant look at the other girls. "Due diligence, lambs," Virgie said, chewing on one side of her mouth to avoid suspect bridgework. "From this humble listening post I cast a wide net."

Deb's pucker was tighter than ever as she stared at Harlee. For now there was a lull in the trailer, computers at the ready and humming for more action. Female voices spoke in near monotones on the police scanner.

Harlee said, "Three nights ago at Treasure Island I recognized someone you probably don't know about."

Virgie smiled, mildly curious, confident that she was wrong.

"We were at the first show of *Mystere*." Devon nodded. "And she was standing next to us at one of the concession stands. I didn't place her right away, because she's wearing her hair different than when she was on the cover of *People*."

"Oh, a cover girl," Virgie said. "Pro?"

"Do you mean in show business? No. Anyway her hair is way cropped now but cute—oh, when *was* that? She hasn't been in the news for—"

"Months and months," Devon said with a shrug.

"Almost as if she's been, you know, in hiding." Harlee and Devon having a dialogue now.

"Certainly couldn't blame her, after all the notoriety," Devon said, choosing the exact buzzword to gain Virgie's full attention.

Deborah had scooted her chair close to Bluesie and was saying something in an ear that had what looked like a miniature Fabergé egg dangling from the lobe.

"Notorious, is she?" Virgie said, licking a bit of fudge from her fingertips before picking up her Virginia Slim from the ashtray.

That prompted a perplexed frown, Harlee shaking her head, still looking to Devon for guidance. "I never forget a face, but—"

"And I'm *so* good about names," Devon said. "Something to do with paradise, that was the association I—"

"Eden!" Harlee exclaimed. "It was Eden Warren—no, I mean, like that; War-wear—*Waring*!"

Virgie was at a loss, for all of three seconds.

Deborah said, "That girl in California who had a premonition, a DC-10 about to crash—"

"Oh, yes. The psychic. If you care to believe such twaddle."

"Oh, I definitely believe she's for real!" Harlee said. "She saved the lives of everyone at her graduation."

Remaining dubious, Virgie said, "Her PR may have exaggerated her prowess. When I was younger I often had remarkably accurate hunches that always seemed to coincide with my monthlies."

"I'll bet the *Enquirer* or the *Star* would still be interested. Or how about *Sixty Minutes*?"

Virgie nodded, preoccupied.

"So how many, um, dimes could Eden Waring be worth?"

"Well—she isn't news anymore, but I grant you the tabloids have always been keen on certain subjects. For tab readers the paranormal probably ranks as high on a list of obsessive fixations as celebrity face-lifts and who's gay. Especially if there's a religious angle. Catholics adore gory stigmata and plaster madonnas that shed tears. Is Eden Waring the goods? Who knows? But I shall give her a shot on what has been a slow evening thus far."

"Bitchin'," Harlee enthused.

Virgie grinned at the girls. "Should your tip prove out, there would be a nice gift certificate for each of you."

"Dolce and Gabbana?" Devon said, her ordinarily mild gray eyes afire as if she had glimpsed the Holy Grail.

"One never knows, does one?" Virgie said teasingly. "Let me get to work on this." With fluent mousework she soon had stripped every mention and image of Eden Waring from several Internet sites. She iso'd three magazine cover photos of Eden, including a blowup of her in cap and gown from the Cal Shasta graduation-ceremony video.

DOES THIS GIRL POSSESS GODLIKE POWERS? the *Enquirer* had boldly speculated at every supermarket checkout line in America. Her photo paired with a shot of the smoking ruins of a DC-10.

Virgie said, "If Eden Waring is still in Las Vegas—could she be hoping to cash in by putting together a lounge act? Ah, the fifteen minutes of fame. If she is here, we will all know before the sun has risen."

"She could be using an alias," Devon pointed out.

"And she's definitely changed her look." Harlee peered critically at the *People* cover. "I suppose they don't have killer makeup boutiques or decent stylists in that small town she's from."

"Spare me a few minutes and make a rough sketch of the 'new' Eden, and Bluesie will composite a revised portrait. Within the hour we will have ten thousand pair of eyes on the streets of Vegas eager for a glimpse of our heroine. Devon, my sweet?"

"Yes, Virgie?"

"Poor Snowjob had *all* of his yearly shots today, and I fear he's still half out of it; but he must go for his walk. If you would be so obliging."

"Not to worry. Is he in the house?"

"Snoozing in his little bed at the foot of my bed. Mind you don't stray from my immediate neighborhood. Some of the apartment people are trash, and they keep the most ferocious dogs imaginable."

"Oh, I'm good at looking out for myself," Devon said.

When she returned from walking Virgie's bichon frise, Deborah the Goth girl was out of the trailer, lounging against the side of Devon's powder-blue Jag in the driveway, toking.

"On my break," she explained, staring at Devon through a domino mask of eyeliner, a hint of mischief or devious purpose in her small smile. "Want a hit?"

"No, thank you."

"Didn't think so. What *are* you guys into, Teen Virgins for Christ?"

"Don't lean on my car like that. I just had it detailed."

"Don't worry," Deborah said, a spike-rimmed leather bracelet on her left wrist resting on the trunk, "I won't scratch it."

"It wouldn't worry me if you did; but it could be a matter of considerable anguish to Y-O-U, dipshit."

Deborah shrugged, then took a step away from the Jaguar.

"I've wondered why you two keep coming around, sucking up to ol' Virg. Like long lost whatever. Harlee and Devon. I never caught her last name, but I ran the Jag plates so I know a lot more about you. Probably not news, but Virgie is worth a mean chunk of change in spite of this sore-thumb place. But I figured you're not running some sort of scam. Don't have to. The Jag's not a rental, it's all yours. A nice gift from your daddy? R. Duke Wisdom. Guarantor of your black Amex card. Big in real estate. Not as rich as Kerkorian or Wynn, but Duke can pee in their pools. Oh, wait a minute. *He* can't be your father. You were born in Ireland."

"Yes, I was."

"So what's with the Czech passport?"

"You've had busy fingers since last we visited."

"It's what I do. I delve."

"Clever Debbie. You see, my history is a bit complicated."

"Tell me about it. Not that I really care. So what *is* your angle? You can't be in love with Virgie's winning personality. All the god-damn fudge and trinkets for the pooch, just setting her up. What for?" Deborah inhaled deeply from the remnant of roach in her clip and waited. Feathery lavender hair and tarbrush eyelashes, enough silver rings in one ear to hang a shower curtain.

Devon sighed. "I must put Snowjob in his bed. Good night, Deborah."

Deb exhaled, winks of fire in her glossy pupils. "Let me leave you with a message. I got here first. Virgie won't be around all that much longer, not with that coal miner's cough and her sewer-pipe arteries."

"Oh, I see. Is that the message, sweetie?"

"Part of it. The rest is, don't bother coming around anymore. It's my territory."

Devon picked up Snowjob for a flurry of kisses, and murmured, "I do hate to see you fall into the wrong hands, Snowie." She looked regretfully at Deborah. "I'm afraid you've become rather a nuisance to us."

"Oh . . . big woo. I'm intimidated. My knees are knocking. Listen, bitch. I'm tight with guys; when they get through with you, you'll feel like you've had a jackhammer up your ass for two days."

"Sounds intriguing."

Harlee was saying goodbye to Virgie in the doorway of the cara-van. "I'm glad we had this little talk, Deborah," Devon said with a pleasant smile. "Now I know why I don't L-I-K-E you."

She went into the house to tuck Snowjob in for the night, Deb smirking behind her back. Devon felt the smirk like a cigarette burn.

Because Eden was new to Las Vegas, Cody Olds suggested Picasso for dinner to his date, then phoned for a reservation at halftime of the Lakers–Spurs game. Waiting time for a table at Picasso could be three weeks. For Cody, no problem.

They were met at Bellagio by a senior-staff casino wrangler named Angelique, who was so smartly turned out that Eden momentarily felt like a candidate for a fashion mercy killing. Then she decided she probably wasn't all that pathetic. Some of the looks that appeared to be for her alone validated an afternoon of shopping. She was wearing a brown corduroy pants suit and a shirt from Versace with butternut lace-up boots. She hadn't been rich long enough not to be chilled to the bone by what she'd paid.

Her major fashion statement was Simba, the rugged walking stick Tom Sherard had left in her keeping. The gold lion's head, big enough to fill her hand like a baseball, glittered in the lights of Bellagio's canopy, which resembled a nineteenth-century European train shed. The lion's head was solid, anciently wrought gold. Eden had explained her need for the cane with a telltale limp; an old knee injury aggravated during her early-morning workout. Both the lion's head and the mopane wood had spiritual and supernatural qualities, which she didn't attempt to explain to Cody. She had tried, for a few larky moments, to imagine what his reaction would be (this no-nonsense, straight-shootin' son of the West) if she described one use the stick had been put to a few days ago at the Apostolic Palace in the Vatican. Oh, sure. Maybe in their sunset years side by side in rockers at the old-folks' home—"Cody dear, did I ever mention the time I killed some demons and saved the Pope's life?" But growing old together wasn't in the picture. She hadn't decided yet, in spite of acute loneliness and confusion of the heart, whether she cared to see him again. But the night was young.

* * *

(Having touched on the subject of ancient things with strange and otherworldly properties, it might be an appropriate time [while Cody and Eden enjoy a relaxed dinner with a warm aura of mutual attraction at their table] to bring up Mickey the Mechanic from Paramus, New Jersey, who accidentally [yes, accidentally; Mickey was always gifted with his hands but just did slide through high school] built a time machine in his garage one weekend when the oak and sumac leaves were turning a deep red in his side yard. The year was 1973.)

When asked in another time and another place how he had done it, Mickey tugged in distraction at a few strands of hair on his otherwise bald pate and said, "Must've been the goddamn spark plugs."

Mickey was speaking of a set of what at first had appeared to be ordinary auto plugs, eight of them, that were the prizes in one of his wife, Annette's, flea market "Crackerjack boxes," as Mickey called them. Annette was a devoted collector of bargain *objets*. This box was oblong, eight inches by six by two and a half inches deep. She had picked it up from the back of a cluttered card table at a bazaar in Old Tappan. The bronze box was heavily inscribed with minute pictographs. One that could be identified without a magnifying glass depicted a man in breastplate and regal headdress standing in a horseless chariot as it overflew the sun.

Annette suspected that the box had something in it, perhaps valuable, probably not. Anyway the box had been carefully soldered shut. She paid four dollars for it and, when she arrived home, asked Mickey if he could get the box open. Mick glanced at it, said sure, maybe tomorrow, he was busy right now.

Regardless of how many hints Annette laid on Mickey, the bronze box remained untouched on his workbench until, two Saturdays later, a neighbor who taught metaphysics at Montclair State College dropped by to borrow a ratchet-handle extension and noticed it.

"Those etchings, they look like hieroglyphs," Riley the college prof said, weighing the box in the palm of one hand.

"What's that?" Mickey said from underneath the '55 Chevy

Nomad he'd picked up for a couple of hundred bucks and was devoting hundreds of hours of his spare time to restoration, that showroom gleam. A cast iron P-glide trans was suspended on the shop hoist. Mickey resumed cursing whoever had put the Nomad's flexplate in backward. Some jackleg with no brains.

"The Old Egyptian system of writing. Where did you get this box, Mick?"

"Dunno. Ask Annette."

Mickey slid out from under the chassis that was up on jacks, wiped his hands on garage waste, picked up a shop manual, and began paging through it beneath his work light.

Riley shook the box close to his ear.

"I think something's inside."

"Yeah? Haven't had the chance to open it. You notice how somebody wanted to make it a tough job, with all that soldering."

"What I think? This little box of Annette's could be a find, Mick. Friend of my father-in-law at Rutgers, he's a noted Egyptologist. You okay to have him take a crack at reading these inscriptions?"

Mickey shook the bronze box himself as if it were a wind-up toy that needed coaxing to speak to him.

"Yeah. I hear something. Annette paid four bucks, she said."

"Could be a steal. If it's Old Egyptian, collectors might pay a bundle for it. Maybe a museum. Depends on what's inside, you know?"

"Collectors, huh. This Egypt guy at Rutgers, what? We call him, make an appointment? Suppose he's busy Saturdays? If you don't have nothing else to do, Riles."

"Now I'm excited," Riley said. "Definitely, could be a find."

The Egyptologist at the New Brunswick campus had a German name Mickey couldn't pronounce even after hearing it twice. He had a workroom in the basement of an old building. No mummies on hand, but there was quite a collection of scrolls and shards in cases with glass tops. The Egyptologist gave Annette's box the eagle eye for a couple of minutes and said, "Fake."

"What d'ya mean?" Mickey said. He was a little stunned. His hopes had been high.

"Meaning this box is not authentic. There are no such phonograms in Egyptian writing. Nor is it hieratic script. Hittite? No. The box is not so old. Worn. A copy. What dynasty? Where? Hm."

He placed the box beneath a large magnifying glass ringed with strong full-spectrum lighting, studied the inscriptions, made copies on a pad. Mickey looked at Riley, smiling uneasily. There were more cone lights above the Egyptologist's worktable, hot enough to bring sweat to the Mick's shiny dome, which was crisscrossed with strands of hair that looked like dried incisions made by a crazed surgeon.

"So can you read any of that?"

The Egyptologist looked up.

"There is consistency of symbology, the construction of symbol groups, and notations that are demotic rather than symbolic. But it is gibberish to me. An elaborate fraud, or else predating any known system of writing. Ha-ha, impossible. As for boss man in the chariot, I get only that he flies to the stars—between worlds, perhaps. Hm. Here is something I miss before. Look here, please, through my glass."

Mickey was directed by the Egyptologist's enormous finger to a tiny stamped inscription near one soldered seam of the box. It read SOUVENIR OF THE CHICAGO WORLD'S FAIR.

"That fair was in 1893," the Egyptologist said. "'The White City,' it was called. Dedicated to the marvels of electricity. The dawn of a new age." He turned off the worktable lights. "Sorry to doom your expectations." He said it with a smile that could be described as secretly pleased.

On the drive back to Paramus, Riley said, "Shoot. Anyway, I'm convinced there's something inside."

"More souvenir bullshit," Mickey said. But he was wondering about the meticulous soldering job.

In his garage workshop Mickey clamped the bronze box in a vise and went to work with a grinding wheel. The metal that had been used for the soldering was surprisingly hard. Mickey and Riley took turns with the grinder but by the time they had the box open it was getting dark and Annette had appeared on the back-porch steps calling Mickey to supper.

"Why go to all this trouble to seal the box?" Riley had said more than once. "Maybe it's a find after all. Jewelry."

Neither of them had a quick comment when they discovered the eight spark plugs with minutely etched glyphs on the porcelain insulators. The center and side electrodes of each plug appeared to be silver. Mickey tried to bite into one with the blade of a jackknife but was unable to score the metal. Silver? No way.

The plugs were neatly nested in their own woven case within the bronze box. Whatever the material was, it crumbled at a touch.

After turning one of the plugs over and over in his hands Mickey said, "Special set, probably. But no specs. If this is a hoax, what's the point?"

"Eighteen ninety-three? Those were still horse-and-buggy days. Did they make spark plugs back then?"

"No. But I guess they had flying chariots a zillion years ago."

Mickey put the spark plugs with a clutter of odds-and-ends jars on a shelf behind his workbench and went into the house to eat, in a surly mood as he handed over the bronze box to Annette. Not knowing the point of things made his head ache. But he couldn't stop thinking about those spark plugs. His hands felt cramped and tingly. He washed them with Boraxo at the kitchen sink and used Corn Huskers Lotion on his calluses. The tingling persisted. When he sat down at the table and touched his fork he felt a shock. The fork glowed for a couple of seconds. His heart flivvered like a just-netted trout.

Mickey pushed his chair back and studied his tingling spatulate fingertips. Annette was taking a standing rib roast out of the oven—a once-a-month treat, prices of meat being what they were—and didn't notice the expression of dismay on her husband's face. As always, because Mick had never been much of a conversationalist, she filled the inevitable long silences of their house, now that the girls, Janelle and Maureen, had departed, with as much verbal stuffing as she could dish up. Mickey seldom apprehended a tenth of what Annette had to say. One of his two remaining obligations as her husband was to grunt or nod in the right places, say, "That so?" or something equally encouraging when Annette ran short of breath.

Annette put the roast on the lazy Susan with the scalloped potatoes and succotash and Parker House rolls, caught sight of Mickey sitting with his hands lax in his lap, staring at the fork that first had buzzed him, then had momentarily glowed like the red foil Sacred Heart in the bosom of Jesus on the wall calender behind Mickey's head.

"What's wrong? You look like you've got a pain, Mickey."

He raised his head. "Huh?"

"I said you look like you got a pain." Her voice rose in anticipation of ominous news. "Are you hiding something from me, Mickey? Was it bad news your last checkup you don't want me to know?"

"For chrissake, Annette. I'm sound as a silver dollar. Told you that already." He looked at the platter with the roast and carving tools on it. Reached out gingerly and touched the sterling knife handle. No unpleasant jolt. Mickey swallowed. "Why don't I go ahead and—"

"Thanks and praise come first," Annette reminded him, settling her bulk into a chair opposite the Mick.

Mickey hitched his captain's chair closer to the table. Flexed his hands before joining them prayerfully. The tingling was barely perceptible now. Elbows on the table, Mickey bowed his head.

"*A' sha'fh nas altuk dif g'la sum ba-Reis s'ha'k baas . . .*"

Annette's head shot up, her ginger eyes like jumbo aggies. "Whaaaat?"

Distracted from his prayer, Mickey frowned at her.

"Whaddya mean, what?"

"*What* was that you were saying?"

"Whaddya—I said, 'Lord, we humbly thank you for this wonderful—' Like I always say at the table, for chrissake. The goddamn *blessing.*"

Annette raised a hand in an abrupt chopping motion, folded three fingers, shook the remaining finger at him. "I'm not in the mood tonight for hijinks, Mickey! Not with little Danny in a hospital suffering from nasal diptheria, and God knows I should *be* there right now helping Janelle with the other children—"

"He's only in the hospital for two–three days. Resting comfortable, didn't Janny say, no need for you to fly all the way out to

Phoenix, not to mention the expense—what in hell'd I do, get you going off on me like that?"

"*Please.* Talking nonsense when you should be thanking God. Just asking for trouble we don't need. God has his likes and dislikes. Talking in tongues! Maybe in some churches that's common practice, but I happen to believe our Lord finds it offensive. Those charismatics, now don't get me started. If you weren't in the mood to ask the blessing—"

"I said it already, most of it! In plain English."

He looked too amazed and indignant to be keeping up a pretense. Annette dropped her hatchet hand, although her lips remained tight.

"Did you not *hear* yourself?"

"Hear myself what? This is nuts. Supper's cooling, and all you can think about is I didn't ask the blessing right?"

Annette stared at Mickey for several more seconds. The Mick staring right back at her, righteous in his hurt; Annette's displeasure lost impetus. She shook her head, then her eyes wandered in a puzzled way. She hunched her shoulders.

"Well, but I . . . I . . . I thought I heard . . ."

"Can I carve now?" Mickey asked, with an edge of sarcasm.

"I guess . . . just upset, Janelle and the kids on my mind, didn't hear you correctly. Or, or . . ."

"Aw, forget about it, Nettie. 'S okay. Let's eat. What's for dessert, by the way?"

"Oh, Mickey, your weight; *not* that I'm criticizing. You know Dr. Chopra said—"

Mickey gave her a wink. Forgive and forget, even if she did get a little peculiar from time to time. Not like when she was wearing those hormone patches, of course. That had been a rough couple of years. "Bet you made something anyhow. Let me give it a guess. Those Macintoshes were in the window greenhouse yesterday? Apple cobbler?"

"But no whipped cream. And I mean that." A playful finger waggle this time.

"Sure. I can get along without whipped," the Mick said.

※　※　※

After he'd finished eating his supper, what was still eating Mickey was speculation about those spark plugs. In spite of having spontaneously spoken a seriously dead language at the table, about which he hadn't a tittle of recollection, Mickey had no insights into the origin of the curious plugs—although he was no longer thinking hoax, and to hell with the so-called expert at Rutgers.

Having solved the mystery of why the Chevy Nomad's torque converter bolts had been too short and reversed the flexplate to fix the problem, Mickey loaded the heavy Powerglide transmission onto the trans jack in his well-equipped home shop and reassembled the unit. His nephew Pat, who lived a couple of blocks over, had fled his house again. Patrick didn't have much to do with his father, a much younger half-brother of Mick's who was raising his three sons with a cruel tongue, the back of his hand, and total contempt for their existence. Pat was fifteen, undersized for his age, a pepperpot kid with scrambled hair and bowed legs and a squashed nose that gave him a goblin look. *So ugly he was cute,* Annette often said of Patrick, when she was sure it wouldn't get back to him. Mick didn't mind having the kid around, although he had too many opinions about everything. Patrick was taking automotive courses at the trade high school he attended, with the notion of making his way in life like his uncle Mickey, as a shop foreman for a new-car dealer.

Patrick sat on a metal stool eating apple cobbler (with plenty of whipped cream) while Mickey put the finishing touches on the Nomad's power train and lowered the car on its jacks. He still had a lot of work to do on the resto: replace corroded trim and the windshield, install new seats, apply several coats of deep-gloss lacquer to the body.

"Does it RUN yet?" Pat asked him. Slow to mature physically, his voice was just now changing, hitting hoarse high notes, giving a few adult grumbles.

"Yeah, ought to."

"How about we take it for a spin?"

Why not? Mickey thought. A new battery and ignition were in place. All that was lacking were spark plugs.

Spark plugs. Mickey took a lot of time wiping his hands, a curious smile on his face that had Patrick looking at him with his head cocked.

"What's wrong, Uncle Mick?"

"Wrong? Oh, she'll *run,* all right, with that 265 block. I was just wondering where'd be the best place to let her out."

But Patrick had made up his mind for him. The Mick had a drawerful of factory sparks. He went through the boxes already half certain he didn't have a set with the Nomad's specs. Already it was too late to drop by the parts house on route 17. He shook his head.

"I forgot to buy plugs," he told Patrick. "So maybe tomorrow, huh?"

Patrick was down from the stool, setting the meticulously cleaned-out cobbler dish on a corner of the workbench. He noticed the spark plugs from the 1893 World's Fair box Mickey had left there.

"What about these? They any good?"

"Oh, those. They're, whaddya call, prototypes. Never made it into production, far as I know."

"They look okay. Why don't you SEE—" Patrick cleared his throat, "if one of 'em fits the Nomad?"

"Patrick, don't touch!"

The boy jerked his fingers away from the crumbling nest of spark plugs. He looked back at Mickey. "Jeez."

"You could get a shock is what I mean."

Patrick looked as if he thought he was being ribbed.

"They're not wired up to anything."

"Well, they're, uh, like I said, not ordinary plugs. So let's just forget taking the Nomad out tonight."

"C'mon. Try *one.* I mean, it could fit. Wouldn't take us long to gap the rest of 'em, wire 'em up." He sensed indecision on Mickey's part. "How long've you been working on that heap, ALMOST three months? Don't you want to find out what she'll do, that straight stretch down by the old Lackawanna switchyard?"

Mickey eyed the neat rows of spark plugs, the odd gift in the Crackerjack box. His own heart sparked. Couldn't do any harm. Plugs fit or they don't. No trouble to find out.

"Hand me my plug wrench, Pat."

While Patrick was retrieving the wrench from the tool caddy, Mick selected one of the plugs at random from its nest. The number-one cylinder was up front of the engine, on the passenger side. He already had pulled the old plugs and cleaned out the sockets. He checked the "prototype" for signs of trouble: a hairline insulator crack, worn electrodes. The plug looked perfect, never used.

"What's all that writing on the insulator?" Patrick asked. "Looks Arabic or something. Russian?"

"Dunno. Hand me my feeler gauge too. There's no gap specs. Might as well make sure the plug's gapped right before I try to seat it."

"You want some antiseize compound?"

Mick gave his nephew a look. "I sure don't want a stuck plug ruining the engine threads. Told you a dozen times how easy it is to do that."

"I know, I know. You feeling all right, Uncle Mickey?"

"What's that supposed to mean? I look sick to you?"

Patrick handed the antiseize compound to Mickey. "You're sweating a lot, that's all."

"N'da 'sha el muq L'lash," Mickey said, the alien spark plug tight in his right fist.

"Huh?"

"Prime rib for dinner. I could use a Alka-Seltzer. Run in the house, get me one, okay? Tell Annette we're probably going down to the Lackawanna yard, run up the mill a time or two."

"Sure," Patrick said, still wondering if the strange sounds his uncle had uttered were partly due to heartburn. He took off for the house, untied sneaker laces flapping.

Mickey coated the plug threads with the aerosol spray. His pulses were noticeably fast, particularly in his temples. He gave the number-one cylinder socket a blast from the air hose, failed to raise a speck of grit. Then he gently inserted the plug, even more gently gave it a twist. Snug. The plug turned easily. Mickey straightened and wiped his forehead.

"Sak m'aa ce'ef'taq," he said with a worshipful smile. *"Vl'tuur, Reis."*

Annette was on the back-porch steps sweeping leaves away when Mickey drove the Nomad out of the garage, Patrick proud beside him on the worn-out front seat. The engine rumbled low and throaty.

"I'll drop Pat off at his house on the way home," he said to his wife.

"How long will you be?"

"Ten, ten thirty," Mickey said. "Want I should pick up something at the Quik-Shop?"

"If you want a beer while you watch the wrestling."

"Right," Mickey said. He pulled out of the short driveway beside their brick and shingle Cape Cod, turned right on Edgefield, headed south. Annette went back into the house, took an orange from the fridge, peeled and ate it slowly, having usurped Mickey's Barcalounger in the den to watch *The Mary Tyler Moore Show.*

It was ten minutes past five Sunday morning when Annette, alone all night and wrung out from nerves, decided she had better call the state police.

11:10 P.M.

Eden and Cody Olds, having canceled their early-morning wager, amicably agreed to split the considerable tab for dinner at Picasso. For Eden, two hours had slipped by quickly, an indication that she was having a relaxed time with a guy whom she was on good terms with, but not stuck on himself; who told entertaining stories about his upbringing on an Arizona ranch. He was okay with the fact that she didn't want to say a lot about herself. Maybe he was wondering how a young woman raised by foster parents in Northern California, middle class all the way, happened to be staying in luxury accommodations at a Vegas megaresort, with private detectives enhancing the already-considerable security. He didn't ask. He wasn't inhibited by Eden's spells of reserve that bordered on wariness, secrecy. Also, Cody was in no hurry to come on to her, if he intended to do so. Eden couldn't read his intentions but she had the impression that he was not the kind to jump into a relationship. So he had the experience to sense a wounded spirit and an instinct for knowing how to josh her out of a complex mood when one rose from the depths of her heart to her eyes.

He was partners, Cody said, with a couple of other investors, in art galleries: Vegas, Santa Fe, Newport Beach, California. They were mounting a show and he would be in town for a few more days. Eden smiled and said nothing about her plans.

As for her night out, basketball and a great dinner, Eden knew she'd needed it and felt less guilty about not spending the time with Bertie. Before they left Bellagio she made another call from the ladies' lounge at Picasso and talked to Bertie's brother Kieti, who was staying the night with her in the hospital suite to which she'd been moved, ensuring stricter privacy. More Blackwelder operatives protected Bertie there. She was still only semiconscious but she had recognized Kieti and her father and had communicated with them through hand squeezes. Vital signs were strong. Eden decided to skip a late visit and see Bertie first thing in the morning.

There were no messages from Tom Sherard, either on her cell phone or on the machine at the hotel bungalow.

Eden and Cody took the escalator to the first floor. Outside, the Dancing Waters show was on; they'd seen it several times from their table in the restaurant. But they watched again, not talking or needing to, comfortable in silence, neither wanting to break off the evening just yet.

"So where's your gallery?" Eden asked.

"At the Venetian."

"I'd like to see it. If it's not too late."

"There's no 'too late' in Vegas. Our crew is probably still there settin' up. The show is Wednesday night. Celebrities. Champagne. News coverage. You're invited."

She had looked away at "news coverage" but smiled nonetheless.

"Why, thank you. Now which way is the Venetian? I'm just a tourist."

"Up the Strip about a mile, opposite the Mirage. We can take a hotel limo."

"Good night for a walk," Eden observed.

"What about your knee?"

"I'm wearing a brace."

"And you've got mighty Leo to lean on. Okay, we walk."

At the Venetian there was a squall line of teenagers and other idol-aters behind velvet ropes, flashcubes greeting celebrity arrivals: a gala was in progress. A twenty-year-old alley cat emerged from one stretch limousine that looked big enough to hold both houses of Congress. She was barely dressed in a silvery something, instantly selling her body to the cameras. The latest infection of showbiz mendacity: but no amount of choreographed overexposure and fervid flackery could breathe into her pale flame a meteor's bright instant of talent.

On the Rialto Bridge over the driveway Eden suppressed a shudder of dismay at the size of the crowd, turning her face toward the canal side of the hotel while fits of rapture pursued the girl and her youthful entourage inside.

But not everyone's attention was focused on the pop diva with the pipsqueak voice. Only Cody noticed the slight, bearded man with a pro rig whose camera was aimed at them from a cobbled sidewalk beside Las Vegas Boulevard. Cody was not an unknown face around Las Vegas. On the other hand, the papas were not likely to consider him newsworthy . . . unless he happened to be with someone who was. This shooter was taking a lot of pictures. So he had to be devoting his time to getting a good candid of Cody's companion.

At the Lakers game she had kept her shades on—the lights, she said. And lowered her head whenever the roving cameras at courtside appeared to pan their way.

Instinctively Cody placed himself in the papa's line of sight, putting an arm around Eden. The unease he saw in her eyes when she glanced at him wasn't because of the casual embrace; at least he didn't think so.

"Crowds get to you?" he said now.

"Yeah. I—"

"No explanations necessary. The Venetian shops and Canaletto's closed around eleven, so there's probably only a few strollers in St. Mark's Square, where the gallery is."

"Okay."

When the Metro police car appeared behind Devon's Jag outside the gated entrance to the Lincoln Grayle Theatre, Harlee pulled out her handkerchief and began working up some tears. Earthmovers were roaring not far away. Work lights provided a near-daylight emanation on the broken face of the mountain, a scattered glitter where the theatre's facade and terrace had been.

The officer on the twelve–eight shift wasn't many years older than their bogus birth certificates made Mordaunt's Fetchlings out to be. With his flashlight he examined two knockout-lovely but sorrowing faces.

"Guys, you shouldn't be parked here so close, with those monster trucks coming and going." He shone his light around the interior of the scrupulously maintained luxury sedan, didn't see so much as an empty soda can. No telltale sweetness of squantch. "Car's acting okay? You waiting for someone?" Then with a second pass of his light up front he saw a box of votive candles in Harlee's lap. "Oh."

"D y'think it's for real?" Harlee sobbed. "He's buried in his car, like they said on the news, under that pile of boulders? But he *can't* be dead. Oh, he just can't be."

Devon, her own eyes leaking, blew into her handkerchief. "We loved him *so much.*"

"No telling what happened to Mr. Grayle. What are the candles for—plan on holding a vigil?"

Harlee nodded.

"Well, like I said, it's not safe here. So I have to ask you to move on. Don't give up on Grayle yet. There's always hope. He was one slick magician, so they say. Never made it to one of his shows."

Harlee smiled and dabbed at her eyes.

"How long d'you think it will take to get all of the rubble out of there?"

"Beats me. They been going at it since about ten this morning."

One of the dump trucks, of a size usually found in open-pit mines, rumbled up to the gates and flashed its lights. Inside the gate-house, a Grayle company security guard let the truck through. When it passed on the other side of the parkway from Devon's Jag, which was already dusty, more dirt sifted down over the windshield.

The cop knocked on the roof and Devon smiled obediently, shifted out of Park, and made a U-turn to follow the dump truck. She needed high beams to see through the pall of dust.

"Damn, look, my car's a M-E-S-S. I won't be able to sleep until I've washed my baby. Where do you want to go now, Harlee?"

"Linc's house. There's something I have to find, and he just might have left it there."

Harlee's cell phone chimed "The Bells of St. Mary's."

"Hi, Reese. Yes. No, I'm not sure I'll be back tonight. Okay. Okay . . . I'll leave it up to you. He's had a tough day, so if he needs a little something just fix him up, give him a nimble fuck, then cry on his shoulder and tell him you've never done anything like that before but it was *won*derful, he eats that shit up. Tell him you're only thirteen; that will really give Bronc a guilty thrill."

"The General asking where you are?" Devon said, grinning.

"The guys told him you took sick and I'm with you at the emergency. I doubt if he's up to gobbling a piece of Reese tonight. He's way stressed. The remainder of the Great One's Elite 88 will be jetting in tomorrow for a summit. Superlawyers and financiers. Those who really rule the world."

"TWRW," Devon said. "Think they'll try to defect, or get their hands on the G-O-L-D?"

"Bronc's job is to keep them in line, even though he's not a Malterran. But most of the gold is secure inside the mountain, first thing

I checked. The Great One didn't trust a soul with his stash but me. And of course I trust you, my heart. My own beautiful treasure."

"Love you too, infinity. But . . . what if TWRW get onto us?"

"Bad Old Souls or not, there isn't one of them we can't handle."

"Wish I had your confidence. They give me the creeps."

"Fuck 'em. Mess with Harlee and Devon, they'll regret it. Listen, light of my life. The Great One *will* return. We must hold that thought. Can't let ourselves forget for one instant that he's somewhere—I don't mean under a rock slide—and no matter where he's been taken or what shape he's in, he exists now and forever, he's *aware.* I just have to establish a channel of communication."

The phone again.

"*Virgie*! Hi! No, matter of fact we're just cruisin'. Stopped at the In-N-Out Burger by UNLV for malts, and we're about to call it a night." Harlee listened for a few seconds, her expression becoming beatific. "*Really*? So soon? Oh, that is just the most amazing— Uh-huh. Sure! Devon has one in her car, just a sec, Virgie."

Harlee pushed a button on the Jaguar's dash and Devon's laptop slid out of its slot, opening up. "It's devonoflaherty, at hotmail. Oh, I'm so excited."

"*Tell* me," Devon said, wanting to share the excitement.

"Virgie thinks she's nailed EW," Harlee whispered. "Sending us pix right now."

Within twenty seconds the face of Eden Waring, enhanced, appeared on the laptop screen.

"Virgie . . . yes! I'm one hundred percent sure it's her. Where was this taken? Yeah? A few minutes ago? And who is the guy she's with? Could she be staying with him at the Venetian? Oh, just curious. Sure, I'll hold on." Harlee looked exultantly at Devon as her excitement ran rich; she nibbled at her lower lip. Devon smiled fondly and winked, one eye on the road. She was a careful driver.

Virgie Lovechild came back to Harlee.

"Cody Olds? Old, like in ancient? Who's he? Oh. Never heard of him but I think I know the gallery. Good-looking dude. Well, Virgie—did Dev and I come through for you? You mean it? The pix are worth *how much*? No, no, no! Wouldn't dream. Gift certificates will be *fantastico*. Thank you thank you thank you. Love you, Virgie. Night."

Devon said, "Change your mind about going up to Linc's P-A-D?" She didn't much want to make the drive late at night. The mountain road up through Kyle Canyon was a bitch.

"No. Eden Waring will keep. Could you pull over to the median for a minute?" Harlee was acting jittery in her seat. "Right now, please, nobody's coming."

"What's up?"

"Silly. You know how I get. Gotta pee, gotta pee."

OCTOBER 28 · 12:05 A.M

My grandaddy Truett Olds was a collector of western art," Cody said, showing Eden around the fifteen-hundred-square-foot gallery. "Edward Borein, Wyeth, Charles Russell. We had a couple of Remingtons in here a month or so ago. Depends on what becomes available at estate sales. That's a Borein there." He pointed to a framed painting with a brass nameplate. "A variation of *Holding Up the Stage*. Over here are a couple of Wyeths. But for the most part we showcase contemporary artists like Terri Kelly Moyers, Tom Browning, and our star this week, Carrie Ballantyne. Carrie's subjects just seem to jump out of the frame at you, like this little cowgirl here in her dusty, sweat-streaked Stetson."

They had the gallery, which was across the canal from the faux St. Mark's Square within the vastness of the Venetian hotel, to themselves. The gallery was toward the end of a shopping concourse that ranged from pricey stores like Movado and Burberry to Krispy Kreme doughnuts. They were eating the last of the Krispy Kremes from a box of two dozen that had been left behind by the crew preparing for Wednesday's show and washing them down with milk from a carton in the office fridge.

"Is there a lot of interest in western art?"

"Booming. We sell eighty, ninety works a month. We'll open a fourth gallery in Telluride this winter. When I was about to get into the business my mother said I should specialize in native American art forms. I told her, Ma, there isn't much money in bumper stickers, comic books, or Navajo blankets." He waited for the laugh, but Eden's broad smile was satisfaction enough. "We sell original oils and drawings, some sculpture. No prints or lithos. Our prices encourage serious collecting. Seven dimes and up, depending on the size of the piece and the artist's reputation. A little oil by Howard Terpning, miniature actually, can fetch up to thirty dimes."

"You don't mean ten cents."

"Sorry. That's Vegas lingo for a thousand dollars."

"I like this one," Eden said, looking up at a large painting of a gunfight in an Old West saloon. "It has a lot of, I suppose this is the wrong word, energy. I feel like I'm off to the side in a shadowy corner, wearing net stockings and garters and holding my ears."

"Now that would be one of the sincerest compliments anyone's ever paid me."

"*You* painted the gunfighter?"

"My signature's in the right-hand corner if you look hard enough. That's Bill Tilghman, by the way, with the .45. A peace officer, not a gunfighter. He killed a cardsharp in Fort Smith, Arkansas, who was fool enough to draw on him. The trail herder in the rain with his tired cow pony is mine too; and the bronc buster losin' his seat at the Prescott Frontier Days Rodeo is my second cousin Averill Shadow Fox."

"So you're a *painter*."

"That kinda sounds like you might be impressed."

Eden smiled and nodded, absorbed in his work. "How long have you been doing this, Cody?"

"I sketched a lot from the time I was too old to eat my crayons. Drawing just kind of became important to me as I grew up. I studied for a year at the California School of Fine Arts, where they told me I had talent, and I've done workshops in Scottsdale, learning craft.

Painting's a good substitute for not puttin' down roots; I'm a wanderer by nature. Disappointed the hell out of my old man for not bein' a rancher born. But like I told you: can't sit a horse too well these days, and I never could get the hang of flyin' a helicopter like my youngest brother, Trey, who learned in the Navy."

"Helicopter?"

"Well, that's twenty-first-century ranchin', if it's a big enough spread. Reckon ours is."

"So you must have this studio with great north light and groupies to bring you coffee and give you shoulder rubs when you can barely get your brush up after a hard day. Sorry. That didn't come out quite right. I thought a little humor. But I blew it. Okay, from bed to worse." She scowled down at the foam cup she was holding. "What's *in* this milk?"

"Plein air's more my style," Cody said amiably. "So I work out of an RV. Not much room for groupies, but I could use a good Chinese chef."

Eden said, crimson in her cheeks, "Right. So, uh, your studio is an RV."

"Well, I travel a lot. Like that old Hank Snow song, I've been everywhere, man. Breathed the desert air. Indio to Winnemuca, Coeur d'Alene to the Sand Hills country. And, always, home again. For a little while."

"When you miss your mother's cooking?"

"Ma was always a total loss in the kitchen. Her true vocation is the law, now that she has no more kids to raise."

"Big family?"

"All those brothers and sisters. I lose track sometimes."

"Bet you don't," Eden said, now willing to look at him again. With a smile, but a shade of sadness came and went in her eyes. She didn't mind if he saw.

"Still close to your own family?"

"My . . . foster parents. Parent," Eden corrected. "Only one left. Never knew my biological parents."

"Who did you lose recently?"

"Riley. Heart attack, a few months ago. He was a large-animal vet in Innisfall."

"Northern California. I've been through there. Pretty country up that way. So you've always lived in Innisfall." He hesitated for a few moments, but not as if he needed confirmation. Then he said, "Full ride at Cal State Shasta. The Lady Wolves. All-Conference first team your senior year."

Eden seemed to back away from him without actually moving.

"Athletic Department's Web page?"

"Yeah. The local paper too. After that I did a Google."

Eden took a long slow breath, let it out.

"Why, Cody?"

"To try to understand . . . Eve . . . Eden Waring, better."

She lowered her head, then gave him a look, self-mockery and despair.

"At least you know I'm not wanted for beheading hitchhikers with a dull ax."

He smiled cautiously.

"I . . . just need to be left alone, Cody. Truly. Let that be the most important part of your understanding."

He nodded, but looked perplexed, something on the tip of his tongue he couldn't come out with until after a couple of halting starts.

"I have to help you," he said finally.

"Excuse me?"

"Early this mornin' when I saw you shooting buckets I thought you were someone I'd like to know. Passing thought. I probably see or meet a dozen women a day, in Vegas anyway, who I'd like to get to know better. But, one thing or another; and I'm no pickup artist, that's for sure. I used to have a bad case of the shys. I wasn't goin' to make a move on you, either. Then . . . this is tough to explain. It was like something picked me up by the scruff of the neck, an ol' puppy dog, and shoved me out there on the court with you."

"Woof woof. That is *so* sweet. Original, too."

"I know I'm not sayin' this well—"

"It was fate. And you couldn't fight it." But she regretted her tone.

A certain meanness. That hotheaded desire to get back at a player who had elbowed her on the court. He didn't deserve ridicule even if he was sounding a little off the wall. Obsessive. But he had weathered her defensive retaliation okay, lifting his chin a little, squaring oxbow shoulders. He spoke calmly.

"I have to help you. I don't know the why of it. Hasn't got a damn thing to do with whether I'm attracted to you or not. Or how you might come to feel about me. But I *am* goin' to do my level best to—"

"You have some glaze from the last doughnut on your mustache," she said. Trying to distract him. He was making her dizzy.

"Protect you." He bit it off with the chill-factor eyes of a Bill Tilghman, who would pull a gun when he had to.

"Whoa, Cody." But Eden felt unexpectedly, along with a surge of blood to her hairline, warmth. Pleasure. Maybe it had to do with all of the drama of the Wild West surrounding them, Cody's milieu: proud hard-living men with a lot of backbone. *Hombres.*

"Somethin' else. I dreamed about you when I was catchin' a nap this afternoon. I don't think I could begin to explain what that was all about. Navajo legend and symbolism. I'm part Navajo, I guess I didn't tell you. Wolf Spider clan."

"Oh really?" Eden nodded, feeling a little off the wall herself. "I've never been much attracted to men with mustaches," she said, as if she were apologizing. "Cody, now let's put an end to this. I'm *involved* with someone."

"Figured you had to be. But it doesn't make any difference."

"Who, by the way, could probably do a better job of protecting me than you ever— Oh, hell. Why are we doing this? I don't want to put you down. Challenge your manhood. It was such a fun evening, and I needed—"

"I had to tell you," he said. "Didn't think it would be right to put it off. Don't blame you for the way you're takin' it. But you'll get used to the idea."

"What idea?"

"Havin' me around. Lookin' after you."

"Wait a—"

"No, that's the way it has to be. But only until I'm sure you'll be okay, that no harm's coming your way."

Three or four seconds passed before Eden realized her mouth was open. She closed it.

"There *is* something in the milk."

Cody smiled, tension gone from his stance now that he had declared himself.

"He's not around right now, is he?" Cody asked.

"What? Who?"

"Fella you say you're involved with."

"No. Tom had to—leave Vegas suddenly. On business."

"When will he be back?"

"I— He didn't tell me. A couple of days. Don't think what you're thinking."

"What about those private detectives who are standin' watch outside your villa at Bahìa? Tom hire them?"

"Yes. They're from Blackwelder. Very reliable. So you see, Cody—"

"Why do you need them? Is it just the paparazzi? I understand how you don't want more of the publicity you've had already, some of it real tacky if you don't mind my sayin'."

"For sure I don't want any more publicity. Didn't ask for what I've had already."

"I figured that, changin' your name and appearance." He studied her. "You look tuckered, Eden, and I know I am." He took out his handkerchief and whisked it over his mustache to dislodge the flakes of doughnut icing. "I could shave this off if you're wanting me to."

"Oh, no. Please. Not on *my* account."

"What we both need is to get a good night's sleep. Maybe play some hoops in the mornin' if your knee's up to it. Then—"

"Cody? Listen to me? I have a friend in the hospital who *I* have to look out for, and some of her family is in town."

"I'm real good at not gettin' in anybody's way. It's not just that you're publicity shy, is it?"

"Cody, I am going to find myself a cab in a couple of minutes and, no hard feelings, our relationship ends when the door of that cab closes."

"You truly are in some kind of danger, aren't you?"

Eden turned away from Cody, not angry, just giving up on trying to talk to him. She walked toward the gallery's mall entrance, an echo to her footsteps, then faltered. Remembering that she had left Simba, her walking stick, in the gallery's office, leaning against a desk. She took a couple of more steps, favoring her knee, then stopped and shook her head.

"Bet it hurts more than you've let on," Cody observed.

She turned back to him and shrugged, exasperated. "My knee's okay. I can make all the moves I need to."

"One of those paparazzi outside the hotel took an interest in you when we got here. The new-look Eden didn't appear to fool him. He was snapping away until I stepped between you and his camera."

Eden's lips compressed. The implication dug into her like a biting fly.

"They know, then. They know I'm still here."

He watched her trying to get a grip and making a bad job of it.

"Who knows?"

"Can't tell you that, Cody. Just some bad guys. I mean really, really bad guys. Do the Navajo believe in evil spirits?"

"Not a matter of belief. They just are; they exist."

"Las Vegas is a fun place to visit, I guess. But there are people— giving them the benefit of the doubt—who live here and who are evil in ways beyond your comprehension. Maybe thousands of them, Cody. And they probably all believe their world would be a better, safer place without Eden Waring in it."

"How's that?" Cody asked, moving slowly toward her now.

"Because two nights ago I killed their son-of-a-bitch unholy leader. Their so-called Great One."

"This some kind of cult you're talking about?"

"Was the Third Reich a cult?"

"How did you—"

"I just took it to him. Big time. I was a hit. Man, I brought the h-house down." She trembled and her eyes lost luster and she seemed about to keel over on her weak side but by then Cody had her, taking her weight against him while Eden rattled on. "And your notion of protecting me from the wrath of Mordaunt's legion is very dear and I will always cherish you for it but, Cody, *no,* you can't, I won't let you! I did have my doubts a little while ago but now I don't think you're in the least delusional."

"Thanks."

"I do some dreaming myself, you see, and some of those dreams can be doozies. Las Vegas is doomed, by the way. It will be destroyed. That little landslide out there on the mountain was just a prelude. And we'll all go down with it."

"Should I skip next month's payment on my condo?"

"What's happened, I think something has *touched* you, Cody. Supernatural, whatever. I have a hunch about what or who it was but *they* shouldn't have involved you even though Bertie's down and helpless and Tom, damn him, has gone to Christ knows where and probably he's in danger himself. You are innocent and proud and tough but when they come after me they will kill you with no fuss and no quarter. You would not have a prayer against some of the powerful forces gathering in this place. The plagues of Egypt were bad, or so I was taught in Sunday school: but trust me, what Vegas has in store would make Pharaoh feel like a lottery winner."

"Real biblical, huh?"

"Yes. Now please let me go. I can take care of myself."

"Maybe once you explain how, I'll believe it. Meantime I'm stickin' by you."

Eden's left eye was turning in. She chewed her lower lip.

"Did you dope my milk?"

"No, ma'am."

"Can't you even look insulted that I'd think such a thing?"

"You don't mean it," Cody said peaceably.

"Please please *please.* I want—I think I—I feel so dopey! What do I have to say to get through to you?"

"Just take it a little easy, now. Got yourself worked up to a near frazzle. Natural-born grit, which I see you have a-plenty of, darlin', will only carry you so far. Then you're smart if you just call it quits for a while. Already half past quittin' time tonight. Now what you should do is come along home with me. I'm supposin' that villa at Bahìa is not as safe for you as it might oughta be. Nothing against those Blackwelders. From what I know about them they're a first-rate organization. But you need to have yourself a restful undisturbed night in a location I can personally guarantee. Tomorrow we'll talk more about pesky bad-hat guys."

"Pesky bad-hat guys?" Eden laughed dismally, then blinked tears for a few moments. "Somehow . . . everything you say just sounds so damn reassuring, so—so *reasonable*. And you're way too big for me to beat up." Eden shook her head, perplexed and forlorn. "I can't insult you and I sure can't fight you. And . . . I'm all through trying to argue with you. So I'll go. You're a fool to get involved with me, but I won't say it again." Instead she said, through clenched teeth, "God, *stubborn*; no wonder you don't get along with women."

He smiled. "Who said I didn't?"

"And get this straight, Wild Bill Bufferlo. Even though I admire your . . . artistic ability, I'm no pushover groper. Grouper. *You* know."

"Who said you were?"

OCTOBER 29 · 12:37 A.M.

Harlee Nations had all the key cards to pass through the high gates of Lincoln Grayle's estate on the western heights of Charleston Mountain, and thereafter to bum around inside all she pleased. Her privileges included access to the Magician's living quarters. The two guards on night patrol knew Harlee and didn't challenge her or Devon. The household staff was asleep or watching late-night television on their floor. The interminable, annoying Christmas music had been turned off. They heard only the high wail of the wind, a lament at this hour, punctuated by the yowl of a cougar in deep forest nearby.

Devon had visited the stacked house on the high slope on other occasions and was past being in awe of its size and architectural ingenuity. The views remained fresh to her eye. Stars were clustered on the bowl of heaven like bright rain about to fall.

Devon watched Conan O'Brien, whom she cherished for his cowlick, while Harlee prowled the two levels of Grayle's suite, unlocking cabinets, exploring walk-in closets. Trepidation became frustration when she failed to locate the red crystal skull.

"Did you and Linc ever?" Devon said, looking at the large bed, dozens of pillows, that was made for romping. Gold and black motif, a script G in the center of the flashy silk spread.

"Silly. I told you he couldn't get it on with women. Not while he's in his human persona."

"Well, then?" Devon said, giving Harlee an arch look.

"No, thankew. He was like way too furry for me in one of his alter shapes. I mean, Jesus, you saw what was on those surveillance tapes. Take one for the team and all that, but shit you not I have my limits. Besides, Linc can't go there all that often. Shape-shifting's not an exact science. Every time he has to make a shift it drains his life force, not to mention adds years to his face. If he wants to maintain icon status in Las Vegas, he'd better keep his good body and his looks. Wayne and Tony can't sing a lick anymore and Tom must be swiveling on his second set of hip joints, but their wills to survive are strong. Long as they can pile on the suntan makeup, their celebrity knoweth not the grave."

"Oh, are those still the originals? I heard that they were cloned. Rumor has it that Tom is planning a sibling act."

"Jones and the Clones?"

Devon made a running jump and bounced giddily in the center of the Great One's bed. Harlee frowned slightly but didn't scold her. She continued to look around the excessively mirrored chamber, the tip of a little finger between her teeth as she nibbled the nail. A habit that had accompanied the structuring of her own, teen persona. Bit her nails, had weepy spells.

"I could use a N-A-P," Devon said. She blissfully closed her eyes.

Before long Harlee crept onto the bed with her. They held hands, lying side by side, Harlee looking at herself in a smoke-toned ceiling mirror, each panel, twenty in all, flecked with pure gold.

"So what do we do N-O-W?" Devon murmured.

"Shhh." Harlee's heart was racing, which it often did when she was this close to Devon. But this time it wasn't an urge to smooch and tickle and drive each other bats with their fluent tongues. Her mind had a late-hour blankness, but her body was totally alive, mysteriously vibrant. The Magician had lain there only a day or so ago. And he was not the only one. She sensed a recent, reluctant female presence. Hostility. The vibes all a-jangle, riling her nerves.

Harlee continued to look up, as if the expanse of mirror held a world of answers. And—*for sure*—it was almost as if she could see him: the familiar form of Lincoln Grayle, but shadow-stretched. She might have been viewing him through a murky prism.

Staring wearied her eyes; Harlee covered them with her free hand. Tiny pips of light grew faint and disappeared as a growing power emanated from the cup of her palm. Refreshing her vision, spreading inward to the brain, the subconscious of Seeing. When she lifted her hand from her face she discovered that she had risen a couple of feet above the silk-covered bed, still lightly tethered by Devon's hand. Devon was fast asleep.

Above Harlee the bits of gold in the mirror twinkled; she could see more clearly what was going on inside the smoky surface. Not unlike sitting in the last seat of the front row watching a movie at an uncomfortably oblique angle. The dialogue was coming through okay. Because now there were two of them, the Magician slim in black jeans and a Harlequin-style black-and-gold sweater.

The girl lying on the bed in the vision that fully absorbed Harlee as she drifted closer to the mirrored ceiling was (she thought) none other than Eden Waring. Dressed in designer pj's a little large on her graceful body. They must have belonged to the Magician.

Harlee hovered, nose almost against the cool glass, watching them as she might have watched a show of exotic one-dimensional fish in an aquarium.

The Avatar wasn't peaceful in the ultraviolet light that illuminated her; she writhed in elongated misery, pajama tops riding up over her breasts.

Harlee heard her say, *Just turn the lamp off for a little while. I promise I'll—*

The Magician said, *Stay? But you can't make promises to me, Gwen. Can you?*

(Gwen? Harlee thought, at first confused, then astounded. But she was the exact image of—)

And the Magician said, *It's Eden who makes all of the decisions for her dpg.*

(Dpg? . . . A doppelganger! Harlee felt such a jolt at this revelation that it seemed for an instant she would decompress or something, yield to the grab of gravity and tumble twelve feet back to the bed where Devon lay obliviously in slumber. She took a deep steadying breath and resumed her clairvoyant, dreambody float.)

Sure. You have it all figured out. Without Eden I'm a big nothing!

And you hate the restrictions of your situation. You even hate your homebody, at times.

(Gwen didn't reply. Harlee assumed from her expression that, imprisoned by black light and too weak to blink away her tears, she hated everybody.)

What if we can get you free of Eden, so that you can be Gwen in more than name only? That's a promise I can make.

Like hell you can! You don't understand doppelgangers at all. Neither does your so-called expert, whoever that is.

Someone you know well, I believe. Maybe it's time for him to come in.

(Harlee was intrigued by Gwen's new visitors. She knew one of them: Dr. Marcus Woolwine, in residence at the Magician's house. Gwen obviously knew him as well, and reacted badly to his presence.)

Oh! God!

Hello, Gwen. Such a great pleasure to see you again. I would like to apologize for some of the things I once said to you. "A soulless facade, a fake, a nonbeing." But, after all. It wasn't easy being forced to consume humble pie—a man of my stature in the remodeling business.

(The man who had followed Woolwine into the bedroom was a Chinese nurse or physician. Harlee could only verify that he wore OR scrubs. He had with him a hospital cart that seemed to be loaded with meds and bags of IV solutions that hung from a short pole. Gwen looked horrified. Harlee couldn't blame her, sympathized in fact, considering what she'd seen of and heard about Marcus Woolwine: a scientist/necromancer who wore vaguely sinister mirror sunglasses. *Like, so decades ago,* Harlee thought contemptuously. Archvillain in a James Bond oldie. Aside from his lack of fashion sense, Woolwine was unpleasantly squat and bowlegged and the shape of his gleaming bald head made Harlee think of a bronzed horse turd.

And Dr. Woolwine wouldn't stop talking.)

From the day we both, ah, found it sensible to flee from Plenty Coups, my interest in you has grown with each passing hour. I have the good fortune now to be in the employ of a man who shares my fascination with doppelgangers.

Gwen screamed, *What are you going to do to me?*

(The Magician sat on the bed and affectionately ran a hand over Gwen's head. Harlee felt a hot pang of jealousy where she lay flat to the glitzy ceiling, on the outside looking in.)

You'll soon have the life you've always wanted. Disengaged at last, freed from the tyranny of a homebody. For your freedom, ALL I ask in return is a favor.

Do you a favor? I'd rather vomit in my own eyes!

But we'll talk more about that when I see you tomorrow.

The thirty-car freight train, with all cars of the rolling stock built to the specifications of bunkers on wheels, approaches the outer limits of North Las Vegas at a sedate thirty miles per hour, in a light mist that has begun to fall on the high desert. It is a long, somber, unmarked, and funereal train, en route from the eastern United States for nearly a week, bearing hives of radioactive ghosts to an earthly Acheron called the Yucca Mountain repository.

Not the first such train to reach the Vegas area. In the past few months others have traveled here through nearly every state: metropolitan centers like Rochester, Cincinnati, KC, Spokane, Denver. Never moving faster than fifty miles an hour, the trains are preceded by mobile track and rail X-ray equipment, observed by spotter airplanes or helicopter gunships that watch over them every mile of the way. All the trains are unscheduled; for security reasons they travel mostly at night. Every precaution is taken to prevent accidents, which the DOE knows inevitably will occur: at least twenty thousand shipments will be necessary to dispose of eighty-five thousand metric tons of waste, a figure that increases yearly.

Yucca Mountain is located on federal land about 100 miles northwest of Dazzle City, an area of approximately 230 square miles under the control of the U.S. Department of Energy, the U.S. Air Force, and the Bureau of Land Management. Yucca Mountain, cresting at just under five thousand feet, is, in geological terminology, a ridge formed by layers of volcanic rock, or tuff. Tuff is compressed ash deposited by the eruptions of local volcanoes between eleven and fourteen million years ago. The volcanoes are now extinct. Yucca Mountain, from any vantage point, is totally nondescript.

In the 1950s this portion of the Nellis Air Force Range was used as an underground test site for low-to-medium-yield nuclear devices.

After testing activity was suspended, more than six thousand seismic "events" around Yucca Mountain were recorded over three decades. One was a magnitude 5.2 on the Richter scale. In 1992 that earthquake caused at least a million dollars' worth of damage to government buildings on the site.

Nevertheless, proceeding from House Resolution 1270, the Nuclear Waste Policy Act of 1997, Yucca Mountain, Nevada, was designated as the permanent repository for pyramiding stockpiles of high-level nuclear waste from decades of bomb-making or reactor operations throughout the United States.

Yucca Mountain has not (as of this night in October) officially been certified by the federal government. But political reality being what it is (Nevada is severely underrepresented in Washington), this is pretty much a fait accompli. Nevada, you've got the desert, we've got the waste. Enjoy.

Three hundred miles of seamless rails extending from the Union Pacific main line at a dot on the map called Caliente, near the Utah border, are planned for the final hauling of the waste from everywhere in the United States to lonely if earthquake-prone Yucca. Meanwhile, urgent demands created by unreported "incidents" related to stockpiles of spent fuel rods close to major urban areas and an equally urgent need to test storage and transfer facilities have prompted these premature, clandestine (and illegal) midnight runs through the heart of populous Clark County to a rail yard where the hazardous materials are off-loaded onto trucks for the final one-hundred-mile trip up U.S. 95 to the still-under-construction repository. About $7 billion of a proposed $29 billion budget has already been spent far below the surface of Yucca Mountain.

As for the hazard level of the surreptitiously transported materials:

The first recorded year in history was about six millennia ago. Nuclear "waste" is still highly toxic, and will continue to be hot, hot, hot for another ten thousand years. But it's anyone's best guess. Handling the hot stuff (i.e., from train to truck) by remote control and behind heavy shielding is mandatory. With no protective shielding, "spent" fuel will kill an exposed person standing within three feet of it in about ten seconds. Even when it is stored in shipping casks, irradiated fuel emits 10 millirems per hour of low-level gamma radiation.

This radiation is harmful to human genes, depending on how long one is exposed to a truck or a train standing in a rail yard waiting to be unloaded.

The shipment aboard the latest thirty-car train, mandated on a can't-wait basis but now about to be stopped at the Craig Road crossing of the U Pac by a small but disciplined band of no-nukes activists and ordinary Vegas citizens opposed to "Mobile Chernobyls" passing through their middle-class neighborhoods, is contained in large-capacity casks designed to hold together for a thousand years. But, for practical reasons, none of the fully loaded spent fuel casks has ever been tested, except for computer simulations, for their ability to withstand violent earthquake shocks, explosive stress, long-burning fires at temperatures above 1425 degrees F, or well-mounted assaults by terrorists with armor-piercing missiles.

An attempt by a homegrown terrorist group to derail one of the first trains (consisting of ordinary, not new, and unprotected rolling stock) with its cargo for Acheron prompted the DOE to rethink its long-term strategy for transporting the stuff, and to clamp down on news stories about the attempted derailment. A few Internet Web sites did report the story; in most cases rumors substituted for facts.

It was a fearsome fact, however, that any accident causing spillage of toxic waste could send an invisible cloud of radionuclides downwind from the accident site, with fallout continuing over a wide area for centuries. Over largely uninhabited Nevada desert, or Wisconsin dairyland. Or downtown Oklahoma City.

The demonstration at Craig Avenue is efficiently dismantled almost as fast as it materializes. Armored vehicles cordon off the area. The flatbed truck driven onto the track in the path of the anticipated Mobile Chernobyl is pushed out of the way by a heavy-duty tow truck. A minor TV actor who loses his balance and falls out of the bed of the demonstrators' truck suffers a broken wrist. Diehards throwing their bodies across the gleaming rails are nipped and savaged to their feet by attack dogs and are herded—backing up, cowering—to a line of military transports. In only two or three minutes the melee is resolved: there are no more bullhorn voices, shouts, epithets, crudely lettered placards denouncing the DOE or the entire Big Oil-Military/Industrial-WTO-IMF conspiracy that has kept the world from settling into a harmonic of lasting peace, nature unspoiled, and love-thy-neighbor. Effigies of politicos currently on the most-hated list are removed along with now-bedraggled and rump-bitten demonstrators locked into plastic wrist restraints. They will spend a few days incommunicado in a barracks at nearby Nellis Air Force Base. No one is trying valiantly to sing "We Shall Overcome." The mist falls in a smear of spotlights, floodlights, red lights, blue lights. Mobile Chernobyl. There are riot police faceless behind reflectant shields, closely spaced on both sides of the crossing. They carry SP-5s and other hard-nosed weaponry. Then a heavy thrum of approaching diesel engines. The local media, tipped off by the leadership of the demonstrators, then warned off by federal honchos, spokesmen for deep-background agencies hardly anyone has ever heard of, have dutifully looked the other way. A matter of homeland security. The train is unscheduled. It was never here. Stick to the familiar, the mundane, those human-interest stories heavy on the aw-gee and warm-fuzzy that everyone is following already, on their morning newscasts. Lincoln Grayle, the first alternate Mr. Las Vegas, is still missing. But we're all praying, Kevin. Yes, we are, Susie. A long-unemployed software designer from Silicon Valley has fed a dollar slot at the Barbary Coast and hit a progressive jackpot worth a little over four million. That's what Las Vegas is all about. No major traffic tieups to report this morning. Afternoon temperatures are expected to be in the midsixties. This is what Las Vegans want to hear at seven a.m. while they bathe, shave, brew coffee, get the kids off to school. Eight thousand new residents moved in last month, beating the previous month's record influx. The tourists can't get enough of whatever it is they came here for. But they're coming in droves. What recession? Sure, the suicide hotlines are humming 24/7, but let's keep it rosy. On *Eye-Opener*

Las Vegas our own Portia Harpring is going to give you homemakers valuable tips on how to carve those Halloween jack o' lanterns. — Gosh, just can't believe it's Halloween already, Kevin! I can connect with that, Susie. Now let's find out what Dr. Steve has to say about our air quality today.

CHARLESTON MOUNTAIN • 2:28 A.M.

Dr. Marcus Woolwine was awakened by a hand tugging at his shoulder. Two beauties were sitting on either side of him on his spine-friendly Swedish bed. His sleep mask had been pulled up to the crown of his bald head. After a couple of woozy waking-up moments he recognized Harlee Nations. He couldn't place the other luscious teenager, who was holding the point of a stiletto against his carotid artery. Presumably not in jest.

"Good morning," Harlee said. "Where is Eden Waring's doppelganger, Dr. Woolwine?"

"Wha'?"

"Come on, wake up. The doppelganger, or dpg, or whatever. Is she here?"

". . . No." His eyes were on the knife wielder. She had a delicious scent he couldn't place. A touch of heather. As for the stiletto— "What are you doing in my bedroom? Who are you? I have a pacemaker. Please put that—instrument—away."

Harlee said, "Dr. Woolwine, all I have to do is wink my left eye twice"—she demo'd by blinking it once, which caused him to flinch and turn glacial—"and Devon will push that stiletto through your neck like a pin through a voodoo doll."

"But—why are you threatening—"

"The doppelganger—what does she call herself, Gwen?—*was* here two or three days ago. Linc wanted something from her. A favor, didn't he say? What was that favor, Dr. Woolwine?"

"I have a pacemaker," he said again in a pleading tone. "You've interrupted my sleep! Who do you think you are?"

"A special friend of Lincoln Grayle's. From long before he took that persona for his own."

Woolwine turned his head carefully so as not to joggle the stiletto. He was still getting the Borgia stare from Devon while he evaluated Harlee. Scientific obsession percolated into his eyes. Not just another bewitching young face. A specimen, a literal throwback, rare fauna rich with implications. His fear stopped flowing out of him like damp from an old grave.

"You must be . . . a Fetchling."

"We both are."

"Amazing. Such lovely skin. Neither of you looks a day over sixteen."

"Physically we're not. Now what about Gwen?"

"You're wrong. She's no longer here. She is, as far as I know, time-traveling."

"Oh. How does she do that?" Devon said.

"If you know anything about doppelgangers—"

"I don't know much," Harlee said. "Fill us in."

"Of course. It isn't necessary to bully me in order to secure my cooperation."

"We couldn't be sure you wouldn't give us a tussle."

"I am eighty-four years old. I deplore violence."

"Supa-dupa." Harlee glanced down at Devon, who smiled slightly and withdrew the stiletto from the throbbing pulse in Woolwine's crinkly neck, which he then massaged tenderly. Without the glowering authority of his specs, his eyes looked lonely. Befuddled.

"Thank you for not cutting my throat," he said with desperate politeness, his voice breaking like a breadstick.

"Would you care for a glass of water, Dr. Woolwine?"

"Yes, please, if it isn't too much trouble."

Devon replaced her stiletto in its forearm scabbard up her left sleeve and got off the bed to pour spring water from a carafe. Woolwine sat up to gulp some of it. He wore Picasso–print pajama bottoms, blue and white birds and a seascape, but his chest was bare. He had age spots but retained good skin tone and his muscles were not at all stringy. Looked to be a hale old fucker, Harlee thought.

"About this time-travel business," she said. "I've always regarded it as pure bumshuck."

Woolwine shrugged. "Seeing is not believing in this case. However: perhaps you'd like to have a peek into the suite Gwen occupied before she was blitzed out of here by whatever fluctuation in the space/time structure or superluminal hyperspace phenomena was required to return her to the past."

"That explains a lot," Harlee said as Devon crossed her eyes comically.

"My dear," Woolwine said with a sigh, "hyperdimensional space and plasma physics are not in my area of expertise."

"Bumshuck?" Devon said, now doubling over in a mime of hysterical mirth.

"If one of you wouldn't mind bringing me my robe and slippers," Woolwine said.

There was subdued cornice lighting in every room of the suite that Woolwine opened to the Fetchlings, moonglow from the terrace. He stood aside, making no move to go in. Air flowing from inside the suite had the heady freshness of negatively charged ions. Harlee felt the down on her forearms stirring, a tickle around the lips, giddiness in her breast as if she were about to board a diabolical thrill ride as yet certified only for crash-test dummies.

"After you, Doctor," Harlee said courteously.

"I'll just remain here in the hall. I have—"

"A pacemaker," Devon said, as if she'd caught a hint of sly treachery waiting within. One lives for hundreds of years under mostly Machiavellian circumstances, one learns a few things. "What of it?"

"The torsion field inside is of a magnitude that could shut my pacemaker down. Or the reverse, accelerate it until my heart explodes like a gerbil in a microwave."

"Gross," Harlee said. "Could you, like, explain 'torsion field' in terms accessible to *Star Trek* junkies?"

"My *dear*. Let's just say that the dynamics are necessary for reaching the fifth dimension: hyperspace."

"O-kay. And that's where Eden Waring's doppelganger went?"

"Hopefully," he said with a tremulous smile. "If not to pieces. By the way—touch nothing inside, and stay well away from the holographic image."

"There's a holographic image?"

"It serves Gwen as a touchstone; without it she may be unable to find her way back."

"Roger that," Harlee said. "Now exactly why did you bring us up here?"

"To verify my assertion that Gwen is not presently available to you. Why don't the three of us do lunch sometime? I'd love to get to know you better. Perhaps you might be willing to part with a few of your secrets for maintaining eternal youth." He smiled again, covetously, then trembled, as if his pacemaker had gone a little haywire on him.

Devon said, "It involves propitiating Astarte with burnt offerings of goat, kine, and over-the-hill rock-band drummers."

"You can go back to bed," Harlee told Woolwine. "We'll lock up here."

"Remember: touch nothing."

They watched him pad silently back down the hall to the elevator.

"Now why do you suppose he's told us that?" Devon said. "Perhaps it's reverse psychology."

"He could be genuinely anxious about our welfare. After all, we possess the secrets of eternal youth."

"This is rather scary, don't you think?" Devon said, looking into the suite but not seeing much other than oriental furnishings and a nice Hokusai wood-block print of abalone fisherwomen on one wall.

"Well, as long as we're here," Harlee said.

No sooner had she laid eyes on the ruby crystal skull on the writing table than Harlee knew she had to have it, even though she'd been warned. But she talked it over with Devon while they stood a respectful eight feet away, at the perimeter of the time-and-space-bending energy field that emanated from the skull's radiant depths.

"It's humming," Devon said. "D'you hear it? Isn't it humming?"

"'You Go To My Head'?" Harlee suggested.

"Get on. I'm not amused. And quite apart from its undeniable ghastly charisma, I don't trust that beastie."

The dynamic field wasn't visible, but they were aware of it from the fizz across their skins, a sensation of heat lamps in the frontal lobes, and the look of each other's neatly arranged bones beneath glowing violet flesh.

"We should get started," Harlee said.

"Don't be foolish. It's putting out enough energy to zap Chicago into orbit."

"But it *knows* me," Harlee said, a charmed look in her eyes as she rubbed the tickle on her lower lip. "I've been with it before, although not during working hours."

"Whatever do you mean by 'been with it'? In a romantic sense? You and the skull have a history?"

"Oh, silly. Mordaunt introduced us. We hit it off right away, vibrationally."

"Nonetheless, I'm opposed to disturbing it. Obviously the Great One had an urgent purpose, allowing the doppelganger to use his skull for that boost into hyperspace."

"I'm just going to borrow it for a little while," Harlee said, heavy-lidded, a mesmeric glaze to her eyes. "The old purpose isn't as urgent as the new purpose. I must get in touch with him. I'll put the skull back exactly where it is now. No harm done."

"At least turn it off before you touch it."

"Turn it off?" Harlee said, her tone peevish. "I don't know what turns it *on.*"

"I can't stand it when my hair frizzes like this. Also I'm feeling strangely violated. To put it another way, I am jolly well freaking O-U-T out."

"None of that, now."

"There is a definable atmosphere of malevolence in this room, Harlee."

"We have to center ourselves. Focus on the larger purpose."

"If you distract that snarky flaming skull from another purpose—lesser though it may be—is there a possibility it could become angry with you?"

"The Great One is depending on us, Devon. Us, and us alone."

"Our last glimpses of him in those surveillance tapes make me a wee pessimistic about his chances for getting out of this latest snafu."

"It's the Irish in you, my love. Irish souls, forever dripping melancholy rain. Remember, I did suggest you add a Latin strain to your bloodline during your most recent tune-up. Flamenco-style zest."

"I have zest. It's just a cooler kind of zest."

"We're going to do this, and we're going to pull it off. Now don't sulk, I need you. Just hold on. Don't let me be snatched into another dimension."

"Gerbils in microwave ovens," Devon said. Then she moaned in dismay, long arms locked around Harlee's waist, her head tucked into the small of the other girl's back as Harlee moved determinedly to the writing table and into the full tumult of the torsion field that enveloped it. The hairs on Devon's head stood out, fiery at the tips from St. Elmo's dancing fire, straining at their roots. Her bones resonated to the low hum from the hypercomplex structure of the crystal skull.

Harlee cried out.

"What's happening?" Devon said, unable or afraid to look herself. "What do you see?"

"Buff guys in singlets with lyres and lutes."

"I hate it when you're being a smart-ass."

She felt Harlee tugging against her embrace, reaching out and down to the skull. Devon braced for both of them. A thrill running through her body, like an orgasm she was enjoying in twilight sleep. She couldn't think anymore, struck dumb by momentum, a gale in the mind. The delights of orgasm faded. She felt as cold and depleted as a corpse, but continued to hold on with eerie strength to Harlee Nations.

Abruptly both of them were hurled backward with tremendous

force, Harlee landing on Devon with a scream. Devon's head hit the terra-cotta floor and rebounded in a blaze of sky-high sparklers, melting into blackness.

She came to with Harlee kneeling beside her, shaking her gently. The light in the room had a surreal quality, a shower of moonbeams to Devon's hazy-dazy eyes. Then she felt snow pelting her blooded face and throat. It was snowing quite heavily in the room. The humming had stopped. The crystal skull sat tamely in the crook of Harlee's other arm, benignly grotesque, with a look of empty caverns.

"Got it!" Harlee said gleefully, snowflakes massing on her brows.

Devon tried moving.

"Oh. Ouch. *Damn.*"

"Anything broken?"

"I don't know. Help me to sit up." Devon was shivering, her teeth clicking rhythmically. The terrace doors stood open, but the snow was a local phenomenon, falling from directly above their heads. Nature rioting in some manic and inexplicable mode. "What's c-causing this blizzard?"

"No idea. Could it be a stage effect Linc stored in here, then forgot about?"

Devon concentrated on her breathing. Some twinges, but not as if broken rib ends were macerating soft tissue. Harlee helped her to her feet.

"Am I b-bleeding?" Devon chattered. "I got such a whack."

"I think that's just melting snow running down your neck." Harlee wiped, licked her finger. "Yep."

"Let's g-get out of here." She looked through the softly hissing snowfall past Harlee at the overturned writing table. The chair was gone. "Harlee?"

Harlee turned to look. Then they looked at each other. Harlee put the tip of the little finger of her free hand between her lips and bit delicately at the nail. Devon noticed that she had acquired a skunk stripe in her coffee-bean-brown hair, a reminder that they had heedlessly ruptured an entire cosmology. And got away with it, so far.

Minimum consequences. But Devon dreaded the first inspection of her own person that she would be compelled to make when she came to a mirror.

"The hologram's gone," Devon said. "That can't be good."

"For someone," Harlee said. "Oh, well. She was no business of ours anyway."

TWO

JUBILATION COUNTY, GEORGIA* · JULY 22, 1926 · 1530 HOURS MOBIUS TIME

Cap'n Hobbs ridin' here
Black-horse rider
Buckshot in his gun, huh!

Hammers on the Dumas line
Buddy don't you fall, huh!
Jesus done forgot his longtime man
Oh buddy don't you fall

Crazy in my head, huh!
Hurtin' in my soul
Hear that hammer ring, boy
Down in the dark hour's dream

His name was Jericho Smith.

The others on his chain, the guards around them each broiling day, knew that much about him, but not much more. What they knew best was to leave him alone.

Not that Smith was dangerous or a troublemaker, not one of those hapless convicts on the squad chain who made life even more difficult for themselves with an incautious word, a slack work ethic, or a wrong look at a harassing guard, which earned punishment brutal beyond the pains of a long day's labor with hammers, shovels, pickaxes. There were other Negroes on his chain with powerful frames, but Smith was the tallest, his shoulders wider, his arms more powerful than any of the rest. He set a tireless pace at the track-laying site with his nine-pound hammer while the labor gang's slow chorus accompanied the spike-driving, steel-ringing strokes. *Hammers on the Dumas line.*

*Parallel Universe Archival ref. p. 702581-MW (Fresno Vortex series)

Smith knew what those words meant, because the straight stretch of railroad track was where he had spent all of his conscious life. The track that came out of the woods half a mile to the west, lying alongside a flat cotton field and a red-dirt road straight as the track itself. He knew west because that was where the sun set every day. He didn't know where Dumas was. He knew only the horizon and the chain and the eighty dark men he worked with, the narrow road and the dusty cotton field. The birds on the telephone wire and the insects in the dry weeds of the ditch. The same clouds in the same sky, day after day. The heat and sweat and moaning and work. The brutal guards, the man on the black horse who ruled the guards and whose name was Hobbs. A thin man with war wounds crudely layered over, waxen, part of his face wrenched sideways, one eye rigidly pale as ice. Wore jodhpurs and polished brown boots and a campaign hat. Tobacco in one cheek. Smith knew just when Cap'n Hobbs would lean down from the saddle and spit vilely in the dust. All day long. The same times, the same way.

The Dumas line seemed never to get any longer, for all their hard work and track laying. Every day he swung the same hammer at the same spikes in the same place until it was time, sun growing red in the sky, to lay 'em down.

But who was Jesus? he sometimes wondered. And what were those dreams of the dark hour?

It was the dark hour during which he lay down on a thin filthy mattress (*know it musta been a bedbug, chinch can't bite that hard*), his head on a pillow covered with an evil-smelling flour sack, the collective sweat and grime of his days, linked to the "building chain" after the prisoners' evening feed of fried sowbelly, cornpone, and sorghum, their unvarying meal. Lay down as he knew he must but not to sleep. Or if he slept he had no memory of what sleep was like. Close his eyes and open them again to the rousting cry, still dark outside, torches in the prison-camp yard, trucks waiting, pee and eat and go to the squad chain, jolt down another rutted clay road to the Dumas line, wait for a glimmer of light in the east to pick 'em up and go to work.

Smith never spoke to any of the other prisoners during the short ride to the Dumas line or while they rested after the midday feed. Yet he knew all about them without having to ask, just as he knew every-thing he could want to know about the guards and Hobbs, the black-horse rider. He knew names and knew their crimes, much of them petty although there were men on his chain who had committed rape or murder. He knew secrets and torments. They just came to him, unbidden, like flies to the dried salt on his skin. He knew about sweet-hearts, children, despair.

What he knew nothing about was himself. Where he had come from, why he was there.

Hobbs leaning down from his saddle to spit, straightening with an angry sweep of his good eye, looking out for the men he would remove from the chain that evening, give them the strop, ten slashes to bare buttocks. Or, if he was in a particularly evil frame of mind, there was the unspeakable torture of the "jack," a medieval pillory in which prisoners were locked into wooden stocks, then left to hang in midair by their wrists and ankles until they passed out.

The sweat began to sting their eyes by nine in the morning.

Wiping it off here!

Wipe it off.

Smith couldn't tell time, and of course he had no need to, but he knew exactly at what point in his daily labors the mule wagons would plod by on the road. He knew when the six crows would float down to alight, one at a time, on the sagging telephone line. He knew when, having raised his hammer above his strong shoulders for the hundredth or two hundredth time, he would catch a glimpse of a hawk in full wingspread above the pine woods and marvel at its free-dom. He knew when he would shift his eyes and find Cap'n Hobbs looking hard at him, and he knew with that little push he could give things in his mind the captain's good eye would be made to shift away from him, and there would be no blood-biting lash for Jericho Smith after the day's work, no pickshack locked to his already-burdened legs, no sweatbox assigned out of idle malice. Bored and ignorant men could turn vicious on a whim.

Yet they all sensed it was wise to leave Smith alone.

The man chained to his immediate right had stolen twelve dollars from a market to feed his children. He had been sentenced to eight years on the chain.

Smith wondered, at a certain time of each day, what his sentence was for, and how long it would last.

The thief had developed a hernia working on the chain. Smith knew exactly when he would sink to his knees, paralyzed from agony, and the guards would come to take him off the chain, cursing him as they loaded him roughly into the back of one of the prison-camp trucks.

Screams.

Jesus done forgot his longtime man.

Smith wondered where the prisoner with the hernia was taken, yet he was always there in the torchlit yard the next day, which was this day, and the day before, waiting patiently to become another link on the chain.

Smith knew how easily he could get off the chain if he wanted to. In that bright corner of his mind where he instinctively Knew Things he had seen himself sever the links just by concentrating for a few seconds. But what was the reason for leaving the chain? Where would he go? Tomorrow, inevitably, he would be back in the yard. They all would, even those who had come from "somewhere." Towns and homes and families they thought about day-long, their hopes and silent cries for release passing through Smith's receptive mind.

But he had nowhere to go. Dreams, memories were denied him. The chain—the first and final place—was home, just as tomorrow was today, and today was yesterday. He was there simply to endure.

Oh buddy don't you fall.

The man with the hernia had been taken away.

Hobbs, scowling, leaned out past his horse to spit chewed tobacco. And Smith raised his hammer.

As he had done countless times before, as he always would do.

Then he noticed, out of the corner of his eye, something completely unexpected, compelling in its newness. Something *different*.

He stood there transfixed, arm and shoulder muscles bulging.

Crazy in my head, huh! went the refrain up and down the squad chain.

But, as they grunted *huh!* in rhythmic expectation of the hammer's fall, Smith was motionless. Men with hammers and pickaxes faltered and stared at him in stark disbelief.

A taxi had appeared on the road and was slowing opposite the chain gang on the embankment.

Smith couldn't read and had no concept of what the words DUMAS TAXI slanting through a yellow shield on a front door of the taxi meant. But in the part of his brain that Knew Things he was aware that this day was meant to be different, with consequences to himself.

The black horse threw back its head, reacting as if a bee had wandered up its nose. Cap'n Hobbs nearly lost his seat.

A back door opened, and a young woman in a summer dress and a wide-brimmed hat stepped out onto the rusty road. She held the crown of the hat to her head because of a sudden breeze and gazed up at the chain gang.

"God damn you, Smith! Starin' at a white woman there? Nigger, you bring that hammer *down*!"

Smith.

The young woman smiled, and looked in his direction.

In his mind where he Knew Things, Jericho Smith heard her voice: *You're Smith? Come on then. We've got places to go.*

The breeze freshened; red dust blew. Smith laid his hammer down.

Walked away from the shackles and chains that fell from his ankles like paper cutouts.

Shocked silence, punctuated by the cocking of hammers on Cap'n Hobbs's eight-gauge sawed-off.

Smith glanced at him and the dust rose in a furious cloud and swept Hobbs away from his horse, lifted him twenty feet into the air, while Smith shrugged a biting fly from a sweaty shoulder and walked on down the embankment toward the waiting girl.

He jumped the ditch while most of the men on the gang and the guards watched Hobbs cartwheel through the dirt maelstrom that surrounded him. His horse wheeled and ran. A few of the prisoners were more intrigued by Smith, who had paused to speak to the girl. She gestured to the open door of the taxi.

A boy of fifteen or so with hard-to-comb blond hair and more than a touch of hobgoblin in his face, so ugly he was sort of cute, looked out of the taxi with a cranky expression, said impatiently, "C'mon, it's time to go! Leave late, get there late."

The young woman held out a hand to Jericho Smith.

"I'm Gwen," she said. "For Guinevere. And the stinkpot's right. We'd better be going, it took me long enough to find you."

"Who am I?" Smith said uncertainly.

"Big guy, we'll talk about it on the way."

"I have to do somethin' first."

Smith turned, looked hard at the long line of prisoners on the railroad embankment and at the brutal guards—who seemed not anxious to fire on him, standing as close as he was to the pretty young woman.

The chain writhed and upended a score of prisoners before flying harmlessly to pieces, freeing them. A few of the men turned to the guards, who lowered their guns and backed away. But the rest of the former prisoners just stared at their feet for several seconds before layin' them down a final time and scrambling away from the never-to-be-finished Dumas line.

For the first time in his harsh existence Smith felt the unfamiliar tug of facial muscles. He was smiling. In the mind sanctuary where he had always Known Things, recognition stirred as he looked again at Gwen.

"I don't know who I am," he said. "But I know who I want to be."

"And who is that?"

"You will do," Jericho Smith said.

Patrick, the fifteen-yeard-old nephew of Mickey the Mechanic, both of whom had last been seen in the vicinity of Paramus, New Jersey, on a chilly October night in 1973, took his eyes off the red-clay road along which he was driving a borrowed taxicab at seventy-plus, and said in a breaking voice to Gwen in the backseat, "It's HAPpening like you said IT would!"

"Just drive," she told him, a steely but preoccupied look in her eyes. The recent chain-gang lifer named Smith was in the seat next to her, slumped now, his eyes closed, sweat trails through the dust on his dark beautifully boned face. But even at their speed and with the windows down the odor coming off his scarred work-gang-hardened body and tattered clothing was hard to bear.

Hovering above the straight road a couple of miles behind them a booming blackened tempest was growing in size, lightning bolts hurled earthward as if a petulant god were cleaning house.

"B-b-but it's getting BIGger."

"Keep your eyes on the damn road," Gwen snarled when they came within a foot of plunging into a milkweed-infested ditch on the right side. More soothingly she said, "It's nothing, trust me. Just a localized backlash from taking Smith off the chain. It won't follow us into town."

"B-b-but you said the universe might implode."

"That was a worst-case scenario, Patrick. And I had a bitch of a headache this morning. The universe didn't implode when you borrowed this taxi, did it? No."

"B-b-but does this mean TOMORROW I'll steal the taxi again and we'll go out to the Dumas line and—"

"No, it doesn't, Patrick. I tried to explain to you. There are certain allowable anomalies within a paradox. Tomorrow will be like *yesterday* for you, the same old yesterday since you and Mick got dumped here. I'll be gone. When you wake up in the morning you won't remember that Auntie Gwen was ever here."

"B-b-b—"

"Patrick. Stop it. Stuttering gets to be a habit. That would not be an allowable anomaly, and you'll stutter for the rest of your—"

"You said you'd help Uncle Mick and me g-g-get out of here!"

"Keep your eyes," Gwen reminded him again. The boy's distress genuinely troubled her. Tears spilling from those red-rimmed blue orbs, smearing all over his freckled runty-endearing face. *There is no way out. For you.* She swallowed the words. Couldn't say it. He might drive them smack into a telegraph pole. How much soul-destroying frustration could a fifteen-year-old endure? Maybe tomorrow—or his next yesterday, or whatever you wanted to call Patrick's Mobius existence within this tab version of Jubilation County, July 23, 1926—he'd take precipitously to serious moonshine like his uncle Mickey had. Certainly an allowable anomaly. But there would be no escaping in a Chevy Nomad with a set of mysteriously enabling spark plugs engineered by a thirty-fourth millennium, before Christ, time tinkerer, who had not been sucked into the Fresno Vortex. At least not on his first jaunt through space/time to modern-era earth, circa 1893.

Even if the Nomad's power sources hadn't been exhausted, like the motive powers of all the other erstwhile time machines (towed to and stacked up in the rear acreage of Wick Hooser's scrapyard on Stinking Weasel Creek), leaving this Jubilation County by mechanical means might not be a permissible anomaly. That could cause an implosion of the universe, and Gwen knew it. But there was no genius around who could rejigger and properly calibrate the flighty Nomad or any other machines invented in planetary habitats scattered around Universal System MW. Their inventors, unsavory specimens of pseudoparenchyma for the most part, had long gone to dust after winding up in the Vortex, done in by what was for them a poisonously inhospitable atmosphere. Just as well, for the sake of the sanity of longtime Jubilationers who were not psychologically equipped to deal with the sight of beings that flitted through piney woods jellylike and luminous as ball lightning, or gaseous slimeballs trudging along their streets. The Vortex had, in the life span of several suns, attracted a few recombinent but reasonably earthlike bipeds of great intellectual and scientific prowess. Unfortunately they, or those, had been incarcerated in the dim third-floor cells of the courthouse and jail, and were largely forgotten by country folk for whom the future was forever today.

Next to Gwen in the backseat of the jouncing taxi, Jericho Smith, with a last flutter of his eyelashes and relaxation of muscles that unfortunately included the sphincter, stopped breathing. His labors were done.

Gwen regarded the handsome but no longer necessary human being with a pang of nostalgia and even a tear; she was a woman after all. But everything that Smith had been extraphysically, Gwen now was. She was perilously close to psychic overload, like a bird of paradise ravaged by a pterodactyl (roughly describing the transfer of Mordaunt's feminine soul to its new host), but purest ecstasy of a vibrational intensity known only to gods fallen and unfallen calmed her. Apocatastasis, or restitution of a vital soul, was now in part accomplished. Job well done. (And wouldn't there be some long faces at the Vatican when this news was passed around the Consistory of the Twelve!) Time to get out of Jubilation County—

"Patrick? Slow down and pull off into the woods."

"Huh? What's wrong?" He glanced back again, and his face wrinkled in disgust.

"Yes, I know. I'm afraid poor Smith has left us."

"You mean he's d-dead?"

"Oh, Patrick. Help me get him out of the taxi. He'll be drying up in a few minutes."

"D-d-d—"

"Dust to dust. But he won't be needing a grave."

"Shouldn't w-we TAKE him to—"

"No, Patrick. And you wouldn't want to return this taxi you hotwired with a fresh corpse inside. Even though, of course, tomorrow none of this will have happened."

Together they wrestled Jericho Smith's remains out of the taxi and laid him on the shady side of a two-foot-thick pitch-knobby Georgia pine, so old that its later branches were now ninety feet from the ground, like broken rungs of a ladder. Birds flitted through the tall trees. Same old birds, same old tunes. Same old sunshine. Jubilation County was a pleasant enough place to live, but unfortunately Patrick didn't appreciate his immortality, stuck as he was at an awkward age.

"Should we SAY somethin'?" he wanted to know. His face was flushed, trickling beads of sweat.

"I'm not religious. And this is not a funeral. Call him lucky to have laid that hammer down for good. Except, of course, tomorrow he'll be right back on the old squad chain. Minus a little something I off-loaded from him. Drive on back to town, Patrick. I now am what I came here to be. And I should be getting along."

"By YOURself? But y-you said—"

"Patrick, I know I promised I'd look over that old heap of yours, but believe me, sweetie, it's no use. I don't have the power to budge it. The Vortex swallowed you, and all of the others who once had bright ideas about how to travel through time. But Fresno's Vortex— if the old bluesman was right—can't spit you out again. Sorry."

"Then how will you—"

"Hey, Pat, I'm a hundred percent flesh and blood but I'm not a real girl. I'm a *doppel*ganger." He stared at her with glimmer eyes, uncomprehending. Gwen breathed deeply and made another try. "I'm, like, part of a set. I have a homebody, my mirror image but in a through-the-looking-glass way, follow that so far?" Openmouthed, Patrick nodded a little. Transfixed, aghast, as stiff in his limbs as a toad-eating dog. "—Even though my homebody and me are presently not on good terms, and I plan for us to stay kaput. I got doctored up by a little guy who's like the mad scientist in those old horror flicks. So if I took my clothes off right now I'd just be naked, not invisible." Patrick blinked. "Nix, that wasn't intended to be a turn-on, I'm not taking off my clothes." She flashed a smile. "Okay. Let me just say that as a doppelganger I have special faculties. For one thing, I can time-trip to my heart's desire, change over from one universe to another, even one that retrogrades every twenty-four hours. How? It's, um, like changing escalators that are side by side virtually forever, and that go up and up forever too. That's the easy part, but getting back to where you started isn't. Too tricky to explain that part right now. No time. I like you a lot, kid, and I know you've got this red-hot adolescent crush on me, but I'm leaving and unfortunately you have to stay. Please don't start bawling. Keep your chin up. I doubt that tomorrow you'll—"

All Patrick saw was a twinkle in the afternoon air. At night it could have been a meteor burning up in the atmosphere. But Gwen grabbed herself below the breasts with a howl, twisted 180 degrees in torment, and tripped over the outstretched feet of Jericho Smith. She sprawled headlong, clutching the place where she had been struck or bitten.

"What was *that*?" Patrick said. "HorseFLY? Gwen, you okay?"

She dragged herself to her feet, still doubled over.

"Do you need a doctor?"

"No," she gasped, getting her breath back. "Now will you please shut *up*?"

"But what happened?"

Gwen straightened slowly, not replying. She rubbed her solar plexus while painfully regaining her breath. She walked away from Patrick, talking oddly but not to him.

"Okay, what the hell did happen? *Yes* I know I've lost it! Felt like jerking an arrowhead out of me. What am I going to do? I don't *know* what I'm going to do about it! Someone must've touched the skull or dared to move it. Linc would never do that! But I don't have a— Yes. There's life force all around me. Thousands of naked souls, but I can't use them. No, no, *wrong*. Nature *does* forbid it! We're talking Celestial Law. Draining souls for our use is *not* an option. Anyway they couldn't provide enough whoomph to break us away from the Fresno Vortex. Get us back to where *I* came from. Even with a lot of hyperdimensional power I couldn't calibrate a destination mechanically. I *need* the skull. I need my simulacrum. Otherwise we are truly and totally *fucked*!"

Wandering, her back to Patrick, head nodding and becking like someone sorely tetched.

Patrick called, "Who are you t-t-talking to?"

The look she gave him was as jarring as a hard slap and backed him up a couple of steps. In a hurry. Gwen shook her head ferociously, sunlit hair lashing her face. She breathed in nasally snarls. Then her hands dropped from her violated breast. Her head shakes gradually became less agitated until a kind of hopeless calm settled over her. She was crying. She wiped away her tears and looked at her wet fingers in amazement and then dismay.

"Doppelgangers don't cry! But I'm not—not a dpg anymore! Only half. Worse than nothing. Oh what a mistake! I'm stuck here too. I wish I wish I wish I could be a full doppelganger again! *But it was that sneaking bastard Woolwine.* Implanting some nanotech gizmo in my neck that altered my magnetic field just enough—and now I'm disconnected from my homebody! I can't go back to Eden. She can't find me to bring *us* back!"

Gwen brushed away more tears and Patrick's florid face came into better focus. He looked terrified, his mouth twitching out of control.

"Wha-what's got INto you, Gwen?" Then he had an inkling that it might have been the wrong question.

Not much change in her face, but he smelled something unpleasant wafting his way: a stewpot stench of garlic, sulfur, wolfsbane. Her eyes had tightened as if stitches had been taken; they seemed elongated. They yellowed like fall leaves as he stared. Pat felt a rush of blood to his temples, as if he'd been upended and, while dangling, was being ruthlessly inspected.

"*A fit's upon our Gwen; her mind has gone amiss. Besotted, anguished, prison'd in despair, unsuitable for sense. Faith, she suffers not in abatement, whilst I, unchafed by low fortune, resolute, enduring as the Phoenix, claim sovereignty: two persons kindred in one, yet remarking only for myself.*"

The voice was different from Gwen's, contralto, cultured, the style of language familiar to him. It had rolled off the tongue of Mr. Whippet, Patrick's tenth-grade English teacher, who savored every syllable. *Julius Caesar* had been the text.

Patrick blinked and took a peek to make sure his feet were on the ground. When he looked, she seemed to have shot up to a height of nine feet or more. Looking down at him with the keenness of a raptor eyeing a pip of a sparrow. Patrick's chapped lips parted, but he couldn't speak. Something compelled him to glance over at the gnarly old pine where he and Gwen (*suffering not in abatement?*) had laid out Jericho Smith. There no longer was an impressively muscled body. What remained of Smith was the tattered clothing he had worn, his high-topped shapeless work shoes leaking smoke. Char and ash had sifted out through popped stitching or the worn places of the soles.

"Ay, there be sadness in the mute farewell of death. He was always a man, not the cur chains made a' him."

The mixture of smells, with an additive of blackened flesh, was overpowering. Patrick gagged and looked back and up and was jolted to his toes. Her hair was now silver and smoke, spun out around a reptilian head and lushly spiderwebbed, a ghostly nightmare of a 'do. Especially because there seemed to be spiders scurrying out of it.

Patrick had no spit but managed to say, "Who ARE y-you?"

"I have oft preferred the name Delilah."

Her right hand moved quickly down as if from an unreeling length of arm and, vinelike, stroked him across the forehead. A light touch, but it froze all of Patrick except for his bladder: the bottom dropped out and in shock and humiliation he gushed down one leg. His eyes were tightly shut. When he opened them again and thawed enough to grimly unknot his sneakers, the Delilah-thing had resumed Gwen's normal size and appearance. The stench of sulfur and wolfsbane dissipated. She pretended not to notice what he'd done. This creaturely Delilah. It made Patrick hate her all the more. He pulled the saturated pant leg of his railroader overalls away from his thigh and held it like that while he walked stiffly through the tall pines and across sunblaze drowsing pasture and cannonballed off the bank into a two-acre pond. He pinched his nose shut and kept his head under water while sitting on the mucky bottom, but before he ran out of breath and started gulping he knew it was no use, he didn't have the gumption to drown himself. And if he did, who would look after his uncle Mick?

Delilah as Gwen (and much more pleasing to the eye) was sitting on a running board of the yellow taxi. She looked up with a smile of apology when he returned dripping and muddied, carrying his tied-together sneakers over one shoulder.

"My pardon, young sir. 'Twas confounding of the senses inspired me thus to foul and furious craft. Thou hast no cause to be affrighted."

"I'm not," he said. "I wasn't." Trying to sell the lie with a sneer that failed. "Just please don't EVer do that thing again. With the hair." He shuddered, although not because of a failure of nerve. He was wet and miserable. "Is G-Gwen okay?"

"She sleeps in mild repose 'pon Lethe's bosom, whilst in her bor-row'd shape I dwell, no longer captive, destiny eclipsed, my greater soul forsaken, interr'd in grief by enemies whose villainy abideth in holy bones."

"Uh, yeah. *Borrowed?* Are you ever going to leave Gwen aLONE?"

"Ay, good Patrick. I swear this world that cheats and beggars Time will not long contain us."

"So what do we do?"

She folded her hands, sat gazing at something greatly distant, or inward.

"For now, I knowest not."

"Oh, great," Patrick muttered, sitting on the rear bumper to put his sneakers on.

LAS VEGAS · 7:20 A.M.

Eden Waring in Cody Olds's pied à terre, fast asleep one moment, wide-eyed the next, alone in the middle of the bed, staring at a streak of rosy sunrise across the ceiling. Reliving the emotional process through which she had been persuaded to be there for the remainder of the night. Dammit: the man just hadn't taken no for an answer. Obnoxious seduction tactics, in a lesser breed. But where

Cody hailed from, a roughshod remnant of knighthood might be in vogue. One of those codes of the West she'd heard about. So giving up and giving herself over (in a restricted sense) to Cody had become an act of trust. Determination, tact, propriety—Eden now reversed an earlier opinion of him. He certainly would be hell with the women he chose. In his modest-size aerie he'd brewed tea and shown her the layout, where things were. Some women's necessities too, in the bathroom. He didn't collect trophy dainties, leftovers from whistle-stops by long-necked toothy beauties as common around Vegas as jackrabbits in the sagebrush. That tendency might have put an impassable knot in the slender thread of their relationship. He'd given her an old flannel shirt, XXL, as a substitute for pajamas, which he said he didn't own. But she had always been partial to men's shirts for sleepwear. And what a sleep! On a featherbed, nearest thing to heaven for sheer bliss. The bedroom air, cleaned by an ionic purifier, was as sweet and bracing as morningtime in a breezy cedar wood.

If she had dreamed, then for once she couldn't remember. There was nothing at the back of her mind to scribble down in apprehension or cold terror as she'd been compelled to do since childhood: her prophetic dreams.

The drapes parted at the touch of a button on a bedside console. The bedroom was simply furnished, country French in wormy chestnut, but the walls were chockablock with paintings by artists whom Cody admired and/or represented. Old-timers, newcomers. Frank McCarthy, Roger Hayden Johnson, Carrie Fell. Dried-out frontier faces dark as figs, rugged, empty, transfixing vistas. Eroded pinnacles stained bloodred by a setting sun. Cody had included only one of his paintings. A sharply ruled still life. Pastel. Meadowlark with an apple on a windowsill. Pale blues and yellows and that bright green apple. A French influence, Eden thought, remembering from a college course a painter she had particularly liked, Aristide Maillol.

Eden stretched and gave her weak knee a careful massage. No bad twinges this morning. Then she reached for her cell phone and alerted the Blackwelder people who had spent the night watching over an empty villa at Bahìa, letting them know she was awake and in good company. They knew where she had slept and probably were think-ing she was an easy lay, but what of it? They were paid to guarantee her safety, not pass judgment on her character. By now they would have a dossier on Cody Olds, maybe his entire family. She didn't think she would need to review it. For the moment she wanted only to hear Cody's pleasingly gruff, no-bull voice again—and what was that hearty campfire odor seeping into the bedroom, bacon on a grill?

My hero, Eden thought, without irony or malice, and sprang out of bed. No headaches, less anxiety, just glad to have a day like this one to seize. And how long had it been since she'd felt that good, on reasonably friendly terms with herself?

Used the bathroom and went dressed as she was, shirttail to the back of her knees, barefoot, to the kitchen and breakfast nook that featured a bow window with a view of mountains in tones of sand and gray and blue. All the sky that she could see given over to heat-less sunblaze the color of still champagne.

Cody was dishing diced peppers, chilies, and tomatoes into a bowl with several eggs he'd whisked, leaving in the yolks. No fad diets for him. He wore a tucked-in T-shirt with beltless jeans low on his hips. He hadn't heard her coming. His attention was divided between the gas range and a small plasma-screen TV on the range counter. And of course the local news had to be focusing again on the efforts to recover the possible remains of Lincoln Grayle from the recent ava-lanche in the Spring Mountains. Eden clenched her hands at her sides, recalling that she had said something to Cody about bringing down Mordaunt's house—although she wasn't certain if she'd said "Mordaunt" or mentioned any name, Grayle's in particular.

"Good morning," she said.

He turned to acknowledge her with less of a sunny smile than she'd hoped for. But after a quick appraisal he seemed to like her exceedingly well in his ratty old shirt, a button missing where her navel would be.

"Morning. Sleep okay?"

"Out like a light. Dead to the world. All those other clichés."

"Did I forget to set out a spare hairbrush?" He looked rumpled and transient himself from sleeping on the sofa.

Eden shook her tousled head self-consciously. "I have a brush, thanks. I rolled out just as God intended me this morning. Do I suffer in comparison with someone else?" She didn't think so. There were no framed sweethearts in his condo, only family photos.

"Now you know that God made you just fine. Do you have a likin' for Denver omelets?"

"I don't know. What goes into a Denver omelet?"

"Depends mostly on what's left over in the fridge," he said, with a smile that still didn't come easily. Trying to be casual and so far missing a note or two. Maybe he hadn't done much sleeping himself, wondering just what he had back there in his bedroom.

"Yummy," Eden said with a deliberate lack of enthusiasm. She couldn't avoid looking at the TV, where someone named Skarbeck, USMC ret., who apparently was associated with Lincoln Grayle Enterprises, was being interviewed on CNN. He looked as if he could split rocks with his chin. Dyed-red hair, and Eden didn't like his eyes much. Too canny and watchful, as if he'd never heard a straight answer. Or given one.

Cody poured the omelet makings into a heated pan, turned thick strips of bacon on the range grill, and gave most of his attention to the TV news while Eden curled the toes of one foot and then the other. She was still at the threshold of the open kitchen with its medieval-looking pewter hood over the range and a gourmet's selection of hanging pots and pans. She sighed.

"Cody, have you decided you really want me here, or should I go put on my clothes and call for backup?"

He looked around at her like a man interrupted in midargument with himself.

"You know, I've had the time to do some heavy thinkin' on that little matter."

"Sure." Her toes were tight, her lips tighter, bloodless.

"I want you here," he said. "No need to bring it up again."

Eden started to speak, couldn't, nodded, then put her heart into an ultimatum, or a plea.

"Well—if you accept me, listen, it's just who I am, no frills, no bull-shit, and—there are things I have to explain that won't go down easy."

"Right now?"

"Yes. I think so. Because—" Her eyes, nervous, darted to the TV screen again.

"You recognize that honcho's on the news?"

"No."

"Pardon, just somethin' about your expression. I thought he might be one of those bad-hat guys you mentioned last night."

"That was your terminology. *Pesky* bad-hat guys. What do you call a 'bad hat,' anyway?"

"Well, if it's fur on the outside and there's a big feather, that's a bad hat L.A.–pimp style. But most of the time the hat has to be black and worn with the brim rolled cocky and low to the eyes. What about the Magician that's not accounted for, Lincoln Grayle? You acquainted with him?"

"Was. I met him in Africa." She was suddenly cold from nerves. Swallowing raw fear. "Cody, do you ever drink before breakfast?"

"There's always a first time."

"Why don't you fix us a couple of snorts from that bottle of brandy you keep there on the counter for flaming crepes or whatever?"

Cody took down crystal snifters from a china cabinet and poured two ounces apiece.

"Now I think we ought to sit down while we have our brandies," Eden said.

Cody held out a hand and escorted her to the round table, place settings for two. He closed the half shutters to mute the sun brightness in the breakfast nook.

"This isn't going to be good, is it?" Cody said, turning his chair around and straddling it, still managing to look cheerful and ready for the hard fastball. Then he let her take her time. After a couple of minutes Eden stopped staring into the bell glass like a defrocked oracle, raised the glass, and drank her brandy neat. Cody did the same. He hadn't taken his eyes off her.

"Have any bad dreams last night?" he asked.

"No."

"I dreamed I got blown up on a yacht off Saudi Arabia." Cody looked perplexed.

"Have you ever been to Saudi Arabia?"

"I can find all the sand that's ever going to interest me in Arizona." Cody excused himself from the table to attend to breakfast, taking the bacon off the grill, putting slices of sourdough bread in a toaster oven. "Any notion what my dream was about?"

"Huh-uh. I'm only good at interpreting my own dreams."

"*Real* good at it? Any chance you could be wrong about Las Vegas bitin' the Big One?"

"Oh, that." She shrugged. "No, sir. I'm sorry. Did I upset you?"

Cody whistled dolefully. "You might say it gave me pause."

Eden licked around the thin rim of her snifter, coaxed a last drop onto her tongue, brought forth shivery music with a flick of a fingernail.

"I never drank except for an occasional beer until a couple of months ago. In Africa. You should go there, to paint, but be careful. Africa sneaks into your soul. It's breathtaking and devastating and so very cruel to the lonely." She drew a pensive breath. "But I suppose you could say that about anywhere."

She reached for the bottle of Rémy Martin and poured herself another generous round, the same for Cody. He watched her. "I think I like it too much. That's a reason to quit. But not a good enough reason yet."

"I expect there's something you need to put out of your head real bad."

Eden smiled ruefully, swallowed, stared at him.

"That magician's dead, isn't he?" Cody said.

"He'd better be."

"You had something to do with that?"

"Everything to do with that."

Cody slid the omelet into a warming dish with a spatula and sat down again. He lifted his glass and studied her through the bell curve. Eden looked steadily back at him and sipped her brandy. The picture of tranquility. Or about to explode into hysterics. He couldn't tell which.

"You sure can go a long time without blinking, can't you? Well, did he deserve it?"

"Oh boy. Did he ever."

"Personal matter?" he said, and had to clear his throat. Larynx knotting up on him.

"It was highly personal. It also involved the fate of the human race, unless I was reading him wrong. Don't think so. We all might be a little better off today. Can't say for sure, yet. That doesn't depend entirely on me. You can stare a long time without blinking, too. Time out."

They both blinked. They were leaning toward each other now, elbows on the café-style table, faces little more than a foot apart. Immersed in each other's aura.

"I don't know if I can follow that," Cody said, in a state of mind that could be called white-knuckle perplexed. "How did you—"

"Cody, there is nothing in the entire Book of Revelation as vile and evil as Mordaunt—the Magician—was, or is. The Magician, whom you know as Lincoln Grayle, is gone for good but not Mordaunt, Grayle's oversoul. He's only . . . contained. So you see I'm not a murderer, really. I *do* have supernatural powers. Those in the occult underworld call me the Avatar." She searched his face to decide if she should go on or just abandon her attempt at an explanation. He nodded with an expression of assent neither skeptical nor patronizing, so she took a second-wind breath and kept going. "An *honorary* position, I didn't have to campaign for it. But Avatars must assume a certain amount of responsibility for opposing the evil ones who would enjoy seeing the world go up in flames. In fact it's their calling. And what do the bad-hat guys care, it isn't *their* world." Eden finished her second brandy, which had kick but didn't prop her up as she'd hoped. She was sagging in morale and feeling like Tinkerbell low on glisten and pixie dust. Her nipples had puckered beneath his shirt. Of all times. Wordless, obviously listening for something he hadn't heard yet, Cody had that effect on her: stature and bounty, his wide-shouldered maleness. But still they were a long way from the right time, if ever.

Eden set her glass down and said with a rueful tic of the lips, "Does drinking before breakfast make me an alcoholic?" There was a change in his eyes, a softness, benevolence. "What would you like to hear now?" she said. "How I came by my supernatural powers? Now there's a story you never read in *People* magazine."

Cody relaxed a little, sitting back in his chair, looking buffeted but not blown off her—their—course. He studied Eden's face, cheekily flushed now, her brow damply alight, from the brandy or from the stress of wringing out her heart.

"There's a long line of sorcerers on my ma's side of the family," Cody said at last. "Diviners, mushroom eaters. An old uncle who turned himself into a raven at night, or so the story goes. What I saw of him when I was little, I could believe it. Even so—I can tell you'll take some gettin' used to."

"Where would you like me to start?" Eden said, bare feet on the lower rung of her chair, toes gripping. She felt so densely naked to his gaze that she might as well not have been wearing the shirt. Naked and cherished but not for sexual reasons: one of those born-again numbers, beginning of a ritual of purging and then acceptance into a new, protective tribe.

"What about your graduation day?" Cody said. "From what I picked up online, isn't that how it all began?"

"Yes. May twenty-eighth. Red Wolves Stadium. Eleven thirty in the morning. That was—" she seemed surprised to think of it, "only five months ago. Seems like five centuries. You know what? I never did get my diploma."

Unexpectedly, tears filled her eyes and she just let it happen, the hot drizzles. But she kept her head up, wincing a little, sniffing. Lashes matting, vision blurred. She avoided his eyes.

"And so far, graduate school has just been h-hell on wheels."

Cody nodded understandingly and handed her a paper napkin.

Eden blew her nose. So she'd let him see her cry. There was only one intimacy more privileged than that.

"No sense lettin' good chow turn cold." He got up from the table. "S'posin' we eat now. There's plenty time for more talk."

"You really want me to stink up your day, don't you, Cody Olds?"

"Might happen. But only if you could beat me at a game of five-card stud."

"Gambling man," she said softly. Eden wadded the napkin in her fist, tapped the fist on the tabletop. Smiled. "Taking a gamble on me."

"No, ma'am," Cody said from the kitchen. "I always have found it profitable just to bide my time and trust my instincts. Would you be wantin' strawberry jam on your toast, or cinnamon and sugar?"

"Cinnamon toast! Haven't had it since I was a kid. And coffee black, please."

4:45 P.M.

They are coming now, the vanguard of Mordaunt's Elite 88, to the high desert, like flies to butter.

Within the next forty-eight hours, before nightfall of Halloween (a killer of a coincidence, but how fitting), all of the 88ers—minus three who now are in the stale of their antiquity and were warned not to fly long distances, and a select handful whose presence in Las Vegas, should they be detected, would be exceptionally newsworthy—will have convened at Lincoln Grayle's secluded Snow Lake Ranch to assess the damage done to the Great One's domain by the upstart Avatar, a new menace to their sacrosanct society.

One by one they enter Vegas airspace, flashing silver in the westering sun: potentate 747s from the Mideast; smaller, merely cushy, mogul-style Boeings, Gulfstreams, or Bombardiers from Montreal, Jakarta, Johannesburg, Prague, Sao Paulo. Two members of the 88 already live full-time or have residences in Dazzle City, having funneled billions into its development.

The Elite 88 is a men's club. Always has been, since the days of long-dead languages. Through millennia there have been a few women, expelled from their wombs in blood and wrath, born and reborn without the impedimenta of morals, mercy, or compassion, who would qualify on equal terms. But when one of them appears, the ranks of the already-empowered close against her. Such women are destined to be subservient to Mordaunt, most often employed as Fetchlings, their reward those dewy states of optimal youth while they assume roles as doxies and consorts to pathologically ruthless and ambitious men who are cultivated, financed, and promoted by the 88 to pinnacles of democratic or despotic power, where they can do the worst possible harm to the remainder of mankind.

The 88 are nearly all Malterrans: souls who lived in miserable darkness and discord on their invisible (from earth's perspective) planet until rare, favorable galactic events permitted a few at a time to escape Malterra's warp and weave, channeled by Mordaunt into a personal orbit, forever in thrall to his sinister halo effect.

Deus Inversus, the darkness of God.

Present whereabouts unknown.

General Bronc Skarbeck, born on an Army base in Arkansas and depressingly mortal compared to the Malterran Elite, who enjoy secrets and privileges of extended life denied him, is not in the club. The irony of his situation isn't lost on Bronc. But (as he reminded himself while shaving early this morning) he is not just Mordaunt's nigger, by a long shot. Bronc knows all of the 88 on sight and by reputation, although he has met few of them personally. They will, he knows, instinctively dislike and mistrust him. His own instincts and training for brute command tell him that without the Magician directing the day-to-day business of the 88, they are little more than a faithless mob. Unenergized. A new *Deus Inversus* will not routinely be elected, like a Vicar of Rome when one of the Church's Gods-on-earth withdraws to heaven's pomp and ermine clouds. The Elite (Skarbeck is reasonably sure) have no experience in acting independently of Mordaunt's will and desires. This crucial fact, he calculates, automatically increases his status and opportunity. He has spent his career in duties of crisis and spit-and-polish organization.

Can't whip a group of spoiled lap cats into shape and keep the Magician's global street game running? *Please.*

Bronc had opted for a limo and driver for most of his hectic day as he shuttled between McCarran, the offices of Lincoln Grayle Enterprises at Bellagio, and Snow Lake Ranch. During these time-outs he reviewed his phone messages, placed urgent calls, kept tabs on the removal work in progress at the avalanche site.

Harlee hadn't made it home last night but had checked in with him twice today. Her dearest friend, Devon O'Flaherty, was still in the hospital. Food poisoning, Harlee said. None of the other girls at the cookout seemed to have been stricken. One of their number who had stayed overnight at Casa Skarbeck crept into his round bed at two thirty a.m., nude and warm and limber as a gymnast, with a smile of worship on her heart-shaped face. Saying how she had admired him from afar. Out of fidelity to Harl and assuming the two girls would trade notes, he ought to have sent her away. But then, dear God, the clutch and velvet of her compact body, breast and pubes plump and smooth as little cupids: before he could get his sanity back it was Molly-over-the-windmill. And not much snooze time after, holding the adorable one in his arms, groin burning and throbbing. Her name was Reese. She had said she was from Iowa. Probably a runaway, he thought, not caring much.

Bronc sipped a neat scotch on his third trip out to the ranch and turned off all phones for a few minutes, following the last call placed to him within the hour by Dr. Marcus Woolwine. The biogeneticist hadn't left a message on the other two occasions, so Bronc assumed that whatever it was could wait. Then he undid the belt of his trousers, unzipped, and pulled out the cold pack he'd been wearing snugged up behind his balls. He adjusted the orthopedic seat of his silent-as-the-grave Maybach, eyes closing for a brief nap while he was chauffeured through the westbound traffic and on past Red Rock Canyon to the ranch.

At precisely five o'clock, the lone Bureau of Land Management ranger still on duty at the Red Rock Canyon visitor's center locked up, then drove his pickup north on the scenic highway, on the lookout for stragglers. He found one in the front seat of a powder-blue Jaguar parked at the Sandstone Quarry overlook.

Devon glanced up from the movie she was watching on the DVD player in her lap when his face appeared outside her tinted windshield like something surfacing in a murky aquarium. She gave a little start, then put her flick on hold, removed her Bose noise-canceling head-phones, and put down the window on the passenger side. The temper-ature outside had dropped a good fifteen degrees since midafternoon.

"Oh, you *scared* me."

"I'm sorry, miss. Couldn't be real sure anyone was inside. Look, it's ten past five, and—"

"Oh, that late?" Devon looked back to find the lowered sun at the edge of the gray mountains, fossil dumps from the deep seas of pre-history.

"Meaning you ought to have been out of here ten minutes ago. There's no overnight camping in Red Rock."

Devon frowned prettily. "But I'm still waiting for someone. She went up that trail, oh, it must have been two hours ago."

The ranger glanced at the Calico trailhead and a shadow assembly of Aztec sandstone, the deep rust of rocks and promontories as wrin-kled as a baby's bottom. He blinked mildly in the red flush of sun-down. He was approaching middle age and drastic hair loss, but he had a trim hiker's body and most of his youthful good looks. The terrain of his sun-cured face was not seriously marred by some tiny dark moles surrounding his squint blue eyes like inklings and omens. He had large sinew-ribbed hands, resting now on her windowsill. Devon liked men with big hands; usually it meant everything else was big too.

"That so? Who is she?"

"Her name's Harlee. She's my best chum."

"Hiking by herself? How come you didn't go along?"

"I would've, but I sprained my knee getting off an elevator at the Palm a couple of days ago." Devon sighed. "Wouldn't you know, I'm a great dancer; but I can't walk up a flight of steps without stum-bling. How do you account for that?"

The ranger shrugged. He was still looking up the trail to the Calico Tanks area of the canyon, hoping to see the missing hiker on her way out. He wore a name tag on his jacket. He was Herbert Cush-ing Jr.

"Two hours? She ought to be back by now, it's only about a hour and a half round trip."

"Harlee said she wanted to be at the top at exactly five sixteen this afternoon."

He didn't look thrilled by the news. "If your friend doesn't start down from the *tinaja* right away, it'll be almost full dark when she gets back here."

"Oh, she's prepared. Flashlight and extra batteries in her backpack. Harlee's in wonderful condition too: she's a champion fencer in her age group. She does excel at rock climbing and the like. She won't get lost."

"What did she want to be up there for at five sixteen?"

"Harlee is into harmonic convergences."

The ranger glanced down at the slender hand that lay atop his. "Harmonic—? What are those?"

"You know, really great vibes. The collective unconscious of peace and love. Healing the earth. There's an international movement. Purification rituals. Like in the sixties—or so I've been told. The dawning of the Age of Aquarius. Were you born then, Herbert? By the way, my name is Devon."

"Born in 'sixty-two," he said. "I remember some of that flower-child business. Then there was Woodstock. My sister went. It rained. Naked people wallowing in mud. Minivans painted psychedelic-like. Well, I wish your friend wasn't out there by herself, is all. Maybe I ought to take a run up to the Tanks and—"

Devon carefully tightened her hold on him. "Oh, I don't think it's at *all* necessary. I'm very sorry that you've been delayed, Herbert." Devon shuddered delicately. They'd reached the point where he wasn't able to take his eyes off her for more than a second or two. "I shouldn't like to be left alone here. Harlee can take care of herself. Really." She shuddered again, an excuse for gripping his hand more tightly. "There seems to be a frightfully keen nip in the air."

"Yeah, it can drop below freezing in the canyon this time of the year. Well. I didn't have that much going tonight. It's my wife's sister's wedding anniversary but we probably won't go over there, they haven't been getting along all that great anyhow."

"Could I persuade you to let me wait at the visitor's center with you until Harlee comes down? I'll leave my car for her."

"It's my business to see that both of you are okay. I can leave you at the center, but then I need to get on up the trail myself, just in case."

"Would there be any coffee?"

"If you'd like some. Suppose I could, uh, make fresh."

So he was a shy one and she had him on the verge of stammers. In under five minutes Devon had raised his awareness of, and desire for, her to critical mass. Forty-four. Those heebie-jeebie midlife-crisis years. Particularly strong for men who had been married way back in their young twenties, as Devon suspected of Herbert Cushing Jr. Devon sympathized, while continuing to mold the putty she had in her hand.

"You won't get into trouble, will you, I mean because of us?"

"No. I'm in charge here, is pretty much how it goes."

Devon lowered and raised butterfly wings of dusky eyelashes.

"I've a confession to make. I have always loved the name Herbert. It's so—authentic: your name gleams with strength and valor. Nowadays the boys one meets are all Seans and Justins. Totally devoid of personality."

"Devon is, uh. A real pretty name." The ranger helped her out of the car. "Mind my asking, how do you get that white stripe through your hair like that? Bleach?"

"No, it's hereditary," Devon fibbed.

She left the keys in the Jag for Harlee, fully confident that Herbert wouldn't be coming back. They were crossing to his BLM pickup truck, the time five sixteen p.m., when a streak like an arrow from the stars fell through cloudless indigo sky to touch down on the summit of the Calico Tanks.

The ranger whistled. "See that?"

"Surely did," Devon said, giving her underlip a pensive bite. She could only hope that Harlee had survived it. The sky above the Tanks was stained a rosy apricot shade that faded slowly. Then there was another arrow, rising this time like pyrotechnics, curving up and over their heads and down to the horizon, where it was lost to view.

Herbert continued to stare at the sky in amazement.

"First one looked like a meteor. But I never did see anything like that other light, and we get all manner of natural phenomena out this way."

"I believe the first phase of the harmonic convergence has come off successfully," Devon said.

"First phase? What's the rest of it supposed to be like?"

"Oh, Herbert. I don't think I could begin to describe all that to you."

When she thought the once-incandescent red crystal skull had cooled enough to be touched, Harlee Nations approached it slowly along the rim of the sacred site, marked by petroglyphs, above the *tinaja*. Ten feet away from the skull she removed welder's goggles. In spite of the protection they'd afforded, her eyes still smarted from the solar brilliance of two flashes an instant apart. Incoming, outgoing.

A wonder that the earth hadn't spasmed in an isostatic rebound or shifted on its axis. But Harlee surmised that the galactic beam, generated by a phenomenon known to all the ancient races as the Fiery Chariot, its passage triggered by a configuration of the hot-blooded planet Mars to the galactic center in the fire sign of Sagittarius, the Centaurian archer, hadn't actually touched the earth. According to the lore she had soaked up in the Magician's library earlier in the day. The potentially shattering power of the beam had been gobbled by that little wonder of a skull and flung out again in Mordaunt's direction. South of the Calico Tanks and perhaps far out to sea, reckoning from the angle of deflection.

If it ultimately had connected with anything but the fishes she couldn't say.

But if Mordaunt had needed the juice to free himself from his glass tomb and the ruby skull hadn't botched the job, he had it now.

Seated on the edge of a desk in the office of the visitors' center, leaning toward Ranger Herb with her panty hose around one ankle while she fumbled behind her back with the catches of her bra, Devon said in a tremulous voice, "Be gentle with me." His stuck-out penis felt as hot as a fireplace poker on the tender inside of one knee. Finally and a little impatiently she pushed his hands away and lay back, heels wide apart against the edge of the desktop, a languid forearm covering her eyes while, with her other hand, she pulled him down on top of her. Really, he was a lovely man.

Harlee was leaning against the side of Devon's car with her arms folded, admiring the pinkish hue of a sickle moon with the evening star at its southern tip, when Devon appeared in the doorway of the visitors' center, turned to give a sizable hunk of ranger a lingering smooch, then came skipping blithely across the parking lot.

"Nice to see you in one piece," she said.

"Can't trust you for one minute," Harlee said good-naturedly. No pang of jealously. No interest in sex herself, at least for now. Her calves hurt from strenuous hiking. She was looking forward to a meal, a hot bath, a sound night's sleep.

"How often does one have the opportunity to fulfill the ultimate sexual fantasy of the middle-aged male? And besides, I was a little randy myself."

Harlee yawned, then smiled sardonically.

"Now don't make me feel cheap," Devon scolded.

CONCORDIA HOSPITAL · 6:00 P.M.

At a news conference devoted to the condition of supermodel Bertie Nkambe, which remained critical, a hospital spokeswoman told the twenty or so media representatives keeping tabs on Concordia's celebrated patient, "This afternoon at three o'clock Miss Nkambe was taken off the ventilator for ninety minutes. The fact that she was able to breathe on her own for so considerable a period of time is a very positive development. She still was unable to speak while off the ventilator, but she continues to be responsive to family members and medical staff when she is awake."

Bertie might not have been making recognizable sounds with the breathing tube out of her throat, but she and Eden chatted at length subvocally during Eden's second visit of the day.

—What happened to the guy with the broad shoulders who was with you this morning? Did you tell me his name? I can't remember.

—Oh, Cody had some business at his gallery. He'll meet me here in a little while.

—Cody, hmm. So what's up with you and Big Tex?

—He's from New Mexico. Nothing, really.

—You spent the night at his place and the whole day with him but it's nothing.

—Last night, God, I was whacked out and he was decent enough not to put on any moves. Cody is . . . easy to be around. Easy to talk to. He sort of has an instinct for knowing how to . . . rub where it hurts. Emotionally, I mean. He just takes my mind off a lot of stuff, that's all. God's gift, or maybe Leoncaro had something to do with . . . us, I don't know.

—Are you sure you trust him?

—He hasn't given me any reason not to, Bertie.

—Be certain that you keep Simba with you at all times.

Eden looked around at a tall hospital volunteer who had backed into the room with an apologetic smile, pulling after her yet another cart laden with flowers. The girl had an oval face with the coloring and piquancy of Asian bloodlines, and dusky-blond shoulder-length hair.

"Oh—those are supposed to go to the cancer wing."

"I'm *sorry.* Nobody said anything. But I just started as a volunteer this afternoon."

"Otherwise we'd be up to our ears. But please leave the cards so Bertie will know who to thank later."

The exotically beautiful girl looked sympathetically at Bertie, who, with her eyes closed, lay partially elevated in the bed.

"I think she is *so* wonderful. What a terrible thing. She'll be all right, won't she? I'll say a prayer in chapel on my break."

"That's very good of you—"

"My name's Flicka. Are you Bertie's best friend?"

"I hope so."

"I feel like I've seen you before. Are you in the movies?"

"No. I'm just plain no-talent Eve Bell."

"Very nice to meet you. I'll see that these flowers are taken to the cancer wing. I can't bear to go over there myself. I guess I'll have to get used to it. Is there anything else I can do for you? Something to eat from the cafeteria?"

"No, I'm fine. Flicka. That's an unusual name."

"My father was from Helsinki and my mother was born in Macao. She was part Chinese and part Thai. But they aren't with me any-more."

"Oh, I'm sorry. How old are you, Flicka?"

"I'll be seventeen in a couple of months. I'm a model too, I mean I'm trying to be, but I have a problem with my hips, so, you know, I really haven't made it big, like Miss Nkambe. Imagine being born on a farm in Africa. Whenever I watch TV and see those poor starving kids over there, I can't help but cry. I mean I'd love to be skinny like that, but not with all those flies and death and stuff."

"Sure. Flicka, if you wouldn't mind? My visiting time is almost up, and—"

"I *apologize*! I didn't mean to intrude. I'll just come by from time to time while on my shift, see if there's anything."

When the girl had gone, Bertie said, —What's wrong with her hips?

—A little wide in the beam for runway, but even so she'd ace the next Victoria's Secret collection. When are Joseph and Kieti coming back?

—Not tonight. They've both got jet lag and there's no need for them to hang around here watching me snooze. Kieti's restless for long-stemmed American beauties, and how long can you keep my pop away from a VIP baccarat room?

—So do you want me to—?

—No. Find yourself a good time. But as soon as you hear from Tom—

—I'll get back to you right away.

—You don't have any idea where he went with the dear departed?

—'Fraid I don't, Bertie, and I'm antsy too.

—Feeling a little tired now. This self-healing process takes a lot out of me, and I sure could use a New York cut smothered in grilled shitakis.

—How much longer, do you think?

—I could walk out of here two days from now. But the docs would find that peculiar. I don't want to attract unwanted attention to myself.

—Two days! You recuperate faster than Wile E. Coyote.

Eden leaned over the bed to kiss Bertie's cheek.

—I'd better. I think you're going to need me. Eden, I've been thinking about Gwen.

—I sure haven't.

—Remember when we met with Leoncaro in the Pope's study? We were speculating what might have become of your dpg after the Magician had her kidnapped off a street in Rome?

—Sure. Sebastiano said Grayle might have wanted her because doppelgangers can travel back and forth in time. And *I* said—

—Only if it was something you wanted her to do.

—That's right. I'm in control of Gwen.

—Eden!

—Doesn't count unless I say her full name out loud, after which she is no longer a doppelganger. Good riddance. But releasing her is my decision alone. Meanwhile—

—You don't know where she is. How do you usually keep in touch with Gwen?

—Kind of a mystery. It's not a conscious thing. There's no secret password. Largely visceral, I think. Sometimes she shows up for no good reason. She can be a pest about that.

—There must always be a reason, even if neither of you is sure what it is.

—I guess so.

—How long has it been since either of us saw her? My sense of time is screwed up. It's the painkillers and anticonvulsants. Bad for my short-term memory too. I'd get them to cut the dosages but I still need to be on oxygen part-time, the lung that took a hit isn't behaving.

—Best thing is for you to get out of here soon as you can. About Gwen—

—What if the Magician found a way to separate her from you? Didn't MORG have her doped up at Plenty Coups? What was the name of that bowlegged little guy with the mirror sunglasses?

—Bertie, I didn't get all of that, you're not coming through clearly. I did finally penetrate the fog around Gwen when I found the time. Before that I spent forty hours straight, as you know, trying to locate a weapon of mass destruction. I get your point, but I don't buy Gwen being under Mordaunt's control, no matter what combination of hypnotics he might have her on. Anyway, he's gone and eventually she'll wake up and I'll get her back on the beam. *Bertie?*

But there was nothing more from Bertie. Her eyelids didn't move. She'd drifted off to sleep and there was little else to hear but the huffing of the ventilator. Eden gave Bertie another kiss and called for the nurse waiting outside. In the sitting room of the suite she alerted Cody Olds on her cell phone. There was a team of Blackwelder ops ensuring Bertie's privacy. One of them escorted Eden to the lower level of the parking garage to wait for Cody. Eden taking time now to devote to her dpg, concentrating on her, wishing for that telltale buzzy feeling around her navel, a signal that they were hooking up or that Gwen was about to put in an appearance. Nothing came of the effort. Eden felt a slight, dismal sense of loss. As if she actually missed her doppelganger. What if something very bad had happened that wasn't really Gwen's fault? And what *was* the name of that bowlegged little guy with the mirror sunglasses?

With four more Blackwelders keeping them company in a huge Hummer behind Cody's little cartoon-comedy Prius, they drove to dinner at a restaurant called Stakes, owned by a couple of his friends. Past a little white chapel like wedding-cake art, host to many a grievous mistake of the heart. A billboard thirty feet high, advertising the

Follies, sweetmeats spangled in feather frosting, leggy as newborn colts. Intersection with flares, an SUV on its back amid metal trash and pulverized glass like a scream gone to glitter, blue lights everywhere. Emerging into the slipstream of light-show ecstasies on Las Vegas Boulevard. It was a weeknight in the off-season, if Vegas could be said to have an off-season, but still there were throngs crossing the street and the boardwalk by the hotel that featured pirate ships doing battle in an artificial lagoon. Eden and Cody both silent while they waited on a light to turn green, Eden looking far down the Strip and wondering if she was on another hard road to disillusion or if she had the right to hope for something better. Cody glancing at her just then with a gleam of intimacy that caused her heart to swell. Whatever was in her future, this moment would do. Besides, as Tom Sherard had said to her (speaking from the experience of the big-game hunter he once was), nothing invites danger like our own fears.

In their breaks from volunteer work at Concordia Hospital, Flicka and three others from Harlee Nations's crew put their heads together in the section of the cafeteria leased to a fast-food chain after they had fended off a couple of interns who, sensing opportunity, had made a move to join them.

"So she was right there when I came in with the flowers," Flicka said. "Beside the bed with her head bowed, lips moving as if she was saying a prayer for the Supa. I was, like, totally ginked. The Avatar. Awesome."

"So do we let Harlee know?" Reese said.

"Lotsa luck," Nic said, with her customary feline petulance. "Her cell's been turned off all day. I don't know where she and Devon are."

"Meanwhile . . ." Honeydew said, and let the suggestion hang while they worked on a Big Mac (Honeydew, with her supercharged metabolism and zit-proof skin) and char-grilled chicken salads (everyone else).

Flicka sipped her Coke, looking at each of them in turn. The vote seemed to be in.

"It's easy to get past the private cops," she said, after a mild belch. "Just bring a wagonload of flowers. There's a nurse probably twenty-four/seven, but I only need to get rid of her like, three minutes, fill in while she takes a sandbox break, whatever."

"Three minutes?" Reese said. She was wearing a pink turtleneck under her jumper to cover up a hickey Bronc Skarbeck had bestowed the night before. Bad bed manners on his part. Like he was trying to suck the chrome off a trailer hitch. Those lusty old guys with hearts as frail as paper lanterns, caution to the winds when they get a whiff of warm quail in the nest. But at least he'd had superior body tone. "How will you do it?"

"No problemo. The Supa's on drip lines. Unconscious, most of the time."

"Give her what?" Nic asked, her thickly made-up foxy eyes avid for the details. "An extra helping of morph?"

Flicka reacted with disdain to this unwitting slur on her prowess as a poisoner. "Severely contracted pupils," she said. "Dead giveaway, so to speak."

"Doesn't belladonna dilate the pupils back again?"

"That's too much fuss, when there are time constraints," Flicka said. She looked as cool as Dracula snacking on a frozen bloodsicle. "And there's no need to get cute with toxins when . . ."

They had another would-be visitor, one of those arrogant brain-digger types, exuding surgical star power and personality in his OR scrubs. Coming on to them heart-to-hearty.

"Hi, girls. What are we being so serious about over here in the corner?"

Honeydew took the lead, her eyes opening as wide and blue as morning glories.

"Looky here, y'all. A *real* doctor."

"Talking to *us*."

"I am totally blown."

"Turn out de lights, I's done seen hebben."

"Do you suppose docky want to fuckus?"

Reese said breathlessly, "Let us now synchronize our orgasms, and all come together."

"*Come to-gethherr,*" they harmonized, turning heads all over the cafeteria.

"Hey, uh, girls, I just—"

"It *is* a little hairy, though, wouldn't you say, Honeydew?"

"Like my daddy's bear-paw slippers."

"Eyebrows, yecchh."

"Keeps itself up, though. Cute buns."

"What d'you say, Nic—want to get down and dirty with it?"

"Like I want a cactus growin' on my lip."

Without a trace of expression on any of their gorgeous faces they watched the back of their victim's neck glowing red as he walked quickly away from the table with his tray, then returned to the business of Bertie Nkambe.

"I'll use digoxin," Flicka announced, as if she'd made up her mind during the diversion.

Nic's full underlip was in bicker mode. Flicka shortstopped her by saying, "The Supa's heart gives out, that's all. Because of the severity of her wounds there won't be any questions as to why she died."

"What about mass spectrometric analysis or immunoassay?" Nic said authoritatively.

Flicka smiled patiently. "There's a flaw in forensic pathology. Toxicologists can't find poison unless they know they're looking for it. It's a matter of professional oversight, and who is going to suspect?"

The other two girls nodded, but Nic said stubbornly, "Harlee's got to okay the offing of the Supa."

"Well, the Great One wanted her out of the way, didn't he?" Reese said. "Not for us to wonder why. Maybe she's, you know, paranormal too? Maybe we should go ahead and finish the job that Cornell what's-his-name botched."

"Girlfriends, do any of us need Harlee seriously pissed because we didn't consult her about Nkambe?"

They all looked thoughtfully at Nic. No one wanted Harlee pissed. Any of them could be banished from the crew on her whim, denied the benefits of spectrochrome therapy, without which they would be dreadful hags in no time. And it was lonely out there, beyond the comforting warmth of Harlee's affections.

Honeydew said, "Why don't you try her cell phone again, Nic?"

"She knows we've been calling," Flicka argued. "Maybe she just doesn't want to be bothered. No rush. I wouldn't try to do it tonight anyway. There'll be a new load of flowers to deliver tomorrow. I'll need one of you to divert whoever's in the suite with Nkambe while I do the deed. Nic, are you going to finish your salad?"

"No, you can have it. I can't eat. I'm all bloated and cramping up. Periods are really bad at our age, aren't they?"

"Consider the alternative," Reese advised.

LAS VEGAS · OCTOBER 30 · 2:12 A.M.

At the threshold of Harlee's room, General Bronc Skarbeck, lavishly decorated veteran of wars, skirmishes, and occupations, suffered the first failure of nerve of his life. It was unexpected, and a shock to his ego. And Harlee hadn't uttered a word or offered a look to bring him down so drastically.

She was, in fact, alone in her bedroom with its scatter of teen magazines and posters of hardbody striplings nonchalant in low-riding denim and baggy camo, as austere in her sleep as a stone saint atop a tomb. She breathed through her lips with a faint sibilance. Her Mac was on, and humming. She had mail. A fragrant candle by her bed had burned down to a nub of flame in a soft caldera. She looked as if she had been asleep for hours, her dreamtime spanning centuries he could scarcely imagine, drawn from wells of personal experience.

So Marcus Woolwine believed, or would have Bronc believe: one revelation among many during a truly fascinating conversation they'd had at the end of Bronc's long day. No denying that Woolwine was a sharp old bastard who had explored boggling possibilities of the occult during his long career. On the other hand, past a certain age even the most brilliant minds could spring leaks, pissing away accumulated wisdom, scientific objectivity, or just plain common sense. Therefore, Woolwine's tales of Fetchlings might have been romantically conceived while the old boy was immersed in a sub-delirium's depths like a nearly extinct blowfish.

The ruby crystal skull was missing from the Magician's house, however. The room in which it was keeping the doppelganger's holo-gram company had been violently disturbed. Because Harlee had made a late-night visit with her friend Devon (confirmed by surveil-lance tapes), Bronc had no choice but to find out what was going on.

The white streak in her hair (some new fad that was de rigueur within her set?) might have given him pause, that sinking feeling. It was somehow ferocious, alien, in the ghost light of the computer screen. So Bronc imagined as he closed the door behind him and approached Harlee's bed. Or else attributed his reluctance to ask questions of her to fatigue. His eyes felt dry and grainy beneath the lids. Alertness was smudged, and he had a burnt-coffee backtaste in his raspy throat. Just stay rational, even-handed. Ask only what he had to know. No staying the night. His heart hung in his chest like an anvil and his balls felt even heavier, with soreness and unpleasant heat. Maybe it was testicular cancer he really needed to worry about. No, just too much screwing lately.

Braver now, settling into her lambency on the edge of the bed. He didn't care to know more about Harlee than the eye beheld, his senses could absorb. All else must be denied. He would savage the world to keep her. On his terms.

The terms he was about to negotiate.

Harlee opened her eyes a few moments after he gripped a bare shoulder, then increased the pressure of his grip.

"Ohhh, Daddy," she said, in her intimate movie-goddess whisper voice, looking up into his fuming eyes. "You're home." She smiled faintly. "But I'm so awfully tired tonight. I haven't had a bath and I feel all bloaty, it must have been something—" Her eyes squinched a little as he applied more pressure, then she lightly bit her lower lip. "What's wrong?"

"Tell me," Skarbeck said.

"T-tell you what?"

"That you love me."

"I do. Oh, I love you, Daddy! But you're hurting me."

Skarbeck eased up a little as, with his left hand, he laid his beat-up old service .45 on the pillow next to Harlee's, where she could see it out of the corner of her eye. See the hammer cocked back. His hand remained on the worn checkered butt of his automatic, not gripping it, just lying there, a hand deeply freckled with age spots.

Harlee looked at the weapon for several seconds—the blunt estrangement it represented—licked her lower lip bodingly, looked into his eyes, a gaze of profound despair.

"But what have I *done?*"

"I don't know yet. Love, or whatever you want to call it, is one thing. Loyalty, trust—those matter more."

"You know you can trust me." Harlee shrugged slightly. Her cheeks looked a little feverish. She cleared her throat, then spoke in her normal voice. One pretense abandoned. Not useful, given the situation. "So, did you and Dr. Woolwine have a tête-à-tête?"

"Yes. What were you to Lincoln Grayle?"

Her eyelids closed in dark sorrow. "His servant."

"Why did he give you to me?"

"I think you know."

"Pillow secrets?"

"More than that, I hope," she said, with a tremor in her throat. "Haven't I been good for you? I'm the daughter-whore you needed— Daddy. The sexual excitement you can't be without. At no risk to you."

With his right hand Bronc slapped her smartly but not too hard, just enough to turn her head. She spilled a single tear. He put the hand on her breast and squeezed a nipple. Harlee moaned.

"I can *smell* your gun! I've always hated guns. I know you've killed men with it. I don't want to die! Oh please. If you pinch me any harder I'll piss my bed."

Bronc withdrew his tingling hand, smiling ironically.

"You don't sound much like an immortal—a, what's the term, Fetchling?"

"But we're *all* human! Nine months in the womb, same as you and Socrates and Jesus. We love, we hate, we get diseases, some of us go mad . . . what I'm saying is, we have no superpowers."

"But you live—"

"Long, but not forever! Meanwhile I can choose where and how I want to live, how I want to look, who I want to be. For a price."

"You're bad, aren't you?" Bronc said, with a subdued, worshipful expression.

"Yes. I *have* been bad. Sometimes. But I like parakeets and kittens."

"Whatever he asked of you, the Great One—" Bronc grimaced. "You did it?"

"Yesss. Don't ask me any more."

"God, you are something! I know I ought to kill you. Quite frankly. But I'm not afraid of you. Let's get real here. Harlee, the Magician is dead. Understand? Gone, gone, gone."

More tears flowed from her hazy green eyes. She lay still with her lips parted, crying, not speaking.

Bronc pulled his .45 back from the other pillow. In a sudden spasm of anger or loathing Harlee wadded that supposedly soiled pillow and flung it across the bedroom. Then she lay with her face in profile to Skarbeck, knees drawn up. He thought of kittens and parakeets and Harlee's petilant laughter, the purity of her voice enlivening an otherwise empty house. He thought of her pleasing touches at his nape or along the seam of his scrotum. How perfect she was, for the age she claimed to be. Her rondure and milk-sweet kidskin, the still-serrated edges of two front teeth that he could see through lips like lush petals. His young pretty, his plaything, his sensuous treasure: his undoing, should he not keep his wits about him.

"Harlee, where's the ruby crystal skull?"

"Ohhh . . . it's in a shoe box under my bed."

"Good Christ!"

"It's nothing to be afraid of." She sat up, sullenly hugging her breasts. All teenager again. "The Great One asked me to take care of it for him." Harlee shrugged. "I don't know why that dickhead Woolwine had it."

Skarbeck didn't enlighten her. "What exactly does the skull do?"

"Do? *I* don't know. Sometimes if you stare at it, you see stuff."

"Like looking into a crystal ball?"

"I guess so." Harlee suppressed a yawn, gave him a quick look. Of course she was lying. She wanted him to know she was lying. It was a minor exercise in the subtleties of control. Bronc almost felt married.

"Like I said, the Magician's gone, Harlee. But that leaves you and me—only—just *where* does it leave us? I have a question. Be truthful. Grayle must have trusted someone else with access to his vault. Is it you?"

"I don't know anything about—"

He fired a shot past her left ear and into the silk-upholstered headboard. Close enough that she had to have heard the disturbance in the air, like a whir of insect wings, that the bullet made in passing just before the loud report rang in their heads.

Harlee jumped in fright, one hand going to her ear, the other diving to her demure nest. That little problem she had. But she could bunk in with him for the remainder of the night. And be of service, if only to rub his tired back.

"Bronc, you shit!" Harlee squirmed in humiliation and outrage, soaking her sheets.

He cocked the .45.

"Don't!" she said, now holding her head in both hands, clenching her teeth.

"Well?"

"I can get into the vault. Full body scan required. A *live* body, of course." She looked up defiantly.

He lowered the hammer and put the .45 away.

"Long as you understand that I'm the man now. You need *me* to stay alive, Harlee. I need for you to show me how I can live longer. And incredibly rich, of course." He didn't miss the slight curling of her lip. "I want to cancel my life insurance. I don't want to read obituaries anymore. I hate funerals. It's a corrupt old planet, but you can't beat the perks. Depending on how well we work together, no reason why the two of us can't have our fill of the cream off the top. Is there?"

Skarbeck smiled encouragingly, having spoon-fed the message. He settled back to watch her lap it up.

Eden Waring came out of Cody's bedroom like someone roused from sleep by a nearby detonation or a scream in the night: she looked edgy, vaguely dismayed, disoriented.

He looked up from the draftsman's table where he had been sketching, laying out a future painting.

"Everything okay?"

She made a disagreeable face. "I hate my dreams. *Hate* them. I need something to write with."

Cody gave her a legal pad and a pen from his rolltop desk. She sat on a sofa with a Wolf Spider clan blanket for a throw and almost tucked her right leg under her before remembering that his roomy flannel shirt still didn't cover all that much. There was a large coffee-table book, Georgia O'Keeffe's paintings, bleached skull with horns like a bleak mountain range against a sere blue sky on the dust jacket. She looked at it, shuddered, turned the book over. Using it as a lap desk, she began furiously to write, her face still bunched in an expression of loathing and dread.

Cody wanted sympathetically to give her a hug, but he went to the kitchen instead. Two thirty in the morning. He wasn't sleepy; still energized from the quiet solid hours of creative work. He puttered around making tea. When it had brewed he returned to relaxing and daydreaming in the L-shaped room that was filled with books, paintings, sculpture, bright throw rugs on the oak floor. He didn't have much in the way of furniture: the sofa bed for visitors, a comfortable lounge chair for reading. Good full-spectrum lighting was Cody's priority.

Two steaming cups on a tray and a bottle of Courvoisier in case Eden felt the need of a strengthener. She had put the legal pad on the beveled glass that covered a sand painting and was stretching to work a kink out of one shoulder. Her expression not serene but less troubled. There was a sleep crease on one ruddy cheek. Her strawberry-blond hair needed a few licks. He adored her, a bolt to the heart that had him feeling dizzily as if his next step would be off a cliff. *Whoa now, Cody.* He glanced at the legal pad. Facedown. Well, if she wanted him to know—

"Thanks," Eden said, taking the cup of tea from him, considering the brandy, deciding she didn't want to get started. "I know I must be a terrible houseguest. Keeping you up at all hours. Was I—making a lot of noise in my sleep?"

"Didn't hear you. But I'm good at shutting out the world when I'm drawing."

"Oh. Can I see?"

"Sure."

She admired his charcoal and pencil sketches. Figures and faces, mostly Indian. "There's something about your Navajo woman with the two small boys. Are they twins? And I think I know her face."

"Probably seen it a few thousand times in the mirror."

"Is that what I'd look like if my hair was darker and braided? Am I going to be in a Cody Olds painting?"

"Don't know how far I'll go with it. I was meaning to get away from the figurative for a while and do a narrative, but with objects, not people. Then you came along, and a dream I had inspired me to—try this one. How long do your dreams stay with you?"

"Not long, fortunately, after I write them down and put them away. But there are those dreams that keep coming back, pressing me for answers."

"Do you see the same thing over and over?"

"No. The images change, but the symbology is linked from dream to dream."

"Prophetic dreams, you called them."

"The worst ones, yeah."

"Real booger bears. Rivers of fire in the streets of Las Vegas." Wanting her to open up; but he instinctively knew he couldn't keep pulling on that thread without unraveling the relationship.

Eden had looked away from him. Then she went to the shutters over the single large window behind his drafting table and opened them.

"Not in the streets," she said. "What are those mountains out there?"

"Don't know what they're called. I don't believe they're volcanic. So there's not much chance of—"

"And it won't be rivers of fire. Do you keep a Bible around, Cody?"

He found it in a bookcase, long unopened, a gift from a high school teammate who was now an itinerant evangelist in rural Texas.

Eden sat on one side of the sofa and turned to the end of the Bible, the last pages of Revelation. After a couple of minutes she found the passage she'd been looking for.

"'And I saw a woman sit upon a scarlet-colored beast,'" she read aloud in a dry monotone, "'full of names of blasphemy, having seven heads and ten horns.'" She sighed and laid the book facedown on one knee, looking bleakly off as if she had no further need to see, fingers of one hand on the twisted chunk of metal she wore like a talisman on a gold chain outside Cody's old shirt. Pressing it lightly against her solar plexus. He had wondered about it, this talisman, although there were many other things about Eden Waring that intrigued him more.

After a while Eden said, "I skipped Sunday school and church most of the time when I was growing up because I already knew . . . mysteries below heaven, the truth of the afterlife, just about every-thing they weren't teaching from the New Testament."

"From your own dreams?"

"Yes."

Cody stretched out in his leather lounger and reached up to turn off the reading lamp above his head.

"Did you see this scarlet beast in your dream tonight?"

"No. Because the beast is gone, and anyhow St. John's vision doesn't jibe with . . . my knowledge of things as they are. It wasn't scarlet, either. It had the body of a tiger, dark gray with black stripes, and only one head, but that was the head of a jackal or hyena. Ugly enough, in its fashion. The beast was the alter shape of the Magician, and its purpose was to mate with me."

"Why you?" Cody said, after a few jolting beats of his heart.

"To combine our powers in a third entity, beast of woman born, ruler of the Long Darkness, the tribulation of mankind the Bible also refers to."

Cody swallowed some cognac, looking a little unhappy.

Eden said, "If you want to call the cops, I promise I'll go quietly."

"I already told you, I'm in for the long haul. You just keep coming up with . . . But I don't read you any way but truthful. I like to think I know people pretty damn well."

"Listen, Cody. My mom is a clinical psychologist. She could tell you about patients who are intelligent, well spoken, and so plausible in their delusions they could beat a lie detector every time. I could be one of them."

"Then I must be delusional myself. I'm dreaming all of this, right?"

He got up from his chair, crossed to the sofa, lifted Eden straight up, and kissed her. Eden's resistance lasted a couple of seconds. The kiss went on for a while, until she got her toes on the floor.

Cody said, when he pulled his face back inches from hers, "Finally got to the part of the dream I'm liking best."

Eden touched his mustache, his lips, eyes losing focus. "Don't get me going. I'm—"

"Involved. I know. With this Tom fella who's run off on you."

"No, he *hasn't*! Dammit, Cody, I'm sure he took the were-beast away, with the help of . . . others. A friend in Rome. This wasn't the first beast the Church has had to dispose of. Tom is making sure the thing is buried, and stays buried forever."

"So that would make two of you who have seen it."

"And Bertie. And Tom's houseman and others at Shungwaya. I wasn't there the first time it came calling on me. Cody, let go now."

He let her go. She stayed close.

"First time I kissed a girl," Cody said, "I counted to myself. One Mississippi, two Mississippi . . . Like I was holding my breath under water."

Eden snickered. "I was chewing gum, and I didn't know what to do with it. I must've swallowed it, because we were really lip-locked. I'd better have a drink now. Short one?"

"Okay. So if the beast wasn't in your dreams, what did you see that upset you so much?"

"The feminine half of Mordaunt's soul. Tom and Bertie also saw her, or *it,* in Africa just a couple of weeks ago, mounted on the were-beast that had come there looking for me. She was naked, wrists bound by silver shackles. Her body unmistakably a woman's. But her face, they said, was unformed, a specter. Tonight I had a better look at her in my dream. She was walking on a mountain of human souls and bones, and that mountain was called Acheron. Unshackled at last, pulling down stars with her one hand, unearthing lightning from the depths of the mountain with the other, combining celestial and man-made power into a fury of pure energy that crackled from her fingertips. She wove a web of fire above the mountain and the desert and down to the city of the desert; and all of the souls inside the great city looked up and they cried out, 'Alas, alas, Babylon,' because none could escape."

Cody brought her a glass of cognac. He had to put it in her hand and close the fingers of that hand. She was perspiring, pulses visible in her throat, at her temples. A vein was huge below her right temple, throbbing. Eden had him worried. She seemed to be at critical mass from the emotional heavy lifting. He wiped perspiration from her forehead with the back of his hand, held the glass to her lips. The cognac went down okay. A swallow, two, then a long sigh.

"You don't have to tell me any more."

"But I do! I knew her name: Delilah. I've known it since I was a child. It's an old, old name cursed and despised for the treachery and evil it embodies. And in my dream I knew her face: because, my friend, Delilah's face was mine."

Eden had another swallow of cognac. A little of it dribbled down her chin and a small drop splashed on the talisman. She stared at Cody with a funereal sadness, eyes smudged like moth-burn on a lampshade.

"So you see, Cody: I'm the avenger, but also the destroyer, hated everywhere I'm known."

"Bull. Your name is Eden. And there's not a speck of evil in you."

"Only half right. I'm Eden the gym rat who learned to live with her bad dreams until they started to come true, Eden who only wants a sane and quiet life and who I think is half in love with a cowboy from New Mexico who, wouldn't you know, turns out to be a wonderful kisser. Dammit, I am *that* girl! But here comes my deepest dark secret: there is another one of me, and oh, Cody, I'm afraid of what she's become, was tricked into becoming by the Magician. Because now one of us is fated to kill the other."

OCTOBER 30 · 13° 42' N, 91° 14' W · 0350 HOURS ZULU

Off the coast of Guatemala, steaming north in a heavy Pacific sea at fifteen knots, the captain of the tanker *Culebra,* awakened by the A.B. on watch, came into the wheelhouse. His name was Dellarovere, thirty-six years at sea. He went directly to the radar on the nearly pitch-dark bridge 116 feet above the sea and looked at the target north of *Culebra*'s position.

"She's not responding to the radio?"

"No, sir. Not for the last eight–ten minutes."

"Appears to be making no headway?"

"She's been set to starboard about a quarter mile since we first noticed her."

Dellarovere got on the radio himself. "Calling the vessel approximately thirteen forty-five north, ninety-one ten west. This is the northbound ship ten miles south of you. Over." He listened. The heavily loaded tanker was rolling nearly fifteen degrees in a quartering sea. There was continued radio silence from the unknown vessel.

"Crew of damned Greeks," the A.B. volunteered. Greeks, along with Haitians, were routinely credited by seagoing men as the worst sailors on the planet. The captain glanced at him. The A.B. was going through initial collision-avoidance procedures, using a grease pencil on the plotting head positioned over the ten-centimeter radar screen.

The captain, feeling both annoyed and uneasy about the ship that seemed to be adrift in their path, tried the radio again, with the same result. Then he telephoned the bow lookout, who was about two football fields away from the bridgehouse. But there was too much rain for the lookout to report a sighting.

"Course change, Captain?" the mate asked casually.

Collisions at sea, in spite of all the sailing room oceans provided, were not a rarity. The size of the ship—for instance, a VLCC like the *Culebra*, carrying 140,000 tons of crude oil from Maracaibo by way of Cape Horn—had something to do with the chance of collision. The *Culebra*, at reduced speed in confused seas, was slow to answer the helm. They had not yet invented a braking system for Very Large Crude Carriers at sea. It could take upward of two minutes to achieve full astern in an emergency.

"Apparently their course is anyone's guess." Dellarovere didn't have to think about it. "Put the ship on hand." The mate pushed a button to take the *Culebra* off autopilot. "Bring her port one eight zero. Maintain speed."

"One eight zero," the quartermaster said.

Dellarovere took binoculars from a locker and used them to look out through one of the spinning glass circles in the window in front of the helm, which offered a clearer view through rain. But there was nothing out there in the dark to focus on.

"Target eight and one half miles, Captain. I don't know if ten degrees will do it at present speed."

"We'll want to pass close enough to find out if she's lost her plant and not under command," the captain said. Radio silence could mean complete lack of electrical. He ordered the *Culebra*'s radio operator to be roused from sleep. He would have preferred to stay well away from the unknown vessel. But he could not bypass a distressed ship at sea. She was, potentially, huge trouble. Too much chance of going zero CPA in a force-8 gale. ("CPA" meant closest point of approach. "Zero CPA" was self-explanatory.)

The A.B. whistled aimlessly and punched up Trial Maneuver on the Collision Avoidance System software. The captain made another phone call, this one for coffee. He raised his binoculars again. They were a little more than four miles from the target on the radar screen when he picked up a momentary pinkish glow nearly dead ahead in the brawling sea.

A flare.

ABOARD THE *STELLA SALAMIS*

Approximately twenty minutes before the southbound container ship had appeared as a blip on the *Culebra*'s radar, Tom Sherard was awakened on the cabin deck by what seemed to be every siren and alarm aboard. The ship was rolling deeper than it had been an hour ago, when he'd gone to sleep with a reading light on over his bunk. Not nearly so rough then. A moonlit sky was still visible through his porthole. Now he was pinned against the shallow rail around the bunk on its open side, gripping it with one hand to keep from being thrown to the deck. The light had dimmed as if it were about to go out.

Sherard didn't know what the alarms meant. Man overboard, fire below, or some other catastrophe only a fast-developing storm at sea could provide. He had the deep-sink feeling of any first-time seagoer in the midst of a gale: his last meal churning acid into his throat; hair raising, borderline terror enhanced by the ship's sluggish responses—complaining, struggling, punch-drunk from rivet-popping blows.

Sherard was already fully clothed. When he was halfway to the door of his cabin the lights went out. Disoriented in the total darkness, he lost his balance and like a kid in a funhouse with everything awry he slammed against the bulkhead with the next long roll of the ship to starboard. A few seconds later the emergency generator kicked on, adding a saffron glow that cast no shadows.

The entire house, five stories high, reverberated to a booming of steel against steel on the forward deck. Similar low-light wattage prevailed in the narrow passageway outside. Sherard lurched from wall to wall, tipsy as an old clown in a flickering silent movie. Two doors hung open along the passageway. First mate's quarters, and the door to the corner room by the steep open stairs to the upper decks that was usually occupied by the chief engineer. If he was already below, then that's where the emergency was, Sherard thought. But he reckoned that the captain would be on the bridge. The best man to ask about their situation, and if there was any danger. Like the ship going ventral, as old salts would say.

He started up the stairs toward the wheelhouse, two stories above cabin deck. Holding on to the railing with both hands. During a brief lull of the sirens he heard what could have been pans flying around the galley three decks below. An acrid odor like burned rubber came up from the fire room of the vessel. A sensation of rising heat. He heard no voices of urgent command or shouts of distress, which he accepted as encouraging, in spite of the unnerving clang of steel forward—as if containers had pulled loose from pad eyes and were being thrown around the deck by the storm.

The *Stella Salamis* was German built. Captain Riklis, who was very fond of her, had elaborated on her good points: sensitive to the helm even at slow speed, with a sharp bow for riding out rough weather, anything short of a force-12 hurricane. Whatever their problem of the moment, Sherard knew there would be an almost preternatural calm in the wheelhouse shared by the captain, chief mate, and quartermaster.

The bow was lifting as he climbed, until it seemed as if he were nearly vertical on the stairs. He lost his footing and clung helplessly to the rails until the bow smashed down into a trough. There was a sensation of traveling precariously sideways for a few seconds. Nearly five hundred feet of hardy steel ship being batted around like a plastic toy in a child's bath. But the ship rolled stubbornly upright and he got his feet under him, took a deep breath. Then the bow begin to lift again. Sherard looked up at the darkened bridge deck in time to catch a glimpse of a body in free fall.

Instinctively he reached with his right hand to try to arrest the plunge of whoever had lost his balance up there, bracing for the impact in the narrow stairwell.

Sherard hooked an arm but couldn't get a grip, because the arm was slick with oil. Or so he thought until the seaman's slowed momentum caused his nearly severed, bald head to yaw in Sherard's direction. He reeked of spilled blood. The arm slipping through Sherard's grasp was handless. Prongs of bone ends, and then the dead sailor was gone, falling the rest of the way down iron steps, skull hammering the deck.

For a few shocked moments Sherard couldn't move. Then he wiped his sticky hand on his cargo pants and continued on to the bridge.

There were two doors with a passage between them so that at night the wheelhouse would always be dark. In that passage he stumbled across another body. The rubber runner on the floor was coated with gore.

By then he knew. The *Stella Salamis* had acquired, in midvoyage and through what supernatural intervention he couldn't imagine, an Entity in Addition to Crew.

The door behind him opened to a shrieking blast of squall weather. Guaranteed to freeze the piss and marrow of the most intrepid. He turned in horror, body at his feet, a monster in the mind, throwing up a hand to block some of the webbed glare from a three-battery flashlight.

"So it's you," Captain Riklis said. "I was hoping . . . you would still be alive." Sherard could barely make him out behind the light. His voice had the cramped breathless quality of a man in considerable pain. "I doubt there is another living soul aboard. So I will need . . . your help."

"Lower your light! You're blinding me."

Riklis changed the beam angle, revealing the body on the deck, back of its head missing, most of a gaunt rib cage wetly exposed, ribbons of flesh. He thought it might have been the radio operator.

"Where is it?" Sherard said. "Where did it go?"

Riklis blinked slowly, like a man surfacing from a depth of ether, or devastating shock. "I don't know."

"I'll need a weapon."

"I have . . . a handgun. But we both know . . . the were-beast can-not be destroyed."

They heard an anguished scream from somewhere well below the bridge deck. The captain smiled horridly. "So there may be others still. But the beast will sniff them out. We must hurry while it is . . . occupied."

Sherard clung to a handrail as the *Stella Salamis* rolled heavily, clumsily. With the steering system out of control, the ship had lost all momentum and was taking seas as high as the boat deck. Riklis lost his grip on everything but the Maglite, hit the deck with a pained outcry, and slid helplessly in Sherard's direction. When he was able to gauge the ship's pitch and get his feet under him, his trimly bearded face was a study in lost humanity, in the stupefaction of extreme terror. There was a wet blood swath on his blouse, from under one arm to the beltline.

"Captain, you have to get your ship under command!"

"Too late. Now you must help me."

"Help you do *what*?"

"Open the seacocks. The *Stella Salamis* must never be allowed to make port with . . . that foul thing aboard. Even though it can't be killed, at least it will be . . . contained. Neutralized. Entombed within a rusting hulk at six thousand fathoms for two or three hun-dred years."

"Bollocks. The were-beast was entombed already, in glass and steel. What makes you think an abyss will hold it?"

"There is no other way."

"There is always a way! First get on the radio and find out if there's help, another ship, nearby."

"I destroyed the radio a few moments ago."

In the shaky light, multiple shadows looming around them, Sher-ard studied the captain angrily. "You bloody fool. Sink the ship, what chance do we have in seas like this?"

Riklis shook his head wanly. His eyes told that his mind was spin-ning out of control. A little fresh blood had appeared at one corner of his mouth.

"But *we* don't matter. Please. I was injured. I'm losing blood . . . my strength. We can't delay."

The sirens had stopped. Sherard barely noticed.

"I'm not helping to scuttle your ship! We may have a monster to deal with, nonetheless it's flesh and bone and fucking brain matter. I've wounded it before! Now I'm finishing the job."

"How? You've seen it. Enormous. The strength to wrench a lashed-down spare propeller from the deck and hurl it to the wheelhouse windows. Capshaw, Jarkko, they died instantly. Then . . . it climbed the outside of the wheelhouse after me."

"I'll need a flare gun," Sherard said. "Then gasoline, kerosene—*where*?"

"I have a flare gun . . . in my office below. Kerosene is stored near the paint lockers on the shelter deck. But it's dangerous there. You'll wash overboard, even with a lifeline. Or be battered to death."

"Show me!"

Riklis looked dimly at Sherard. The blood from his mouth had matted in his beard. He nodded, not as if he had real hope, and gestured for Sherard to follow him. Sherard picked up the revolver Riklis had dropped on the deck and looked at it briefly. Smith & Wesson .38. He smiled grimly and handed it back to the captain.

"Keep it for your own protection. Aim for the eyes if it comes to that."

Riklis said something in another language that might have been Latin, then feebly made the sign of the cross. The *Stella Salamis* yawed and plunged sickeningly into a wave trough. The entire house vibrated like a struck bell as loose containers caromed around the foredeck.

Open the seacocks? As far as Sherard was concerned, the ship was a goner already. But with luck they all wouldn't go to the bottom before his showdown with the so-called Great One.

Eden Waring went barefoot into the condo kitchen to reheat the water in the kettle and make more soothing tea for her parched throat and overworked larynx. When she returned to Cody, who was laid out in the lounger that was designed to pamper his once-broken back, she found that at last she had talked the man to sleep. Eden felt sheepish about it, the outpouring of her recent life and woes, but also strangely blissful, unburdened, much closer to him in this quiet hour. She also had opened the books on her life back home in Innisfall, where for most of her childhood and adolescent years she'd felt like an imposter, dutifully mimicking other girls her age, adopting some of their trivial obsessions and cliquish vernacular, while her mind seethed with the breadth of her occult knowledge. Just trying to fit in and, once she realized how good she could become, to work hard, excel at sports. Softball, tennis, and particularly basketball granted status and popularity. Made it easier to ignore her sometimes-glimpses of that other, alien Eden, sidelined, but observing with cool patience and authority. Waiting for their special time together: graduation day, when Eden Waring was yanked nakedly out of the closet and flash-fried by the media. *Awesome* was the word. And devastating to her psyche. Had Cody understood? Seemed to. He asked questions that expressed his need to relate the magical and otherworldly to what he'd already observed and instinctively felt about her, affirming the rightness of his uncritical judgment.

Except for Betts, her foster mother, Eden had never imagined having the confidence to entrust her secrets to another. She was out of words now, but not out of heart. Her heart was a balloon, one of those hot-air, lofty, cloud-skimming balloons. She sat on the sofa and sipped her tea, yawned occasionally, and studied Cody in his sleep as if every passing moment afforded some new insight, added to her quickening fondness and frank sexual interest.

She set the cup aside finally and closed her eyes, put a pillow beneath her head. It would not be possible, she knew, for a very long time, if ever. But she had a romantic yearning to go home again. Take Cody with her. *It's just me, Eden. Look what I found!* Saying to all of them, *He's a good man and not afraid of me. So what do you have to fear?*

Wishful thinking. A fantasy, for now. But the notion served its purpose, and charmed her to sleep.

ABOARD THE *STELLA SALAMIS* · 0420 HOURS ZULU

Tom Sherard had seen the movie when he was at boarding school in Nairobi. Age twelve. It was a flawed 16-millimeter print of Howard Hawks's *The Thing from Another World.* Delicious chills and jump-out-of-your-seat scares, classmates spooking one another when the cleverly calculated tension became unbearable. The girls screaming and covering their eyes half the time, when they weren't surreptitiously holding hands with boys they had crushes on. *The Thing.* Manlike but huge, a superstrong and intelligent vegetable, it had been chipped out of ice near its crashed flying saucer in a remote Arctic snowscape, then transported by dog sled to a remote scientific facility. Where, wouldn't you know it, its ice casket was partly melted by an electric blanket. The Thing itself thawed out. The scientists and military personnel inside the sprawling station were hostages to a blizzard outside: nowhere to go, prey for the monster that thrived on—what else—the blood of animals.

It was that long-ago movie Sherard had had in mind when he tied himself securely to the bolted-down table in the officers' dining room. Exhausted, as battered as if he'd been in a back-alley brawl from the wallowing of a helmless ship in a gale. The Pacific Ocean and not the Arctic wastelands, but still nowhere to go while he waited for the monster he'd tried to lure, using a loud hailer to be heard above the bellowing thud of containers against the house—probably half of the containers on the decks had come unlashed—and the dull groanings of hull plates, some of which might have been popping rivets at each blow from the huge seas. The radar mast was long gone, carried away by a fifty-foot wave. The house leaked torrents with every steep roll. Water flowed across the galley deck a couple of feet deep at times. Sherard had been soaked for a good twenty minutes, iced to the bone. His hands grew numb as he gripped the loud hailer.

"MAGICIAN! This is Sherard!" Bravado reverberating around the distressed freighter, metallic words whipped away by the winds. "I'm in the officers' dining room! Dining room! Waiting for you! Come and get me, you filthy misbegotten bastard! I'll kill you as many times as I have to, devil! DEVIL!"

All of it designed to enflame the were-beast's lust for revenge. *If* it hadn't been washed overboard. *If* it truly had a desire to tear him to pieces, the apparent fate of the rest of the crew.

But Sherard's taunts and invitation had been ignored; now he was shaking too badly, too hoarse to call anymore. At each steep roll of the ship it seemed to Sherard that the *Stella Salamis* must at last break in half. Although he wore a flotation vest, he would drown before he could hope to free himself from the ropes binding him to the leg of the metal table.

He hadn't thought about Riklis for several minutes. Didn't know if the captain was alive or dead somewhere on the galley deck, in one of the dining rooms or the salon. Riklis had been losing blood steadily while they put together a makeshift plan to confront the monster. But Sherard's field of vision was limited to what the bloody glow of an emergency light, mounted on a bulkhead, afforded.

There was another light, or at least a faint shining like the first glimmer of dawn, which he had seen through a starboard porthole as the ship struggled to right itself. As if out there in the gale another ship loomed, fixing the *Stella Salamis* in the beam of a searchlight. Sherard was fascinated. Waiting for the momentary glow in the porthole glass was like waiting for the face of God to appear. When he didn't see it he felt a rip of despair in his chest.

"You should see what the two of you have done to me, Hunter!"

The thing was in the doorway between the galley and the dining room. All but filling the space with his awkward-looking bulk. Still partly the feline beast from about the waist down. But holding on with a human hand. The shape of the head was familiar. So was the voice of Lincoln Grayle.

"Our pleasure," Sherard said, then repeated it, because he knew the Magician hadn't heard him the first time. The ship rolled a good fifty degrees, and this time it seemed to Sherard that they must turn upside down—but that terrifying moment passed; the *Stella Salamis* stayed groaningly on keel. Sherard saw that blip of light through the porthole glass again. Just enough light to afford him a glimpse of the state the Magician was in. He felt both horror and satisfaction.

"HOW DID YOU GET OUT?" he said, straining to be heard.

"A power was granted to me! I used it!"

"What . . . power? The lightning that struck your container?"

"It wasn't lightning. Where is she? Are you hiding the bitch Avatar from me?"

Sherard managed to laugh. "Don't know when you've had enough? You're bloody . . . stupid. And you look like shit!"

"I'll catch up to Eden later! When I'm feeling . . . more like my old self. I always win."

"But you . . . can't make it back . . . *can* you? You're stuck between man and monster!" The Magician's once-handsome face looked like a backyard-barbecue accident. "That old . . . black magic doesn't work anymore!"

"How little you know about me!"

"Can't hear you! Come closer! I'm wearing my FUCK YOU GREAT ONE T-shirt tonight!"

Sherard blinked, momentarily focusing on the searchlight out there amid gale seas.

The Magician saw the light too.

"My ride's here. I'll be leaving you now, Hunter!"

"You're going . . . nowhere but down! We go together! Twenty thousand fathoms deep! What power will help you escape from a canyon in the bottom . . . of the ocean?"

The *Stella Salamis* tilted like a carnival ride from the impact of what Sherard reckoned was a rogue wave. Steel plates twisted as they were pulled apart. Water gushed into the house. The Magician was washed from the bulkhead doorway by the incoming flood. He managed to grasp the tilted table with his human hand, clinging there like an over-sized gargoyle off the parapet of a skyscraper. The mismatched entity was a blur to Sherard's salt-stinging eyes. Its tail twitched smartly above one shoulder. It smelled awful, an evolutionary reject expelled from the bowels of a cosmic corruption.

"Taking a souvenir . . . home with me! Your head ought to do. Think that will impress our girl, Great White Hunter?"

Sherard had no fear left in him. Beheaded or drowned, what difference? Looking into the face of the Magician, he saw in his mind that old scary movie unspooling; comfortingly he recalled the light-boned girl pressed against him as they sat on the commissary floor. He'd given her a deeper visceral thrill by solemnly kissing her hand as they watched the movie, licking a fingernail as if it were a piece of hard candy. She was the daughter of the Swedish ambassador to Kenya. Pale, pale blond with lashes as fine as spider's silk, lips that tended to blister in the equatorial sun. Soon after they both turned thirteen he slept with her on a double safari cot. The innocent, primal bliss of first sex. Outside their tent, grunts and coughs and eerie cries of nocturnal prowlers in the bush.

Paradise he had known at an early age: now, on a doomed ship with the were-beast in his face, he wondered just what God was up to, why God believed he deserved a hell more bizarre than human imagination could invent.

The besieged characters in *The Thing* had figured out a way to electrocute their nemesis, cooking it down to a stew of vegetation.

Moral was, Sherard thought, when the going got tough . . . the tough set the table and had dinner.

He and Riklis had cooked up a plan of their own, but Riklis probably was a goner. And Sherard was deathly cold. He couldn't feel his fingers beneath the flotation vest. He had lost touch with his only hope of survival.

The were-beast's claws gripped his throat. The Magician, always theatrical, taking a little time, wanting Sherard to break emotionally before he died, to scream and scream again.

Her name was Sigrid.

Sherard hadn't thought about his first love in a long while. But hers was a fine memory to hold in his mind during those few seconds before the muscles of his throat were severed and his life blew out through torn arteries.

Still the Magician hesitated, as if he had reconsidered killing Sherard. Or had another fate in mind. His own, perhaps.

Something bit into Sherard's numbed forebrain like an egg-laying insect.

Unlike the rest of him, Sherard's sense of smell wasn't frozen. He caught the reek of acetone an instant before the captain of the *Stella Salamis,* more dead than alive, loomed behind the were-beast. Riklis was tethered to a line of his own. It kept him from being swept down the tilted, back-broke deck in the next torrent of sea and washed overboard.

He held an open can of highly flammable acetone above his head.

The were-beast sniffed it too. It turned its misshapen head with a cry of rage.

The table to which Sherard had tied himself was coming free of the deck. The entire house of the *Stella Salamis* seemed to be pulling apart in the sledgehammer seas. The light from whatever ship was out there appeared again to reveal the dark, sensual eyes in the head of the were-beast, a grotesque reminder of what and whom Lincoln Grayle had been but could never be again.

With a snarl of arrogance the were-beast released Sherard's neck and swung its claws while holding on to its perch with the human hand.

Riklis's head was crushed to pulp above the brow line as the gallon of acetone showered the were-beast. Blinded by the volatile solvent, it howled in agony.

Riklis vanished in a fresh incoming deluge. The swallowing sea surged from all directions, though doorways and splitting bulkheads.

Sherard, groping beneath the flotation vest, found the butt of the Kilgore flare gun hidden there. It was loaded with a twenty-thousand-candlepower parachute flare.

The table was set. A moment or two left, he hoped. Time to turn up the heat on the main course.

He yanked the Kilgore from beneath his vest and fired point-blank at the were-beast, just before the table was wrenched loose in an upheaval of deck plates and washed toward a widening breach in the starboard bulkhead.

The last thing Sherard saw was a livid explosion in which the were-beast's shape was revealed like a glow-in-the-dark skeleton painted on a child's Halloween costume. Then it disappeared in an expanding explosion like dawn in paradise, or a beacon atop a watchtower in hell. Then Sherard, still holding on to his pistol, rode a jet surge along with the uprooted table into darkness, powerless in that crush of water.

Yet he sensed that somehow, in spite of being engulfed, thrust down into drowning depths, he was meant to survive.

No. Not just survive.

To reign.

JUBILATION COUNTY, GEORGIA · JULY 23, 1926 · 1740 HOURS MOBIUS TIME

Over HERE!" Patrick called, in his creaky elevator of a voice.

He was somewhere beyond a precariously stacked still-life composed of busted machine parts, galvanized scrap metal, iron trusswork, and sheaves of old barrel hoops in Wick Hooser's junkyard, all of it coated with a fine red dust. The junkyard was by Stinking Weasel Creek, which was only a weedy trickle at summer's baking zenith. The temperature at this hour was, as always, oppressive, an unbreathing ninety-six degrees.

The feminine half of Mordaunt's soul, who called herself Delilah and who was getting around in Gwen's sultry purloined body, had paused to remove a shoe and shake some grit from the toe. She slapped a mosquito taking blood from the side of Gwen's neck and felt something hard, like a larger piece of grit, beneath the skin. She didn't think anything of it and caught up to Patrick, whom she found in that part of Wick's junkyard devoted to abandoned time machines.

There was an oleophilic globe that flinched and hissed when approached; two metallic plates that revolved in the air and passed mysteriously through each other like the joining and unjoining of magician's rings; there were armatures of highly polished brass and copper coils and cogwheels and levers. There was a child's treehouse with TIME MACHINE—KEP OUT painted over the doorway. Patrick had often wondered about that one. All standing useless now, the pride of beings who had invented them on far-flung worlds, then taken them out—so to speak—for a little spin.

Straight into Jonas Fresno's notorious Vortex.

And then there was the red '55 Chevy Nomad.

Patrick's expression was habitually glum whenever he circled the Nomad, kicked a softening tire, brushed off a little dust. The same routine every day. Usually he sat inside for a little while, dreaming of home, idly turning the key in the ignition. On, off. On again. No spark. No thrum of life beneath the hood. Vacancy in his heart, a drip of tears from red-rimmed eyes.

Today his expression was a kindling of delight and awe as he beckoned to Delilah.

"Here's a NEW one!" His mouth was ajar as he looked up and up, at a multihued timeship looking not unlike a huge cellophane butterfly, wings quaking slightly as if reacting to the solar winds. The centerpiece of the magnificently spindly machine was a golden seat, infant-size if judged by human proportions, occupied by an also-spindly creature that resembled an inky scrawl of blood vessels in the human brain. The creature was held in place by girdles of scintillating space debris, like those that compose the rings of Saturn. It did not appear to have survived the jaunt from wherever or whatever to the center of the Vortex: the common fate of many time-travelers unsuited to the torpor of a Jubilation County summer's day.

"*Look you, boy,*" Delilah said, standing beside Patrick and gazing full-bewildered at this marvel. "*If Time's hand dost stay the change from day to day to ending doom, which thou swear'st to be true of your unlikely world, how cometh something 'new,' as you proclaim this nollygost?*"

"'Nollygost'? That's a good word," Patrick said happily. "Well, as Gwen exPLAINED it to me, all *these* are allowable uh-uh-un-nomalies. Because of the Vortex that pulls them in from"—Patrick circled a freckled hand overhead—"just about everywhere."

Delilah looked around at the array of time machines. She scratched the itch of the mosquito bite on the side of Gwen's neck. The rake of nails produced a little blood.

"*A way in, but no escape? FIE! Be it riddle or paradox, I say 'tis false. Such beliefs are the poor baggage of poppinjays, untutor'd boys of little kidney. I am DELILAH! Neither couched nor enfeebl'd by cunning paradox, born not to fret in my own grease, bawl my sorrows to the scowling Fates! I am Delilah! Bearing brain to wither confoundest argument, armored by degree of will known only to the Amazon. Mark me, I am purpos'd to see the enfolding Vortex, and study on't. Thus to reverse the mystery and bid Time release us from this stagnant abode. Like kingly Alex on swift Bocephus, I shall not be long detained.*"

"Do you really think—? I mean, GWEN explained that the Vortex is like a black hole, only, you know, it's actually brass and much smaller. But the same PRINciple applies in a microregion of space/time."

When Delilah let go of her towering temper, it was a sight that reminded him too vividly of spiders in spun clouds of freakish hair.

"*Prate not to me another syllable! No more pimpering tattle! Hence, I say! Scrofulous sulk, pewling of diddled strumpet, importunate buzzling!*"

"Oh, jeez," Patrick lamented. "Problem is, you see, I'm n-not even sure the Vortex is open this t-time of the day."

Fresno's Vortex was on the other side of Jubilation County in a rural area settled largely by Negroes. Patrick had discovered, before they left the junkyard, a flat tire on the taxi that needed patching, so with one thing or another and Delilah looking daggers at him because of the delay, it was after six o'clock Mobius Time when he pulled up near a 1926 Franklin sports coupe that glowed in its spiff newness as shadows from the pine grove around them lengthened and the tone and mood of the day acquired a more mellow, golding patina.

Patrick, an antique-auto buff, gazed reverently for a few moments at the rakish, boat-tail speedster. Without looking under the engine cowling he knew it had an air-cooled six-cylinder engine. This was one of the models with a heavily chromed, dummy radiator grille. The all-wood chassis was painted apple green. Pat didn't think Jonas Fresno had ever driven it very far, but he was too bashful to ask.

"*I mark there seems to be a fit upon thee,*" Delilah said impatiently.

Patrick roused himself from his appreciative swoon, then hopped out to go around the fuming front end of the taxi to open the door for Delilah. He hadn't let on to her—tried to say as few words as possible only when spoken to—but he came every night to the Vortex, in order to retrieve his besotted uncle Mickey and guide him stumbling into the backseat of the same taxi he had no business driving around in now. An allowable anomaly, for sure. Otherwise the world as he and all of Jubilation County's citizens knew it to be would have imploded the instant he turned the key in the ignition, before he could drive the taxi away from its parking spot on the south side of the courthouse.

But he wondered with a run of shudders and gooseflesh what could happen if he wasn't careful to have the taxi back in its customary place before that all-important twelfth stroke of midnight from the clock in the courthouse tower.

Delilah looked at him, looked all around in disbelief and fulminating displeasure. Eyes settling finally on the ramshackle, nearly windowless, and unpainted honky-tonk with a line of fatted crows idling on the swaybacked tin roof.

"*What is this hovel I see before me?*"

Patrick drew in a fortifying breath of air.

"This is it! Jonas Fresno's Vortex." He endured a coldly lifted eyebrow. "I mean, I never actually described what the Vortex was like, DID I? But it's the real thing, you'll see."

"*Unconscionable caitiff! Must I call 'pon the crows to dig at thy liver?*"

"Caitiff" sounded like some breed of big dog to Patrick. He was sure that it was better than being called "pewling of diddled strumpet," which sounded just plain nasty.

"Come on inside. Jonas is here." He laughed uneasily. "I guess he's ALways here. So if you have questions you wanta—"

But Delilah had turned her back on him and crossed her arms. The crows were leaving the roof as she angrily tapped a foot on the rutted red clay of the doorway. Six bombastic crows flapping fell wings that flashed in rosy sunlight. Their caws hard mirth to silence the trilling of other birds nearby.

"No, wait! You have to LISten to Jonas! Listen to him and the others; then you'll *know*!"

Patrick cowered from the incoming glide of the largest of the crows. As it passed over the showroom–perfect Franklin Sport coupe, the crow thoughtfully released a glob of whitewash aimed at the stylishly vented hood, as yet unsoiled by the merest film of red Georgia earth. Patrick had wrapped his arms around his head, forgetfully leaving his liver open to attack, but even as he ducked to avoid the rush of the malevolent bird he saw the pud of shitbomb miss the speedster.

Although *miss* wasn't the right word. The pud simply stopped falling and remained suspended a few inches above the engine cowling before side-slipping gooily as if down the slope of an invisible tent covering the fender-mounted spare tire. It spattered harmlessly on the hard ground. Where, Patrick now noticed as the crow circled and again glided toward him, the red clay around the coupe already was plentifully marked with past droppings.

Delilah also had followed the shitbomb as it went astray. She jammed both little fingers of Gwen's hands inelegantly into the corners of Gwen's mouth and whistled shrilly. The threatening crows departed in vocal disappointment. Delilah wiped some spit and looked at Patrick forgivingly.

"*'Twas base of me to act so hastily,*" she said. "*I am now content there be a touch o' antick to this place.*"

"I TRIED to—"

From inside Jonas Fresno's seedy honky-tonk came the sound of a trumpet, fingered with such authority and soaring élan that even the crows flocking to roost in a nearby tree fell silent, deferring to the majesty of a golden horn.

Delilah listened with cocked head; presently Gwen's toes began to tap a more agreeable rhythm. Patrick's anxieties became muted. When the trumpet paused, Delilah frowned and addressed the unseen hornman.

"O! Pray do not resolve that strain! I am smitten. Take breath, and play again the hot condition of thy blood."

"That was Jonas," Patrick informed her, and enthused, "He's just practicing. Great, DON'cha think? But wait until you hear them all. The Jubilation Joymakers. My unca Mickey calls them the 'Hotlicks Six.'"

"Hot licks?"

"Jonas on trumpet, natch. Shadrach Delhomme on bass, Delaware Joe Parker on trombone, Roscoe Raines on skins and ivories, Saint Vincent Poitrine on clarinet, with Jimmie 'Ducks' Clyborn playing banjo. C'mon, we'll go inside. It's early yet but we can have ourselves a couple of sodas, I'm DYing of thirst. How about you and, uh, Gwen?"

"Yea, we do thirst. Yet I know not what you mean by 'soda.' A goodly sherris-sack, or stronger distillation?"

"'Strong stuff'? It's illegal, but the Vortex has that too. Only you have to be CAREful about drinking moonshine."

"'Moonshine'? It sounds most agreeable. We go hence, then, to the fellow that hath the gift of spheres in a bawdy, hallow'd horn."

Well, I dunno," Jonas Fresno said, making a circle with a long finger in a small spill of beer, then touching the finger to his lower lip. "We can play 'em down from the skies okay, been doin' jus' that for the longest time. But play 'em back up to where they comes from? Don't rightly know how to do that. Seein' as I can't 'zackly tell how I latches on to 'em in the fuss place. It be all in the horn. How it was made, and how it be played."

"But," Patrick said, popping a few boiled peanuts into his 7-UP, "you NEVer *had* to do it before! Because when they're in the Vortex, either the machines or their inventors get damaged. Me and Uncle Mickey made it through the Vortex okay. I mean, it's not all that different from New Jersey around here. But the NOmad won't start anymore."

He looked unhappily at his uncle Mickey, soused as usual at the far end of the bar, face in hands and mumbling to himself.

With Gwen's hand Delilah irritably scratched at the side of her neck where there was still a lump and a rash from the mosquito bite. She looked from Patrick to Jonas Fresno, fascinated but perplexed, biding her time.

"Aw, honey," Letty Fresno said to Delilah as she approached their table, carrying a platter in each hand. Baby-backs, hot corn bread, and vinegar greens. "You ought not be scratchin' thataway, give yo'self a fever in the blood befo' you knows it." She set the platters down and leaned over the table for a closer look. "Umm-umm." Delilah eyed her warily. "I gots blue ointment in the kitchen, good fo' all kinds of cuts and burns. Draws the torment right out. But go 'head, chil', eat yo'self somethin' fuss, you is lookin' half starved to me."

Jonas Fresno stroked his pure-white Uncle Sam goatee and looked at Letty.

"Woman, you done studied on such things. You think it could be?"

"What that now?" She was a tall lean freckled high-yellow woman with a crooked back and flesh like beeswax, or summer squash ripened on the vine. On the back of her head she had a tight bun of hair as white as Jonas's beard. Her left eyelid was sewn down tautly over an empty socket. On that parchmentlike lid was tattooed the blue facsimile of a wide-awake eye. Through the piratical flap of skin (Patrick had observed) a light sometimes gleamed like the mysterious lens of a far-gazer.

"Meanin', toot time-travelers—like these yere folk—back to they's own time 'n' place?"

The idea startled, then seemed to intrigue Letty Fresno. She didn't comment right away. Patrick held his breath. Delilah watched her with an expression of suppressed mirth, and had another sip of moonshine from a nearly emptied cup.

Letty made up her mind. She shook her head regretfully.

"No. It don't seem possible to me."

"Why NOT?" Patrick said, dismayed, his dream of home vanishing like soap bubbles.

"Oh, lamb. Don't you see? If you done come here in somethin', no matter what kind of contraption it be—and Jonas and me, we done seen a mighty lot of odd contraptions fall outer the sky when his mighty horn reach up and nab 'em—" Letty chuckled. "What I be sayin', you jess cain't traipse on back to where you been, if'n you don't gots nothin' to ride there *in.*"

Jonas nodded. "Makin' sense to me." He glanced at the eight-by-eight-foot bandstand raised a few inches above the honky-tonk's warped old pine-board floor. The bandstand was crowded with instrument cases, an upright piano, a drum set, and a standing bass fiddle. Saint Vincent Poitrine, an elf of a man in shirtsleeves and a brown fedora, had appeared from nowhere to clear his throat, insert the mouthpiece of his shining clarinet, and begin to noodle. The sundown light coming through tall plantation shutters behind the bandstand illuminated a standing microphone as if it were a round gold-toned web woven by a metal spider.

Delilah hiccupped loudly. They all looked at her, Patrick through eyes that were brimming over. Delilah smiled a little giddily.

"Jonas—" Letty said, with a formidably censorious brow.

"Aw, now. She done axed me fo' the good stuff. 'Shine ain't 'zackly a ladylike 'freshment, but I done figured, what harm?"

"So y-you're saying we're STUCK here?" Patrick wailed at Letty, his hopes betrayed once more.

"*Moonshine? It is potation fair-named, that with the sting of physick doth bring forth humours of the blood and merrily prick the senses. Such amusement I have not had in a pissing-while! Look you, goat-bearded fellow; dost apprehend what bodies forth upon the empty air? O riotous visions! I see ten thousand, nay, ten millions of twinkling lights all raving before me, like the eyes of Holofernes proffer'd on a serving plate.*"

"My, my, how she can talk that talk," Jonas marveled.

"Oh, great," Patrick said sullenly. "Now she's as soused as Unca Mickey."

On the bandstand, Shadrach Delhomme, beside whose great shapeless bulk the standing bass looked almost cello-size, began to find rhythm of his own. Knuckly old hands love-thumping the mellowed curvy wood, fingers thrumming taut guts.

"'*Soused*'?" Delilah hiccupped again, a hand going to Gwen's belly. "*Sure, I know thy meaning. But always beware: Delilah hath wit to spare.*" And she winked at them.

"Don't nobody want to be eatin' my good ribs and corn bread?" Letty complained. "Jonas, here's Roscoe now, and Ducks too. It be gettin' on time fo' the broadcast."

"I'm eatin," Jonas said. He smacked his lips and tucked a saucy napkin under his chin. Patrick began to chew lugubriously on a rib bone. Only Delilah's plate went unfilled. She was scratching furiously again at the wound on Gwen's neck.

"Honey, I can see that itch 'bout to devil the life out o' you. Come on back to the kitchen, then, let me doctor it up. Then you can pay 'tention to yo' appetite instead."

"*It hath me tetchy,*" Delilah acknowledged, "*and burthened as if 'twere angry canker. Mistress, my thanks.*" And she followed Letty to the kitchen.

LAS VEGAS · OCTOBER 31 · 8:20 P.M.

Devon, look, it's her!"

Harlee and her best friend were passing the Gallery of Western Art on their way to the Italian restaurant across the canal within the Venetian Hotel, where Harlee's crew customarily gathered for dinner on Thursday nights. The occasion at the gallery was an invitation-only show. Smart-casual dress, with some Houtie-style, rodeo-parade regalia optional.

Eden Waring had augmented her hair with a fall; she was wearing a black mantilla and triangular native-art gold earrings with a short-sleeved blouse, green sash, and ankle-length black skirt, but Harlee hadn't had to look twice to pick her out of the crowd. In fact, Eden had seldom been off her mind for the past couple of days.

"It sure is," Devon said, and they stopped along with other strollers on the concourse to take in the festive scene. "Looking bloody marvelous, I must say. But what is she doing with a cane, has she injured herself?"

Harlee didn't reply. She was laser-focused on Eden. A scowl crept onto her face. Below them a gondola went by, the gondolier singing a tenor aria that echoed from the vault of the faux St. Mark's Square.

After a minute of silence Harlee said, her piss-and-vinegar expression replaced by a look of wry resolve, "Devon, why don't you go on to Canaletto's? I'll be there in twenty minutes."

"What are you going to do?"

"If fate has brought Eden and me together, must be a good reason, don't you think?"

"Harlee—it's called playing with F-I-R-E."

"No, no, Bronc said I should buddy up to the Avatar! He made it a priority, in fact. He wants to turn Waring over to Marcus Wool-wine for the good doctor's brand of R and R."

"Bronc has a fucking screw loose."

Harlee said in her breathless, brainless-bombshell voice, "But I *always* do what Bronc wants, like a good li'l scout."

"'Twas only yesterday you wanted to kill him."

"Still do," Harlee said, being Harlee again. "Oh yes. Bronc came close to shooting off my left ear. I'm still half deaf on that side. He made me wet my bed! Bronc's horseplay with his .45 moved him all the way up to number two on my shit list, but Eden Waring is still numero uno. Woolwine isn't going to get his hands on her. Rest assured. Eden Waring is *mine.*"

"But—you aren't ready to—"

"Will be soon. Matter of fact, I think we'll drive up to Ferdie Younger's place tomorrow. He called me a couple of days ago to say he had something new and rare to show me. Good old Ferdie. He said the pain that his new little friends inflict is—it's just so fucking incredible, the victims beg for death. The venom of those nasties consists of eleven different chemicals and enzymes that, among other things . . ." Harlee paused, letting the suspense build, ". . . dissolve human flesh."

"Harlee! We are about to have our dinner."

Harlee turned her head to look somberly at Devon.

"But that would be a fair payback, don't you think, for the agonies the Great One must still suffer?"

"Yes. I feel his pain too, Harlee." Devon sighed. "Whatever you have in mind. I simply don't relish hearing the gory details."

"But it's what we *do,* love. Have always done. Will do again . . . and again. Of *course* we sometimes feel sympathy for some of those souls who have recklessly made their lives dispensable; we're not inhuman monsters." Harlee looked back at the gallery, Eden's mantilla topsail above the crowd. "There's no harm chatting with her. It will make access easier when her time does come. I want to look into her eyes. I want *her* to look, in all innocence and unknowing, into *my* eyes."

"You don't have a crush on her, do you?" Devon asked suspiciously.

"In a complex way, I suppose I do. It's almost inevitable, a part of the age-old syndrome. The captive and her jailer. The stalker and the stalked. I get delicious chills."

"As long as you don't get burned. How are you going to manage, though? It looks as if they're being rather strict about invitation-only."

"You silly. I may have forgotten my invitation, but I *did* remember to bring my checkbook."

Eden deftly plucked a crab roll from a passing caterer's tray and nibbled while listening to Cody's father, Eloy Olds, talk his way through part of the family genealogy. He'd sired seven children with two wives. Five of his married children had thus far provided him with seventeen grandchildren. As Eloy had but seventy-two well-lived years, he said he was looking forward to at least a baker's dozen more while he still had the faculty to remember all their names.

"Course, I'm losin' brain cells now faster than hell is gainin' politicians. Come from a sizable family yourself, Eden?"

"No, I'm an only child."

Eloy snagged the arm of a caterer and handed over his empty glass. "Bull Run, straight up, son." Eloy was a towering man in his dress boots. He carried enough gut to keep him back on his bulldog-ger heels most of the time. He had an untamed handlebar mustache, a thick sun-silvered head of hair cut like a thatched roof, a beefeater complexion, and one droopy eyelid that gave him a droll look as he peered down his weather-pocked nose at her.

"That an heirloom walking stick you have with you?"

"I think it's probably very old. It belongs to my—to a dear friend. He's from Kenya. He lent it to me because my knee goes out on me from time to time."

"Kenya? Did some huntin' there one time. Met Mr. Hemingway. He autographed me a book a' his'n. I think I've read durn near all he ever wrote. Agatha Christie too, particularly the Poirots, but I never had the honor of knowin' her. Well, I read a lot for pleasure, but you know, they say if a man stays mentally active, it keeps the little gray cells from dryin' out. But chess or games a' chance don't appeal. Keep myself amused, I make up these little songs when I find myself in the saddle for a long stretch."

"Daddy's had three of his tunes on the gospel-music charts," Cody said, pausing on his circuit of the gallery. "Which one hit the top ten on *Billboard*'s list, Eloy?"

"That was 'Jesus Hot-Wired My Heart (and I'm drivin' straight to heaven)'."

He had a voice that carried, despite being near basso in quality. A woman with blue eyes in a Navajo face and a straight fall of hair to below the small of her back turned her head with a smile and sang in a Dolly Parton soprano:

> *"Back on the road to glory,*
> *And I know his way is right."*

Eloy did a slight double take, then came back with:

> *"Lost my key to the heavenly*
> *kingdom*
> *And my soul was out of gas."*

And the woman sang:

> *"But Jesus got me up and runnin'*
> *Now I'm travelin' Angel-class."*

The man she was with, slim in a dark suit and a bolo tie, was a tenor. The three of them harmonized, shutting down most of the conversations in the packed gallery.

> *"Well, the devil's shoutin'*
> *'Detour!'*
> *Yes he's a tempting sight.*
> *But I'll see pearly gates*
> *a-flashin'*
> *In my high beams tonight!"*

"You can tell we're not a stuffy bunch," Cody said, grinning at Eden.

"Nikki Lea!" Eloy said, peering through the crowd. "That you, honey?"

"Put on your glasses, Daddy."

"Didn't have no idea you was gonna be here."

"Daddy, I told you twice on the phone I was headin' up to Carmel for the weekend. My old roomie from Arizona State is fixin' to marry again."

"That would be the Korean gal with the mustang temper? Shoot. Somebody oughter tell the groom to start lacin' up his combat boots."

"Having a good time?" Cody asked Eden.

"I've got a mad crush on your daddy," she said sweetly. "You can go away. Call me sometime." Eden suppressed a mild belch with her fist. "And those delicious crab rolls are making a pig out of me."

"How about a beer?"

"No, I'll stick with champagne."

"You can have mine," Harlee Nations said cheerily. "I haven't touched it yet."

Eden glanced at her, mildly startled. She hadn't been aware of the girl, who was standing at her left elbow and just a little behind Eden. Seemed to have appeared in a faint aura of pixie dust, or maybe that was a visual effect from the champagne she'd already drunk. Eden looked back at Cody as he squeezed her shoulder and moved on to work the room and sell paintings. Then she looked again at Harlee, who held the champagne flute out to her.

"Anyway," Harlee advised Eden, "I don't have any fatal diseases."

And not a filling in her teeth; her smile was a dazzler. Eden smiled back. "Sure doesn't look that way. Thanks."

"I'm Harlee. Not like the motorcycle, but with two *es*?"

"Gotcha. I'm Eve."

"Ohhhh—you know? I have always *loved* that name! It has such a peaceful sound, like a gentle wind blowing through trees. Like in the Garden of, you know, Eden."

Eden almost said *no shit* but held her tongue because Harlee didn't seem to be trying too hard or putting her on. Just her age, maybe, accounting for an earnest, unsophisticated poetic streak. Eden guessed that Harlee was about sixteen. Sage-green eyes and that vividly dimpled smile. A good tan for the end of October. Wholesome teen-model looks. She was wise enough to go easy on the eyeliner and lip gloss.

When Eden accepted the champagne flute, Harlee reached past her, stuck out her hand a little bashfully to Eloy Olds, and reintroduced herself. "I just love Christian rock. And old-time gospel music."

"You don't say. Are you born-again, girl?"

"No-o. Not exactly."

"Read your Bible?"

"Yes, sir, I do. Every day. You just have to have faith in terrible times like these. I could talk about Jesus all day! That is a *huge* diamond you're wearing, if you don't mind my saying."

"'Bout six karats, I'd allow."

"It looks pink in this light. Excuse me, just can't help myself. I love diamonds."

"Never met a young lady who didn't."

"Oh—I didn't *mean* anything. Now I'm embarrassed, Mr. Olds."

"You just call me Eloy. Nothin' to be embarrassed about. Diamonds was made for little beauties like yourself." A caterer brought Eloy his crystal tumbler of Bull Run bourbon. "Fetch Miss Harlee a glass of the bubbly," Eloy said, twinkling at her several degrees brighter than the flashy pink diamond. "You did say you was of drinkin' age, darlin'?"

Harlee hunched her shoulders slightly and looked down with an abashed smile.

"Only at weddings, sir."

"Well. Can't be no harm in havin' a sip or two in honor of Nikki Lea's friend, who is about to go 'round the course for the third time. That is, if it's okay with your folks." Eloy looked around. "Where they be at?"

"I'm by myself. I was passing by outside with—friends, and I—I've always loved Western art, so—" Harlee peeked around, then looked up in a conspiratorial manner at Eloy, "I snuck in."

Eloy rumbled with laughter. "We won't tell nobody."

Harlee had charm aplenty, Eden noted, and used it with care. She relied on that great smile to light up her immediate surroundings. And she could wear clothes: a nifty Hermès number tonight, basic black, with a coral cashmere sweater around her shoulders. Just a kid. But she made Eden, age twenty-two, feel antique and a little dreary. She drank half the champagne in the glass Harlee had given her.

Eloy had slipped off his diamond pinkie ring in order to let Harlee have a better look at it. Her face was alight with gemstone passion. Eloy's face glowed a little redder, more pridefully, than it had before Harlee showed up. Talk about charmed. She did seem to have an easy way with men of a dignified age. Eden's ears were ringing as she finished her third glass of champagne in a single swallow. She smiled but said little even when Harlee roped her back into the conversation. It slowly dawned on Eden that, unfair as her judgment might be, there was just something about Harlee she didn't care for. And no, she was not a bit jealous of the girl's verve and flawless good looks.

By the time the party was winding down and Cody returned to them, it seemed that Eloy had included Harlee in their dinner plans for the evening.

Spectacular, Eden thought a little glumly.

She drained another glass of champagne while it was still available.

Waiting at their banquette table in Canaletto with the other girls in the crew of Fetchlings, all supernally lovely and all but Nic shimmering with hybrid vigor, Devon received a text message on her cell phone from Harlee.

"We should go ahead and eat," Devon said, dropping her Nokia back into her clutch purse. "Harlee can't make it tonight."

"What's going on?" Nic demanded. In one of her surly moods. Her jaw was swollen on the left side. She bit down on a breadstick and winced. "She-it! Next time I do me a full-body makeover, it'll be without wisdom teeth."

"Is Harlee okay?" Reese asked.

Devon smiled calmly despite a pinch of unease. "Yes. Something came up." From her seat in the restaurant Devon could tell that the party at the gallery was over. The guests had begun to drift out onto the shopping concourse that bordered the indoor canal. She didn't see Harlee. "Not to worry. She'll tell us all about it tomorrow."

I gots a good hold on it now," the one-eyed Letty Fresno said to Delilah. She had been fishing with needle-nose tweezers in the expanded wound on Gwen's neck that a mosquito invisibly had begun, sucking its gullet full. Gwen's hands took a hard purchase on the pump handle of the sink, Delilah moaning softly *aye aye aye* through gritted teeth.

Then the buried thing popped out and Letty, astounded, studied it, turning up the flame of an acetylene lantern: it was a bit of metal or ceramic-coated metal smaller in diameter than the head of a thumbtack.

"Reckon how that bitty thing come to be buried in yo' neck with only a trace of a scar? Never have seen the like befo'."

Delilah silently requested and Gwen poured more 'shine for them in their tin cup. While they drank the potent stuff Delilah pondered the pill-like object. She had no comment.

Letty handed Gwen a wad of cotton cut from clean flour sacking to press against the oozing wound. She took the 'shine jug away.

"Watch yo'self. The hangover be worse than a nest o' yellajackets let loose in yo' brain. Now hold tight to the bandage while's I make a poultice for that li'l wound. Three–four days, oughter heal jes' fine."

In the nearly empty honky-tonk the Jubilation Joymakers, propelled by Jonas Fresno's hard-driving trumpet, rollicked through "My Baby Don't Wear No Shoes." Letty's expression was pure bliss, as if she hadn't heard them play that number on an infinite number of nights before this one.

"My *man*," she said. "Ain't never been a finer trumpet in all the realm of God Almighty! It do light the sun, uh-wah-hum. It paint the moon and the flowers of paradise. The *Mona Lisa* too."

"*Verily, it doth impose motion on this hive of slumbers,*" Delilah observed. After polishing off yet another large cup of 'shine, Gwen's eyes, which had grown hazy, began to roll a little. Fortunately she was sitting down.

"Uh-wah-huh-uh-huh!" Letty sang, nodding and switching her hips while her fingers prepared a concoction of smears from several odd-size jars she took from a cabinet. Delilah studied the implant removed from Gwen's neck. Gwen's eyelashes fluttered. The button gave her the jumps, as if she were connected to the distant source of an eerie power. With a fingertip she stroked Dr. Marcus Woolwine's MFIU (Magnetic Flux Inhibitor Unit) as Delilah tried to divine its internal intricacies.

"What it be tellin' you?" Letty asked softly, applying the poultice to Gwen's neck. And, with a touch of sorceress wiles: "Tell me what you be seein', chile. Ol' Letty knows you be seein' somethin' mighty interestin'."

Gwen was pale, but she had stopped trembling.

"*Ravens,*" said Delilah. "*Thick as old enemies, that rise like blood of spring blooming in a gusher. Faith, I am poxed, bearing scars of vile enchantment, too long with a malady that hath no name! My might, my hope, but a drifting planet in aeons of Andromeda. We must be join'd, and soon, within the embattled citadel. If not, our cause is lost.*"

"Got yo'self a young man where you comes from?" Letty asked sympathetically. She taped another square of cotton sack over the now-sterile wound. Gwen's body trembled anew, with concern and passion. She closed her left hand on the tiny MFIU.

"*Aye, the citadel be manly, of good bone and comely flesh for beguilement's sake. But 'tis mere accoutrement, a player on the mortal stage. The sunder'd soul is what I spake of, scepter and crown. Which, once united, rules the empty paradise of man's eclipse.*"

"Hm. Don't rightly know if I grasp yo' meanin'."

Delilah smiled sadly and shrugged Gwen's shoulders.

"*Conjure mother—for I know thee to be one with the antick arts— I speak of my life in twilight drear. My blood is black, my tears but snow whilst twin souls dwell apart, made separate by abyss of flaw like mirror crack'd.*"

Following the roust-the-house syncopation of "My Baby Don't

Wear No Shoes," the Jubilation Joymakers segued to a bluesy but still swinging mode, introduced by Jimmie "Ducks" Clyborn doubling on barrelhouse piano. Delaware Joe Parker's trombone backed him up with gliding swoops before Jonas Fresno stepped in, low-down but with a touch of wounded swagger to his legendary horn: "Rat Alley Moan." Roscoe Raines's vocals were a raw shout, accompanied by his thunderous percussion—like something heard pounding away in six feet of grave on a stormy cemetery midnight.

> *"Well Well my momma leavin'*
> *me now*
> *Don't give me no money*
> *Say I don't need that cocaine no-how!"*

Letty studied the puzzled, downcast face of Gwen the doppelganger. Gwen's hand was pressed against her solar plexus.

"So you needs to kick this starbox and find yo' way home." Letty shook her head. "Wisht I had some good news to tell." She nodded to the blues shout filling their ears. "I does know somethin' 'bout this-yere time-travel business. It be hard, sho' 'nuf, or any fool could likely do it." Gwen bit her lip and nodded. "You see, 'time' be sticky stuff. Like that big ol' cobweb hangin' in the corner there I keeps meanin' to broom down? Lose yo' way in time, jes' might get tangled up fo'ever. Now, you takes a time machine, no matter how queer-lookin' some be to *our* eyes, they all works the same way: like a radio. Uh-huh. Thas's truth. You tunes in to where it is you wants to go, then ride that wave, honey. Got somethin' to do with how far them waves travel, you una'stand. And how many of 'em they be. Reckon nobody can say fo' sure. The Jubilation Joymakers, they don't go travelin' through time, but they music does. Travels on 'n' on through the heavenly cosmos, 'cause it don't never fade nor die. They gots a wave be strictly all they own. *Powerful* when they's hittin' they best licks. Now that wave, it cross over many another wave out there somewheres, know what I'm sayin'? Gets tangled up . . . and that's how I believe them time-travel folks go astray." Unable to refrain from getting with the music, Letty cakewalked around her kitchen. "Should the likes of a traveler-wave run afoul of 'Bear Cat Papa' or 'Stay Away from My Chickenhouse' way way out there in the dark lonesome, look out! Lawdy me, *how* they do come! A-tumblin' and a-skitterin' down like flies into the Jubilation wave-web, bless they uncanny bodies an' strange li'l hearts. Jes' you listen to them mens play! Oh, they pumpin' it up fiercely now! I hears 'em ever night, mind; still that music fit to raise the short hairs of a dead mans on his coolin' board. It gets me to sashayin' thisaway. And thataway. Mercy!"

At last out of breath and strut, she left off for a glass of well water at the sink. Letty sipped her water and splashed some on her over-heated brow and gazed contentedly out the kitchen window. There was a full moon above the spear-tip pines like a great yellow pearl in a buccaneer's treasure cave. Stars beaming their own attractive magic, beckoning to the proud, the unwary.

"Funny thing," Letty resumed in a confidential tone, "and I ain't told this to all that many folks—Jonas and me, we got us selves a time machine. Uhhh-huh." Letty looked back over one shoulder. There was a light like a twitching electrified filament behind her sewn-down lid. "What you think 'bout that? Well, it be jes' a-settin' 'round the Vortex goin' on near fo'ever. But they ain't no place Jonas and me rather be. Jubilation County suit us *fine.* Anyhow, we don't know what make it go. Only know it mus' be a time machine. 'Cause of all the clocks inside, and gadgets galore." Letty whistled low "And they's somethin' else." She leaned toward them. "A scary, grinnin' thing! Be made of crystal, reckon. But glowin' like the devil's own two eyes."

Gwen's head, which had been nodding, was still. She looked more or less alertly at the old conjure woman.

"I be mos' 'fraid to look at it my ownself. 'Fraid o' what I might see deep down in them empty sockets." Gwen's lips parted and her breathing quickened as Letty turned her face away from them, grinning her own, skull-like sly grin. "You could maybe have a peek at it, if it is you ain't believin' me."

Gwen fell off her chair, wobbled to her feet, braced herself against the table.

"I believe you!" It was Gwen speaking for a change, her voice slurred. But her eyes focused on Letty and she trembled with excitement. "Show me—your machine! If it's wha' I think it is, I can make that sumbitch *work*!"

LAS VEGAS · OCTOBER 31 · 9:40 P.M.

Halloween night in Vegas didn't compare to New Year's Eve for revels, but still there were a fair number of costumed visitors to the Venetian Hotel's upscale restaurant row and casino. Inside Emeril's, at a table near the one occupied by Cody Olds and his guests, a dozen people were dressed for a masque.

Eden's absence from the table had stretched to nearly fifteen minutes, and with the arrival of their main courses Cody frowned and looked concerned. Harlee caught his eye.

"Want me to check on her?"

"Maybe that would be a good idea."

Harlee found the women's lounge empty except for Eden, who was in the rearmost stall. The door was closed. Harlee rapped discreetly.

"Eve? It's me. Dinner's here. You doing all right? Cody was getting worried about you."

"A little stomach upset. Touch of the flu, or something. I'll be right there."

"I don't have anything with me but some Motrin," Harlee said. "Could it be that?"

"No. I just finished my last period." Eden rose from the toilet seat and flushed. She came out slowly, licking her underlip. She had a wad of toilet tissue in one fist. She had tried to wipe all the blood off her neck, but without a mirror she'd left a couple of streaks, one down to her collarbone.

"Omigod, what HAPpened?" Harlee said, taking hold of her by an elbow.

"I dunno. Just started bleeding for no reason."

"You're a little wobbly. Sit down over here, Eve."

She led Eden to a plush-cushioned bench in an alcove, helped herself to a linen towel from a stack beside dual gold sinks, wet the towel, and returned to Eden. She gently removed what blood remained, looked for a wound. There wasn't one. It was as if she had bled from her pores. Harlee was perplexed, Eden rock-tense and downcast, hands clenched in her lap. She felt cold to Harlee.

Harlee bathed her cheeks and forehead with the warm wet towel. Eden smiled wanly at her.

"There's no cut," Harlee said, peering close. "I thought maybe your earring had a sharp edge. . . ."

"No."

"And you keep your nails short, like me. Was there a lot of blood?"

"Seemed like it."

"Nothing now. Did you . . . have you ever bled like this before?"

"I'm not one of *those,* Harlee."

"Oh! I didn't mean anything. I'm sorry."

"It's okay."

"Do you want to go home? I don't think Cody can get away right now, but I could take you."

"I don't want to abandon him. I'll be fine. Maybe nothing's going to happen after all."

Harlee looked sharply at her.

"What d'you mean?"

"Oh, nothing. I'm just feeling a little spooked. Spooky. But why not? It's Halloween, isn't it?" Eden smiled wryly.

Two women came into the lounge, chatting. Both wore harlequin-style masks. Harlee sat down beside Eden and put a hand on her wrist. The two women went into the stall reserved for the handicapped. They rustled around in there, giggling softly.

"You had a premonition, didn't you?" Harlee said quietly.

"Why do you say that?"

"I . . . this is hard to explain, but I pick up things about people. I'm only sixteen—I'll be seventeen in January—but even when I was just a little kid I had premonitions." Harlee, feeling emboldened and taking a chance that Eden wasn't a mind-fucker (among her other, documented talents) or had no peeping ability, made up a story on the spot. "When I was six and just starting school—I'd been in first grade a couple of weeks—one morning I refused to get on the school bus. I cried and threw a tantrum, like my mom was trying to feed me to a shredder. And you know? That day the school bus lost a tire and wobbled off a bridge down the hill from our house. A couple of my classmates drowned in the creek." Harlee fetched a convincing shudder. "I didn't see in my mind's eye what was going to happen to the bus. I just had a shuddery cold feeling, knowing something bad—I still cry whenever I—" And now for a few tears.

Eden looked sympathetically at her as Harlee carefully blotted her eyes.

"We do have something in common, I guess."

"You too? Somehow I was so *sure.* As soon as I saw you, Eve."

Harlee again blotted her tears with the towel that had Eden's blood on it. "I must be a mess," she moaned.

"No, you're not."

Harlee rested her head on Eden's shoulder, sniffing and wiping her nose, childlike, on the back of a wrist.

"Our dinner's probably getting stone cold. Did you order the fish too?"

"Uh-huh. But I'm not all that hungry."

One of the women in the handicapped stall was groaning. Harlee pressed a little closer to Eden. Trying to keep certain thoughts in the hideout cellar of her mind.

"I told you mine," she said. "Want to tell me yours?"

"I didn't say I had a premonition," Eden said guardedly.

"But you *did,* didn't you? And the bleeding—that was part of it?"

"I'm not a religious ecstatic, Harlee. But there are things about me I'd find difficult to explain to you."

After a few moments Harlee said, "That's okay. I just get so confused about myself, and lonely. Like I have the biggest secret in the world I can't possibly tell, either. I thought—you would be the one to understand."

"I'm a good listener, Harlee. Maybe this isn't the time or place."

"Does that mean someday you'll, like, trust me? Like best friends? And neither of us will feel so lonely anymore?"

"Let's see what happens, Harlee. Thanks for coming to my rescue. We ought to get back to the others, or I'll really have some explaining—"

The massive displacement they experienced as they were walking out of the women's lounge wasn't an explosion, although it rattled their bones. Nor was it like an earthquake, because the floor didn't rock and roll and the ornate ceiling didn't collapse on their heads. It was an extended optical effect, a dizzying space warp, as if they'd been shot in the wink of an eye to a funhouse chamber mounted on a gyroscope and filled with slidey mirrors, the sound effects therein like the roar of a turbulent sea.

The immediate result was vertigo. One of the masked women from the handicapped stall staggered past them bare to the waist, nipples like pink neon. She vomited on herself. Harlee clung fiercely to Eden, clawing for purchase as they too staggered giddily, fell down, got to their knees, toppled again. They heard screams and the *pops* of breaking glassware and, distantly, the hectic music of a Dixieland band going full-throttle.

The optical and aural effects lasted, perhaps, seven or eight seconds. Vertigo continued for a longer spell. There was serious barfing going on in Emeril's elegant restaurant. Those on their feet were reeling around like Bedlamites inventing a dance.

"What the *fuck* was that?" Harlee said. "The last time I—" Then she turned her head sharply aside to pitch her own cookies.

With an effort Eden kept her dinner salad down. She got slowly to her feet, bracing herself with the aid of Simba, her walking stick. Something came rolling across the floor toward her and she lurched aside, her knee twinging sharply; she was panicked as a child until she recognized a Halloween pumpkin with a goofy, gap-toothed smile carved on it.

Eden looked around, and felt her navel buzzing like a defective doorbell.

But almost as soon as she'd received the surefire signal that she and her doppelganger were about to become united again, the connection abruptly was broken. Leaving Eden feeling puzzled and still unsteady, with her mouth putrid-dry and her head thundering. Exactly as if she'd awakened from a binge with an all-time champ of a hangover.

J. P. O'Hara, ex-DEA and now deputy director of security at the Venetian, happened to be crossing the main lobby on his rounds, heading to the casino and restaurant row, when the phenomenon occurred.

Once his disordered senses, including depth perception, were fractionally restored, the first thing he focused on was a shimmering corona like an aurora borealis, extending nearly the full breadth of the concourse near the casino. The corona rose in a spire that seemed to pierce the sixty-five-foot frescoed ceiling. The spire was also ablaze, like an enormous stalagmite of ice with the sun shining through it. Mildly vaporous, it showered golden droplets. He thought a little dizzily, *Theatrical effect.* But way out of place here. And what had caused an immensely expensive replica of a doge's palace to waver like a match flame in a sudden breeze?

O'Hara shook his head a couple of times, wincing, his heart pumping into overdrive. He used his walkie as he glanced around for casualties, damage, terrorists with automatic weapons.

"All security, all security, main lobby on the double! Guests down. Guests down. We need medical! No, I don't know what the hell—no, no, couldn't have been an explosion. No smoke, no rubble. Condition is *orange.* Might be a diversion for a casino robbery. We're in lockdown, repeat, *lockdown.* Alert Metro but let's hold the god-damn SWATs until I get a read on this!"

He was stumbling toward the still-bright corona, weaving to avoid dozens of people prostrate along the concourse. But they all seemed to be stirring, sitting up. Half of them were being sick all over themselves. Panic? Not yet. Thank you, Jesus and Mary.

He felt steady enough on his pins to jog. The spire above the seething borealis, like Technicolor fog across the floor, was beginning to evanesce, spindrift in the air. If any of it was poisonous, the victims closest to the borealis didn't appear to be gassed.

O'Hara sidestepped puddles of vomit, trying to talk soothingly to the staggered or crawling victims. Thinking, *Lawsuits.* But who could say the hotel was liable? Not his problem anyway. The long lobby floor was an optical illusion in shades of yellow and brown marble: the illusion that one was climbing steps.

"Everybody stay down, just stay down please!" He spoke again to security control. "Hank—not sure what it was—is—but—hold on a sec—think I see—no, that can't be!"

But there it was as he approached the main entrance to the Venetian's casino. Dimly visible within the radiant borealis but—unmistakably— an antique motorcar. Not a sedan. It had racy lines. A mid-1920s sport coupe.

And he thought he saw a woman, shadowy beside the car. Or—his vision wasn't perfect yet—it could have been the shape of someone at the threshold of the casino, where there was a lot of milling around. Like wacky revelers in shadows and fog. He heard muted cries. But no hysteria yet.

The woman appeared to be holding something in the crook of an arm. An object with a radiance all its own. Like an oddly shaped jar filled with brilliant rubies.

Someone lurched against O'Hara. He looked away, two seconds, looked again for the ghostly woman. Shadows aplenty in the borealis, but she was gone, and so was the ruby light he had glimpsed.

Never mind. He had another, longer look at the antique car sitting just outside the casino floor. What a beauty. He felt both dazzled and a little angry. If the car was part of a show promo or some charity event, security had been left out of the know.

As the borealis continued to fade and a degree of calm spread, a red-haired boy, midteens probably, crawled unsteadily out of the speedster and leaned weakly against the open driver's door. Someone else, O'Hara saw, remained inside, not moving.

The boy raised his head and looked around. Still acting stunned. His voice had a squeaky break to it.

"Gwe-ENNNN?" he called. He took a couple of steps and stumbled against a man twice his size. The man wore a cream-colored Stetson and had that well-heeled, oilpatch look.

He caught Patrick and steadied him. "Hey, son, turn on your headlights," he said, laughing.

There was another one, same size, same Stetson. Identical twins. Family name Tustin. Val and— O'Hara shook his head, his brain still a little dopey, as if he'd spent four hours at the dentist. *Cleve* was the other twin. They were high rollers exclusive to the Venetian, therefore among thirty or so of the hotel's most valued guests.

Patrick took in the tall lookalike men and all the security, then glanced behind him at the casino, big as a carnival lot and in the thinning fog as unreal to his eyes as a trompe l'oeil painting.

"Is this your car?" O'Hara demanded.

Patrick looked vaguely at him and at the security badge. Inside the car, his uncle Mickey stirred and moaned softly.

"Hey, not so fast," Cleve Tustin said with a gold-lined smile. "We saw it first."

Val, who was still holding Patrick on his feet, said to O'Hara, "Mean to tell us the hotel don't own it?"

"Well—I—I—couldn't really say right this moment, Mr. Tustin; but if you and your brother are interested I'll certainly look into the matter of ownership."

"It's m-mine," Patrick said in a low tone. "MINE and my uncle Mickey's."

"What's your name?" O'Hara barked at Patrick. "And how did you get this car in here? You don't look old enough to— I think you'd better come with me, I want some answers right now!"

Val Tustin literally placed Patrick under his wing, and looked at O'Hara a shade coolly.

"Well, now. With all the fireworks under control, maybe you need to give the boy a little time to collect himself. Catch his breath. What did you say your name was, son?"

"P-P-Patrick."

"Pleased to know you, Patrick. I'm Val. This here's Cleve, the ugly twin. We collect rare cars. You ever laid eyes on a '26 Franklin coupe in showroom condition, Cleve? Me neither. Like to make you an offer, Patrick, you and your uncle. We could talk about it over dinner if that's agreeable to the two a you."

Patrick shuddered; his eyes squinched and tears fell.

"W-where am I?" he said, almost inaudibly. "ANother damn V-Vortex? This CAN'T be a real p-place."

The mysterious but largely localized disturbance on the main floor of the Venetian between the immense casino and restaurant row, which had been caused by the precipitous arrival of Jonas Fresno's own sports-model time machine, had barely been felt around the reproduction of St. Mark's Square on an upper level of the hotel.

Harlee Nations's crew, doing some shopping on the concourse along the quarter mile of indoor canal, thought, as did everyone else nearby, that the unusual vibration and funhouse-mirror warping of perspective had to have been the result of a minor quake. The singing gondolier whose voice filled the concourse scarcely muffed a note. The water in the canal had slopped against the brick sides, then settled back placidly. That was the extent of the disturbance in their neighborhood.

Only Flicka, something of a klutz anyway, had lost her balance. She ended up sprawled on one of the arched bridges over the canal. She sat there for a few minutes holding her head during a spell of dizziness, refusing medical attention. Devon brought her a cup of water.

"Must have been the *zuppa di pesce*," Flicka muttered.

Devon, Honeydew, and Reese went into Banana Republic to browse. Nic chatted with a Marine in dress uniform. A gondolier standing in the prow of his boat grinned up at Flicka before ducking his head as he passed under the bridge. His single passenger, seated at the other end, didn't look at Flicka. Her eyes were closed. She looked pale and exhausted. The ruby skull cradled in her lap glowered like a graven image in a novelty-store window.

Flicka, astonished, got to her feet and leaned over the railing on the other side of the bridge as the gondola glided away. Then she called to Devon, who was trying on a safari-style shirt dress in the store. Flicka motioned frantically when Devon looked around. Devon left the store with the other two girls and crossed to the canal in time to see the woman with the ruby skull.

"Omigod!" she whispered.

"Yes."

The others joined them.

"What's wrong with you two?" Nic demanded. She was cranky from her impacted wisdom tooth in spite of the Darvon she'd been taking.

Flicka pointed and continued to whisper. "There goes the Avatar."

"Omigod!" Reese said. "You sure?"

Devon nodded. "Harlee and I saw her earlier tonight at that gallery opposite St. Mark's. There was a party. Harlee crashed so she could—" Devon paused, frowned. "But the Av was dressed differently then."

"Where's Harlee now?" Honeydew asked.

"Don't know." She also didn't know if that was something to be concerned about as she watched the departing gondola disappear around a bend in the canal. Devon's pulses raced. Something wrong here. "*Wait* a minute." She was focused on the red crystal skull. The last time she'd seen it, the skull had been in Harlee's possession. Devon quickly became anxious. Her thoughts skipped past the skull to that holographic image of Eden Waring's doppelganger she'd seen at Linc's place on Charleston Mountain.

What had the dpg hologram been wearing? Devon had a fantastic memory for clothes, if not always for faces. She recalled a ribbed, dark brown or black mock-turtleneck sweater, hip-length over casual plaid slacks. Yes, and leather Nikes or Reeboks. No jewelry. And the Avatar riding in the gondola—hadn't she been wearing an identical sweater?

Devon gathered the crew around her.

"That wasn't the Avatar we saw in that gondola! It was her doppelganger."

"A what?"

"C'mon, Devon."

"No, I'm double-damn certain of it."

"How do you know she was a doppel—whatever. Goober," Reese said, and snickered.

Nic said, "Everybody has one, you gink. Fetchlings included. They're mirror images. We just can't get them to show themselves to us. Only Avatars can summon their dpg's."

"It's not a Black Art," Flicka said. "Is it?"

"This is all real confusin'," Honeydew drawled. "And a little scary. *Two* of them? What kind of power does one of these doppelgangers have?"

Nic yawned. "I think they just have to do what they're told," she suggested. Her last couple of painkillers had her on the nod at last. She propped herself against lanky Flicka, who adored Nic even when she was moody or caustic. Flicka nuzzled the back of her favorite lover's head.

"We can talk about dpg's another time," Devon said. "Flicka, take Nic home, give her a bath, and put an ice pack on that jaw before she goes to sleep. You two have a job to do on Bertie Nkambe tomorrow."

"Tomorrow? I'm havin' dental surgery tomorrow!"

"Right, then. The day after tomorrow. But don't delay any longer, chums, should they decide to move the Supa to another hospital or a private clinic. Honeydew, you and Reese come with me."

"Where to?"

"We must catch up to that doppelganger."

"Uh-oh," Honeydew said. "Why?"

"We need to learn how she came by that crystal skull. Harlee's supposed to have it, but—"

"What's so important about the skull?" Reese asked as the three Fetchlings hurried along the concourse toward the loggia that overlooked the Strip.

"The Great One is depending on it," Devon said. "That's all I need to know."

Dr. Marcus Woolwine had been looking up on the Web an article from a back issue of *Scientific American* when he was distracted by a knock on the door of his suite. A Limey houseman told him he had visitors in the first-floor great room of the Magician's mountain home.

The visitors were three very attractive young women the houseman hadn't seen before, who were escorting Lincoln Grayle's female guest of a few days ago. Woolwine received that news with a ripple of electricity up his spine as he pulled on a velvet robe. The houseman went on to observe that Eden Waring's dpg had appeared unable to stand erect without assistance. And, oh yes, she had with her—was hanging on to with a death grip as it were—an exotic-looking red crystal skull that, frankly, had given the houseman the willies.

Woolwine made haste down to the great room, which had a large circular fireplace in the middle of it, an artificial log fire blazing beneath a dome of tempered bronzed glass.

Gwen was seated on a sectional sofa between two of the girls whom Woolwine didn't know. The other girl was Devon, the gray-eyed Irish Fetchling whose presence gave him a reminiscent chill as he recalled the stiletto she carried beneath a sleeve of her blouse. Nevertheless he smiled at her.

"My dear!" He looked in astonishment at Gwen, who was gazing at him as if he had appeared within a mantle of thick fog, trying to recall who he was. "Wherever did you find Gwen? I'd all but given up hope—" His gaze lingered, fascinated, on the red skull Gwen held in her lap.

"We found her at the Venetian. Gliding westbound in a gondola."

"Well, Gwen," Woolwine said, drawing closer to her, wary of a circulating sparkle like tiny orbiting worlds within the electric depths of the red skull, "I'm amazed that you were able to bring yourself back."

"Back from where?" asked a fair, toothy girl with a sun goddess's fluffed corona of white-blond hair. Another Fetchling, he assumed.

"Honeydew, I've already explained," Devon said patiently, as if the fair one were a couple of bananas shy of a bunch. "She was time-traveling in hyperspace. Doppelgangers often take a notion to do that." Dev looked at Woolwine. "At least that's what Dr. Woolwine told Harlee and me while we were here the other night."

Woolwine nodded. "I spoke the solemn truth. By the way, I'm also delighted to see you again. Devon, is it?"

"*Who is yon dwarfish fellow?*" Delilah asked, before Gwen's eyes glazed and her head began to loll.

"It's all right, lovey," Devon said to her. "You know him. He's a doctor. *Your* doctor. He'll look after you until you're feeling ever so much better."

"What's wrong with her?" Woolwine said. "Not ill, is she?"

"Just out of it."

"Maybe she suffered reentry problems," said Reese, who was on the other side of Gwen with a helpful arm around the dpg's shoulders. "Like, coming in from hyperspace, couldn't that knock a kidney loose or something? I'm only speculating."

"Smell her breath," Honeydew objected mildly. "She's snockered. I'm talkin' totally blitzed, y'all."

Delilah began to sing, softly, "My Baby Don't Wear No Shoes."

"Extraordinary," Woolwine said, his hairless scalp tingling. He decided to retreat from the cosmically active skull, afraid that his pacemaker might misbehave.

"Whatever the problem, a good night's sleep is the best thing for her," Devon said. She looked pointedly at Woolwine. Her Borgia stare. "She *will* be all right here? We've all become rather F-O-N-D of Gwen."

"Even though she can be funny-talkin'," Honeydew observed. "I mean funny like Elizabethan hip-hop."

"I'll be personally responsible for her," Woolwine said, "in the absence of our host." He was looking now at the taped gauzelike patch on the side of Gwen's neck where he had implanted his Magnetic Flux Inhibitor Unit, which sequestered Gwen from her home-body's beck and call. Was it still there? If not, who had excised it, Gwen herself? Too many mysteries all at once, and he was up past his usual bedtime. "If I may presume," he continued, with a blithe smile at Devon, "you have all been so thoughtful thus far, but from the look of her Gwen ought to be put to bed immediately. I'll give her a little something to ensure sound rejuvenating sleep. All of you are welcome to stay the night—or for as long as you like. Of course, we are at the threshold of a potential tragedy—"

Devon shook her head, russet hair aswirl. "Don't say that! The Gr—Lincoln Grayle is not dead! He isn't missing either, in spite of what everyone thinks. He will be back, and quite soon."

"That's wonderful news. So you've heard from—"

"No. Not us. But Harlee—I think Harlee knows for sure. I trust Harlee."

"Wonderful news," Woolwine repeated, looking unenlightened.

Gwen's eyes had been closed; now she looked back at him, then all around the great room with its dome of fire and corner shadows. For now Woolwine was gratified to have Gwen back, more interested in her than he was in Lincoln Grayle's whereabouts. Gwen presented to him, in his eighth decade, a unique opportunity that had gone unexplored in the limited time they'd already spent together. As for the refreshing night's sleep he'd proposed—he had the expertise and chemical means to keep Gwen isolated, docile, and fully under his control for as long as he wished. Assuming that Lincoln Grayle had no further use for her. But Grayle, in spite of Devon's assurances, was most likely in a highly pulverized state beneath tons of concrete and rock at the foot of the mountain that bore his name.

Gwen was still staring aimlessly, but for the most part in his direction. Her eyes were devoid of recognition, although momentarily Marcus Woolwine had a sense of someone or something else lying beneath her drink-blurred surface, like a crocodile waiting on lunch in a stagnant lagoon. How curious. He smiled at her.

"I don't relish that drive back down the mountain at this late hour," Devon said to Woolwine. The other girls nodded sleepily. "We will stay the night, then." To Reese and Honeydew she said, "Right. Let's get her off to B-E-D, darlings."

I'm really not in a hurry to see you again," Harlee said coolly to Bronc Skarbeck on her cell phone.

"I can understand that. After the—the way I talked to you. But—"

"It was the gun that freaked me so bad, Bronc. Really, how could you?"

"Stupid of me. Can't explain why. Jealous, I guess. Knowing what I now know about you."

She sensed, although his voice didn't exactly give him away—stumbling over a word here and there—that the General had been drinking. Hitting the Irish hard. Even so he couldn't sleep. So there was an underlying emotional cause not entirely centered on her absence from his house.

"I'm a real person. I have my ups and downs. My feelings get hurt. I need some space." After a few moments she added in a warmer tone, "Daddy."

"I understand. But we're a *team*, Harlee. All we have is each other right now. Let's not lose sight of—" His voice broke unexpectedly. "I really need to be with you tonight. I have enemies. But that's not the worst of it. Where are you?"

"At Devon's." She said nothing about meeting Eden Waring, subsequently bonding with the Avatar. "Just hanging out. What *is* the worst?"

"I have cancer."

"Oh, Bronc!" Part concern, part *you're shitting me.*

"True."

"Have you seen a specialist?"

"I went to a lab. My PSA was eleven! I've got this burning sensation—"

"Bronc, you're going to a specialist tomorrow if I have to drag you myself."

"They'll only tell me I'm going to die."

"You went to one of those freelance labs? They make mistakes all the time. Just calm down."

He began sobbing heavily. "It's too late for specialists. You're the only one who can help me. Please, Harlee. Get rid of my cancer."

She felt there was something not quite genuine in the fear he was trying to convey.

"I'm no fucking faith healer!"

"But you possess . . . secrets."

"Bronc, we are not going to get into that at this time, especially on the phone."

"All right. Whatever you say. Just be by my side tonight, that's all I'm asking."

Harlee thought it over. Devon hadn't checked in and wasn't accessible on her cell. Harlee didn't know when Dev might show at her own digs. And she was curious to explore, not the state of Bronc's health, which had been problematic since they'd met, but his reference to "enemies." With the Elite 88 sequestered at Snow Lake ranch for one of their rare conclaves, leaderless on this occasion, Harlee could well imagine the level of intrigue: the 88 were close enough to billions of dollars in gold to give each man's greed a radioactive glow.

Maybe she was making a mistake in staying aloof from Bronc at this critical time. Her counsel could be worthwhile. What she lacked in experience dealing with Mordaunt's disciples, she made up in wits and daring. One reason why the Great One valued her so highly. Other than Mordaunt himself, only Harlee could access his great vault without bringing the rest of the mountain down in a further cataclysm, sealing the cache forever.

Okay, then. Time to revert to Bronc Skarbeck's "transition object"—as a clinical psychologist might view her in assessing the relationship. Transition to what, a second go at puberty?

Harlee smiled.

"Now, I don't want you to take another drink," she admonished the already-foundering Skarbeck. "And put a pot of coffee on, Daddy. I'll be there in twenty minutes."

THREE

WHAT BEAST COULDST THOU BE, THAT
WERE NOT SUBJECT TO A BEAST?

—WILLIAM SHAKESPEARE, *TIMON OF ATHENS:* IV, III

Patrick O'Doul, the fifteen-year-old erstwhile time-traveler, awoke in the suite he shared with his uncle Mickey at the Venetian Hotel to find Mickey sprawled on a sofa in the sitting room below, staring at the television. The sound was off. He was vacantly watching a rerun of a NASCAR race on the Speed Channel. Both NASCAR and the tracks where they raced had come a long way in thirty years.

Even in the dim light of the sitting room Pat could tell how red Mickey's eyes were. He'd had little if any sleep; and he'd been crying again. But the sounds of grief he still made from time to time were lodged in his throat.

Pat stretched, got out of bed, used the bathroom, went down the steps into the sitting room, and parted the drapes a couple of feet. The windows faced east and a low spine of gray-blue mountains, above which the sun turned a thin cloud cover incandescent.

The boy cleared his throat and said, "How about I order some breakfast now, Unca Mickey?"

Mickey wet his lips with a furry tongue. Otherwise he didn't move or speak. He hadn't shaved in a while. Patrick had had his hands full keeping Mickey halfway presentable during the last three days. And they'd had a lot of company. But no cops, thanks to the Sainted Mother plus a team of lawyers the Tustin twins had furnished to protect their interests. As for the incident on Halloween that remained unexplained, no one had been injured and no one had shown up to contradict the claim that the Franklin speedster belonged to Mickey and Patrick. To all questions about how they'd suddenly appeared in the Venetian's casino the quick-witted Patrick said repeatedly, "It's a trick. I can't tell you any more." Because magicians were stellar attractions at many hotels, and would-be magicians abounded in Vegas, the explanation was serviceable. The hotel's lawyers had concluded that it was best to paper over (with cash) the inevitable nuisance claims and let the matter quietly go away. They suggested but didn't insist that Mickey and Patrick go away too, and soon.

Patrick was in no hurry. And he loved room service. Today he ordered french toast, crisp bacon, coffee, fruit. Then he sat on the sofa with the Mick, hands clenched between his knees. The night before he'd fallen asleep trying to think of the right words, the right approach to the subject of *home*—or what they had known as home in Paramus, New Jersey, circa 1973.

He had been able to deal with Time's dislocations more forthrightly than his uncle, even in the frustrating Mobius microregion that was Jubilation County. Patrick had a practical streak and wasn't as sentimental as most Irishmen. As far as he was concerned, he and Mickey had hit it lucky just winding up in the same star system with planet earth, let alone only a third of a century in time and two thousand miles from where they'd inadvertently shoved off into a parallel continuum. All thanks to Gwen's nearly dead reckoning and with some help, probably, from that amazing crystal skull.

He'd dreamed about Gwen for the last couple of nights, sweaty anxious dreams. He wondered what had happened to her, and to the hitchhiking entity that had boldly pushed Gwen aside in her own body. Gwen shared some of the blame, Patrick acknowledged; the entity was the reason why she'd shown up in Jubilation County to begin with. But Delilah had turned out to be a lot more hell than Gwen could've anticipated.

Delilah. Someone Patrick did not care to dream about or see in spectral aspect ever again. But it was lousy that Gwen should be so casually dispossessed. The hairs on his forearms stirred; the back of his neck was chilly. Nevertheless, he and Mickey were indebted to Gwen. They had an obligation to locate and try to help her.

Patrick already had an idea of where to start.

First, however, he had to snap Mickey out of his tragic stupor. Get him interested in living again. See the possibilities.

With an advance on the money they would be paid for the Franklin speedster by the Tustin twins (who also were picking up their tab at the Venetian for as long as they wanted to stay), Patrick had looked through the yellow pages and chosen a private eye. His intention was to get an idea of how things were in Paramus in the so-far astonishing (*awesome*) early years of the twenty-first century.

In about three hours (one astonishment was the existence of something called the Internet, where you didn't need detecting skills to learn practically everything about anyone), Patrick had a ten-page report (fax machines, jeez!) filling in the family history.

Sad to say, Mickey's wife, Annette, had passed away in a nursing home just before the stroke of midnight at the turn of the century. Mick's oldest daughter had succumbed to kidney cancer in the prime of her life. The grandkids were all grown, married, scattered. His youngest daughter, who was now older than Mickey, still lived in Arizona. Mickey had perked up at that news and wanted to rush right down there but Patrick cautioned: How do you explain thirty years, no word, and here you are looking just the same? Mickey promptly resumed his funk.

Patrick's dad was living in a double-wide in Punta Gorda, Florida; bald, fat, retired. He looked meaner than ever in the photo supplied by the detective agency. Pat didn't feel he owed his father a visit or much of anything else. As for his mom—maybe he missed her. But she'd had two coronaries and his showing up out of the blue probably would be good for an epic third.

No, neither Patrick nor Mickey could go home again. Patrick had become a time-traveling orphan, which didn't depress him. This was a new, exciting place and time in which to be, and he could resume growing older at the customary pace. He liked the idea of studying magic; becoming a headliner in Vegas. What if he could talk Gwen into joining the act?

They already *had* magic, Patrick had enthused to himself, beyond the imaginations or talent of competing magicians: the power of the ruby skull that Gwen/Delilah had removed from the Franklin speedster. The skull had delivered them from the monotony of Jubilation County in about three heartbeats to the Venetian's casino, and Patrick wouldn't be surprised if with a lot less of a twinkle the skull could transform hoptoads into movie stars.

Breakfast came. Patrick poured coffee for Mickey, bracingly black.

Mickey accepted the cup while barely taking his eyes off the big-screen TV.

"Val and Cleve are thinking about sponsoring a stock car," Patrick said, referring to his new best friends, the Tustin twins. He drenched his french toast in maple syrup. "You could be their crew chief, what d'ya think about that? Those engines: *man,* they gotta be six hundred HORSEpower. Wouldn't you love to get your hands on a mill like that?"

"Huh," Mickey said, beginning to sip his coffee.

"Between them they already own forty-three classic cars. A 1912 Caddy. Tolerances to one one-thousandth of an inch, and no more hand-cranking. Wouldn't you like to see one of those babies aGAIN?"

"Yeah," Mickey said, with a gleam in his eye that was a lot like love. All Cadillacs; Cord L-29s; the Marmon Wasp Indy Cars—those were his fantasy goddesses.

"They're planning to build a museum RIGHT here in Las Vegas! You could be a *big* help. Heck, nobody knows more about restoring classic cars than you do!" Pat heard his uncle's stomach growl. "Want some of this french toast? More here than I can eat."

Mickey glanced at Patrick's plate, and nodded.

"I need to get dressed, get going," Patrick said, reaching for the bacon. Which he ate with his fingers, brushing crumbs off his pajama top.

"Go where?"

"Gotta get started looking for Gwen."

Mickey glanced at his nephew. "But she—"

"Yeah, WALKED away. Not a word to us. But we know she's not in her right mind. I mean, Gwen is in there somewhere, except she's not running things." Patrick drank half of his orange juice, frowning. "I told everybody she was my SISter, okay? And that it was Gwen who designed the trick, I mean the illusion, that they all wanta know about."

"Your sister?"

"Catch up, Unca MICKey! Anyway, I found out yesterday they have probably a thousand cameras in this hotel, what they call digital cameras. Don't ask me how they work, all I know is they don't use film? Everything each CAMera records—" Patrick paused to clear his throat, "is stored in a computer. And if somebody walked in or out of the hotel, say five months ago, the computer can, uh, ISOlate that moment, recall it, and maybe even identify the PERson with something called facial recognition software."

The Mick stared at his nephew until his left eyelid began twitching.

"So the lawyers set it up for me, and the deputy chief of security here at the hotel is gonna help me find Gwen, see which way she went. See if she got into a taxi or somebody picked her up? After all, she does live here, in Las Vegas, which is the reason why we're here too."

Mickey began to shake his head.

"Don't," he said. "Don't do it, Patrick. Leave well enough alone. Don't go near her again! Haven't we had enough misery already?"

"But none of it was GWEN'S fault! And I've got *plans,* Unca Mickey!"

CONCORDIA HOSPITAL · 8:20 A.M.

Eight days after being hit three times by a would-be assassin's bullets, Bertie Nkambe was off the ventilator for good and sitting up in her bed, eating solid food in spite of a sore throat. And sometimes talking, in a whisper, although she still relied mostly on subvocal communication with Eden.

"So how is the self-healing coming along?" Eden asked her.

—I had a stubborn infection to knock down. Both lungs feel good now. All wounds that don't kill you are superficial, I guess. Doesn't mean they don't hurt like a bastard. They should be taking the drains out of my head in a couple of days. Damn, I need to get out of here! So give it to me straight, how're things going with the cowboy?

"Cody? I'll bring him around later to meet you, if that's okay."

—Looking forward to it.

Bertie put down her fork, having finished most of a plate of scrambled eggs. Eden held a glass of juice for Bertie to sip through a straw. She studied Eden's face. That momentary gleam at mention of Cody Olds had vanished from Eden's eyes. She looked doom and gloom again.

"You haven't . . . heard anything from Tom?"

"No."

—What do your dreams tell you?

—Nothing about Tom. I just have a bad feeling I can't shake.

"Gwen?"

Eden shook her head.

—But you're sure she's around?

"Yes. But I can't—you know—get in touch. It was only for those few seconds Halloween night. And my neck was bleeding."

"So she's . . ." Bertie massaged her throat. "In some kind of trouble?"

"Knowing Gwen, that's a cinch. Bertie, Cody's people have a ranch down in Navaholand? Cody offered to drive us and we can stay around his home place as long as we like, until you're fully recovered."

"Sounds . . . like a plan." Bertie resumed subvocally: —You want to get out of Vegas, don't you?

—In the worst way. My skin has been crawling. There's nothing but trouble here. They've had you under so you probably can't sense it, but there's such evil congregating. Worse than when the Magician was alive.

—So why don't you go on? I don't want to hold you up, I'll come later.

—I won't leave without you. That's not open to discussion.

There was a discreet knock at the door. "Come in," Eden said. The door was opened. Flicka looked in from the sitting room.

"Oh, you're sitting up today!" Bertie smiled bravely. "I was just wondering, anything we can do?"

Eden and Bertie saw another hospital volunteer behind Flicka, a mocha-toned black girl with big liquid eyes and great cheekbones, but a tight smile. She had a certain inward watchfulness that bothered Eden. The kind of beauty who came with a big price on her head.

"Is this a bad time?" Flicka asked.

"No," Bertie said.

"I just wanted you to meet Nicole. We work together."

Nic's smile became a little more generous. She didn't say anything. After a few moments Flicka said cheerily, "We'll be here all day, Miss Nkambe. If there's anything at all, just ask for us."

"Thank you," Bertie said.

"Very nice meeting you," Nic said. Her eyes were on the gold lion's-head walking stick Eden had left across the arms of a chair close to Bertie's bed.

When the door closed, Eden looked around at Bertie.

"Guess we're . . . getting to be big buddies," Bertie said of Flicka. "She comes around three or . . . four times a day. Wholesome as butter cookies in spite of . . . those exotic bloodlines."

"Uh-huh. What do you make of the other one?"

"Doesn't seem the . . . volunteer type."

"No," Eden said, "she doesn't. How's your peeping ability?"

"Don't know. Haven't tried. Why?"

"Oh, nothing. I thought I saw—but I'm just jumpy, and out of sorts." She leaned closer to the bed to kiss Bertie's cheek. "I'll be back with the cowboy, when he can spare the time for us."

—You're in love, aren't you?

Eden drew back with a pretense of surprise. "How can you say that?"

"Because," Bertie said with smug good cheer, "I just peeped you."

CHARLESTON MOUNTAIN · 9:24 A.M.

In a large, so-called clean room in the wing of Lincoln Grayle's aerie dedicated to Dr. Marcus Woolwine's work, a room that was for now lit only by ultraviolet light, Eden's doppelganger floated nude and sedated in a shallow bath of liquid twice as buoyant as seawater that bubbled into the glass tank through an aerator. In spite of the sedatives and the presence of black light, which weakened the physical body and kept her immobile, Gwen's eyes were open. The expression in those eyes was one of pure rage.

Bronc Skarbeck sipped coffee and studied the dpg through an observation window.

"What seems to be the problem?" he said to Woolwine.

"You may recall that we talked about Gwen's purpose in traveling through time."

"So you think she actually pulled it off?"

"I have no doubt. But the Gwen that has returned to us isn't who she used to be. She apparently acquired, while in Jubilation County, an entity who has made herself known to me as 'Delilah.'"

"Entity? The feminine half of Mordaunt's soul? Wasn't that how you put it?"

"Precisely."

"You seem afraid, Doctor."

"I admit to some trepidation. I've been exposed to—certain unnerving phenomena in the past forty-eight hours. Not the least of which is a persistent effort to encroach on my own brain."

"But you have her under control, don't you?"

"For now. I'm obliged, however, to increase the entity's dosages on an accelerating schedule." Woolwine rubbed his bald head nervously, as if something were crawling around up there, trying to gain entry into his skull.

"Doses of what?"

"We have her on Depakote, trazadone, and klonopin."

"Jesus. All three at once?"

"Yes."

"If, let's assume, you should lose control of the dpg, what then?"

Woolwine's shrug was like a clonus. "You know what *he* was like. Even in his human persona. Well. This little lady is the rest of Mordaunt. Perhaps the worst half, who can say? And she's not happy."

Skarbeck turned for a look at the EEG monitors, at moving pens that recorded on a scroll the steeps and falls of Gwen's brain waves.

"What I don't need right now is another Mordaunt," he said, frowning. He looked at Woolwine.

"Are you suggesting—?"

"I'm not suggesting. I'm telling you. The mind may be immortal, but the body is flesh and blood. Kill her."

"I thought perhaps a chemical prefrontal lobotomy might—"

"Results uncertain. Kill her. Do it today."

The four recording pens on the EEG scroll began moving at earthquake speed.

NYE COUNTY, NEVADA · 10:34 A.M.

Harlees Nations and Devon O'Flaherty arrived at the high gates of Ferdie Younger's desert homestead in the candy-apple red Humvee that Devon had borrowed from Honeydew to make the rough trip down rocky defiles to the eastern edge of the Mojave, a few miles from the California line. Several unmarked miles from anything resembling a road. Ferdie Younger's avocation demanded both seclusion and privacy.

In front of high chain-link gates midway through a canyon Harlee made a phone call. Presently the lock on the gates clicked open. They proceeded the rest of the way, the passage becoming as narrow a squeeze as a birth canal, and suddenly popped out into Ferdie's valley within ocher cliffs cut and shaped by surging waters of ages past. On the floor of the small valley were four interconnected steel buildings painted desert tan, a windmill, and a squat adobe house with bits of colored glass embedded in the walls, a slant pole roof over the dooryard.

The girls got out, lugging two big hampers filled with deli treats for Ferdie, who came up out of his rocker in the shadows of his veranda and ambled toward them, rancher's frayed straw hat angled down to shield his eyes, thumbs hooked inside his unbelted Wranglers. He circled the Humvee with a grin, admiring it.

"Bitchin' wheels," he said in his high-pitched voice. His own vehicles were a beat-up Land Rover and a five-ton refrigerator truck for transporting sensitive specimens to his hideaway. Ferdie had had a lifelong fascination with small, deadly things. He was small and deadly himself; slim, with a nearly unlined, beardless face, only five feet tall in his scuffed calf-roper boots. He had been able to pass for a teenager well into his thirties, which, along with a knack for making himself unnoticeable, had contributed to success in his vocation. Ferdie was a contract killer of nerve, stealth, and accuracy. He specialized in political wipeouts—although only the occasional victim of one of his assassinations was acknowledged or even rumored to have been murdered. All politicians hated the idea that they were not invulnerable.

When he wasn't doing such work, for which he collected millions, Ferdie spent a lot of time in swamps, rain forests, deserts. A self-taught herpetologist and entomologist, he had published scholarly monographs. For obvious reasons he preferred not to lecture, and except for nightly Internet chats he was largely unknown to his peers. Harlee felt fortunate to have found him at home.

"Snakes or bugs?" Ferdie asked her, after they'd enjoyed a round of delicatessen tidbits and lemonade on his veranda. He showed his gums when he laughed.

Devon shuddered delicately. Harlee said, "You told me when I called that you had something special I might like to see?"

Ferdie nodded delightedly. "They arrived from Japan three weeks ago. Japanese hornets from the pristine forests of the Ashio-Sanchi highlands. Nothing like them has ever been found in this country, of course. Importation for any purpose is strictly banned. Just as well, just as well. Whether they might propagate beyond their natural habitat is an open question. My educated guess is that they have the potential not only to quickly adapt to alien habitats, but to change the world's ecology. The world's ecology." He helped himself to more lemonade. He wasn't alone in his valley. There were housemaids, caretakers, associates, and technicians who worked in the joined buildings, which maintained diverse simulated environments, but they kept out of sight when Ferdie had visitors. "Almost any species can be controlled, of course. Except our own, and the cockroach." Ferdie laughed and laughed, smacking a knee with the palm of one hand, concluding their assassins' picnic.

Inside each of the steel buildings on his property was another complete building, accessible through airlocks. Behind glass walls of large vivariums with their own diurnal cycles were such specimens as recluse spiders, Australian brown snakes, scorpions from five continents, and his latest acquisitions.

"The expense, don't ask," Ferdie said as they paused outside a translucent container the size of two truck trailers. "This is an exact duplicate of a section of Japanese forest, including transplanted chestnut trees. It is now just a few minutes past sunrise within, but soon you'll be able to see them. The queen was dormant 'til just recently, overwintering. Now she's begun to fulfill her natural function. I've released the male hornets to fertilize her, which is their only raison d'être. They'll live just a few days. The female Japanese hornet is the deadly one. Isn't that so often the case?" Ferdie showed his gums again; the girls smiled politely. "Oh, here come a few of them now; they've detected our presence. Be very still or they'll dash themselves to death against the glass trying to get at us. They'll soon go about their business, which is to gather their favorite food—the sap of the young chestnut trees we imported clandestinely."

Devon was fascinated by a couple of the giant hornets, five times the size of ordinary honeybees, as they hovered a foot from where she stood.

"They even look Japanese!" she whispered, as if there weren't a half-inch-thick barrier between her and the hornets. She didn't want the glass to vibrate.

Ferdie Younger also spoke softly. "Surprisingly so, with those gaudy orange and yellow heads, shaped like the masks of warriors. But as I mentioned, the warriors are all female. I've heard that about thirty Japanese hornets can destroy a hive of as many as three thousand of the small European honeybee in a matter of three hours. They have powerful mandibles, as you can see, for slicing and dicing. Slicing and dicing. And they may sting repeatedly, although they themselves are well armored against the stings of other aggressors."

For a couple of minutes they watched the flight of the hornets inside the slowly brightening vivarium. "Too bad they don't seem to do well in captivity. But it has been worth the expense and aggravation of the smuggling process to have this opportunity to record their daily lives for a few weeks. And once they die, they provide delicious meals."

"You *eat* them?" Devon said, making a yechy face.

"Japanese epicurism. Deep fried, the hornets have the succulence of tempura shrimp."

"How do human beings react to their venom?" Harlee asked, getting down to the core business of their visit.

"Ah."

"You said something the other day about intolerable pain."

"Oh, you liked that part." The gums again. And a wink.

"It would be fitting."

"Shouldn't ask, I suppose, whom you have in mind for such biblical tribulation?"

"Her name is Eden Waring."

"Hm. Not familiar."

"Also known as the Avatar. A psychic witch. She's the one who killed Lincoln Grayle."

"She must have unusual powers. So the Magician *is* dead."

"But not the Great One. He's surviving. Somewhere."

Her tone precluded further inquiry. "Well, as to your question. Their venom consists of eleven different chemicals that, among other things, dissolve human flesh. If one is stung about the face, the face will soon decompose. No matter. By then the victims are usually dead from anaphylactic shock. The victims, however, needn't be stung at all."

"No?"

"One mode of attack employed by the hornet is to squirt venom, like a spitting cobra, into the eyes."

Devon hung her head, looking faint.

Ferdie said to Harlee, "So you'd like to acquire a small amount of venom?"

"Uh-uh," Harlee said, with a gesture to the vivarium. "I want *them*."

"Harlee, you're not serious!" Devon said.

"Bet I am." To Ferdie she said, "Can I have, like, half a dozen of the females? By themselves they're no threat to the ecology."

"The discovery of even one dead Japanese hornet in this country would set off alarms. *Alarums.*"

"So what?"

Ferdie shook his head. "Besides, I don't know how long they could be expected to live, outside their preferred environment. Twenty-four hours? Thirty-six?"

"Long enough."

"Harlee—" Devon said in weak protest.

"But how do I transport them without getting stung to death myself? Is there a method of tranquilizing the hornets until I'm ready to put them to use?"

"You are really asking too much of me this time, Harlee."

"You've got dozens of those beasties in there. Can't you spare *six*? Doesn't smoke knock out honeybees without killing them?"

"The accepted method of dealing with them when hives must be moved. And, yes, it worked with our hornets too. Less than twenty-four hours after combs with queen were removed from their forest hideaway, they were installed here. They traveled by chartered jet freighter; the well-being of the hornets was constantly monitored. Still many died en route. So how would you propose to—"

"How about in one of the picnic hampers like we brought?"

"That's *it*," Devon said. "Risk your own neck, but I am having no part of this! Smoked hornets in a picnic hamper? Harlee, you have lost it!"

"Hm," Ferdie said. "It would take some experimentation, but I *am* curious." He smiled. "What are you offering in return, Harlee?"

"Two tickets to *O*. Harder to get than my own sweet pussy."

Ferdie had a good laugh, attracting angry hornets to their corner of the vivarium as the glass panels vibrated.

"And?"

"Ferdie, do you know how much a gold brick weighs?"

"Do you mean the standard size, Johnson Matthey refinery ingot? One kilo."

"You like gold, don't you, Ferdie?"

"You know I do." Ferdie wet his lips. "As it happens . . . I find myself a little short of reserves these days. All that *mordida,* and no one wants dollars anymore."

"As much gold as you can haul from the Great One's vault inside Grayle's Mountain in thirty minutes. I'll use a stopwatch. You can use a wheelbarrow."

"What a surprise you are sometimes, Harlee. So you have access?"

"For now I'm the only one who does."

Ferdie nodded. His decades-old baby face creased in thought and took on a rosy glow as he considered the challenge proposed and the benefits to be reaped.

"If it proves to be doable—moving the hornets by the means you've described—I'll certainly take you up on that. Payment in advance."

Harlee folded her hands at her waist and smiled, eyes downcast.

"I was kidding about my pussy. But, purely as a businessman, you wouldn't be so foolish as to try to fuck with me, would you, Ferdie?"

Ferdie looked uncomfortable. "In spite of the mendacity in the world around us, I've always been a square dealer. A square dealer. Let us say—one kilo of gold for expenses? I'll need to try more than one method for temporarily rendering the hornets hors de combat. Remaining payment will depend on your satisfaction. Let me caution that you may count on having only a few hours of live, lethal hornets at your disposal. I can't guarantee longevity beyond that. Or your safety."

Devon groaned softly.

"Cautious is as cautious does," Harlee said blithely. "So we have a deal. I'll work out the itinerary for my hornets. The kilo of gold will be ready for pickup in town this afternoon."

"Lovely doing business with you, Harlee," Ferdie Younger said.

We'll be making port at Terminal Island in just under three hours," Captain Dellarovere said to his Person in Addition to Crew as they were finishing lunch in the officers' dining room of the huge tanker ship. "Authorities will board us along with the pilot at the sea buoy. I'm sure there will be many questions about the tragic loss of the *Stella Salamis.*"

Holding his coffee mug in both hands, Tom Sherard sipped slowly, eyes narrowed against the sun coming in through a port window. It made the captain's face hard to see. They were alone. The junior officers, as was their habit, had eaten quickly and scattered to prepare for shore time: visits home, waits for new ships.

"I won't have any more to tell the Coast Guard or a board of inquiry than I've been able to tell you," Sherard said. "We took a pounding and were breaking up. The sounds of a ship's plates being pulled apart isn't something I'll ever forget. But they're about the last thing I remember. How I survived when the others weren't so lucky—" He put his mug down and shrugged, feeling sharp pain on his left side where his ribs were heavily taped.

Captain Dellarovere nodded sympathetically. "I've wondered, during your days as a safari guide in Africa, did you have any—how should I say?—close calls? I couldn't help but notice two rather prominent scars like claw marks when our ship's doctor was attending to you."

"There were always those moments of miscalculation," Sherard said dryly, "for which one paid dearly. So there I was on a peaceful sea voyage when my number came up again."

They both seemed to ponder the odds, implications of the miraculous, dark ironies of luck. The captain had a broad weather-creased olive face and a fondness for religious tokens on chains, one of which he fingered now as if a blessing was called for.

"If you have changed your mind about getting in touch with someone before we make port, in order to reassure—"

"I haven't." After a few moments Sherard shifted his gaze and smiled slightly at the captain. "I've always been a loner. My parents are long dead. There is no one in particular in my life. I take companionship where I find it."

"I have been married thirty-one years myself. So you have no plans."

"Only to 'kick back,' as they say in America. Give myself a chance to recover. I feel as if I'm one large bruise."

A seaman came in with a fax that he handed to Dellarovere, who after a few seconds passed it on to Sherard. He tried to read it but found his vision blurring from headache.

The captain helped him out. "Good news, it seems. The consul-general of Kenya in Los Angeles will himself be at the terminal to assist in the process of getting you off the ship. Depending on how long it takes for the U.S. State Department to process a new visa, you could be on your way within forty-eight hours. Meanwhile I'm pleased to have your company on board. I look forward to a tale or two of stalking wild game. Lions, leopards, tigers—but there are no tigers in Africa, are there?"

For an instant the captain glimpsed the chill of an alien spirit sequestered in the hunter's gaze.

"Once there was a tiger," Tom Sherard said. "It had the face and jaws of a hyena."

"Oh," Dellarovere said delightedly. "A *tall* tale!"

CHARLESTON MOUNTAIN · 3:10 P.M.

There was no forewarning of trouble in the Magician's aerie, no terrifying cries for help when it happened. Nothing at all disturbed the tranquil atmosphere in and around the cliff-dwelling house. Of course it was a very large house—twenty thousand square feet, two wings, five cantilevered levels. And Dr. Marcus Woolwine's facility was well apart in one wing from the most populated areas. Whatever the servants were doing, they went on doing without a moment's pause to look up, listen to something alien to that hour or outside the daily established routines of housekeeping. They carried on just as if the master of the house were still in residence, or was soon expected home.

Meanwhile two of Dr. Woolwine's assistants lay bleeding to death on the floor of the room in which Gwen had been floating in that shallow salubrious bath, physically weakened by ultraviolet light, which was kryptonite to all doppelgangers. The several lights suspended above the lab tank had suddenly been shattered with enough violence to drive hot shards through the flesh and vitals of the assistants, cutting loose important moorings to the heart.

Gwen, free of the wires that had monitored her vital signs while she soaked and drowsed, was gone.

A silent alarm summoned Woolwine. He found her by tracking bloody footprints and her other bath drippings, which had turned to glowing gelatinous splatters on a staircase and the marble corridor floor two flights below. She had returned to the suite that Gwen had occupied before time-traveling to Jubilation County a week ago.

Now she stood naked in the bedroom regarding herself agleam and fouled with others' blood in a full-length standing mirror. There were still pieces of tape on her forehead, breasts, and back. She pulled a piece away disconsolately.

"Two of us? Nay, intolerable conceit! I must be one spirit, one host of flesh and blood."

She caught Woolwine's reflection in the mirror when he paused in the bedroom doorway behind her.

"W-what have you *done*?" Woolwine stammered. "They b-bled to death!"

Gwen turned; Delilah spoke.

"'Tis the doctor of deviltry and low cunning. Dull me not with melancholy belchings! Did'st think there was dust of forgetfulness 'pon my brain? Destroy me? Know that I have sorceries undreamt of in thy womb of night, and rue thy bloody disposition."

"But it wasn't *my* idea! I'm a scientist, not a murderer! I could n-never have—I would've f-found a way—who *are* you?"

She laughed.

"Has't thou now cause to steal lustre from a saint? Fodder for jer-lings, attend me, for I have temper to take thee unto torment."

With that, Gwen changed in two blinks of an eye, shooting up in a pall of smoke until her head nearly touched the trey ceiling of the bedroom; her hair went haywire, as if electrified; it seethed with grave-hoar glimmers of haunted night while her jaws elongated like a slathering wolf's.

"Oh my G-God!" Woolwine jabbered, clutching his bald head with both hands.

Hulking, she limped nearer, licking her wolfish lips; saliva burned him where it splattered. Her hands had turned to long paws and longer claws made to tear food from the quivering bodies of just-caught prey.

"I am the dark of nature; ageless, ever increasing, iron hearted, with soul of gall. Foe to all that breeds, lives, breathes upon this orb, all madded naked souls that lack o' shielding spirit."

Woolwine's knees were knocking together; an interesting phenom-enon, since he was conspicuously bowlegged. When she breathed on him his frightened face broke out in pustules like the pills on a cheap sweater.

"D-Don't kill me!"

She inserted a claw into one of his nostrils, levered him to the floor.

"Whatever it is you want, let me h-help you!"

Instead of ripping the needle-pointed claw up through his nostril and into his brain, she paused. Still looming over him, part wolf, part sty of a woman grossly knockered, yellow eyed, foully humid.

"Please—I have a pacemaker!"

Her nostrils dilated as if she'd caught a whiff of some subtle prac-tice on his part.

"Where lies your worth to me?"

Some blood was dripping from the nostril that enclosed half of a claw. Woolwine licked it from his upper lip.

"I can tell you—things you need to know. About your soul mate the Magician, and the girl who destroyed him! Only—*please*—would you go back to being just plain Gwen? There is just so much of this—I can endure!"

"Dead, you say? Ill names this day! Who is guilty of the deed?"

"Your—I mean Gwen's lookalike. Her *home*body! Eden Waring! Ask Gwen about her."

The claw was slowly withdrawn. Woolwine fumbled for a handkerchief and plugged his nostril with it. He felt dizzy and cold. Rocky on his feet, he staggered to a silk-covered chaise and collapsed there. He closed his eyes tightly.

When he was able to open them again he had stopped bleeding and the were-beast stench had faded from the bedroom. Gwen was sitting cross-legged in the middle of a four-poster looking gravely at him.

"Hello, Dr. Woolwine."

"Oh, God. It's *you*. I'm so grateful. But—"

"Delilah said I should talk to you about Eden. But she's listening. Remember that. Tell me everything that's happened while I was gone."

Woolwine clasped his hands to stop them from shaking, cleared his throat, and took her through the events surrounding the death of Lincoln Grayle. Twice while he spoke Gwen reached up to touch the bandage on the other side of her neck from where Letty Fresno had tweezered out Dr. Woolwine's implanted Magnetic Flux Inhibitor Unit. Its removal had facilitated the time-traveler's return from Jubilation County. Now a duplicate MFIU was in place; once again Gwen was beyond the reach of her homebody.

When he had finished his story, neither Gwen nor Delilah said anything. Woolwine fidgeted, thinking of the bled-out bodies in what had formerly been the "clean" room, wondering what to do about them. Meanwhile there was a play of emotion across Gwen's face. Her lips moved soundlessly or compressed palely. Her eyelids fluttered or closed altogether for several seconds at a time. Tremors randomly agitated her body and Woolwine was afraid that one of them would end in another horrid manifestation.

He said timidly, "I'll do whatever you—I mean Delilah—asks. But I need your help too! I can't just have *corpses* lying around upstairs."

There was a pause in the interior dialogue between Gwen and Delilah; it was Delilah who looked out at him as Gwen nodded.

"Bless you," Woolwine said humbly. "Both."

"Lock them away unto stilly night, whence the corses shall be safe removed to clinging earth, death's chill and silence. Betimes, we find ourselves environ'd in cruel dilemma."

"How so?" Woolwine asked cautiously.

"Dost thou not bear a brain? Gwen is chattaled to another; enfeebled; a doppelganger."

"Yes, I know all about her status, but I—"

"Look you, I'll be sworn the Avatar shall die! But not at penalty to ourselves. Now they are separate; yet there is peril in the other's passing, according to primal law. I have tooth that serpents envy, kidney for conquest, spleen of lion's cast, marrow to match the ravening wolf's. But I am powerless to 'scape the fate of mortal flesh, should Gwen vanish o' the instant Death grays the ruddy cheeks of Eden."

"Dilemma, yes, I see. A pickle of a paradox, um-hmm. What do you think we—"

"Ever-fixèd Law inscribes remedy. Gwen will be unfranchised by speaking of her name, to wit: 'Guinevere.'"

"You're saying that it's Eden Waring who has to set her own doppelganger free?"

"Ay. Therefore to this affair you must with haste draw Eden hence."

"I don't know where—"

Gwen levitated, still purely naked, now spraddle-legged, eyes growing long and livid in a suddenly refashioned face. In she-wolf style she growled and pissed at him. Woolwine flinched.

"No, no, just give me a moment to think!" He set his mind to racing, trying to look composed and competent while he riffed prospects or possibilities. A girl who had good reason for not wanting to be noticed. An object of edgy veneration pursued by the mentally unreliable, those who were known in a more distant day as kooks . . . it hit him. He cleared his throat.

"Provided that Eden Waring is still in Las Vegas, there is someone who might, ah, be keeping track of her. Not from the police. Her name is Virgie Lovechild. She makes her living catering to the absurdist fantasies of immature celebrity worshipers."

Gwen settled back on the bed, the tempests in her face subsiding.

"But if Ms. Lovechild is able to help me find her, why not simply—I'm speaking to Gwen now—go to Eden yourself and beg an indulgence? As long as my MFIU is implanted, the master/slave relationship is annulled. The two of you apparently never got along anyway. In short, of what use are you to Eden Waring? Or threat? As long as she remains unaware of your present alliance."

There was a period of silence. Woolwine cleared his throat a couple of times, not taking his eyes from Gwen. She seemed deep in thought, or discourse with Delilah. Woolwine needed his afternoon medication, but he didn't dare make a move to leave the room. Gwen, her eyes milkily placid, seemed unaware of or indifferent to his mounting distress.

She said suddenly and with a happy smile, "Delilah thinks that's a good idea, Dr. Woolwine. Find Eden and arrange a get-together. Not here. In a place, maybe like at Boulder dam, where she won't be suspicious about anything and we can get our deal sorted out. It's okay to explain to her about your magnetic jimmy-jammer or whatever it is because she'll be wondering why she can't recall me. Blame it on the Magician, tell her it was all *his* idea." Gwen paused. "I'm kind of looking forward to this. Just the two of us, like old times." She seemed to get a nudge from Delilah, and her lips pressed together. "Then once she names me and I'm not a doppelganger anymore, Eden will be dead meat. That's a real long drop down the face of that dam."

Excuse me," Patrick O'Doul said, "are you Mr. Olds?"

Cody paused as he was walking into his gallery and looked back at the boy, who had been sitting on a bench on the canal side of the shopping concourse.

"Sure am."

"Could I talk to you? My name's Patrick. I'm here at the hotel with my unca Mickey."

"What about, pardner?"

"I won't take up much of your time." Patrick seemed anxious that Cody not get away. He had nearly sprinted across the concourse from the bench he'd occupied. "It's KIND of important."

Cody remembered when his own voice had changed, settling into a deeper register almost overnight. Right now Patrick was wavering between tenor and soprano.

"Well, come on in. Not a painter, are you?"

"Painter? No, I'm—I'm thinking about being an illusionist. Like my ah, um, SISter."

"Your sister's an illusionist? Would I know her?"

"Yes—well—that's what we need to TALK about. Privately?" Patrick looked around. He seemed jumpy. There were four browsers in the gallery, and a collector who was deep in discussion with a sales associate over a Carrie Ballantyne pencil portrait of a cowgirl about Patrick's age.

"Guess you've got a good start on your future career," Cody said good-humoredly, "because I'm baffled already. I can give you five minutes. Come on back to the office. Where you from, Patrick?"

"PaRAMus, New Jersey. But, uh, not lately."

Fifteen minutes later Cody leaned back in his chair behind one of the desks in the gallery office and looked hard at Patrick's sweaty face. Patrick had chewed his lower lip nearly raw as he talked. And talked. He winced from the sting as he took a sip of Coke. Then his shoulders hunched tightly as he squarely met the skepticism in Cody's appraisal of him.

Cody said, "So you and—*Gwen*—you call her, and your uncle Mickey staged this illusion to get publicity for your act, only it didn't go right and half the patrons along restaurant row were blowing their cookies from the aftershock. Instead of doing cooler time right now, through the good offices of the Tustin boys you got off the hook with the Venetian's brass. But you won't talk about how the illusion is done."

"No, sir."

"Meanwhile your sister is missing. So you spent most of the day lookin' at surveillance files until your eyeballs were bloody tryin' to learn where she went. But guess what: turns out she was with *me* part of the time."

Patrick couldn't decide whether to nod or shake his head.

"Couldn't be," he muttered. "Because—"

"The files showed Gwen and also my date for the evening, who are dead ringers, in two different places at the same instant."

"Yeah."

"That's some story, Patrick. Let me tell you what's wrong with it."

Patrick lowered his head.

"That was no magic trick happened there on the casino floor. I know, I was close-by. It was something real. A phenomenon, far-fetched, out of this world maybe, but *real*. Wasn't it?"

Patrick licked his sore underlip and remained silent.

"Also, I don't know where or how you met, but the one you call Gwen isn't your sister. If you care to level with me about that, I probably won't throw you out of here."

Patrick winced, then shrugged submissively.

"Okay. Maybe we're getting somewhere. Now, mind tellin' what it is you want with me?"

"They're . . . twins, AREn't they?"

"Can't answer that one, Patrick. Just not sure." Cody looked past Patrick at someone who had entered the office. Patrick didn't look around. Cody smiled, his eyes on Patrick again.

"Either you're one of the most accomplished bullshitters I have ever met, or there's truth in you somewhere that's dyin' to come out if you'd only let it."

"You'll just think I'm CRAzy."

"Suppose you start over about this *Gwen* you say you were partnered with. This time tell it to both of us."

Patrick raised his head. Eden Waring had walked around the desk and now stood beside Cody, arms folded. She looked curiously from Cody to Patrick.

5:57 P.M.

Devon phoned Harlee from the salon where she was having her hair tinted and her feet pampered.

"Everything all set with Ferdie?"

"Can't believe how heavy those GD bricks are! And they don't come with handles. Nearly sprained my back getting one out of the, you know. I had to cancel with my fencing master this afternoon. Now I'm heading over to Caesars for a cedar sauna, a synchro, and an oxygen facial. What are your plans, beloved?"

"Ho-hum. No plans. I may pass by Virgie's when I'm done here to see if she's all right."

"How do you mean?"

"Wednesday is her bowling night. Virgie always comes here first for a wash and set. Her routine is virtually set in stone. But Jacques said she missed her three o'clock, and she didn't call to cancel."

"Why don't you give Virgie a call if you're concerned?"

"Oh, I did. Her personal phone is shut off. I don't know what to make of that."

"It's probably nothing. One of her headaches. She smokes too much."

"Harlee, I've been watching the local news here. As yet there's been no word about—"

"Don't. We're both on the air."

"Right. But today *is* the D-A-Y?"

"Nothing to worry about," Harlee assured her. "Flicka doesn't fail."

CONCORDIA HOSPITAL · 6:05 P.M.

Flicka and Nicole brought to the suite Bertie Nkambe's first meal since her October 26 luncheon on the lagoon terrace at Bahìa, where she had been shot. Dinner was a blue cheese soufflé with hash browns specially prepared in the kitchen of Peppermill, the twenty-four-hour breakfast eatery that was a favorite of locals.

As always there were two private detectives from the Blackwelder Organization on shift in the sitting room of Bertie's suite. Old friends of the Fetchlings by now. One of them had a serious crush on Nic that she had effectively promoted during their visits. She stayed outside with the detectives while Flicka rushed the catered meal into Bertie's room.

She was surprised to find Bertie out of bed and sitting on a small sofa, wearing a robe and pajamas. She was still on fluids though, Flicka noted. One of her team of doctors was listening to Bertie's lungs. From his expression both were in working order again.

"Well, surprise!" Flicka said with a happy smile; Bertie responded with a smile of her own while breathing deeply for the doctor. His name was Block or Bach, Flicka couldn't recall. "But aren't you rushing things a bit?"

Bertie touched her forehead to indicate that sitting up out of bed made her a little dizzy, but she was game to try.

Dr. Block or Bach put his stethoscope in a pocket of his hospital coat and said to Bertie, "Pulse and respiration are fast, which is to be expected. I want you back in bed in fifteen minutes. That should give you time to eat. You'll probably find you don't have much appetite at first."

Flicka was setting up the catering cart that Peppermill's kitchen had sent over. One of the perks of celebrity. The hospital had been deluged with get-well and goodwill messages. Flicka knew that Bertie's e-mail box was full every day. The children's wing was overflowing with flowers that Bertie insisted be rerouted when they came in.

Bertie said in a low, hoarse voice, "I'm a pest, but . . . need to go to the loo again."

"Where's Wendy?" Flicka asked. Wendy was Bertie's nurse on this shift.

"She had to make a phone call. Some nonsense about . . . a credit card bill."

Good old Reese, Flicka thought. Reese would have Wendy in knots on the phone for a good fifteen minutes.

"Flicka, that soufflé smells so wonderful," Bertie said, as Flicka lent a hand to raise her from the sofa.

Dr. Black—Flicka straightened out the identity matter with a glance at his hospital ID—made a couple of notations on Bertie's chart, which he left at the foot of the bed.

"My guess is you'll be off fluids in another twenty-four hours. No pole to lug around on your daily walks."

"When do I . . . get this other drain out of my head?"

"I'd say end of the week. By then—and I wouldn't have believed it as recently as Monday night—you'll be good to go."

Flicka glanced at the flaccid IV bag on Bertie's pole.

"She's low on Ringer's," Flicka said authoritatively. "Should I change it? I know how."

"Better leave that to Wendy," Black said, looking at his pager as he left the room. "See you tomorrow morning, Bertie. Enjoy that soufflé."

Alone at last. Flicka needed, she had reckoned, less than three minutes while the Supa was on the pottie and her room was empty. Of course, Bertie's brother Kieti or her father could show up at any time, but Nic was there to handle that situation. She'd already fucked Kieti once, on their first date and even though her wisdom teeth were killing her. Kieti probably thought he was in love.

Bertie Nkambe's last moments on earth had been carefully prepared for. Flicka wondered, even as she chatted amiably with her intended victim on the way to the bathroom, how much time *Entertainment Tonight* would devote to the supermodel's shocking and unexpected demise. She'd been doing so well, according to daily bulletins from the hospital. Tragic. A real tragedy.

As Flicka helped Bertie onto the toilet, then closed the door, Flicka experienced a momentary but profound lack of focus. She knew what it felt like to have her heart skip a beat, but this was the first time her entire brain had suddenly gone off-line.

She took a step away from the bathroom, but couldn't take another.

Suddenly terrified, forgetting what she had in one pocket of her colorful volunteer's smock, Flicka opened her mouth to call Nicole.

And discovered that she couldn't make a sound.

Flicka could see, and also she could hear perfectly well Nic's laughter in the other room as she jollied the Blackwelder guards. But Flicka's mind was one massive jammed gear. She stood in the bedroom as if rendered in bronze, eyes unblinking.

Behind her the bathroom door opened. Bertie came out.

"I haven't done everything to you that I could," Bertie said. "It's just a partial brain lock. I may let you go after you've had a talk with a good friend of mine . . . but that will depend on you, Fetchling."

6:18 P.M.

As if my life isn't complicated enough," Eden said with a weary smile while Cody drove them to Concordia Hospital.

"How much of Patrick's story do we buy?"

Eden laughed. "All of it, or none of it, I guess."

"Means you're buying it," Cody said with a glance at her as they stopped at a red light.

"Cody, what fifteen-year-old could possibly come up with a story so fantastic, but so detailed?"

"The part I liked best was the junkyard full of waylaid time machines."

"What he told us does make sense—when I put it together with everything I already know is true."

"Your doppelganger, Gwen—"

"*Calls* herself Gwen," Eden said with a frown of disapproval.

"—Strayed off the reservation. And she has the ability to time-travel."

"In common with all dpg's. I think probably Gwen had an assist, at least on the way home in that Jazz Age sports car with Pat and Unca Mickey, from the red crystal skull the car came equipped with."

"Nearly forgot about the skull. There's so much else to keep track of."

"Maybe I didn't mention it, but I've seen the skull or one like it in my dreams. My dreams may confuse the hell out of me half the time, but they don't lie."

"Was that the dream where you met up with, how did you put it? The *female* half of Mordaunt's soul? Which could be the same one your friends saw in Africa, stark naked and ridin' on the back of a tiger?"

"Head of a hyena, which technically makes it a were-beast."

"Now there's a sight I'd pay money to see."

"Not if I can help it, darling." Eden sighed. "So Mordaunt's better half is back, possessing Gwen, calling herself Delilah, talking, Pat said, in Elizabethan-era iambic pentameter. She has a lousy temper and can change her shape on a whim. Oh, my."

"Got a few other tricks up her sleeve, maybe. Did you just call me 'darling'?"

"Tricks? Like pulling down stars with one hand, unearthing lightning from Acheron with the other? Combining celestial and man-made power for a hell-on-earth-welcome-to-doomsday-folks scenario? I've wondered about the source of that power—could it be from the heart of the earth, or from the spent nuclear fuel I've heard is already being stored inside Yucca Mountain? I suppose Delilah can do all of these things, being the bitch version of *Deus Inversus,* and who knows what else? Just my luck. Yes. I *did* call you darling. My love. My darling cowboy Cody. The reason that taxi driver behind us is screaming as if he wants to kill you, the light's been green for ten seconds, Cody."

Cody burned some rubber getting through the intersection, a look of disbelief on his face easing into a mellow smile.

They had just driven into the larger of two parking lots at Concordia when a tall girl wearing one of the distinctive paisley smocks of the hospital's volunteer corps roared out from between a couple of large SUVs on a very flash low-rider hardtail and crossed six feet in front of them, cutting across the lot between other vehicles to an exit.

Cody had jammed on the brakes of his little Prius.

"What the hell?"

As he started forward again, a uniformed security guard appeared in all-out pursuit of the motorcyclist, closely followed by one of Bertie Nkambe's Blackwelder bodyguards. Neither had a chance of catching up to Nicole, who disappeared from the lot a few seconds later.

"I've seen that girl!" Eden said, her hands pressed against the dashboard. "She was in Bertie's suite with another volunteer this morning! Oh God, I think something's happened to Bertie!"

Eden was out of the car, sprinting herself in spite of the pain in her bad knee, before Cody could say anything.

AT VIRGIE LOVECHILD'S · 6:35 P.M.

Devon had planned to pull her Jag into Virgie's narrow driveway, but most of the drive was blocked by an RV with a couple of trailered Harleys behind it. She drove on up the block and parked near an apartment building with feather-duster palms in front, illuminated by pink and green floodlights. She walked back to Virgie's compound.

There was a pickup truck with California plates in front of the RV. Two big black dogs in the truck bed who looked and sounded mean enough to kill Red Riding Hood leaped up when Devon approached. She stopped, a cold needle of fear penetrating her heart.

From the carport where Virgie kept her old Chevy a tall kid with shoulder-length unkempt hair and a face as sore and spoiled as Dumpster fruit strolled toward her. He was biker-bar trash. Dangling silver and a death's-head tattoo on his exposed chest, the densely tattooed forearms known as "sleeves."

He whistled sharply to the dogs, who were lunging around in the pickup's bed with barely suppressed violence. It seemed to have an effect on them. They quieted down but didn't take their eyes off Devon.

The kid gurgled down what was left of a quart bottle of beer, dropped it in the yard, and tried to focus on Devon. He had the bright creepy eyes, itchy-twitchy body language, and jaw gyrations of a meth addict. She could smell him from ten feet away.

"You want something?"

"I came to see Virgie."

"Who're you?"

"A friend," Devon said, with a lift of her chin.

He shook his head. "She's not feelin' good enough to have company."

"Virgie's ill?"

"Call it that."

"Who might you be?"

"You don't rec'nize me? I'm Brad Pitt." He tried out a boyish grin.

"Where is Virgie? In the house?"

"Told you. She ain't seein' nobody."

"Well, look who's here!"

Devon turned her head toward the Airstream trailer. The Goth girl named Deborah, whom Virgie employed, stood in the doorway. Her little mouth was bunched. A smirk to go with her smirky tone of voice. Devon suddenly felt very cautious. Insolence thickening the air, the tense murderous dogs. Brad Pitiful lazily flicked his ciga-rette butt in Devon's direction. Sparks flew near her feet. Devon looked at the fiery butt, looked up slowly and steadily at him, saying nothing.

He turned to Deb, shoulders pumping up and down freakily.

"The Brit cunt says she's a friend of Virgie's, about which I never heard nothing. Virgie havin' friends, I mean."

"Devon is Irish," Deborah said, eyes narrowing in Devon's direc-tion. "Or so she would like us to believe. I don't know about the cunt part. Got my suspicions, though." Deb smiled belatedly. "Just messing with you, Devon."

After a few seconds Devon said, "I'll just be leaving now. If you would tell Virgie I stopped by."

She took three slow steps back toward the street, her mouth dry. Keeping an eye on the dogs, who looked ready to leap out of the pickup.

Deborah came down into the yard, saying, "No need to rush off! You want to see Virgie? Could be she's asleep again. Sleep's the best thing for her in her time of grief, but—"

Devon stopped. "Grieving? What's happened here?"

Deborah shook her head, looking sorrowful as she walked toward Devon.

"Not to make a long story of it, Snowjob sneaked out of the house without any of us knowing, and—"

Devon looked again at the dogs growling and shaking the pickup with their murderous energies and was instantly appalled.

"Oh, no! How *dreadful*. Poor Snowie."

"Yeah, Virgie's just all busted up about it."

"I shouldn't wonder. Whose brutes are those?"

"They belong to Chinch here and his Hermosillo honcho Keno Ramirez. Who are friends of mine, dropped by for a visit." Deb resumed smiling. "Same as you and your bud Harlee drop by some-times unexpected? What happened to Snowjob was just one of those tragic misfortunes." Deb sighed. "Chinch and Keno, feeling kind of responsible wouldn't you know, they offered to buy Virgie a puppy to help make up for her loss."

"And them bitchin' frizzies cost an ass 'n' a half," Chinch grumbled with a few uncontrollable head jerks. "Show-dog money, honey."

"But it was for naught," Deb continued in a passable imitation of Devon's gentle brogue. "Virgie's, like, inconsolable. I had to give her something, you know, calm her down."

"Like what?" Devon said.

Deborah looked Devon over, not answering the question.

"You didn't happen to bring Virg a little present, did you, might get her to feeling better? Right now she doesn't want to talk or eat. I don't know what else—"

"Yes. I do have a keepsake for her."

"Swell! Let's go in then."

There was another guy, whom Devon took to be Keno Ramirez, lounging in the shuttered front room of Virgie's bungalow. Big, no neck. He had one of those scary-looking, stone-carving Hispanic faces with hooded dark unmoving eyes that seem never to blink. He was staring at the Cartoon Channel on a wall-mounted LCD screen. Devon had the quick impression that Keno's idea of real entertainment would involve chain saws and live human beings.

A miasma of squantch in the room was almost enough to trigger Devon's gag reflex. She'd just had her hair done and now she'd have to wash it as soon as she got out of there.

"This way," Deborah said, as if she owned the place. She preceded Devon down a tiled hallway to the back of the bungalow, where, mercifully, the air was cleaner and Devon could take a reasonably deep breath. But Chinch and his odor were too close for comfort behind Devon.

Deb opened the door to Virgie's bedroom without knocking, then turned her head to warn Devon, "It ain't a pretty sight."

She remained in the doorway. Devon squeezed past her and looked at Virgie, whose head was propped up on a couple of breadloaf-size squishy pillows on the iron bedstead. Her eyes were closed. Her complexion was cement gray, her face sweaty. In the crook of her right arm lay the remains of Snowjob. The air in the room had a bloody odor. It was difficult to identify what Virgie clung to as a dog.

There was a tray of uneaten food, drying on the plate, placed across the arms of an antique Spanish chair next to the bed. Apparently Virgie had been all day without getting up to visit the bathroom. Devon smelled soiled sheets as she approached the bed.

"Virgie? It's Devon."

Virgie was breathing through her mouth. She didn't respond until Devon was close enough to reach down and touch her cold cheek. Then her breathing accelerated, muscles moved randomly in her face, her eyes peeped open. She looked uncomprehendingly at Devon.

Devon turned to Deborah, who stood watchfully in the doorway, picking with a fingernail at something between her teeth.

"Her color is awful! Are you certain she hasn't had a heart attack?"

"She'll be okay. Shock. You know how she doted on her doggy. Go on, tell Virgie about your present, maybe that'll perk her up."

Devon glanced at the containers of prescription pills that were on the tray. Heavy-duty tranks. She looked at the scales of dried vomit on Virgie's chin.

"Perk up? That's ludicrous. Virgie should be bathed, and it's obvious she requires immediate medical attention. A stay in hospital." Devon reached into her purse for her cell phone. "I'm calling for an ambulance."

"Wouldn't be in a hurry to do that," Deb said with a quick turn of her head. "Chinch, get your ass in here."

Chinch jived into the room with a crooked grin and snatched the cell phone from Devon's hand, slipped it into a pocket of his silver-studded leather vest.

Devon swiftly drew her stiletto from the flat forearm scabbard beneath her sweater. With the point beneath Chinch's stubbly chin where an artery throbbed, she walked him backward into a stucco wall below a ceramic head of the biblical Madonna. Her purposeful expression caused his grin to fade. He looked sideways at Deborah, clenching and unclenching his teeth.

"She means to stick me, Deb. On the border you get where you rec'nize the ones they'll use a fuckin' blade."

Devon retrieved her phone and kept Chinch pinned to the wall, where he jitterbugged like a hung-up marionette.

"You're overreacting," Deb said mildly to Devon. "Like I tried to tell you, what Virgie needs is bed rest, time to get over the trauma. She works too hard anyway. Give her a week, she'll be her old self. Meanwhile Bluesie and I will take care of the business."

"Devon," Virgie said in an exhausted voice, "help me."

Devon didn't dare look around. She motioned Chinch toward the door, the point of the knife denting his throat. He had sense enough to keep his neck muscles taut, which could make it slightly more difficult for Devon to open his throat from ear to ear. If he wasn't afraid of her, at least he had learned respect.

"That's what this is about?" Devon said, recalling her earlier conversation with Deborah. (*"Let me leave with you a message. I got here first. Virgie won't be around all that much longer, not with that coal miner's cough and sewer-pipe arteries."*) "You're taking over Virgie's business? Stoking her with monster chemicals— Oh, I see. Snowjob's demise was no accident, *was* it? But you are not as clever as you think. Not half. I won't allow you to get away with this."

As Deborah moved aside, Devon pushed Chinch out into the poorly lit hall. She heard the dogs. She took a fast look, her blood congealing. The dogs were at the other end of the hall, claws scrabbling on tile. But for now the hulking Keno had them tight-fisted on chain leashes.

"You be steady now," Chinch advised Devon. "That big boarhound's Bobo. The part-rotie bitch is Evangeline. What it is, they're trained to kill when they see a knife. Crotch and throat, bam-bam. So you still wanta stick me?"

Deb walked past Chinch and Devon into the bedroom. Virgie was crying, a faint despairing wail.

"Hey, Virg, just shut up for now, okay? Had about all I care to listen to. I'll get you a drink of water in a minute."

Devon said, "Harlee knows exactly where I am. In case I don't show up at the Caesars spa in the next fifteen minutes."

Chinch put an easy hand on the hand that held the stiletto. Crisis seemed to soothe his nerves.

Devon let him take her stiletto.

Deborah removed the ceramic head of the Madonna from the wall. She walked out of Virgie's room and smashed Devon in the back of her head with it. The heavy but hollow piece broke in two. The dogs were going nuts. Devon crumpled without a sound.

Deb prodded her hard in the ribs with a booted foot.

"Looks like Devon is O-U-T," she said sardonically.

"So what do we do with her?" Chinch said, beginning to twitch again.

"Parrrtyyyy," Keno growled.

"Down south on your own turf," Deborah advised. "Have all the fun you want, guys, but don't tear her a new asshole. Keep her high. Morph, not skag. Make sure she eats and doesn't get dehydrated. Couple weeks, she'll be docile as lovebirds. Clean her up and take her over the border, see what she'll bring from that Ay-rab does his shopping in No Gal for the teenage runaways. We split the proceeds fifty-fifty."

Deborah reached down for Devon's shoulder tote and began to rummage through it. First she found the keys to the Jag. Then she came up with a jeweler's box wrapped in pink tissue.

"What do you know? She wasn't spoofin' about a present for Virgie. Let's have a look." Deb tore off the paper and opened the box. "Expensive, too. From Fred's." She held up the bracelet to the hall ceiling light. "Yep, eighteen karat. It's always good to know people who go first class. I'll drive her car over to Treasure Island and leave it in their garage. Keno, give her a dose of treats *before* she wakes up. Enough so she's nodding but can still walk out of here to the RV with a little help. You don't want to have to carry her; the goddamn neighbors are incredible snoops."

I'm not ready to check out of here," Bertie said. "Another twenty-four, forty-eight hours maybe, before I've built up my strength to the seventh energy body."

"Then security needs to get a hell of a lot tighter," Eden said. "This was way too easy for our friend here."

They both looked at Flicka. The Fetchling sat in an armchair, hands folded in her lap, staring at a landscape on the wall with unblinking eyes. Her expression was one of eerie serenity.

"Are you having any trouble holding her?" Eden said.

"No. My mental body is almost a hundred percent charged. And she's only a Fetchling. They're all beauties, thanks to the spectrochrome therapy. Which can charge up to the fifth energy body and is great for removing dents, wrinkles, and old skin. But none of them have superpowers."

"That's a relief."

"Eden, they're everywhere in Vegas. That was the lure of Mordaunt. The crew Flicka belongs to is typical: six or eight personas, all of which have been around for centuries. I have a few names. Do any of these strike a chord, someone else . . . you may have met lately?"

"Bertie, you're nearly exhausted."

"But we need to do this. Nicole was the one you saw on her bike, trying for a new land-speed record."

"You must have scared her bad."

"A little slippery, I couldn't quite get control of her. And there's Devon, Reese, Honeydew, Harlee—"

"Good grief! Harlee, but not like the motorcycle?"

"Yes."

"She invited herself to a show at Cody's gallery the other night and buddied up to all of us. Especially me. Really charming. She's called me a couple of times since. She wants to do lunch."

Bertie said, "Like the lunch date I had with Charmaine Goferne?" She smiled ruefully, looking at the IV line taped to her wrist. "*That* was special." Bertie paused, and closed her eyes. "I wish Tom were here," she said in a barely audible voice. Eden, sitting beside her on the bed, squeezed her other hand. In the armchair across the room Flicka stirred and blinked as if she were trying to see through a thick fog. Bertie took a tighter grip on her mind and Flicka settled back with a small sigh.

"Anyway—about Harlee. From what I picked up looking through Flicka's recent activities, it's Harlee who runs the crew." Bertie drew a long, pensive breath. "Guess you know what you have to do."

"Avoid her at all costs until we can both get far away from Vegas."

"Uh-uh. You have to dig into Harlee's mind and find out all you can about her. We can't just run. There are still matters to be settled, here and now. We can't allow the Fetchlings to form a bond with Delilah."

"Get into her mind? I don't peep, you know that."

"You're not a natural-born peeper, but you have latent ability. It's your sixth energy body, which you've never paid much attention to. Time to . . . get on with your education as Avatar."

"Time for you to rest. And you never did touch your dinner." Eden looked back at Flicka. "Of course you had this little problem. *Our* problem now." She opened the hypodermic kit that Flicka had brought with her.

"Any idea what this stuff is?"

"Something lethal, that's all I know."

"We have to turn her over to the cops."

"Possession doesn't equal intent, Eden. Any publicity while her lawyers are working on it, the other Fetchlings in Harlee's crew will make themselves scarce."

"You could—"

Bertie smiled faintly at Eden's stern expression.

"Brain-lock? I'm not quite up to it. And it's the next thing to murder anyway." Bertie put a hand on her chest as she breathed. Her eyes closed, opened. "Not up to that, either. We just have to let her go. But with a lesson . . . she'll never forget. Know what I mean?"

"I'm reading you," Eden said grimly.

"There's . . . adhesive tape in the bathroom."

Eden got the tape and a pair of scissors with blunt points, then stood behind Flicka, tearing off several strips of the transparent tape. With those she sealed the Fetchling's mouth and taped her wrists tightly together. While this was going on, Flicka, unable to offer resistance, looked uncomprehendingly at Eden.

"You said they were a 'crew.' How do they live, commune-style?"

"Far from it. They're all kept. Flicka has a penthouse to herself at the Space Odyssey except when her 'Vegas Daddy' is in town. He's a media billionaire in Seattle. Fishing for marlin . . . off Tasmania right now. All set?"

Eden backed away from Flicka's chair, eyed her taping job critically.

"All set."

She reached for the walking stick of stout mopane wood that went everywhere with her. The gold lion's head made a quarter turn toward her face as she held it lightly and horizontally in one hand. Eden closed her eyes briefly.

"Cut her loose, Bertie."

Moments later Flicka jerked sharply in the chair, eyes widening, nostrils pinching in as she drew a huge breath. The expression in her eyes went wild as she struggled to free her taped hands. She leaped to her feet, looking from Bertie on the bed to the stick in Eden's outstretched hand. The muscles in Flicka's throat stood out. She bolted for the door.

"*Simba,*" Eden said.

The stick flew from Eden's hand, turning end over end, and slashed down across Flicka's upper back as she groped for the doorknob. Flicka jerked backward in pain and was struck smartly across one thigh, which hobbled her. She dropped to her knees.

"Good thrashing is enough," Bertie cautioned. "Don't break any bones."

"I know," Eden murmured, expertly deploying the stick, dispassionately watching the action with folded arms as Flicka threw herself helplessly around the carpeted floor, trying to avoid the painful fleshy whacks—most of them to her rear end—and an occasional jab to a calf or arm muscle.

At last she lay weeping with her hands covering her face, thoroughly welted beneath her volunteer's smock. Simba continued to hover over her body at an angle of thirty degrees.

Eden cut the tape away from her mouth with scissors.

"Listen good, Flicka," she said in a big-sister tone of voice. "You think it hurts now, but oh when you wake up in the morning! Anyway, you'll live. A courtesy you don't deserve. Bertie could keep that evil mind of yours in a snakepit for the next two hundred years. Or remember this—either of us can kill you before you're able to blink." Eden passed her left hand, palm down, over the talisman that lay on her breast—only a thumbnail-size wad of grayish metal to Flicka's streaming eyes. "Understand? Nod if you're connecting with me, cutie."

Flicka nodded, making strangled sounds that alternated with whimpering. Her face was flushed and wet.

"Good. You don't have the talent to play in our league. Don't try it again. Still paying attention?"

Flicka nodded hatefully.

"Get up."

Flicka rolled over slowly with a cry of distress and raised herself to her knees. Eden helped her up the rest of the way with the gold lion's head under Flicka's chin. Flicka's eyes rolled nervously.

"I'm bleeding internally," she moaned, wiping a little blood from a corner of her shapely mouth.

"You bit your tongue, that's all. A couple of guys are going to come in here and take you—somewhere. Have a long whirlpool bath with Epsom salts, then alternate ice and heat every fifteen minutes on the bruises. You should be able to get out of bed by this time tomorrow."

Eden released her grip on the walking stick, which remained where it was and kept Flicka's chin angled toward the ceiling.

—How did you get to be such a tough guy? Bertie asked Eden subvocally.

—Four years of Division One basketball. Bertie, let's see Flicka again, say, around eleven tomorrow morning?

—What? Where are you going with—? Oh, I get it.

—Practice, practice, practice. As long as we have ourselves a Fetchling, I should make good use of her.

—So you're going to park her in the bungalow at Bahìa for the night, away from bad influences?

Eden smiled.

"For now we're going to be Flicka's new best friends."

Saying it aloud; Flicka rolled stricken eyes in Eden's direction.

AT VIRGIE LOVECHILD'S · NOVEMBER 4 · 12:53 A.M.

Delilah had insisted that the red crystal skull accompany her wherever she and Gwen went, so it was sitting on the front seat next to Gwen in the Cadillac Escalade. Dr. Marcus Woolwine rode in the back of the SUV as far as he could get from the skull, fearing complications with his pacemaker. Gwen drove because Woolwine had never learned how. The Escalade had an onboard navigator, so Gwen had no problem getting them down from the Magician's fortress on Charleston Mountain en route to the short street behind the Strip and the ever-growing eastward sprawl of megaresorts.

The Strip was where she had problems.

Gwen could drive because dpg's routinely mimicked their homebodies' mundane skills, but she didn't have a license. And she'd never tried to handle anything the size of an Escalade. Heavy southbound traffic on the Strip unnerved her. So did Delilah, who expressed a certain childlike awe at what she was seeing.

"O wondrous sight! How the night dost thrive, with combustion fit to breed Apocalypse!"

Her attention divided, Gwen nearly sideswiped a white limousine with running lights, and partygoers sticking up out of the moon-roof opening like bobble-head dolls.

"The moon is red at midnight, as if it supped on blood! So this is Vegas! Methinks it not unlike a hunting ground, wherein herds of game pay for the privilege of their slaught'ring."

"I don't gamble myself," Woolwine said faintly.

A cultured female voice advised Gwen to make a left turn where Spring Mountain Road became Sands, then a right onto Burbank. Delilah quieted down once they passed the Wynn Resort and crossed under the monorail, which momentarily fascinated her.

The gate across Virgie Lovechild's driveway was closed but not pad-locked. The yard was empty. They heard, faintly, rap music coming from the Airstream trailer parked near the concrete-block wall at the back of Virgie's property. And the low tones of a police/fire radio frequency scanner. There was a party going on in one of the oblong apartment buildings on either side of Virgie's place.

Marcus Woolwine got stiffly out of the Escalade, which Gwen had left across the driveway entrance. He blinked at her. She had the red crystal skull under one arm. Pointless to suggest she leave it behind, he thought. Better to leave both Gwen and Delilah there in the yard while he tried the house. He had seen that there were lights inside.

And, as he found upon entering (the front door stood carelessly or invitingly open, depending on one's purpose in being there), a stuffiness made even less bearable by an assortment of odors that offended his keen nose. Stale but still strong marijuana smoke. A tinge of vomit. Miasma of unwashed animals. Sweetish smear of spilled salsa dip on a low table.

"Hello?"

No reply. But even as he held back on the threshold Woolwine sensed that someone was there. He heard a faint, muffled grunt from the back of the bungalow. Then a sudden loud assault of malevolent hip-hop, as if that someone had dialed the volume of a radio too high while idly looking for a station. It gave Woolwine a violent start. Only about three seconds' worth of the ghetto music, and silence again. But his nerves were slow to settle down.

He took a couple of cautious steps into the living room.

"I'm looking for Virgie Lovechild!" Woolwine called hopefully into the silence.

He heard that small, exasperated-sounding grunt again. As if someone was laboring to accomplish a small task.

Woolwine hunched his shoulders uneasily and proceeded across the front room of the bungalow, crunching corn chips underfoot. He kicked something that gleamed momentarily like a dog's bone as it rebounded from the concertina of a small radiator. The trashiness further offended him. And if there was a bone, where was the dog?

He paused at the entrance to a tiled hallway. On either side, at the end of the hall with its statuary niches, there were two rooms. Lamplight slash through a partially open door to the left revealed another apparent instance of sloppy housekeeping: three or four pieces of broken pottery on the tiles. His eyes shifted from a jagged remnant of a painted face to an indistinct shadow on a bedroom wall beyond the carved door. Someone seemed to be doing an exercise. Which could explain the grunts of effort he'd heard, if not the refusal to answer him.

But the simple explanation could not hold its shape in his mind. A discordancy, a sense of something terribly skewed, emphasized by that pale piece of a saintly face and a single blue eye on the tiles catching the light from inside the room, made his skin prickle.

His instinct, as the grunting came more fiercely to his ears, was to back off, go away with no further attempt to intrude or interrupt what possibly might be a bout of not-altogether-agreeable lovemaking. He was poised to turn when he heard, almost at his feet, a cell phone ring tone.

Woolwine jerked his foot away as if from something deadly and stared down at the compact phone alight and lying against the line of hand-painted baseboard tiles.

As he stared at the cell phone, feeling a creeping numbness along one edge of his tongue and an artery throbbing in his neck, he realized that the abandoned phone wasn't just another instance of general untidiness. Something bad had happened, was still happening, in Virgie Lovechild's house.

The door to the bedroom in front of him opened wide on iron

hinges, the hall brightening a little more from the light of the opaquely shaded lamp within. A girl with a spiky ruff of dark hair, grotesquely overpainted eyes, and a sweaty face was standing there, her breast heaving. She had on headphones that were plugged into an iPod that she wore around her neck.

Behind her, Woolwine glimpsed a still form in tangled bloody bedclothes, head and face hidden beneath a flattened pillow. Those effortful grunting noises he'd heard—the girl had not been exercising but engaging in a more lethal pursuit, smothering the life from whoever it was on the bed.

Deb the Goth girl and Dr. Marcus Woolwine stared at each other with nearly identical expressions of dismay. Deborah's expression changed first, to lip-biting resentment, as if she were anticipating some sort of parental rebuke.

"Who are you? What are you sneaking around here for? What did you *see?*"

"I—I wasn't—I didn't mean—"

Deb pushed the headphones off her ears and waved a temperamental hand as she walked toward him, still trying to get her breathing under control.

Dr. Marcus Woolwine backed up, the only sensible response to the heat and fury he felt emanating from her body. He saw in her darting eyes the trapped wildness of a desperate character, emphasized by the remote heavy beat of hip-hop menace issuing from the headphones. Woolwine knew that few human beings have a taste for cold-blooded murder. He was unable to imagine what had triggered the girl's assault on a presumably helpless, bedridden person. Following the deed she might simply have lapsed into a fugue state, shutting out the immediate past, settling down into some sort of nerveless rote activity. But his unexpected presence had wrenched her back into that other emotional state, which had seen her through the killing frenzy. Of which, Woolwine realized, he could now be an extension, simply an object to be removed from her flight path as quickly and efficiently as possible.

If she'd had a gun, she might already have shot him. Instead, Deborah had her hands and fingernails.

"Stand away, skithy fool!"

Certainly not Deb's voice that he heard. The Goth girl only grunted in her heat as she sprang at him, fingers hooked frighteningly to rip away a significant portion of his face.

She missed, but was close enough to swipe the mirror sunglasses from his face, dash them against the wall as he stumbled and fell back. He landed on his shoulders instead of cracking his skull on the tiles, saving him from a concussion at best. Nevertheless, for a few moments he was in such pain that he couldn't move. Deb kicked his knee and was about to kick him squarely in the groin with a sharp-toed boot when Woolwine saw a thin beam of light like a laser strike her in the forehead. He then was able to scramble out of the Goth girl's path. But she didn't continue after him. She was motionless, as if she'd been hung out to dry on a pink clothesline that went through her head to the wall behind her.

Woolwine continued to put distance between them on all fours, glancing to the front of the house where Gwen/Delilah stood with the cradled crystal skull. The laser beam issued from a cosmic flurry deep inside, from another universe he was incapable of imagining. He looked again at the aghast but silent Deborah and smelled her cooking. A mingling of odors, most prominent of which was bone being ground away as if by a high-speed drill. Wisps of smoke rose from her distended nostrils. He paused, transfixed, continued to stare at her until Deb's eyeballs boiled over and flowed down her cheeks. That was all he cared to see. He pushed himself erect and turned away. When the beam from inside the skull abruptly vanished he heard Deborah fall on her face with a mushy sound.

He said to Gwen/Delilah, "I . . . I don't know what was going on here! It must be Virgie Lovechild in the bedroom! Probably murdered. I think we should leave here as quickly as possible!"

Gwen said, "There's someone in that trailer outside. He may have seen us."

"I can't believe how badly this day has gone!" Woolwine lamented.

"Delilah wants you to wait in the SUV. We'll only be a minute."

"You're not going to—!"

"Yes. We are."

Woolwine was sweating coldly. Unsteady on his bowed legs. He felt his gorge rising.

"This is *not* what we came for."

"Delilah says, 'In delay there lieth no plenty.' And for you to shut up. You'd better get going. She can really fly off the handle at people, you know?"

Gwen turned and walked away with the skull in the crook of her arm. Woolwine followed numbly from the bungalow. He didn't look around as Gwen walked quickly to the Airstream trailer.

He was getting into the back of the Escalade when he thought he saw, in a car parked near the dead end of the block, some movement, a hint of a pale inquiring face behind windshield glass that reflected the tropical neon of a sign advertising an apartment complex.

Woolwine quickly averted his own face, closed the door behind him, and sat hunched over, holding his stomach, trying not to think of what might be going on in that trailer. But not daring to sneak a look. Blood throbbed in his temples. All he could think of was jellied eyeballs and a slogan that the Las Vegas Chamber of Commerce recently had adopted:

What happens in Vegas stays in Vegas.

He hoped that was true, because he didn't plan to stay there for more than a few hours longer. The flickering, stylized palms of the sign reminded him of Rio—the fun capital of Brazil, not the local hotel and casino—and Rio de Janeiro seemed perfectly sized to his immediate ambitions for getting good and lost in a far place.

1:05 A.M.

From where they were sitting in Harlee Nations's red Dodge Viper coupe, Harlee had an obstructed view of what must have been a second intense flash, this one inside the trailer where Virgie Lovechild had conducted her lucrative Pack of Rotsies business for many years.

They were silent as Gwen subsequently reappeared with the red crystal skull, got into the Cadillac Escalade (which Harlee had last seen parked in the garage beneath Lincoln Grayle's aerie) and backed out into the street, headed south, and turned right at the intersection.

Nicole let out the breath she'd been holding. "That was the Avatar?"

Harlee shook her head. "Don't think so." But she couldn't be sure. After all, what were the odds that Eden Waring's doppel-ganger had successfully completed her journey through time, returning spot-on to her point of departure—and without the help of the crystal skull that she and Devon had spirited away not long ago from the dpg's suite at the Magician's house? The same skull Harlee had deposited the day before in the vault at Grayle's Mountain.

In the Great One's absence, Harlee was certain that she alone had access to the vault. Harlee was tired, confused, angry. But not so tired that she couldn't reach the only reasonable conclusion to this mystery: there was more than one of the cosmically powerful crystal skulls in Las Vegas, no matter who they'd just seen driven away from Virgie Lovechild's.

"They're gone," Nic said, yawning tautly. "Are we going to Vir-gie's now?"

"No."

"But Devon—"

"She's not there, Nicole."

"Her *car*'s not there! Doesn't mean—"

Harlee started her Viper. She closed her eyes momentarily, seeing red. Her hands wanted to tremble. She gripped the wheel tightly.

"Just shut up, Nic! I don't know what's become of Devon and I won't know until I hear from her. But I'm not going near Virgie's house. Something went on there tonight, Devon's missing and I have a bad feeling."

Nic moaned softly. "Girl, you are givin' me goose bumps."

Harlee drove down the street, slowly, both of them staring at the walled half acre and the nearly lightless bungalow.

"If it *was* the Avatar we saw, why do you think she was—"

"I don't know!"

"You don't need to be yellin' at me, Harl."

"You're right. Apologies. What are you doing?"

"I'm callin' Flicka again! I'll call her every five minutes until she picks up!"

"Don't bother," Harlee said. "*They've* got her."

With the phone to her ear, Nic shot Harlee a look. "Even if they turned her over to the cops, I mean, what could they prove? And doesn't she get a phone call?"

"She's not in juvie. By *they* I meant the Supa and the Av."

Nic's expression turned dismal. "*Shit.* Voice mail again." She dropped the phone into her tote. "If that's true, what are we gonna do about it?"

"I need time to think this through. I'm going home."

"I don't want to be by myself tonight!"

"Come with me, then."

"I hate bein' around that old guy you livin' with. Drop me at Reese's?"

"Okay."

"What do I tell Reese and Honeydew?"

"We'll put our heads together tomorrow. Right now I need sleep."

Harlee's own phone rang. She glanced at the dashboard display.

"It's Flicka's cell!" Nic said joyously.

"About time," Harlee said, but she hesitated before answering, feeling a twinge of apprehension. Then she took the call.

"This is Harlee. Where—"

"Hi," Eden Waring said cheerily. "Hope I'm not calling you too late, Harlee."

Cody Olds returned from his compact kitchen with two snifters of brandy to find Eden lying knees-up on the sofa and gazing thoughtfully at the ceiling, tossing Flicka's little cell phone from hand to hand. She was bare legged, wearing running shorts and a hooded pullover.

He eased down onto the sofa at her feet, his back giving him problems—from a stressful day and present worries, he thought. Cody put one of the snifters on the floor where it was handy and reached out to nab the phone Eden was playing with. He put it into his shirt pocket. Her reverie interrupted, Eden smiled and sat up facing him. She tucked a big buckskin-covered pillow behind her back and extended a hand for her brandy, waggling fingers mock impatiently.

"Well, it's done," she said. "A short but interesting conversation."

"But was it the smart thing to do?"

Eden sipped her brandy and licked her lips in appreciation.

"What's that line from the *Godfather* movie about enemies?"

"Keep 'em closer than your friends. I wonder if anyone's ever done a follow-up about the success of that strategy."

"She can't hurt me. That's the first lesson Harlee Nations is going to learn."

"I guess you're not about to tell me what it was you did with that Flicka girl."

"No more than she deserved. Cody, they're not—sweet young things. They're *Fetchlings*. They all have histories that would gag a maggot."

Eden extended her long legs across Cody's lap. He winced a little.

"I'm sorry! Is it your back?"

"Yeah. I'm okay."

"Want me to—"

"No, you're fine like you are." He ran a hand from one ankle to the inside of her knee. Hesitated there. Smiled. Left his hand where it was. Three little puncture scars there, repair job on a torn meniscus. "You just get me to seizin' up sometimes, because I don't know yet how I'm supposed to be of any help to you."

"Your bad back is my fault?" she said teasingly. "I thought you fell off a horse."

"You're the horse I keep fallin' off of now."

Eden smiled, sympathetically.

"There's no one else who can be what you are to me, Cody."

They looked at each other for a while. Cody blinked first.

"What?" Eden said, reaching for the hand on her knee and slowly moving it higher.

"Pain in my back went away."

"Good."

"When are you meetin' up with this Fetchling?"

"One thirty tomorrow afternoon."

"In a public place?"

"You bet. I invited her to lunch."

Cody nodded. "Goin' it alone?"

"I'm shielded, Cody. Protected from—any harm they might try to bring to me. But they can eventually get to me through you, if they know we're as close as we are. Can't allow that to happen."

"How do you plan to get this Harlee off your back?"

"Just believe that I can do it."

He nodded slightly. They resumed looking at each other, sipping brandy, smiling about things that didn't need to be put into words.

"Cody, I think I'll go to bed now."

"Sleepy?"

"No. I'm not all that sleepy."

Almost a minute went by.

"What about—"

"His name is Tom Sherard. He's someone—something that I got caught up in because I was afraid and lonely and not at all sure of myself. But some of that's changed now; the rest will be up to you."

"Okay."

She swung her legs together to the floor and stood, stretching, not looking at him.

"Give me five minutes to—brush my teeth, and, like, settle down because my heart's really going now, and—time to get comfortable in my skin, if that makes sense to you."

"Can't say I'm any different, Eden."

"Really? Because I couldn't deal with a lot of—you know, macho stud bullshit right now. My love life has been—oh, I probably shouldn't even bring it up, but. He, my first lover I mean, betrayed me and might've gotten me killed. Tom—wherever he is—I think probably he'll be glad for me. And that's—really all there is to tell. Some love life." She laughed. "God, I'm nervous."

"Go brush your teeth."

"Okay . . . okay. Do you want me to call you when—?"

"I think I'll know when."

"You will, won't you? And that's what I love about you and depend on, so much."

CITTA DEL VATICANO · 0620 HOURS ZULU

Following a working breakfast with the senior Vatican prelates whom he most relied on to keep sand out of the theocratic gears and orchestrate accommodations between secularists and hard-line conservatives within the Holy See, Pope John XXIV takes a twenty-minute breather, alone, in his garden.

The sun has just risen and ground fog is melting away. Leoncaro has a small plastic bag of birdseed with him, which, like a good Franciscan, he scatters at intervals. He is also practiced at bird calls but feels a little embarrassed at the possibility of being overheard. Except when he is secluded in his personal quarters, there always are eyes on him.

Nevertheless, fun is where he can find it during the course of grueling eighteen-hour days. And this morning he has indigestion.

"Back so soon?" he inquires skeptically of Zachary, the Echelon 3 recently dispatched to Las Vegas, who now is achieving modest form within a line of Italian cypresses. "Very well. Report." With a fist Leoncaro suppresses a bubble of gas that has reached his lips. He looks around in the morning glow. There are rosy nuthatches living nearby that he is particularly fond of, but he has yet to see one on his morning walk.

The Caretaker-in-training waxes a little brighter as he falls into step beside his mentor.

"There really was nothing more I could hope to accomplish in Las Vegas," Zach explains. "The bond that has been established between Cody Olds and Eden Waring should prove to be . . . unusually durable."

"Fast work."

"Because they've now reached an inevitable point of intimacy, I didn't feel at all comfortable, you know, hanging around. And there are developments."

Leoncaro broadcasts more birdseed. "Related, perhaps, to recent disturbances in the Mobius microregion colloquially known as 'Jubilation County' that indicate Mordaunt's better half has succeeded in reclaiming her true persona."

"Oh. But aren't there safeguards—"

"Fresno's Vortex. To be sure. I think it unlikely that 'she' managed, by herself, to escape from a Mobius microregion, even taking into consideration her considerable powers. Yet it seems she *has* escaped."

"I don't know if or how this could be related, but—do you recall, Holiness, on my last visit you were telling me all that fascinating stuff about Eden Waring's doppelganger."

"Guinevere. Yes."

"Whom Eden had lost touch with? Well, it's a virtual certainty that the dpg showed up in Vegas a couple of nights ago. Behind the wheel of a 1926 Franklin speedster that suddenly appeared on the casino floor of the Venetian Hotel. Accompanied by atmospheric disturbances that upset quite a few stomachs and had guests reeling all over the—"

"Franklin Sportster? I remember those. I suppose you're going to tell me that Gwen wasn't traveling alone."

"No, Holiness. She had two passengers with her in the car. Inadvertent time-travelers, it seems. Patrick O'Doul and his uncle Mickey, both of whom disappeared from Paramus, New Jersey, present era and macroregion, circa 1973. Something to do with spark plugs in an old—anyway. Patrick eventually spilled the beans to my—to Cody Olds. Explained how they simply vanished. *Poof!* And found themselves—"

"The theatrical gestures are unnecessary, Zach. Now, did you happen to see the car that the doppelganger and her passengers arrived in from Jubilation County?"

"No. But from Patrick's description, it had to be a time machine."

"Specially equipped by Letty Fresno," Leoncaro muses. "No doubt with one of those damnable red crystal skulls. More of Letty's sly deviltry. She and all of her skulls should have been interred aeons ago beneath a frozen methane sea on Neptune."

"Red crystal skull? Now that you mention it, Holiness—"

Leoncaro looks at Zachary with a slight knowing grimace.

"Gwen had it with her?"

Zach nods. "When she was last seen, leaving the hotel. Because of the surveillance network in Las Vegas—which is more comprehensive than that of a supermax prison—anyone who sets foot there is almost immediately recorded."

"Then we can safely assume that Mordaunt's liberated better half has control of Gwen. Who remains beyond Eden's recall. Thus in a position to become the most deadly of the Avatar's enemies. I wonder how this can get any worse."

"What about Mordaunt himself—I mean, Lincoln Grayle?"

"That's another matter. The *Stella Salamis* went down in a Pacific storm short of the undersea canyon that was to have been the final destination of the encrypted were-beast. The *Crucis Aurea* has yet to determine if there were survivors, although another ship was in the area."

"Well—tragic that lives were lost, but the sinking of the ship isn't all bad, is it?"

They walk on, mulling the troublesome turn of events. Leoncaro barely suppresses a belch and says apologetically, "I rarely have sausage for breakfast, and this is the reason why."

Zachary ventures, "Surely the odds that the beast survived are very long."

"The prospect, no matter what the odds, of his soul being made whole is too dreadful to contemplate. And there's the fate of the two girls I rashly sent out there to deal with the late Magician. Their developing powers and, I hope, instinct for teamwork, are impressive. But *Deus Inversus* full-strength is no adversary for amateurs."

"If we're correct in assuming that the feminine soul is presently in human form—" Zachary looks baffled. "But of course doppelgangers aren't human. They're—they're—what exactly *are* they?"

"What matters is that this one, although not fully independent of her homebody, is very dangerous. Celestial Law ensures that her doppelganger may not take Eden's life. But she is a threat to anyone close to Eden, who could be manipulated into naming Gwen, thereby setting her free."

"Bertie Nkambe has made a remarkable comeback from the shooting, but she'll probably be in a weakened condition for a while. As for Cody Olds—" Zachary shakes his head worriedly.

"You were only doing your job," Leoncaro assures him.

"I do feel responsible for him. He would lay down his life for Eden now. Perhaps I should go back to Vegas. Even though I can't directly interfere in human affairs."

"No. Take a breather for now, Zachary. I set all of this in motion. I shall be the one to go to Las Vegas."

Zachary looks around the papal garden, the old stones, the greenery coming to light, and then at the solemn face of his boss.

"But—your schedule here—you don't have a minute free to—"

"I shall just have to be in both places at once."

Zachary purses his lips to whistle, but doesn't.

"You can do that?"

Leoncaro shrugs. "After all, there are only twelve of us, Zachary. Two places at once, merely a matter of training and discipline. Now, being in three places at once—that is a bit of a stretch."

In addition to Bronc Skarbeck's Aston Martin there were a couple of black limos on the parking court of Bronc's house when Harlee arrived home, yawning. Bronc often had visitors at all hours of the night, particularly this week with the Elite 88 in town for uneasy parleys. She took little notice of the limos.

Her unusually sharp and focused mind was blurred with concern for the missing Devon. She was further confused about the import of Eden Waring's phone call. Eden had been cheerful, suspiciously so, but had refused to answer any questions about Flicka, saying only that the Fetchling assassin was for now "a guest" of Eden and Bertie Nkambe.

There were two men in the foyer of the house eating take-out pizza. Limo drivers or bodyguards, Harlee thought, not looking closely enough at their suits, expensive European tailoring that bespoke style. She smiled absently as she walked to the stairs.

In spite of swarthy skin and a few moles they had bland, easily forgettable faces. If you paid little attention to lightless eyes that could outstare a corpse. Harlee felt a stab of uneasiness before one of them spoke to her.

"Are you Harlee?"

She paused, a hand on the stair railing. "Yes."

"The General would like to see you, in his quarters."

Harlee's shoulders dropped. "Not tonight. Could you just tell him—"

A scream of intense agony reverberated through the house. Harlee looked up the stairs, lips parting; then she turned and ran for the front door.

The shorter of the two men, with three gold rings punched into an earlobe, was quick. He caught her by an elbow and did something with her arm that gave her excruciating pain and had her up on her toes, barely able to breathe.

"Walk," he said.

The other one stuffed the last of his pizza into his mouth and chewed it while he followed them upstairs. Harlee grimaced in pain but didn't say anything. They weren't men you could disobey or try to trick. Harlee knew that she and Skarbeck were in a huge bind. She could piece together a scenario without much difficulty.

Pain had cleared her mind. The closer they came to Bronc's suite, the more lucid she became. She had a good idea of what she was going to see inside. Whoever was waiting for her could be manipulated, outwitted; just a matter of experience. For now she made do with squeaks of protest, tears.

There were more men like those who had met her in the foyer. She didn't expend energy trying to impress them with her fear. She let her feet drag, whimpering, as they took her through the bedroom with the round bed the size of a satin-covered helo pad and on into the ornate bath where the ringleaders were presiding over Bronc's torture amid urns of fresh flowers.

Three of them, all members of the Elite 88, who in Mordaunt's absence had united to get their hands on the one thing that would ensure their power over other hostile factions: Mordaunt's gold. They looked at Harlee when she was brought in with poorly concealed impulses of deep greed. She was instantly contemptuous, although she rolled her eyes and favored the situation with a shriek of horror. It *was* a shock to see how they had broken a tough guy like Bronc Skarbeck.

He was kneeling on the bathroom floor, his head and face in a streaky mess of blood, some old, some new. His hands were wired behind his back. His ankles were wired together. They had inserted a silver rod into his anus. Silver provides excellent conductivity. No elaborate devices: wires from the rod had been joined to an ordinary electrical plug, which, when inserted into the outlet next to Bronc's shaving mirror, had caused him to smash his head repeatedly against the tiles.

When she shrieked, one of the ringleaders nodded to the man who had control of her. He let Harlee go. She went to Bronc, who was trying to raise his battered head, look around with blood-clogged eyes, utter coherent words. Harlee slipped in his blood, shrieked again, put a hand on his quivering naked back.

"Sorry," she thought she heard him say.

Harlee stood protectively beside Bronc, aimlessly rubbing bloodied hands on her clothing, urine running down her legs (they'd find that a convincing touch), saying, "Nonono oh *please* don't hurt him any more!"

The spokesman for the little group of Malterran claim jumpers, a bled-out crookback scorpion of a fellow, gray as ashes and apparently living on a charge of lethal belligerence, said, "There should be no need. Now that you've returned." He looked at another of the trio of urbane cutthroats—this one had jowls like pouches of coins low-slung from heavy jawbones. The Scorpion said with a galling smirk, "In every man's life there is at least one day that will haunt him forever. Usually it has to do with a woman." He looked back at Harlee. "A pretty young thing in this case, eh?"

"She's soiled herself," the third man observed. It seemed to excite him. He ejected the remains of a smoked cigarette from an ebony holder and walked over to Harlee, lifted her chin with a thumb. "You are Fetchling? Remarkable. What stories you must have to tell. You should be most entertaining."

Skarbeck was convulsing. One of the torturers slipped the silver rod out of him and tipped him on his side with a foot.

"He's dying! Get him a doctor!" Harlee pleaded.

"Give him a shot of morphine," the Scorpion said to the torturers. "Then cover him. We're through here, aren't we, Egon?"

Addressing the one who had been captivated by Harlee, and who held her immobile.

"*Are* we through here?" the smiling man asked of Harlee, whose chin he held at an acute angle in the air, light pressure on an artery.

"I'll do whatever you want! Just don't let Bronc die, please!"

"You have access to the vault? You would not both be lying to us?"

"Yes. Yes! I can get you in. Please. I'm going to faint."

Egon let her go. Harlee held her throat and made pathetic strangling sounds while assessing her precarious situation. Flight, for now, was out of the question. Too many of them; she wouldn't get far. But they weren't going to hurt her, not seriously. Aside from her supposed entertainment value she was uniquely valuable to these renegades.

Harlee looked in dread at her bloodied hands. "I need—I have to—"

"Of course, darling," the Scorpion said. "Egon will take you to your room to shower and change your clothes. Unless—" He looked around Bronc's bathroom.

"I have my own suite."

Egon walked Harlee down the second-floor gallery and into her digs.

While he was looking around for possible escape routes, Harlee glanced at the picnic hamper that she and Devon had taken to Ferdie Younger's canyon hideaway earlier. Her heart was jumping. The hamper had been returned, probably by messenger, wrapped in pink cellophane with a bow. And there was an envelope inside.

While Egon was out on the balcony judging how far Harlee would have to jump to rocky ground if she was desperate enough (more than twenty feet), Harlee scooped up the hamper and carried it into the bathroom, where she stashed it at the back of her walk-in clothes closet.

She turned on the shower, began pulling off her clothes. Saw Egon in a fogging-up mirror, leaning in the doorway behind her.

"Leave me alone."

"What harm if I watch you undress?"

"No. Get *out.*"

Egon shrugged, smiling. "Oh well. Plenty of time for that later, yes?"

Harlee gave him a look over her shoulder, lips tight together. His smile became a laugh, but he went away, closing the door, but not tightly, behind him.

Once she had stripped, Harlee wrapped herself in a bath sheet and retrieved the hamper from the closet. It was lighter than when it had been filled with toothsome treats for Ferdie. And it felt cold.

Her name in script was on the pink envelope. She opened it.

Dear Harlee:
Caution is your watchword, I should remind you. There are
ten of my beauties. Be aware of the correct number. A mistake
could be deadly for you. For now they are snugly packed in a
section of their hive that is surrounded by dry ice sufficient to
keep them sluggish and unfit for combat. Quite harmless until

warmed to room temperature. Simply attach the nozzle of a portable hair dryer to the case containing their hive. Two minutes, on low heat, will be sufficient to restore them to full potency. Full of vim, vigor, and homicidal inclination. Again, be very cautious. I would miss your stimulating visits.

F.

Very cautious? Well, that was the part that required a lot of thought, while she soaped and loofah'd herself in the steamy shower.

The steam and the attention to her body was making Harlee sleepy, along with the inevitable aftermath of a considerable shock to her system. As soon as she had dried off and put on a terry robe she swallowed a couple of uppers with cognac. She needed a rush to sharpen her perceptions and keep her on her toes, as if for a crucial fencing match.

The pesky Egon looked in on her again without knocking. She was drying her hair. She turned off the dryer and just stared at him until he went away again.

This time Harlee locked the bathroom door. Her pulses had picked up. She felt a keen sense of purpose, a razor's edge of desire for revenge.

In her dressing room she put on thermal underwear, then a fresh white padded fencing costume. She selected a mask and studied herself in an alcove of bright mirrors. Only her hands, feet, and the back of her head were unprotected. She took off the fencing mask, added a fall to her hair, and made of it a thick bun no hornet could penetrate. Fencing gloves and a pair of lace-up, knee-high white leather boots completed her costume.

Then she woke up the Japanese hornets.

Harlee could only hope she'd done it right. She wasn't about to open the hamper to have a look. But she sensed a lethal power astir, down there in the fragment of hive.

Egon knocked imperatively on the bathroom door. "Coming," Harlee said cheerily.

In the bedroom he stared at her costume as she walked briskly past him, fencing mask in one hand, hamper in the other.

"What do you have there? Why are you dressed like that? What's in the hamper?"

"Two thousand dollars' worth of bloody clothing I'm throwing out," Harlee said, not breaking stride. "A few personal things."

"Just leave it."

"Don't be a fool," she said. "Twenty minutes after the house-keeper gets here at seven, there'll be cops all over this hacienda."

He was quick to catch up to Harlee.

"That will not matter to you. Or to Skarbeck."

But Harlee was already on the gallery, quickening her pace to Bronc's suite.

"Stop. What are you up to?" Egon said.

Harlee sobbed. "Is he dead? I just want to see him again."

"Stop!"

"Fuck you," Harlee said, shrugging off his hand and entering the suite. The other men were slow to react to the hamper, the odd costume, the fencing mask. She slipped past them to the double ebony-and-gold doors of Bronc's bathroom. Bronc still lying on the floor inside—looking old, tired, freckled, gray, with filmed-over eyes.

Harlee was grabbed again.

"You will show us what you have—"

"Oh yeah?" Harlee screamed. She turned and flung the hamper at Egon. "You sons of bitches! Take it! Take all of them!"

The lid of the hamper fell open as Egon deflected it to the floor. He bent down to turn the hamper right-side up, then jerked his hand away as if he'd touched a live wire. Harlee saw four or five of the giant samurai hornets clustered on the back of his hand and wrist.

Then she turned and ran, fencing mask going to her face. She vaulted over Bronc's huddled form and ran into the shower enclosure as Egon screamed in shock and terror. Her heart was throbbing up into her throat.

The shower was nearly the size of a horse's stall. She quickly began to turn on the shower jets, hearing screams from other Malterrans as hornets flew at their eyes, blinding them with streams of venom.

Through the angular full-force sprays of water Harlee saw a looming frantic face as one of the men tried to join her in the shower. He got the door open, but she kicked him in the balls and drove him back as one of the great hornets alighted for a moment on a fleshy cheek. He went down, flailing and shrieking. Harlee had never heard another human being make such a sound, not even Bronc Skarbeck with a lightning bolt up his ass.

Fetchling. And so contemptuous of her. So confident of their own status and power.

Their venom (she heard Ferdie Younger say again, recalling his voice perfectly in her mind while she chewed savagely at her lower lip) *consists of eleven different chemicals that, among other things, dissolve human flesh. If one is stung about the face, the face will soon decompose. No matter. By then the victims are usually dead from anaphylactic shock.*

Harlee clenched gloved hands and screamed herself, exultantly.

So how do you like me now, guys?

She couldn't look at her watch, didn't know how much time had gone by before it was absolutely still in Bronc Skarbeck's suite. She let the shower jets run and leaned against a wall, shuddering, staring through steam at Bronc's body. Thinking nostalgically of how he'd obsessed over her, and how he would have approved of this act of vengeance.

But now, with her valuable hornets scattered, their own time short in an alien unforested place, she would have to think of something even more appropriate to avenge the Great One and satisfy her vendetta against Eden Waring. Who also seemed to be taking her too lightly, going by the tone of voice that the Avatar had adopted during their brief phone conversation. Harlee hadn't missed the mild but unmistakable taunting.

Think you're good enough? Take your best shot, kid.

No big deal. Harlee felt enlivened by the rough jets of water stimulating her skin through two layers of stinger-proof clothing. Wonderfully focused. And dispersing wholesale death by hornet had been the best upper of them all.

She wanted to stay on top of this high. She wanted another death. She wanted it *soon.*

The coldest hour of the new day.

At seven thousand feet or better the temperature is within a couple of degrees of freezing.

Two of them sitting on the Magician's terrace outside his six-room suite at the highest level of the cantilevered house. There are clear night views in three directions.

Two spirits, one immortal, the other subservient, within a single body on a chaise lounge, blanket-wrapped. The red filaments of an electric heater mimic in tone the shimmer of the red crystal skull on a table next to the chaise.

She, they, have been lying there for an hour. A storm is building over the cloudless peak of Charleston Mountain. The crystal skull has begun to gorge. Its source of earthly energy (more than suitable to Delilah's needs and purpose) is contained within a much smaller mountain eighty miles northwest. A hidden, unacknowledged source, but available to the attractive power of that cosmic glow-worm of a skull.

Thus, the sky between Charleston and Yucca mountains, previously untouched by weather, displaying a tapestry of stars in the clarity of the high desert, is alive at this hour in the form of a seething, ruddy whirlpool. There are flickerings within the slowly circulating cloud of energy that resemble heat lightning.

Below the cloud, the desert, largely unpopulated.

And certain secret government installations collectively known as Area 51.

There is almost no traffic, commercial or military, in Las Vegas airspace, but a helicopter has crashed on takeoff at Nellis, all of its eletronics compromised. No loss of life, no immediate connection to the appearance of the mystery airborne event, but military meteorologists are among the first to begin a study of the growing phenomenon.

At fifteen thousand feet or so, the cloud is easily visible to anyone on the streets of Vegas. Even at the graveyard hour there are quite a few fun-seekers up and around. Most are spellbound; a few are frightened. Those who try to use their cell phones find that reception is poor to nonexistent.

A Lufthansa 747 freighter from Frankfurt, inbound to McCarran International but still thirty-seven thousand feet above southwest South Dakota and Mount Rushmore, is advised by the FAA's Denver Center to divert to the Salt Lake City area and hold there as long as fuel permits, due to "unstable conditions" generated by the rogue system near Vegas.

Harlee Nations, red-eyed herself and desperate for sleep, is aware of the violent red glow overhead as she drives up the sometimes-difficult road through Kyle Canyon to the Magician's house, where she plans to crash for twelve hours or so. She doesn't make much of the cycloid cloud even when her car's electronics start acting weird short of the gated entrance to the Magician's house.

She gets out of her Viper and trudges across the auto courtyard carrying a backpack with items of clothing and other essentials to get her through a few days.

All lights in the house are out, except one, which attracts her eye: an intense beacon of neonlike pink fulminating on the highest terrace. She has seen its like before. But in spite of her muddled emotional and mental state, she knows very well that she put the crystal skull in the Magician's vault with all the gold that the predacious, now very dead, Malterrans had lusted after.

And only Lincoln Grayle himself could have removed it.

Harlee sobs hopefully on her way up a succession of stairs to the high suite.

Yes, I see it," Bertie Nkambe says to Eden on the phone. She is looking out a north window of her room at the cloud with its carousel of lightning. "I *feel* it, too. What do you think?"

"You know how it goes with me. I dream it a couple of times, then it *happens.*"

"Good-bye, Las Vegas?"

"Good-bye to us as well," Eden says pensively. "Can you speak up, Bertie? I can barely hear you."

"Maybe this is the best Gwen can do," Bertie says. "If that's it, then the two of us can do better."

"No. You're too weak, still. Better leave Gwen to me. She's my responsibility anyway."

"But there's two of them, Eden! And we don't know what powers Delilah survived with." Bertie looks at the cloud again. It seems less formidable than it did a few minutes ago, when she was levitated from sleep by its presence, every nerve in her still-healing body ignited by the attractive force in the depths of the cloud.

"Doesn't matter," Eden says grimly. "I buried *him,* Bertie, and I can damn well bury both of them."

Bertie says after a few moments, "Might not be a good idea, subverting occult law. She's your doppelganger."

"Until I decide otherwise. As for occult law—when she's not just another energy body, she's—nothing, really. It wouldn't be the same as killing myself."

Eden's voice fades momentarily, a ghostly withdrawal.

"Or would it?"

"Let me think about it," Bertie cautions. "There's time. Eden, I think the cloud is losing some of its force. Powering down."

"Seems to be," Eden agrees. "Bertie, I have a hunch what this was about."

"A demonstration?"

"Yes. Staged for us."

4:51 A.M.

By the time the cloud had disappeared, more than seven hundred calls had been received by Las Vegas Metro's emergency lines, an electronic traffic jam that had put the 911 system temporarily out of business.

Bertie was looking at the now benign night sky and yawning, thinking over her conversation with Eden, when there was a knock at her door.

She thought it might be her father or brother. But at this hour—

Bertie's pulses jumped. She hurried to unlock the door.

Tom Sherard stood there wearing a seaman's sweater and Levi's, cuts on his face, fatigue in his gray eyes.

"Tom!" she cried, but even as she reached out to draw him closer, she realized her mistake and backed away, horrified.

She tried to reverse the polarities of his brain but her psychic strength wasn't equal to what Mordaunt could bring to bear on her.

Bertie sank nervelessly to the floor as if her brain were being sucked deep into a whirlpool.

"You won't get her," she murmured, her last coherent thought.

She never saw him smile.

4:54 A.M.

His name was Hector Rosario, and he came from a little place in backroads Guatemala called Joatomala, where he'd spent all but the last six years of his life before joining the ever-growing Latin American migration north to the States. Now he worked night maintenance at Concordia Hospital. He had learned reasonably good English. He was forty-five years old but looked ten years older. He had a wife who earned good money as a chambermaid and three children who attended Vegas public schools. Hector had little formal schooling himself but he was an intuitive man with a quiet way of observing everything that went on around him. In addition to being handy with tools, Hector had certain talents that distinguished him. Hector was descended from a long line of warlocks. Thus, he was accorded the leadership of an ever-expanding community of Hispanic expats, the majority of whom were steeped in occult tradition.

Hector was on his break in the employees' break room in a basement area of the hospital, snacking on beef jerky and drinking a Sprite, when he had a strange nerve-prickling sensation. His hands shook. More alarming, there was a shudder in his mind, as if a stealth intelligence had entered with no fuss and was getting acquainted.

Ay Dios!

Because supernaturalism was the way of his forebears and still a fact of life in the villages back home, Hector had always been comfortable with the juxtaposition of such influences and the Catholicism that he faithfully practiced. Now he bowed his head and grasped the gold crucifix around his neck, praying inaudibly. No one else in the room paid Hector any mind.

Only a few moments passed before it became apparent to Hector that the possessing spirit was both supernal and extraordinarily loving, not a threat to his soul. Hector had a vision of the Holy Father in a showering gold radiance that settled on him like a rich cloak, humbling and calming him. Tears flowed down his cheeks, but his trembling subsided.

"What do you want of me, Holy Father?"

—Just think of me as a Caretaker, Hector. We must work together for a little while. No harm will come to you.

"As you wish, Holiness. But why are you in Las Vegas?"

—Soon, possibly within twenty-four hours, there is going to be a great battle here, an epic battle between good and evil. The city may well be destroyed in the process.

"Dios mio!"

—In fact, it has begun already. There is a Presence in this hospital—

"The Evil One?" Hector began to quake again.

—Not at full power. They're a matched pair. But the Presence within is very dangerous, and we need to expel it quickly.

"I—my family—"

—As soon as we've seen to the present emergency, you must use your authority as a community leader to organize an exodus of all your people from the city.

"But, with all respect, sir—if time is growing short—there are as many as two hundred thousand Latinos in Las Vegas! Not counting tourists. And what of the rest of the population?"

—Hector, if you lived here or were attending a convention and noticed a couple of hundred thousand other people lighting out across the desert in all directions with whatever they could throw into their SUVs, what do you think would be your first impulse?

Hector said with a sickly grin, "To follow? Ah, yes, I see. And I do have authority with my own people. But to reach so many, and quickly, a miracle is required!"

—It's called the Internet, Hector. Now let's get ourselves going. We're needed upstairs.

Mordaunt allowed Bertie sufficient freedom of mind and motion to dress herself and walk without help. Which she did, performing mechanically, eyes open, emtionless. In the sitting room of her hospital suite she saw the two Blackwelder bodyguards whom Mordaunt had brain-locked; she had no memory of who they were. No comprehension of their fate. Full recovery from brain-lock was impossible. Partial recovery took many months.

The night nurses on duty had suffered the same fate at the whim of Mordaunt. The entire floor at nearly five in the morning was very quiet, except for the remote beeps of monitors in other of the luxury units.

"I have a limo waiting downstairs," Mordaunt said in Tom Sherard's voice. But Bertie had only the dimmest memory of what Sherard had sounded like. Of their life together at Shungwaya in Kenya. Of the man he'd been, the love she had had for him.

They were a few steps from the elevator when the doors opened and Hector Rosario walked out.

Mordaunt stopped suddenly and Bertie, feeling the rage, the animus that possessed him, shied away.

Tom Sherard and Hector Rosario, surrogates for *Deus Inversus,* the Darkness of God, and the purest representative of Supernal Light in the galaxy, entities with powers beyond the scope of any human to imagine, studied each other.

Sherard, tall hunter, made a guttural warning sound.

Hector, squat, graying, sad-eyed, said in Spanish, "You are turning up much too often these days, Evil One."

"And you have strayed too far from Rome. Las Vegas is my sanctuary. Its people are *my* people."

"Yet a young woman barely tutored in the Art of the Light defeated you here." Tom Sherard's shoulders hunched. Hector smiled slightly. "What does that tell you about the condition your powers are in?"

The guttural rumblings became a full-throated growl.

Hector sighed, then heard himself say as his chest tightened from a heart swell of contempt, "Oh, piss off. Release the Hunter, release the girl, who is of no use to you, go back to playing the Dark God on the mountain in this neon Gomorrah. No one else needs it or wants it."

"*No,*" Bertie said hoarsely.

They both looked at her, Mordaunt angered by the slippage of his control that allowed her to speak at all. Then they both glimpsed the brief coherent warning that had surfaced in her conscious mind.

Sherard let out a roar that shattered glass cabinet fronts and light boxes at the nurses' station.

Then Hector's eyes filled with a light directed at Sherard's pale eyes. The light blinded him like the noonday sun and sent him helplessly to his knees, the heels of his palms pressed tightly to the orbits of his eyes. But even that wasn't enough to keep the light from his brain. His body convulsed.

"Enough!" Mordaunt shrieked.

"Oh, I don't think so," Hector said, and the light intensified. Sherard collapsing, writhing.

Hector pulled Bertie to her feet and backed with her to the elevator. They left Sherard, and Mordaunt, on the floor holding his head, sheathed in the brilliant light that had surrounded him like a celestial cocoon.

"That will hold him for a little while," Hector said to Bertie, whose eyes were closed. She was breathing harshly. "But soon he'll go in search of Eden's doppelganger. Miss Nkambe, I know you're in considerable pain, but can you talk to me?"

"I'll . . . try. Oh God, why . . . did it have to be . . . Tom?"

"Do you know where the dpg is?"

"No."

"Does Eden?"

"I . . . don't think so."

They reached the main floor. A guard yawning by the entrance looked them over, frowned, crossed the lobby floor toward them.

"Hector, where're you going with her?"

Hector looked him in the eye. The guard did a puzzled double take, blinking, and stood very still.

"Roberto, we'd like to borrow your car. Matter of fact, why don't you drive us?"

"Of course, Don Hector. *A donde vamos?*"

"I'll let you know in a few moments."

The three of them left the hospital and walked toward the employees' parking lot.

Hector said to Bertie, "I know that Eden is with her new friend, the artist. Do you know where he lives?"

"No."

"His name, then?"

"Cody . . . uh, Old. No, Olds."

They got into Roberto's car. "The address of Mr. Cody Olds," Hector said.

"Yes, *jefe.*" Roberto was a cop during the day, desk job in Metro Traffic. He made a phone call, and had Cody Olds's address and phone number in under two minutes.

"*Arriba,*" Hector said, looking back at the main hospital building. He was in the front seat with Roberto. Bertie was lying face-up in the backseat, knees up, groaning softly.

"I'm so sorry, my dear," Hector said to her.

"What . . . are we going to do? What *can* we do, once Mordaunt finds Gwen?"

"Make sure he doesn't."

"Is that . . . a plan?"

"No." Hector looked at Roberto. "Speaking of plans, is there one for the orderly evacuation of Las Vegas in an emergency?"

"Yes, Don Hector. Coordinated with FEMA. Because of the, you know, the proximity of Yucca Mountain."

"That's good news. The evacuation of the city must begin today."

"For what reason?"

"The reason, I believe, will appear in the skies, and no further explanation will be required. The important thing will be to prevent devastating panic."

5:35 A.M.

Over a second cup of black coffee she needed to keep from falling asleep on her feet, Harlee Nations said to Gwen, "Here's my deal. I will set up the meeting between you and Eden when I have lunch with her this afternoon. When you've negotiated with her and she's said the magic word that deprograms you or whatever—"

"Releases me."

"By the way, how can you be so sure that, when you're close to her, she can't regain control? What I've seen, she's one very strong-willed girl."

"Dr. Woolwine has seen to that. Eden and I are on different wavelengths right now. No control is possible. As for strong wills—would you like another look at Delilah?"

"No, thanks. Once was enough." Harlee closed her eyes for a couple of moments. She trembled from fatigue. "And my end of the deal, Eden Waring is *mine*. Not yours, not Dee-Dee's."

"*Jest not with my name,*" Delilah said surlily.

"Okay, sorry. But I get to cut her throat. Agreed?"

"We are sworn. Yet think on't. Is blood your art? Poison speaks slyly, but with an oath of doom."

"Fuck that. I want to watch her bleeding in her own lap. And now I need to go to bed before I pass out. Somebody wake me at noon."

6:45 A.M.

Anyone want more coffee?" Cody asked of the other four people meeting in his spacious RV, which was parked anonymously with half a dozen similar vehicles and some eighteen-wheelers at a truck stop off I-15 south of the Las Vegas airport. Cody's environment-friendly little Prius was in tow behind his RV.

They all declined. The strategy meeting involving Hector, Roberto, Bertie Nkambe, and Eden Waring had been going on for an intense twenty minutes. Cody felt like, and was, an outsider. There was nothing he could contribute.

He sat in the driver's seat next to the Fetchling named Flicka, whom they had picked up at the bungalow on the grounds of the megaresort Bahìa. She didn't look at or speak to him, only stared, as if in an Eden–induced trance, at the rush-hour traffic northbound. Windshields flared as the sun rose. The sky was a dusted-over shade of blue. Inbound traffic at McCarran was picking up.

It was inconceivable to Cody that a metropolitan area of this size could, had to, become a ghost town, like the old boom-and-bust mining camps throughout the West more than a century ago. But Roberto obviously had intimate knowledge of the computer program containing the master evacuation plan for the city. Not only that, he could put it into play and with a few keystrokes render the program irreversible behind the mother of all firewalls. Traffic signals would be locked outbound-green on all major roadways. Incoming flights to McCarran, Executive, North Vegas, and Nellis airfields would automatically be rerouted. TV and radio stations would broadcast nothing but emergency instructions. Hospital evac teams—local, state, federal—would begin removal of the sick and helpless. Casinos would go to lockdown. Looters would be shot with tranquilizer darts. So would anyone else with notions of riding out the storm.

Even with the inevitable attempts at looting, the evacuation might not erupt into chaos. Luck was a large factor. And luck might well depend on what was going on over the heads of the already-spooked evacuees, all of them fearing the worst.

Cody didn't scare easily, but he was scared now. Doomsday scared. And the hell of it was, the two ordinary-looking men and attractive young women who were in charge of one version of doomsday were totally lacking in evangelical fervor. Over coffee and Danish in his luxury motor home they were having a coordinated, quietly efficient discussion about means and ends. Cody heard Hoover Dam mentioned a couple of times.

The exotically lovely Fetchling next to him had begun breathing heavily and chewing her lower lip, drawing blood. After they had marched her into the RV and spent fifteen minutes alone with her in the master bedroom, the girl had emerged wobbly and with drained-looking eyes.

Cody rotated his chair and alerted Eden to the change in the Fetchling.

Eden came limping forward from midcabin. She looked at the agitated Flicka, then placed a hand on her forehead. Flicka quieted immediately, her head falling back on the contoured seat.

"How did you do that?" Cody asked Eden.

She shrugged as if mildly embarrassed. "I don't know. Cody, you don't have to stay with her. You could join us."

"Wouldn't have much to contribute to the powwow. I don't have any special talent for setting the world on fire."

Eden thumped him lightly with a fist, then kissed him.

"Neither do I. But that's not going to happen."

"According to your dreams, Vegas is a candidate for holocaust. Tee-total destruction, as my daddy would say."

"I suppose the definition of destruction could be stretched to include a place where nothing lives but evil, nothing visits but the wind. A shunned place for a thousand years, or as long as human memory endures. That would be the good that comes of all this."

"The bad part?"

"Simple. We lose."

Hector was taking a bathroom break. Bertie was lying quietly on a sofa big enough to accommodate her six-foot frame. Roberto began speaking urgently to his wife on his cell.

"I'm not big on losing," Cody said. "Whatever it is I can do to make this thing work out in our favor, you let me know." He nodded to Flicka. "What's her story?"

"Well, you know about Fetchlings. Flicka had information that was useful. Some luck on our part. When Mordaunt went missing—"

"Thanks to you."

"—Almost all of the Malterran hierarchy from around the world came running in a panic to Las Vegas for a meeting."

"To elect another Mordaunt?"

"I haven't met any of them, but I doubt if there's a Malterran who remotely qualifies as *Deus Inversus*. They're just bad, evil people. The important thing is, almost all of them are still around, out at Mordaunt's Snow Lake Ranch. We have to make sure they stay here. A nice long sojourn with their Prince of Darkness."

"Eden—is there anything you can do about Tom Sherard?"

There was pain in Eden's eyes.

"Oh God. I don't know, Cody. Tom is—he's probably lost to us."

"Along with Gwen?"

"The hell with her," Eden said. "She wants her independence? She can have it. Gladly. And spend the next millennium right here with those we're about to send to Judgment."

6:54 A.M.

The entity known as Mordaunt returned to full consciousness in the emergency wing of Concordia Hospital well before Tom Sherard, the persona he had co-opted, had any power of movement. Still under the protection of the Supreme Light of the Universe, his body was virtually in suspended animation.

It was a risk Mordaunt had always taken while walking the earth in human form. He could transmogrify flesh on a whim, change a mouse into a were-hawk, but not if that flesh was steeped in the Light that nullified his dark powers.

For now, while detectives roamed the hospital trying to learn what had wrecked an entire floor and left four other people in deep comas, Mordaunt could only wait for the Light to wane, the sleeper to awaken. He amused himself with the chronicles of an adventurous life he found in Sherard's brain, and more recent memories of Eden Waring, whom he had possessed just a few days ago.

Mordaunt felt no anger that the one whom he also coveted had lain with another man. No sense of loss. Pragmatically he accepted the fact that he'd badly misjudged Eden and her burgeoning powers. It only made him want her all the more.

And there would be another time.

8:20 A.M.

Well off the road in an unpopulated area of southernmost Nevada, they left Cody's recreational vehicle and walked a third of a mile uphill to a promontory above a dry lake. It was still chilly at this elevation, but windless. The sky was flawlessly blue.

"Why are we here?" Eden asked Hector.

"We're going to make some weather."

Eden and Bertie looked at each other. The walk had been hard on Bertie. She winced at the idea of more exertion, mental or physical.

"I think I should just watch."

Hector smiled sympathetically. Cody set up a camp stool for Bertie, opened a thermos of orange juice. She drank half, nodded gratefully.

"I'm better." She asked Hector, "What kind of weather?"

"Potentially frightening, but harmless. To set the stage for the great exodus from the city."

"They're probably going to be grateful for this, down there in California and Arizona," Cody said.

"I think he means fireworks," Eden said to Bertie with a rueful grin. "No floods. No whirly stuff."

Cody whistled softly to himself. Eden looked to Hector for guidance.

"They're accustomed to sonic booms in the area," Hector said, "because of proximity to military airfields. But dazzling bursts of light from all corners of a clear sky, a display for which there is no rational explanation? That's another matter."

"So you want me to do both?"

Hector nodded.

"Okay. How?"

Hector said, "The talisman you wear is the key to the Dark Energy of the Universe. The sky is clear, the day calm. You don't feel it yet. But concentrate on how you disposed of Mordaunt the first time."

Eden had gooseflesh, and rubbed her bare forearms.

"I remember how the effort knocked me for a loop."

"But you will have learned from that experience how to apply your powers without exhausting yourself or your passions."

"I guess so. Once I've done this—maybe I'm good for twenty minutes or so—what next?"

"The answer to your question lies within the depths of a pair of crystal skulls, once we get our hands on them."

"Gwen had one. I didn't know there were two."

"Unfortunately, yes. But the skulls can be used for our purpose as well as theirs."

"*If* we had them," Bertie said.

"I think Hector wants me to make a deal," Eden said.

Hector beamed. "What a Caretaker you would have made. Not that you're doing badly so far."

9:02 A.M.

A little before nine, Tom Sherard suddenly got up off the table in the emergency-wing cubicle where he'd lain, apparently comatose, for more than three hours. He disconnected himself from an IV drip and the finger clip that monitored vital signs and walked out. He glanced at the nurses' station down the hall, then went the other way, through a pair of automatic doors into the small waiting room. A TV was on. Remote newscast. A legend on the screen read RECORDED EARLIER. The picture showed flashes of brilliant light above a scrubby mountain range. There were no clouds to account for the violent electrical phenomena.

He watched for a few moments, then went outside, looked around to get his bearings, then walked to a parking lot where a chauffeur was sleeping behind the wheel of a limousine.

Sherard knocked on the tinted glass, waking the man. He got into the back of the limo and gave directions.

When the limousine pulled out of the lot, it was followed, not closely, by a dark blue Crown Vic.

Harlee Nations's cell phone played musically on the pillow next to her. She groped for it and focused on the caller ID. Flicka's number. Which meant— Harlee felt a touch of ice at the back of her neck, a pleasurable jolt to the spine.

"I hope you're not a late sleeper," Eden said.

"What time is it?"

"Almost nine thirty."

"I was hoping for another hour or two." Harlee yawned. "I assume you're still with Flicka. Tell me she's okay."

"She'll be happier when she's not peeing blood. Meantime we've done some talking. Whatever became of that red crystal skull you and your pal Devon were playing with a few days ago?"

Harlee was silent for several seconds. "Don't have it," she said at last.

"But you know where it is."

"What if?"

"I want it."

"Like I'll just hand it over to you. A—a sacred object. Priceless."

"Sacred to Mordaunt, you mean? To the Dark Cause?"

"I don't know that much about it. Truth. I'm afraid of it, though. Some things in the universe you don't trifle with. But you don't seem to have learned that."

"If you want to go on enjoying semi-immortality, or whatever you call it, you can't depend on Mordaunt anymore. You've got about twelve hours left, Harlee. Right now I'm the only one who can save your neck. And Flicka's."

Harlee laughed.

"We'll meet at two this afternoon. Bring the crystal skull. When I have it, I'll guarantee you safe passage out of Las Vegas before we put the whole place into lockdown for a thousand years. Nobody else can make you an offer like that."

"*What* are you talking about?"

"Turn on your TV. Any channel. I'll be back in touch."

Cody had been talking on his own cell phone while he drove east on Sunset Road toward the Galleria mall in Henderson.

"Tom Sherard is at Bahìa. He went into the bungalow a few minutes ago and hasn't come out."

Eden only nodded, looking preoccupied.

Five minutes later they pulled into the parking lot at the Galleria.

"There's the Channel Ten mobile unit," Eden said. "Pull up behind it."

"What's the newsgal's name?"

"Lana something."

Eden got out of Cody's RV with Simba in one hand. Channel Ten's roving vid journalist, wearing full makeup, came over to her with her crew.

"Hi," Eden said. "I'm Eden Waring."

"Lana Briscoe. Changed your hairstyle, but I recognize you from file tape."

"Are we on the air, Lana?"

"Make it worth my while and we will be."

"Worth your while. Okay, how's this? The electrical disturbances that began this morning at approximately eight twenty-four and lasted for nineteen minutes are only a prelude of what's in store for Las Vegas. By tonight the disturbances will have become major storms that will knock out all power in the metropolitan area. I'm talking about everything going dark, not just the megaresort glitz. Remember the old movie *The Day the Earth Stood Still*? It's almost here. But it won't last for a day. It will last for centuries."

"Jesus . . . you expect people to *believe* that?"

"Why don't you run the file tape you have on the DC-10 that crashed during my graduation exercises on the twenty-eight of May at 2110 hours? And ask as many of the people as you please who were not in the stadium and missed incineration by a matter of seconds what *they* believe."

"But—how—what's causing these violent storms?"

"Gee, I couldn't answer that one, Lana. I'm just reporting what's in my dreams. If you don't think they're newsworthy after what went on this morning—" Eden shrugged and turned back to the waiting RV.

"No, hey, hold on!"

"You have five more minutes of my time, Lana."

When Eden had returned to the RV and they were rolling again, Hector said to Roberto, "It is time for Level Two of the evacuation plan."

"Yes, Don Hector." Roberto went to work with his laptop computer.

Cody said, "What's Level Two?"

"Mobilize state and local police. National Guard on standby alert. By the way, we have, I think, about ten minutes before they will find and attempt to suppress us." Roberto sighed. "Meanwhile, all of southern Nevada and not just Area 51 has become a no-fly zone." Schematics blipped on and off the laptop screen. "Except for authorized aircraft. All vehicles will be diverted from Hoover Dam at 95 south. All interstate traffic will be turned away at state lines. Hotel security has been notified and the casinos are closing. Did I mention that we have become persons of great interest to every law-enforcement agency on the planet?"

"They probably think it's just some kid hacking away in his bedroom," Bertie said.

Eden's own cell phone played "I Walk the Line." She didn't recognize the originating number.

"This is Eden."

"Would you like Tom Sherard back unharmed?" Mordaunt said in the voice most recognizable to Eden, that of the late Lincoln Grayle.

"Define unharmed, you evil son of a bitch," Eden said.

"Rather woozy, and with the gestures of childhood, for a few days."

"What do *you* want?"

"I know what you're trying to do. But you're out of your depth. Stop this panic attack on a city I happen to love."

"I'm sure you do. You can have it, all of it. You and your Fetchlings and that whole Malterran crowd. I'll bet you outnumber the cockroaches by now. You can have Gwen too, you deserve each other."

As soon as she'd spoken, she wished she hadn't.

"Oh? Gwen is back? That's interesting. Where is she?"

"How would I know. You took her from me, remember?"

"I detect some anxiety in your voice."

"You're the one who has something to worry about."

"You can—and you have—caused me difficulties. I suppose I'll just have to relocate. Join the exodus out of town."

"All by yourself?"

Cody said quietly, as they approached Las Vegas Boulevard South on Sunset, "We've picked up an escort."

Eden looked out at flashing lights keeping pace with them.

"Slow down but keep moving until there's a good place to pull over," Hector advised.

Eden said to Mordaunt, "I don't believe you're willing to settle for half a soul. Because without your better half, we're stronger than you can hope to be. And we *will* find you."

"I'll look forward to that. Another time, then. For now I think I should go home and pack."

Eden put her cell phone away and laid her head back against the seat rest.

"Eden?" Bertie said, sounding frightened.

Eden looked at the police cars on three sides of the RV, saw a helicopter hovering above the boulevard a hundred yards south as Cody turned carefully at the intersection. All other traffic was being held up.

"Mordaunt claims he'll give us Tom if we ease up on him and his crew and his whole damn playground. Whatever we decide, I don't see how we can win. Right now Mordaunt is probably on his way to his old haunt, the Magician's house, which is on a mountain somewhere around here."

"Charleston mountain," Cody said.

"How long would it take him to make the drive from Bahìa?"

"About half an hour—more, if midtown is clogged with traffic. Which it will be."

"Hector—what do you think?"

"Much depends on what, or who, Mordaunt may find when he reaches the house."

Eden nodded. "I think so too. That's probably where he was keeping Gwen, the place she'd come back to." Eden rubbed her forehead. "Okay, then Mordaunt can't be allowed to get to the house."

"They're advising me to pull over," Cody said. He had his motor home geared down to a sedate fifteen miles per hour, and all exterior lights flashing.

Eden took another look at the helicopter.

"Stop right here," she said to Cody, and swiveled around to Hector. "You couldn't simply—"

Hector shook his head. "We are forbidden to take lives, Eden. Mordaunt's protection from the power of a Caretaker always has been the human persona he possesses."

Eden nodded tautly as Cody stopped the RV in the middle of the boulevard. Police immediately closed in. A special weapons team had arrived.

"Now what?" he asked.

"Bertie and I need to talk," Eden said.

In the stateroom at the rear of the motor home the two girls sat side by side on the bed, holding hands.

"What are you going to do?" Bertie asked.

"Play dirty, I guess."

"Can you save Tom?"

"I don't know. I think somehow I have to trick Mordaunt into leaving his body, assuming—one of those shapes he's famous for."

"Together we could—"

Eden squeezed one of Bertie's hands, finding it cold and lifeless. She smiled.

"You can't go, Bertie."

Tears stood out in Bertie's eyes. She lowered her head.

Eden kissed her cheek and stood. She seemed nerveless.

"Fun's about to start," she said. "You don't want to miss it."

When Eden and Hector in his hospital maintenance coveralls stepped down from the motor home all they saw were uniforms, most of them partly hidden behind a phalanx of police cruisers. More cops arriving as they looked around. Eden was carrying Simba, her lion's-head walking stick.

The helicopter was in the street fifty yards south of them, rotors idling. Eden shielded her eyes with one hand, looking at it.

A bullhorn voice told Eden to put Simba down ("the weapon," as it was described) and ordered her and Hector to kneel, hands laced on their heads.

Eden spoke up: "I'd like to talk to whoever is in charge here!"

Two officers closest to Eden and Hector had Tasers out. They wore full riot gear. They closed slowly in a pincher maneuver.

The bullhorn voice repeated its demand.

"What do you think?" Eden asked Hector.

"An exercise in kinematics might be in order."

"Kinematics, right. I don't know what you're talking about, Holiness. I mean, Hector."

"We don't want anyone to be seriously hurt. Velocity, *caro*, not brute force."

One of the encroaching cops fired his Taser at Eden, who hadn't been paying close attention to him. But Simba jumped from the ground and batted the barbs away, causing a crackling flash on contact. The gold lion's head turned on the walking stick and Simba glared at the other cop, jaws open.

Eden said to the cop who was backing away, "He won't hurt you. Now if you're not in charge, get me someone who is, okay?" She resumed her conversation with Hector: "Why don't you show me what you mean by cinematics."

"Kinematics. I'd much rather observe what you've learned in so short a time."

"Hector—"

"*Por Dios!* Just pull the rug from under them. Before they become even more aggressive."

Eden looked at a TV news helicopter circling widely a couple of hundred feet above them, then down at a stretch of tarmac between them and the massed cruisers. She nodded, having gotten Hector's meaning, and touched the talisman between her breasts. Her eyes closed. Her lower lip was folded between her teeth. The bones of her face seemed to stand out beneath the skin, which took on a blue-tinged glow like gas flame.

A ripple began in the asphalt a few feet in front of Eden, mounted swiftly into a wave. It bowled over the cops nearest them, continued on, crested at about three feet beneath the wheels of the parked cruisers and a SWAT van, which rose and fell back haphazardly as the asphalt wave rolled on to the other side of the boulevard.

Eden, breathing hard, sweat beading on her face, said, "Was that good enough?"

"They may not be convinced. Perhaps we need a hostage, should they decide to open fire on us."

"Okay." Eden took a couple of deep breaths. "Simba!"

The walking stick flew like a javelin with jaws to one of the nearby cops as he was getting to his feet. Simba seized him by his outer vest near the back of the neck and lifted him, kicking helplessly, ten feet into the air.

While Simba was bringing the cop to them, Eden focused on one of the empty cruisers and began methodically to compact it, like a barroom show-off folding a beer can. The cruiser made loud buckling and crunching noises as the engine fell out of it. Eden's half-lidded eyes as she concentrated on this feat were like violent electrical storms beneath her blood-suffused brow. The talisman on her breast was incandescent.

When the squared-off cruiser was a third of its original size Eden gave up the effort and brought the suspended cop within a few feet of her raised face, upending him in the air. He made desperate swimming motions with his hands, but Simba's grip was strong.

"Take off your face shield," Eden said to the cop.

He pulled off the helmet and shield and dropped it. He was a young guy, probably not much older than Eden. He was losing his hair and making an effort not to lose his nerve.

"Hi, I'm Eden. This is Hector. What's your name, Officer?"

"Lew . . . Welling," he said in a strangled voice.

"I know this is awkward for you, Lew, but you'll be okay. Can you tell me how many seats that Metro copter over there has?"

"Uh . . . four, I think. Plus pilot."

"Get on your radio and tell everyone that Hector and I are going to borrow the copter because we need to be someplace else in a hurry. I said borrow, not steal. It will be returned. Oh, and tell whoever may be concerned that we're taking you with us. In case your snipers get antsy and try to put a couple of rounds through our heads. Because—now listen to this carefully, Lew—if *I* die, there is no way to prevent Simba—that's my walking stick, I have this knee injury from sports—no way to prevent Simba from wiping out everyone in the vicinity. Beginning with Officer Lew Welling. Also, if the helo tries to take off before we get there, I'll be very angry. You saw what happened to the cruiser."

"Uh-huh."

"That was nothing compared to what I can do if I really put my mind to it, because I have all the Dark Energy of the Universe at my disposal. But this is no Xbox game. Is there anything I've said about potential consequences that you don't fully understand, Lew?"

He didn't understand "Dark Energy," but this didn't seem to be the time or place.

"No . . . ma'am."

"Pass it on." Eden turned to the RV and called to Cody. He appeared in the doorway, looking with a wide disbelieving grin from Eden to the unhappy suspended cop.

"Cody, you can drive on to the ranch now with Bertie."

He shook his head. "Leave you? No."

"*Yes.* I'll meet you there . . . I don't know, when I can."

"What are you doin' to yourself? You look beat all to—"

"I'm good," Eden said, but her eyes leaked tears. "Really, Cody. Please get out of here while they're distracted."

"Eden—"

"Promise," she insisted. "And trust me, Cody. Nothing, nobody, not all the evil this world can come up with, is going to keep me from you for very long. Besides," she added, with a rueful wrinkle of a smile, "don't I deserve a vacation?"

Cody glanced at Hector for help.

"Why does this have to be *her* fight?"

"Because she is the Avatar. And she has the unique power to finish what Mordaunt has started."

Cody gestured, frustrated, helpless.

"Speakin' of evils, what am I supposed to do with the Fetchling?"

"Send her out," Eden said. "There'll be room in the copter for Flicka. I made a deal with Harlee. Now go."

10:12 A.M.

An airborne Channel Three news team was getting it all, feeding every astonishing, unexplainable moment of what had been a standoff on Las Vegas Boulevard South to the audience that regularly tuned in to *The Today Show* locally, and to every NBC afil in the country via the network's News Service uplinks in Charlotte, North Carolina. Eden Waring was a hot item again, although perhaps not good news. Not that anyone trying to interpret the on-camera events had a clear idea of what was happening, or why.

Eden, an unknown middle-aged Hispanic male, a beautiful young woman who had Eurasian bloodlines, and a likewise unidentified Las Vegas Metro policeman with what looked like a long gnarled stick attached to the back of his flak vest were seen getting into the police helicopter, which lifted off less than a minute later and hovered momentarily before turning in a northerly direction.

That's when both the Channel Ten helicopter and a second helo from a rival station new on the scene appeared simultaneously to develop engine trouble: each had to set down quickly. Unable to follow, the news teams focused on the "borrowed" Metro copter as it dwindled to a speck in the sky above suburban Summerlin. Where the streets below were crowded in three directions with outbound traffic—north, west, south, it didn't seem to matter. People were getting the raw news coverage and the speculative message that things were weirdly awry in paradise. Feeding off an atavistic communal urgency, they wanted out of town *now*.

At the aerie of the late Lincoln Grayle on Charleston Mountain, Dr. Marcus Woolwine, still in the process of packing up to prudently join the exodus, watched TV for a couple of minutes with Gwen the dpg and Harlee Nations. Harlee had easily identified Flicka, and kept that knowledge to herself while she pondered what Eden was up to.

"Where do you suppose they're going?" Woolwine said. He was on his third cup of black coffee, and jumpy.

"They're coming *here*," Harlee said with a flash of inspiration as she looked at the doppelganger and her consort, Delilah. "Because Eden knows *you're* here. The question is, how does she know?"

Gwen looked distressed until Delilah offered a contemptuous response.

"*She quickens to a destiny the planets have decreed; anon she comes in blithe folly, with revengeful appetite and blood-sotted cheek, to sport with a ruder power. Pish!*"

"Does anyone want more coffee?" Woolwine asked.

"Maybe you shouldn't be so cocky," Harlee advised Delilah. "Because what I saw her do to the Great One looked pretty damned impressive."

"*Mark me, Fetchling: I am greater than he who proclaimed himself 'Great' whilst I was away.*"

"I believe I'll just be getting along," Marcus Woolwine said with a tense smile.

"*Nay. I may'st have need of thee, unhair'd physicker.*"

"But I'm not well! I have a pacemaker. Too much . . . excitement is bad for me." He looked with loathing at the fulminating red skull in the crook of Gwen's arm. "And so are the vibrations from that . . . artifact."

Delilah gave Woolwine a look that silenced his desire to protest further. He backed out of the room with the translucent dome-capped fireplace in the middle of it and out onto one of the wind-buffeted terraces that were cantilevered over steep wooded slopes of the mountain. He stood with hands clasped behind his back and looked forebodingly at the turbulent superheated sky. The crystal skull was still up to no good, perhaps uncontrollable as it siphoned power from both man-made sources and the magnetic-flux belts that girdled the earth above and within.

In the house, Harlee said to Delilah, "One of those skulls is for sure a cosmic train wreck: even so, it may not have enough oomph to stop Eden. But there is another one. I've been thinking it might be smart to get your hands on it."

"Thou hast seen the other?"

"Yes, and by the way, Eden wants it too. What does that tell you?"

"Where liest this skull?"

"In the Magician's vault, below the ruins of his theatre. I'm the only one around with access. A full-body scan is required."

Delilah studied Harlee, then nodded.

"Go thou hence, Fetchling. Return quickly, that twinn'd skulls may enforce a forkèd plague to wither and oppress the demi-goddess."

"Favor for favor, remember? When you're finished with her, what's left is mine."

10:25 A.M.

There it is," Eden said, pointing to the multistory house on the western face of Charleston Mountain. The police helicopter was at seven thousand feet and two miles distant, approaching from the southwest. The pilot's name was Harry Redmond.

Through binoculars Hector saw Harlee's candy-apple-red muscle car pass through the gates of the house and speed away through tight turns.

"Someone's leaving," he said, and handed the glasses to Eden.

"It might be Harlee. Flicka, what does Harlee drive?"

"Dodge Viper," the girl said sullenly. "Red."

"It's Harlee." To the helicopter pilot Eden said, "Where does that road go?"

"About another eight miles through all those switchbacks, it connects with the main road up Kyle Canyon at Cathedral Rock."

"What's at Cathedral Rock?"

"Hiking trails, picnic area, some cabins to rent."

"I need to get close enough to the Viper to see if anyone else is with Harlee before she reaches Cathedral Rock."

"I can try. Don't know how close I can get for a look-see through all that ponderosa and bristlecone."

Harry Redmond banked the copter right and headed straight for the mountain. The twelve-thousand-foot summit was buried in fulminating cloud. Through the binoculars Eden saw only intermittent flashes of the red car. Harlee was going very fast on a narrow road on which there was little forward visibility through a blanket growth of ancient pines.

"If she don't know the road like the back of her hand," Harry said with a shake of his head. "What I'm saying, there's turns where the dropoff's a thousand feet straight down."

"Crazy," Flicka said. "She's just crazy for speed. I never like to ride with Harlee."

Eden's hands trembled, as if the binoculars she held suddenly weighed like a stack of bricks. She put the glasses down. Her heart shimmied, the beat staggering. She could feel it knocking near her breastbone. *Aftereffects,* she thought. All in all, she didn't feel very well.

She said to the pilot, "Is there a place at Cathedral Rock where you can set the helicopter down?"

"Parking lot, if it's not too crowded."

"What are you thinking?" Hector asked. He had noted her

trembling hands, which were now clasped atop the midpoint of her chest-hugging seat harness.

"I want to be sure Gwen isn't in the car with Harlee. We have enough lead time to stop her at Cathedral Rock."

"If she wants to stop," Flicka said.

Eden smiled slightly.

Harry Redmond flew to the southeast of Griffith Peak, the helicopter making unexpected and scary moves in wind shear at eight thousand feet as they dropped toward Kyle Canyon. Eden felt dismayed to discover that the recreation area at Cathedral Rock was a busy place in what should have been the off-season. The loop road was lined with cars and RVs. There were hikers all over the slopes, some hurrying for shelter beneath a lowering sky that already blackened the western horizon: there was a huge, slow-moving circulating cloud that sparked ominously and stilled birdlife as it sought to swallow the pale sun above the southeasterly slope of the mountain.

Harlee in her Viper was still a few minutes away from them on the gated private road to the Magician's aerie.

At treetop level Harry Redmond was having trouble holding steady in a tricky up-canyon wind while he looked for room on the deck. The chopper was attracting a lot of attention from campers and hikers.

Eden said, "Hector, we need to get those people out of here! Off the mountain and farther down into the canyon where the other campgrounds are."

Officer Welling said with a somber face, "What's gonna happen?" It was the first time he'd spoken since being loaded into the helicopter. He still seemed dazed from the experience of dangling from Simba's gold jaws, but he had been studying Eden. Something about her anxieties—even though he didn't know what was causing them— had struck him as valid.

"To begin with," Eden said, and she was trembling again, "when I get going, with all these trees, there could be a danger of fire."

"Well, me and Harry could probably help move folks out," Welling said. "Soon as he sets 'er down."

Eden smiled, tense as lockjaw.

"Thanks. Look, I'm sorry if I made a bad impression on you and Las Vegas Metro, but—"

"*Bad* impression? My Jesus! I don't have a clue where you're coming from, or what you are."

"Yes, I get that a lot lately," Eden said, and looked away.

"I didn't mean to—"

"Not important now, Lew. Hector and I would appreciate all the help we can get."

"This other girl," Lew said, leaning toward Eden's right ear as much as his harness would allow, "is she like you?"

"No, there isn't anyone else like me, Lew. I'm sui generis."

Lew looked puzzled, then said guardedly, "Is that treatable?"

The pilot put his helicopter down where it wouldn't block the loop road. The gate across the Magician's road was about fifty yards east of them, following the course of the south-loop trail.

As soon as Eden opened the door on her side she realized that the temperature was fifteen or twenty degrees cooler this high on the mountain. She was wearing only a cotton sweater, and began to shiver as soon as she stepped out of the helicopter.

Hector got out next. Eden said, "Harlee's only about three minutes away. The gate will stop or at least slow her down. If she's alone then she can keep going after we've had a few words. If not—"

Eden didn't have a chance to finish the thought. A white limousine had appeared, coming up the canyon road. It looked as out of place in the rustic setting as a wiener wagon at a state funeral.

The limo turned right onto the gravel apron in front of the gated road. Stopped. Backed down forty feet to the paved road and idled there, as if the unseen driver was waiting for instructions.

While the stretch limo sat there a tinted window slid down and Eden saw, in a backseat, Tom Sherard talking on a cell phone. As he talked he turned his head slowly to look at her.

But it wasn't Tom she saw in those hooded eyes.

"Oh my God! Hector!"

"I know."

"What do I do now?"

The gates were opening. Apparently Mordaunt had contacted

someone at the house, or else there was a rolling code activated by the phone call.

As the limo started uphill again and the window rose darkly, Mordaunt raised two fingers to his temple, saluting Eden.

"Stop this, Eden," Hector said quietly. "Whatever the consequences, the possessed cannot be allowed to meet."

"But it's Tom! Mordaunt has control of him, and I don't know what to do!"

Behind her, Flicka laughed. Eden watched the limo pass through the gates, then whirled to stare at the Fetchling. Both of them realizing the same thing at the same time. The limo took up all of the Magician's road and Harlee would never see it in time.

Flicka stifled a scream with her hand.

10:58 A.M.

Ignoring the pain in her bad knee, Eden jogged past Flicka and got into the helicopter with Simba.

"Harry, follow the limo!" she said to the pilot. "Treetop level!"

"Might be askin' for trouble, the thermals they get up here! And that cloud's breedin' something I don't care to fly through."

"But you've got to do this for me!"

He looked at her for several seconds, chewing gum slowly. Harry was a middle-aged man with a lot of freckles on his square face, and a sanguine disposition.

"Who's that in the limo?"

"All I can tell you is he's as bad as bad can get, and he has a hostage who is a very dear friend!"

"Well, all I can do is try," Harry said. "Seeing as how this here is another hostage situation, and you bein' one of the most desperate characters I've ever met."

"Ha ha. Harry, *please.* We're wasting time."

Harry grinned sorrowfully, then devoted his attention to lifting off. They were already pointed in the right direction.

"Even if the limo's full of more-desperate characters, ain't no way I could hope to stop it on that narrow road."

"Let me worry about that."

"I'd put that down to braggin' if I hadn't seen with my own eyes that you got some powerful tricks up your sleeve. You just about made a churchgoer out of me again. Better close our door, honey, it could get rocky real quick."

"Need to leave it open, Harry. Is there a safety rig in case I need to step out onto a skid?"

"Step—? Mercy!" A look convinced him that she was serious. "There under your seat. Line attaches to that eyebolt on the floor. Don't suppose you're wantin' a gun? We carry the Smith .40. Course, if I give it to you, once this is over with and provided I live to tell the tale, I'll have to say as how you overpowered me."

"Really, Harry. Do you think I need a pistol?"

"Just makin' conversation. I am kinda nervous." Harry applied forward cyclic to hover next to a steep shaggy grove of ponderosa, the rotors grabbing at thin air with a sharp slapping noise. "Here comes that limo, just like a caterpillar clingin' to a leaf stem."

"See it. I'm more interested in the red Viper right now. Keep on top of the road for another mile up."

"Fixin' to do, prevent a head-on crash?"

"Yes."

"How?"

"The easy-to-understand version is, I'm going to pull the Viper over and park it until I've attended to my other business."

"From up here you're gonna do that? I hope you don't mind my curiosity."

"You remind me of my foster father," Eden said as the ship climbed higher. Her nose was leaking from the impact of warm turbine exhaust on her sinuses. "He took everything in stride, even though he and Betts always knew about me and my heritage. I never knew my birth mother. They took me from her as soon as I was born. But I saw her in dreams while I was growing up. Then, funny thing, a few months ago she came to me." Eden didn't know why she was rattling on to Harry this way; his attention was rigorously devoted to keeping his helicopter aloft. Probably she was only distracting herself. Thinking now of Gillian Bellaver and their moments together on a windy Montana hilltop, Eden in a psi-active state of her second-energy body. They'd had only a few moments together, little time for Eden to say— She caught sight of the Viper dashing along the road below.

"There she is, Harry!"

"She can drive, I'll give her that. But how lucky does she think she is?"

"Fetchlings who live a couple of hundred years probably get so stinking arrogant they think nothing can hurt them."

"A couple hundred years?"

"Swing us around and go down as close to the road as you can!"

"Problem is, we don't have much density at this altitude, but I'll try'r."

Harry pushed the helo a little too forward and clipped some high branches from a pine. A couple of broken branches whipped in through the doorway. The cold was like teeth in Eden's bones; part of her face felt numb. As the ship swung abruptly, giving her a cleaner line of sight, she nearly went headlong out the door, thinking as she was dumped, *Well shit, Harry,* but she didn't say it: he was doing his best. The safety line yanked Eden back, and she got her feet under her on the deck.

"Can you give me five seconds of steady while I lasso that sports car?"

"While you do *what*?"

Eden placed a hand over the metal talisman on her breast. Harry looked at her long enough to see the glow through her hand as Eden summoned Dark Energy and aimed it mentally at the red convertible. The transference was just another sight Harry was unlikely to forget for the rest of his life.

Eden had a glimpse of Harlee's face as the girl looked at the hovering helicopter. Her hair streamed out behind her in the rotor wash. Eden saw that Harlee was wearing her shoulder harness.

So Harlee stayed with the Viper when control was abruptly taken from her and the Viper assumed a new trajectory, off the road, threading between a couple of massive trees and into space like an untracked roller-coaster car pulling a couple of Gs at a nearly vertical downward angle.

"Oh Lord, she has done bought it!" Harry cried over the intercom.

"No, I've got her," Eden said calmly, as the Viper slowed in its plunge and pulled up, regaining altitude off to the right side of the copter while continuing to lose momentum. There were skeins of bluish light all around the car, resembling a cat's cradle, as the Viper rocked gently, going nowhere, a hundred feet out from the dark forested slope of the mountain.

Harlee still had a death grip on the steering wheel. She looked stunned. Eden couldn't contain a nervous giggle at her expression. Not that she was having all that much fun. There was still far to go, and the effort she had expanded so far had her nauseated.

"Lord God a' mercy!" Harry said, staring in fright at the floating car. "Don't suppose you'd be available for kids' birthday parties?"

Eden tapped Harry on the shoulder as he corrected for both high altitude and a buffeting wind from the growing maelstrom on the crest of the mountain.

"She'll be okay! Nowhere to go until I come back for her! If I do."

"What about that limo?"

"Right. Thanks for reminding me, Harry."

Eden chose a tree, a gnarled, overhanging bristlecone pine that looked as if it had withstood more than its share of lightning strikes. Now it endured another, or something like lightning, that split it nearly in two from a twisted topknot of barren branches to its solid base. Half a ton of riven tree fell hard across the road, blocking it.

"That should slow him down some," Eden said, thinking only of Mordaunt. Not wanting to think of Tom Sherard as a prisoner in the grip of *Deus Inversus.* "Can you take me to the house now, Harry? Ought to be a helicopter pad up there."

"Reckon you're expected?"

Eden looked at the house of the late Lincoln Grayle, only part of it visible, jutting from the side of the mountain with vistas of high desert in three directions. Over the desert and south of Yucca Mountain a new storm had arisen as if it were being sucked out through a fault in the earth: smothering sky, great balls of pure energy spinning, colliding, glaring lethally like radium, a birthing universe. To Eden's eyes the chaos greatly resembled Van Gogh's painting *The Starry Night.*

"Depend on it," Eden said. As fascinated, and as frightened, as she'd ever been.

Eden, wishing she had a plan.

10:47 A.M.

The household staffers who had kept things humming as usual in Lincoln Grayle's still-mysterious absence were now on the run, lugging possessions to a waitng van on the stone-paved auto courtyard. The wild pinball display and fulminating blackness swallowing heaven had them panicked. The terraced levels of the house were lit up by displays of electricity like those emanating from a Tesla coil.

Harry Redmond turned on his landing lights as debris pelted the helicopter. He looked grim from strain while locating the landing pad outside another set of tall gates. He turned his ship ninety degrees, crabbed it sideways, and set it down without a bounce. There was a near-vertical wall of forest less than ten feet from the helo disk. Pinpoint landing. Tall trees swayed violently, loosing a barrage of pine cones.

"You're a genius, Harry!" Eden said over the intercom. "Thanks for the lift!"

"How long you aim to be?" he asked, looking in dismay at the storm. "This is like End of Days! One stout branch comin' down, we're marooned up here!"

"You're not staying, Harry! That van? They can't make it down the mountain! Can you take those people to Cathedral Rock?"

"Better hurry! And whatever it is you got to do up here—best of luck!"

Eden unbuckled and backed out of the helicopter. Between the rotor wash and the whipping winds she had to stay in a crouch while making her way through the gates to the van. Her hair, short as it was, was trying to stand on end. Her fingertips glowed like Saint Elmo's fire.

She waited in the lee of the van while Lincoln Grayle's beleaguered servants scrambled aboard the helicopter. She felt both relief and a sense of abandonment as Harry lifted off. He had offered to come back for her; Eden had refused, knowing how poor his chances would be of making another trip up the mountain.

When she couldn't see the copter anymore Eden put her face down on one arm and sobbed.

"I know you're tired," she heard someone say. A calm voice. Firm but soothing.

Eden's head jerked up as hands gripped her shoulders lightly. She looked around into the eyes of Gillian Bellaver.

"*Mother!*"

10:52 A.M.

The limousine that had been making slow time up the mountain road from Cathedral Rock, nearly too long to negotiate the hairpin switchbacks, finally came to a stop at the smoldering hulk of tree blocking the rest of the way.

"Can't go no further, boss," the limo driver said to his passenger in the backseat. Then he caught sight of the red Dodge Viper that was just hanging around in thin air a hundred feet off the road, laced up in a netting of pure energy. His jaw sagged. He couldn't take his eyes off the Viper and its pretty driver, who was standing on the seat waving her arms at them as if she were in a lifeboat signaling a passing freighter.

Mordaunt laughed at Harlee's predicament, forgetting for the moment who must've been responsible.

The driver opened his door and stepped gingerly out into the road. He looked reluctantly at the storm piled high atop the mountain, looked down at his hands. They were glowing. The skin on the back of his neck crawled.

"They Lawwddd!"

He backed away from the white limo, looking again at Harlee. The girl was using some vile language out there. "Reckon as how I'll just come back for it some other time," he mumbled, referring to the limo. Then he broke into a run down the road, not wasting another look back.

Mordaunt, still laughing, got out, assessing Harlee Nations's situation. Of course she didn't possess a jot of magic and had no powers to extricate herself from the predicament in which the Avatar—who else?—had left her. Not much he could do, either, without shutting off the power that kept the Viper in suspension. But then it would be good-bye Harlee.

Harlee didn't know him, of course. Mordaunt liked the body he was in, the lean well-traveled hunter's body. Although nothing else had been available to him in the crisis—the imminent sinking of the *Stella Salamis*—still he couldn't have wished for better.

"Where did Eden Waring go?" he called to her, in the voice of Lincoln Grayle.

"Linc? The *Great One*?" Harlee reverted to her teen persona, babbling "Omigodomigod get me *out* of this!"

Maybe, Mordaunt thought, instead of trying to recast Eden's spell he could add to it without terminal consequences.

"Better sit down, Harlee. Fasten your seat belt, too."

"WHAT ARE YOU GOING TO—"

"I said, sit."

Harlee slid down in the seat, grabbing for the harness. She felt the Viper rock a little, and let out a wail of fright.

The Viper shot forward toward the road. It would have burned rubber if there had been anything but air beneath the set of performance tires.

The Viper came down hard on the road, two wheels, snarl of electricity around it, and stopped with a jolt against the front bumper of the limo. Harlee's eyes were shut tight. She had a stranglehold on the steering wheel. Her hair crackled on her head. She made a hissing sound through her teeth as Mordaunt approached and cooled the Viper down.

He leaned toward Harlee, sniffing, as her eyes peeped open and she looked up at him.

"Think you c-could hold yours if you drove headfirst off the—"

"Nice to see you again, Harlee. Better change."

Her teeth were chattering. "Ch-change into what?" She noted what Mordaunt was wearing, instantly coveting the seaman's bulky-knit sweater.

"How about letting me have that sweater?"

"Mr. Sherard might catch his death of cold up here."

"He looks like a hardy dude, and anyway you're n-not planning on keeping him, are you?" Mordaunt had to smile. Harlee knew him well. "Didn't think you were. Linc, I'm s-s-suffering. *Please*?"

"Guess I owe you that much, don't I?" He smiled indulgently and pulled the sweater off over Tom Sherard's head, creating a ministorm of static electricity. Harlee got out of the Viper, realizing she had little choice but to strip to the skin. Her knees were knocking. *So cold.* She snuggled gratefully into the sweater, which covered her to the kneecaps. She pressed her thighs together and crossed her arms, hands inside the sleeves of the sweater, leaned against the abandoned limo, and looked at Mordaunt, seeing him through the fixed pupils of Sherard's attractively hooded eyes.

"Where were you going?" Mordaunt asked her.

"I was on my way to the vault. Where I stashed your crystal skull after I used it . . . to break you out of that awful crypt of glass."

"Always so clever and resourceful," Mordaunt said admiringly. "I never had a moment's despair knowing you'd find a way."

Harlee's blood had warmed enough to allow for a flush of pleasure.

Mordaunt frowned and stared at the pinwheeling sky. "But if the skull is in the vault, what's causing *that*?"

"There's another skull, Great One. Identical. The bitch Avatar's doppelganger brought it back with her—along with someone who calls herself Delilah." She looked to Mordaunt for enlightenment.

All he said was, with a trace of sardonic amusement, "*Does* she?"

"And she doesn't respect *you* at all."

Mordaunt had another laugh as he looked up the road.

"I think I'd better get up there before they wreck the house."

"I should get moving myself," Harlee said quickly.

"No. I want you to wait here, Harlee. We'll go together—" He cast another glance at the sky. "After I've finished off Eden Waring."

"But, Great One—I wanted to take care of her myself! Make her suffer for all she did to you."

"Don't you think you're being a little too ambitious, Harlee?"

"No, I don't!" she pouted.

Mordaunt studied Harlee in combat mode for a few moments longer, then nodded. "I do owe you a great debt. All right. Once I've . . . denatured Eden, stripped her of her powers, I'll let you deal with her."

"You can do that? Take away all her powers?"

"Har-lee. I'm amazed that you even asked me that question."

11:05 A.M.

As the electrical storm covering the summit of Charleston Mountain gained in intensity, Gillian Bellaver said to her daughter, "This is all the time I can spend with you."

They were sitting in the sixteen-passenger van, Gillian with an arm around Eden. Who had had a blissful few minutes to be soothed and loved, to recover her strength and courage.

"But I still need you," she said tearfully.

"It's time to take back what belongs to you," Gillian said.

"And you can't help me?"

"I don't have that dispensation, Eden. But you won't need any-one's help from here on. The power that she's generating now will be Delilah's undoing."

"How?"

"Just put her in her place, darling."

"Where's that?" Eden said, with a despairing laugh.

"Once you've seen her you'll know."

"But when will I see *you* again, Mother?"

"In quieter circumstances. A more peaceful place."

Eden was afraid. "Does that mean—"

"That you're going to die? Not here, not today."

Gillian calmed her daughter with a kiss. And was gone instantly, as if she'd never been there, a somnambulist's daydream. Eden shook her head violently, slumped in the seat, and let out a yowl of bereavement.

Something bumped hard into the van. Eden jumped. She turned to see a hand flat against the window and the face of Dr. Marcus Woolwine, mirror glasses askew and reflecting the livid sky. His mouth worked as if he was straining to breathe.

Eden slid back the door and Woolwine tumbled partway inside, fingers digging into the floor mat.

"Help me . . . get me away from here!"

Eden grasped him by his belt, pulled him all the way inside, turned him over.

"Who are you?"

"Marcus Woolwine. And you—must be—"

"Eden." She looked unkindly at him. "*Doctor* Woolwine? I know all about you. You took Gwen away from me once, kept her a pris-oner at Plenty Coups. Are you keeping her from me now?"

"Yes!"

"How?"

"A device that I implanted in her neck. A Magnetic Flux Inhibitor Unit. But I'm not in control of Gwen! This—this creature who calls herself Delilah has Gwen now."

"So I was told. The device is in her neck? Where?"

"Right side. It's only a little more than skin deep. Can you help me now? My pacemaker—"

"Keys are in the ignition, Dr. Woolwine. You'll have to drive yourself. I'm going to be damned busy for a while."

Eden stepped down from the van, no longer interested in Marcus Woolwine, deaf to his pleas and immune to his terror. She looked at the house.

Her doppelganger had appeared on a midlevel terrace in a blitz of electricity that had a baleful tone to it. Gwen held the red crystal skull in the crook of one arm. Eden grimaced at the pulses of energy emanating from the skull, targeting her from a congeries of foul worlds in transit far beyond the skull's earthly depths. At the same time, she was contemptuous of what was being summoned to test her, even before she and Delilah had been formally introduced.

Simba had risen, erect and protective, deflecting the charged bolts hurled Eden's way. Behind her the large van was struck repeatedly and rocked, then toppled. It spun and bounced like an empty tin can in a zephyr down the road until it flew away in darkening space with its lone passenger.

Eden began to shimmer, then neatly to divide, separating into five distinct energy bodies as she, and they, passed through the open gates to the courtyard of the Magician's house. Her other bodies were like teammates in a cosmic game. They literally blocked out for her as she drove for the goal, feeling springy power in her legs and not a twinge from the cartilage-poor knee as she soared from cobbled courtyard to the terrace.

Where Gwen, or the shell of Gwen, was waiting.

So what does one say to her renegade dpg? Eden didn't feel like saying anything, even though Gwen's lips began a humble smile of greeting. Quickly suppressed by Delilah. The doppelganger was just a waxworks replica anyway, compared to Eden's teeming energy bodies.

On the other hand, Eden conceded, not all of this was Gwen's fault. She'd only been headstrong, competitive, independent-minded, and gullible. Precisely Eden's own characteristics, except for gullible.

"Sure, here's the sweet bitch now, cometh in ceremony, appurtenanc'd with Promethean court! Futile justlings; they will avail you not."

Eden shrugged. "I want Gwen, and I'm taking her."

The pupils of Gwen's eyes, mirror images of Eden's, one eye starting to turn in from fatigue, combusted with the heat of Delilah's disdain. It was *so* creepy, staring at herself in mortal thrall. Eden's shoulders contracted. Her gorge was almost in her throat.

"Disprize me of my chattel? Nay, I think not."

"And one more thing," Eden said, taking a calming breath while the dazzling, red-cheeked skull poured its apparently inexhaustible store of complex occultism into the energy bodies surrounding her. "First and last warning: turn that fucking thing off, Delilah."

Gwen's lips were shaped for lethal scorn when Eden shifted her gaze to the mote of the Magnetic Flux Inhibitor Unit beneath the skin of the dpg's neck and zapped it out of there with a bolt of her own energy.

Two things happened instantly.

The corporeal body vanished. Something else appeared in its place: a great writhing tempest, bones and nettles, screeching hell-birds and venomous roil of green-scaled serpents. The tireless orb of red crystal, buoyant in the maelstrom of violence, glared.

But Gwen was saved and Eden knew it; she had felt the familiar homecoming buzz around her navel.

As for Delilah:

Eden heard her mother say it again—

Just put her in her place, darling.

Eden went to work with all the force, passion, and goodness at the disposal of her maturing skills and the Dark Energy of the Universe. First to contain the furious lashings of the Delilah tempest (yet only a part of a larger deadly soul) with its murk and foulness, corruption and evil craft, its primal curse and eternal blasphemy. Unflinching, Eden and her energy bodies denied what the loathsome and now bodiless spirit before her most desired: to take form—as shrike, harpy, banshee, some dark incarnate beast never before seen—and fall upon its tormentor. *Sorry, not today.* Eden blended her own energies with those around the wicked little skull, desaturating them of evil until the tempest was tamed, yanked inside-out and at odds with its worst intentions. Sensing rank fear in the supercharged air around the terrace and above the mountain, Eden with a final thrust sent Delilah into the skull and the damnation that lay beyond it.

Eden had no desire to know where that might be. All she cared about was packing the skull with so much of her own fury that Delilah, no matter how resourceful, could never find a way out.

The red skull fell to the terrace floor, rolled around lopsidedly with that puckish death's-head grin she loathed.

Eden retrieved it carefully, the tip of her walking stick through one eye socket. She held it with an outstretched shaky arm. The skull swarmed with bad feeling but not much potency, smarting off at her. She felt its animus like pinpricks to the heart.

The tempest in the sky had not lessened. Dark, highly charged smoke like that from a runaway prairie fire. It continued to move toward what Eden assumed was a city in full panic mode, feeding on what the magnetic earth and that cache of buried radioactivity within Yucca Mountain provided.

As she had witnessed in her dreams. But there was nothing she could do to stop it.

Eden leaned away from gritty blasts of wind circulating around the house and vomited some bile mixed with blood. That scared her. She was seriously drained but there was no stopping now. A mate to Delilah's prison skull existed, and she had to find it.

Then there was Mordaunt.

With Tom Sherard's fate to be resolved.

With the taste of blood on her lips, Eden was certain that she wasn't far from dying. What Delilah had contemptuously referred to as her "Promethean court" only flickered now in Eden's waning energy field, specters composed of scattering sparks.

Keeping the skull far enough away that its oscillations couldn't drain her further, Eden turned and was shocked to see, in the glass of a sliding door, that her hair had gone as white as a snowfield.

At the least, Eden reckoned, she could use a good hour to recover somewhat before any more confrontations. The rest of the week, even better. She yearned for just one last look at the face of her new love, whom she had banished from what might remain of her life.

But someone was waiting for her in the courtyard, and it wasn't Cody Olds.

Eden found stairs and went down slowly, walked outside on the cobbles, and aimed the skewered skull at her nemesis.

"I'd better have that," Mordaunt said pleasantly.

Eden found that shaking her head was brute labor. Still she managed not to let him see her tremble.

"Have a rough time of it with Delilah? What's become of her, anyway?"

"You'll have a chance to talk things over with her. But . . . not here."

Mordaunt lost his breezy attitude as he looked hard at the skull. Tom Sherard's wide shoulders drew together slightly. Otherwise there was no reaction by the body she knew so well and that the Magician inhabited. Eden wondered if enough of Tom remained to recognize her given the state she was in. Or to know her voice.

She tapped a depth of anger she'd thought was exhausted.

"Why couldn't you just have left him alone?"

"Because," Mordaunt said, "he shot me. Also there was nothing else available when my ship was going down. So Delilah and I are as far apart as ever?"

"Do you want the bad news first? There's no way . . . you are ever going to get her back."

He thought it over.

"Then why don't I just leave that to you?"

"Make a trade, that's what you're saying?"

"You're weak, Eden, weaker than you know. Better take it."

"Let me talk to Tom."

"You want to hear him beg for his life? Eden, that's so penny-dreadful they wouldn't use it on *One Life to Live*. Besides, I'm not a sadist. I'm basically a businessman. So let's get our business done, and he's all yours."

Eden said with wild-eyed suspicion, "You've destroyed his mind, haven't you? He *can't* talk to me!"

"Destroyed? I'm not a mind-fucker either; I just set him aside for a while. You know how it works. Are you being irrational on purpose?

Calm down. I know Delilah must've put you through the wringer but for both our sakes stay focused."

His tone was almost flippant, but she sensed anxiety, and knew very well what made him anxious. Probably he wasn't lying about Tom; for now he needed his host. "No harm has come to your lover. So give me Delilah. Okay, please."

"First let go of Tom for a few moments! That's all I'm asking now. Let him say something to me so I'll know he's all right!"

Eden went down on her good knee and set the skull on the cobbles. She looked up at the blazing sky.

"So help me I'll turn this thing into a bag of marbles!"

Mordaunt, carelessly perhaps, had told her what she needed to know. And now—

"Tom?"

The face of Tom Sherard lost its stoic blandness; the faraway gaze came closer. Looking down at her, he shrugged painfully, as if in response to an immense weight he bore.

"Hi . . . kiddo."

"Tom!"

He blinked at her, raised his eyes to the hell on the mountain, looked again at Eden. He smiled wryly.

"Okay, that ought to be enough," Mordaunt said impatiently, and the muscles in Tom's face began to slacken.

"Tom, what do you want me to do?" Eden cried, mentally grabbing him back from Mordaunt's attempt at control, digging in mulishly so that Tom grimaced in pain. Then he exerted his own will in concert with Eden's efforts. In his eyes Eden saw the savvy hunter who has caught a flicker of quarry in deep brush.

"You've got the shot," Tom Sherard said. "Take it, Eden."

Mordaunt went recklessly into Tom's brain, now in a destroying mood as Eden sobbed and took over the rest, the corporeal Tom Sherard, destroying too, reducing what was dear and human to her to bright and starry dust that was quickly flying on the wind, scattered skyward.

And there stood Mordaunt where Sherard had been—naked, hunchbacked, wolfen, long in the snout and with tall pricking ears.

The thing was instantly in motion, springing at Eden. But the talisman on her breast glowed furiously and repulsed it. The renewed brightness coalesced into a phalanx of Eden's energy bodies. Five pairs of hands flung Mordaunt to the ground before he could lope away. Her supernatural Furies resisted Mordaunt's every desperate, cunning effort to shape-shift and elude them as they dragged him howling to the radiant red skull.

"You wanted to be with Delilah? Go to her," Eden said, then closed her ears and mind to Mordaunt's shrieks.

Within the fireball of skull a curious glimmer of a face appeared. The were-creature's screams abated when he saw it. What he saw made him cringe, more whipped dog than wolf now.

It was a high-yellow face inside the skull, the skin lavishly freckled. The left eyelid was sewn into place over an empty socket. And upon that lid was a vivid blue-eyed tattoo.

In spite of the rising wind Eden was certain that she heard high notes from a supernal horn.

The face inside the skull was split by a nearly toothless grin.

"You, Mordaunt," Eden heard Letty Fresno say. "High time you be gettin' back to where y'all belong!"

A gleam appeared behind the tattooed eyelid, soon became as bright as the talisman on Eden's breast. Then the light beamed from the crystal skull and exploded with such force around the shaggy form of Mordaunt that Eden was momentarily blinded. She fell forward on her elbows and curled with a sigh into fetal position, her senses tuned to a last, long held, purifying high note that only the amazing Jonas Fresno had ever reached.

A horn man whom she'd never laid eyes on; but she recognized his genius as well as a sympathetic spirit. Captivated by Jonas's spell, she felt renewed, forgiven.

Once Eden was able to stand without being knocked sprawling by wind, with no idea of how much time had passed, she found herself alone with the crystal skull. No energy bodies protectively surrounded her. But there was no vestige of Mordaunt either, no residue of his evil. Her navel quivered suggestively, but she didn't want to hear from Gwen. As far as Eden was concerned her doppelganger was banished until—and maybe she was hoping for too much—Gwen learned to stay out of trouble.

The virulent storm brewed from nuclear waste appeared to have spread considerably while she lay dull-witted and motionless on the driveway. *Too bad for Las Vegas,* Eden thought without remorse or regrets. If the lights of Glitter Gulch hadn't gone out already they would before long. Permanently. No big loss to the culture, although inevitably there were good people who would be greatly inconvenienced, forced to resume their lives as refugees.

She refused to blame herself. The overlying storm was only one aspect of the evil that had infiltrated and possessed that gaudy nightmare of a town. She couldn't have reversed it even if she had been in a more forgiving mood. She was weak, crapped out—according to the lingo of the gamester's land.

Weak, but alive.

They would probably rebuild Vegas or a cheesy replica somewhere else someday. There was always enough money. And, like her doppelganger, the majority of human beings were slow learners.

Eden looked at the crystal skull that had, in two separate gulps, swallowed the soul of *Deus Inversus.* In the aftermath the skull seemed almost benign. Eden presumed that the Caretakers would be pleased with her. There was no message, no astral e-mail to consult, but she knew she wasn't supposed to leave the skull lying around. As long as this one and the other skull—wherever Harlee Nations was keeping it—were available to those remnants of Mordaunt's followers like the Fetchlings, there was risk that the evil they contained could find another outlet.

So don't be a slow learner, Eden said to herself. *You're tired, you feel a hundred years old, you don't have the power left to light a match, but finish it. Get rid of the damned skulls!*

With that she picked the skull up in one hand, palming it, index and middle fingers curled in the eye sockets, and began to walk. She was wobbly, aimless, empty-headed, needing to pause frequently to take deep harsh breaths as she made her way with the aid of her walking stick down toward Cathedral Rock.

Eden felt as if she were sleepwalking, her conscious mind detached from her shuddering body and trailing behind like a balloon on a string. She daydreamed of Africa, the spacious veranda of the house at Shungwaya shaded by thatched roofs, the shimmer of the nearby lake, heat haze through which far-off animals moved evanescently to water. Dreaming of lazy days that had served to make her whole once before, a book in her lap or binoculars with which to study birdlife. Or leisurely conversations with Bertie or Tom—Tom, whom she had sacrificed because there was no other way. Whose bravery in retrospect was more than she could bear to dwell on, else she would just quit here and now, petrified with despair, abandoning hope of making it back to the sanctuary of the Kenya homestead. . . .

The red Viper convertible she had left floating in air was back on the narrow road, parked and empty in front of the white limousine. Eden stared at it uneasily, her mind working much too slowly. Only Mordaunt could have rescued his harlot Fetchling, she reasoned, but where—

And she was slow to turn, to recognize that she had trapped herself between one long side of the limo and the precipice that began six feet away at the edge of the road.

The limousine door that Harlee flung open behind Eden knocked her flat. Simba flew end over end from her hand. If her two numbed fingers hadn't been gripping the skull like a bowling ball she would have lost control of that too. Her bad knee had struck a rock; the pain had the effect of clearing her mind. But as she tried to turn over, Harlee was on top of her, screaming, tearing the talisman from Eden's breast and flinging it aside.

"*Bitch!* Where is he? What did you do to the Great One?"

Harlee had a screwdriver from the car's tool kit in the other hand. Most of her weight was on Eden. A knee dug into Eden's groin. Eden squalled in pain. Harlee hesitated for a moment to relish her advantage, perhaps hoping also to raise fear in Eden's eyes.

"Now you see me and now—you don't!" Harlee cried, striking at Eden's left eye with the screwdriver.

Born with a lot of quick from birth, reflexes and stamina reinforced by thousands of hours in the gym and on the running track, Eden reacted, in spite of her depleted state, fast enough to deflect the first strike. But Harlee was young and quick herself. The second hard strike drove the eight-inch shaft of the screwdriver through the palm of Eden's right hand.

As Harlee worked to yank the screwdriver free, Eden smashed her in the side of the head with the crystal skull. Harlee fell back against the limo. Eden pulled her hand free of the impaling screwdriver. But she couldn't power up fast enough to seize the advantage, cave in the Fetchling's forehead with another blow from the skull.

Simba was out of sight, out of reach of her acquisitive power— what remained of it was no more than a guttering candle flame about to be extinguished forever.

Eden didn't hear the gunshot; she couldn't hear much of anything. But the screwdriver, aimed again at her left eye, disappeared, along with about a third of Harlee's hand, transformed into a red smudge the size of a blooming rose on the side of the limousine.

Harlee, staring wide-eyed at her crudely semiamputated hand, was trying to scream again. She could only make a drawn-out windy sound of horror.

Eden struggled painfully upright on her good knee and saw Cody Olds come around the front of the Viper sports car, a long-barreled .45 Colt's Frontier model revolver in his shooting hand. At a bend in the road a little distance beyond the Viper stood his Toyota Prius, driver's door standing open.

Striding toward them, he paused to pick up Simba from the road, keeping the Colt aimed at Harlee's head. But the Fetchling had no fight left in her. She was crying hysterically.

"Cody," Eden said, making an effort to keep her chin up, "what— are you doing here?"

He glanced at her, shocked and concerned about her appearance. The white hair, the deeply hollowed eyes.

"If you thought I was going to go off and leave you on your say-so, there's plenty you still need to learn about me."

"So glad—you didn't listen. So happy to see you."

"Who is this?" he said with a glance at the Fetchling he'd shot.

"Meet Harlee Nations."

Harlee screamed at Cody, "My hand! Look what you did to my fucking hand!"

Seeming to forget about Eden, she scrambled awkwardly toward Cody, cradling the wounded hand against her breast. He cocked his six-shooter with his thumb, gave her a warning look.

"She one of those supernaturals?" Cody asked Eden.

"No. Don't shoot her again, luv. There's something I need to find out."

"You're bleeding all over yourself, Eden."

"Not serious. Hurts like hell. She stuck me with that screwdriver."

Eden intercepted Harlee and stopped her yelping, sprawling progress in Cody's direction. She grabbed a handful of the Fetchling's hair and yanked her head up and back.

Mad with pain and frustration, Harlee spat at her.

"That's cute," Eden said calmly. "Listen, Harlee. I want to know where the other skull is."

"I'm bleeding to death! I need a doctor!"

"We'll get you to a doctor. Where's the goddamn skull?"

Harlee glared at Eden, moaning, then rolled her eyes to Cody when he placed the muzzle of the Colt against the side of her head.

"You can't have it! You'll never get your hands on it!"

"Tell me why," Eden said, tightening her grip on the Fetchling's hair

"It's in his vault. The Great One's vault! Nobody—can get in there but us!"

"What vault where?"

"His theatre. Below his dressing suite."

"Take us."

"Don't waste your time," Harlee sneered. "No way inside. Without—all of me." She raised her wounded hand in dread. "But I'm not perfect anymore! I can't *fix this.* I can't grow another hand!"

Cody looked at Eden. "Reckon she's talking about a full body scan, or all ten fingerprints for biometric access?"

With a frenzied laugh Harlee lunged off the ground, shoving Eden momentarily off-balance. Eden's grip on the Fetchling loosened. Some of Harlee's hair tore off her head along with a patch of scalp as she bolted past Eden and leaped from the side of the road, space-walked momentarily with a scream, and was gone.

Eden recovered quickly enough to get over there and see Harlee crashing down through the green pinnacle of a fat old ponderosa pine. The Fetchling tumbled and plummeted farther until she was abruptly jerked to a stop, a jagged bare branch socketed in Harlee's soft underjaw, protruding through the top of her head.

Behind Eden, Cody lowered the Colt's hammer and stuck it inside his belt, whistling regretfully.

"Guess that makes her the winner. The hard way."

"That's not a come bet," Eden said. She turned and took Simba from Cody's other hand. "Let's go."

"Think you can get into that vault?"

"I don't know. I know I have to try."

4:35 P.M.

There was no power available at the ruins of Lincoln Grayle's theatre on Spring Mountain other than what an on-site generator supplied for work lights. The elevator that Eden and Cody located in a back wall of the late Magician's roomy wardrobe was inoperable. No juice, and also a biometric scan apparently was required.

With an electric torch Cody eventually uncovered a shaft for emergency use while Eden with her throbbing hand remained quietly in the spectrochrome chamber where the Magician and his cohorts regularly restored their vigor through application of colored lights. Eden had no idea how any of it worked. Her energy level seemed to be building slowly as she and the ruby crystal skull she had placed on the chamber's table faced each other. The skull retained a faint interior starburst glow. It seemed to perk up the chunky talisman Eden had restored to her breast. Now and then she imagined she heard that eerie, confident trumpet solo.

"Want to come take a look at the vault?" Cody said as he returned to the spectrochrome chamber. "You need to be real careful climbing down there with that hand of yours."

Eden had bandaged her palm from the first-aid kit Cody kept in the Prius, but the puncture wound was still oozing blood and fluid. A couple of her fingers on that hand didn't work at all.

"I'll be okay." Eden flashed her own light at the bank of colored lights above the table. "I wonder if there's an instruction manual. I might be able to turn my hair back to its natural color."

"That's all you have to worry about?"

"Well—I must look like hell to you, cowboy."

"You're not so bad with white hair," he said diplomatically. "Let's do this and get out of here. All those costumes and masks and stuff— spooky."

"He won't be back, Cody."

Cody looked at the crystal skull. "Don't trust that thing. Looks like it's winking at us."

Eden didn't know how much time they had. Or what came next. She bound the skull up in a long scarf and Cody helped her arrange the sling across her body. He went first down the shaft hewn from solid rock, frequently looking up, wary of Eden slipping and taking them both twenty feet to the bottom.

In the illumination from their flashlights Eden had a critical look at herself in the mirrorlike surface of the vault door installed in a grotto. It was chilly down there, probably less than sixty degrees.

"How do you suppose they got a vault that size down here?" Cody said. "Remember when they opened that vault of Al Capone's on television a few years ago? Nothing in it but an empty beer bottle. Could the Fetchling have been lyin' to you?"

"No," Eden said. "The other skull is in there. I feel it. But—" Cody watched her. Eden licked her crusted lips. "I just don't know what happens when—the two of them get together."

"Then let's don't trouble to find out," he said uneasily. "Throw that one you got already into Havasu and we'll go fishin'."

Eden smiled, a loving smile for him, but shook her head. She walked toward the vault until she had nearly merged with her reflection, then raised her good hand and touched the door with spread fingers. Her head nodded forward slightly. Her eyes closed.

After almost a minute had passed she pushed experimentally with her fingers. The talisman on her breast seemed to explode with light that turned Cody away, shielding his eyes. But not before he saw the door waver like a midday's desert mirage. He had only a glimpse of a shadowy Eden as she appeared to walk through the two feet of steel door and into the vault.

Talk about spooky: Cody shuddered. He wanted to call to her, but he couldn't make a sound.

Stuffy inside the vault. But well lit, due to the energy pulsing from her talisman. Eden looked around without much curiosity, seeing pallets of gold bars, as many as two thousand of them. Gold didn't interest her. But the red crystal skull glowing atop one of the pallets, lonely as a lighthouse, did.

She took off the sling she'd fashioned from the Magician's theatrical scarf and, working awkwardly with her stiffened punctured hand, unwrapped the skull she had brought. The two skulls hummed to each other in their mysterious, conspiratorial ways. She left the newcomer on the floor and took down its twin from the pallet, placing it a few feet opposite the first one.

Just leave them there like that?

No good, Eden thought. In time perhaps the vault would be breached by those who had reason to suspect the treasure it contained, also liberating the skulls. To be sold, perhaps, to a collector of Grayle arcana. Or to someone steeped in the occult who one way or another had the means to let loose this evil in the world.

But even with the skulls safely interred there remained enough evil out there beyond the dead city to keep Eden Waring, the Avatar, busy for her lifetime. The familiar, pervasive evils employed by men of bad will for millennia.

After a while the glitter of gold gave her an idea.

Eden smiled skeptically. She wasn't at all sure she had enough access to the Dark Energy that would be needed to seal the skulls in a golden coffin, and still make her escape.

Obviously it wouldn't do to trap herself. She experimented at first and found that she was able, precariously, to levitate. Not exactly like a feather in a freshet, but far enough above the vault floor to keep from being entombed herself—

—As she began to melt the stacked horde of gold, turning bricks into slow molten flows that ran down from the pallets to pool on the floor, engulfing the skulls, filling every socket and crevice and grinning mouth.

When they were completely covered there were pallets of gold bars to spare. She continued to melt them until the heat building up in the vault threatened to overcome her.

Cody was sitting with his back against a rock wall of the grotto in near darkness, the batteries of his electric torch almost drained, when the vault door ten feet away did its high-noon-on-the-desert mirage thing and Eden tumbled out of the vault. She landed awkwardly on her wrapped bloody hand and bad knee and yelped in pain. Her body glowed as if it were radioactive.

"Don't touch me, Cody; not yet," she warned him, and lay still on her side for a couple of minutes. Cody kneeled beside her until she was cool enough for him to put a tentative hand on her.

"You'll be okay?"

"Yes."

"What did you do in there?"

"Buried the skulls in liquid gold. They're probably indestructible, but—maybe for a few centuries—"

Cody helped her to sit up. Eden wincing but not complaining. She had something else on her mind.

"Cody, when you introduce me to your mom, maybe you better not say anything about—this? Me? I mean, break it to her slowly?"

Cody sat back on his heels and laughed.

Eden misinterpreted his laughter. "You *are* going to introduce me to your mother. Trust me, I can do something about my hair."

"Eden, we're practically buried in the middle of a mountain here—" He took hold of her by the waist and stood, set her on her feet. "Those flashlight batteries are failing and if we do get out I'm not sure my car will start again."

"Oh, we'll be okay. But would you promise me—"

Cody put her on the ladder, aiming the weakened torch beam upward.

"No problem. Just get going."

"One good thing," she said as they climbed, Cody giving her an occasional boost when she faltered. "You've seen all there is to see. I don't have any more surprises."

"I have been wonderin' about—watch your step!—that doppelganger of yours. You know, like how it'll be, havin' her around."

"Gwen? Oh, no. Uh-uh. Put her out of your mind, Cody! She's banished. It's just you and me, Cody Olds. Listen. I have a great idea. We hide out for about a week before I meet your mother and by then—hell, Cody, maybe life can actually be fun again."

"I can help you with that."

"I know you will," Eden said. Having reached the top of the ladder she was breathing hard as she stood. But also flushed with a sensation that wasn't far from happiness. She extended her good hand and found his as he climbed out of the hole in the rock, took a hard purchase for herself. "Cowboy, I'm counting on it."